YOU SHOULD'VE
KEPT DRIVING

by

M. A. Savino

Cover

By

Frina Art

Dearest readers,

This book contains triggers.
This is your only warning.
I'm not going into details because it will take all day.
All I can say is, if you have any triggers at all, just don't
read it. Stop now and pick something more YA.
If you continue reading and are triggered, you were
warned. Please don't punish the author with a bad review
because you couldn't handle it.

Sincerely,
Willow, the MC of this story.

P.S. There are no children or animals in this story. Geez,
I'm not a monster.

This is an NC-17 (formerly X) rated novel.
Reader discretion is advised.

This is an NC-17 (formerly X) rated novel.
Reader discretion is advised.

Oh, foolish boys. They can't see the danger that is right in front of them.

Do they really think finding women for their trafficking business could be so easy?

Blinded by my beauty and alluring eyes, they ignore the pit in their stomachs and kidnap me anyway.

What a glorious mistake they have made.

They should've kept driving. But they made a conscious decision, locking in their fates.

Come to me my sweet victims, and take me into your lair...

Chapter One
Flat Tire

Taking me was a mistake, but they don't know it yet. I'm quiet as they whisper in the shadows and wonder why I am unafraid.

My stomach growls, and I glance down. I didn't get a chance to eat dinner, thanks to these morons. They snatched me from behind as I changed my tire on the side of the road. Then stabbed me in the thigh with a needle and tied my hands and feet to this old ass bed.

A cool breeze floats through an open door to the left of my captors, shifting the fine hairs on my bare feet. I lift my head and peer through the doorway. Inside, a metal ladder connects to an opening in the ceiling. Rain drizzles through the hole and shimmers in intermittent rays of sunshine.

We're underground.

Above me, pipes and cables come together and split off in multiple directions. I crank my neck and glance at the closed door behind me. To my right, a small sink, a refrigerator-freezer combo, an electric stove, and multiple shelves filled with seasonings and different cooking oils fill the space.

The men's voices grow louder as they move in and out of the shadows, intermittently stepping under a bulb hanging from the ceiling, arguing. Both have blonde hair and piercing blue eyes.

Brothers.

One is younger, maybe in his early twenties, shorter, and twitchy as fuck. His bony tattooed hands shake as his presumed brother grabs them. Where one man is short, this man is large—tall, thick, muscular shoulders, a trimmed goatee, and tattoos flowing from his upper arm to his wrist.

"Calm the fuck down, Benny. What's your problem?"

Benny? What a sissy name. It suits his wimpy, disheveled appearance—wrinkled pants, stained shirt, and dirty shoes.

Benny's eyes dart from mine to his brothers. "I'm telling you, Griff, this one's different. I mean, look at her."

Both men turn towards me. I keep my smile to myself. On the outside, I'm stoic and emotionless—breathing rhythmic and steady.

Griff is short for Griffin. His name doesn't suit his physique. His massive arms test the strength of the army green T-shirt stretched over them, and his camouflage-covered legs tilt outward like a cowboy who just dismounted his horse.

He walks away from Benny, leans against the stove, and crosses his arms. Judging by the crow's feet around his eyes, he must be pushing thirty.

His eyes lock on mine. "So, she's tough; breaking her will take more work." Griffin shrugs his shoulders.

Break me? That's comical. I've been broken since birth.

"Take off her clothes, Benny. Let's see how she enjoys being naked."

I love being naked. *Let's do it.*

"You take the lead on this one." Benny passes a blue-handled pair of scissors to his brother.

Griffin rolls his eyes, snatches the scissors, and steps towards me. "Fucking pussy."

This should be fun.

Griffin slices down each side of my designer black trousers, cutting around my bound ankles, and yanks them out from under me. His blade knicks my abdomen as he cuts away my blouse. He smudges the crimson liquid, stares at it for a brief second, and sucks it off his finger.

2

A man after my own heart.

Benny stands beside him. They stare at the white lace lingerie hugging my perfect size eight frame. I've never been tiny, but my hourglass body and heart-shaped ass raise plenty of eyebrows.

Griffin swipes my long black hair away from my green eyes, mounts me, and gropes my breasts. The scent of fruity bubble gum emanates from his breath.

I relieve myself, releasing the pressure on my bladder.

"What the fuck?" Griffin jumps up and examines the wet spot on the front of his pants.

That will teach him to touch without permission.

He growls and slaps me across the face. My eyes gleam as he hits me a second time. I bite down on my gag, unable to stop my grin.

Griffin seizes me by the cheekbones, crushing them in his grasp. "You will be on your hands and knees begging me not to kill you very soon."

I snort, and he punches my upper thigh. He furrows his brow as I cackle at his foolish attempt to hurt me.

"I told you." Benny points at Griffin and then at me. "She didn't even flinch. Something's wrong with her. Let's get rid of her now, before…"

He grabs Benny by his shirt and pulls him close to his chest. "Before what, Benny?" Griffin squints his fierce eyes.

Ah…the alpha male shows himself. Makes sense. Benny Boy is the weak underling living in the shadows of his dominant, masculine brother for years—wanting to be strong like him. The problem is that Benny doesn't have the physique and commanding presence Griffin does, and he never will.

"Griff, I'm trying to tell you something isn't right. And you always say if something doesn't feel right, don't do it. Well, something is off with her."

Griffin releases his brother, seizes a ceramic coffee mug from the counter, and throws it into the wall, shattering it into pieces beside me. A ceramic flake lands on my shoulder.

"If you want to bow out, that's fine, but don't try to weasel your way back in later. When the time comes, she's mine, and mine alone to sell."

Sell? Do they intend to sell me like a piece of property? Good luck with that. I'm condemned.

Benny throws his hands in the air. "You can fucking have her." He enters the room with the exit and wraps his fingers around the first ladder rung. "You're making a mistake." Benny glances at me, and slips on the first step, bumping his head.

I smile at him, and he scowls.

Griffin shakes his head as Benny climbs out of sight. A loud bang echoes through the room as the hatch to the surface slams closed. Griffin glares at the yellow stain on my underwear and the sheets beneath me. He picks up the scissors from the counter, yanks my bra straps, and cuts them. After removing my bra, he tosses the shears on the mattress, grabs the front of my underwear, and rips them off by hand.

He turns and drops my damaged clothing inside a small trash can by the sink.

My eyes fixate on his ass. It couldn't be more perfect. I want to grab each cheek in my hands and chomp on them.

Nom, nom.

When he turns back around, my eyes are stuck on the bulge between his legs.

His eyes follow mine to the still-wet part of his pants. "I need a fucking shower and so do you."

I give him a seductive wink.

He snatches the scissors from beside me and presses them against my throat. "You think you're funny?"

I raise my eyebrows and nod.

I'm fucking hysterical.

He cuts the ropes away from my hands, grabs a set of handcuffs from his back pocket, and secures my wrists in front of me. "You won't for long."

After cutting my legs free, he drags me up by my hair and pushes me ahead of him. "Walk."

I dance towards the closed door, excited about the change of scenery. The metallic partition screeches open, revealing two more doors across from each other.

It's a game show. The prize behind door number one is...

We walk through door number two, revealing a bathroom with a large stand-up shower, a wall sink, and a toilet. Griffin raises my arms over my head and attaches me to a hook by the shower head. He steps out of sight, leaving me alone.

All the floors I've seen thus far are concrete, painted gray, and cold under my feet. The bright white walls call to me with their blank canvases. I could paint down here for days. My fingers twitch at the thought.

Warm water splashes over my head startling me. I tilt my head down, and let the warmth soothe the tension in my neck. After all this manhandling, I'll need to make an appointment with my chiropractor.

I stare at a greenish-yellow, irregular-shaped speck on the opposing shower wall. Someone blew their nose in the shower, and the nasal contaminant stuck to the wall like dried mashed potatoes in a bowl. It was probably Benny. He seems like the type. The rest of the shower walls are clean and booger-free.

Griffin reappears and steps in front of me, naked. His body is as beautiful as I imagined—chiseled, muscular, tan, and hairless. Even his balls are bare. A chain tattoo weaves around his left calf and stops at a woman wearing a neck shackle with her mouth open to the left of his perfectly shaped dangling cock. Despite the chill in the air, it keeps its colossal size. He backs his ass into me as he drenches his hair, turns back around, grabs the soap, and washes his quads.

Those legs…

I could wrap them around my face for the rest of my life and still not be satisfied. I need them near me, on me…in me. I want to take his inner thighs, one by one, into my mouth and bite into them like a vampire.

My mouth waters.

The possibilities are endless.

He hesitates when I lick my lips and shakes his head when our eyes lock. I don't look away, but he does. He lathers up the washcloth and slaps it against my skin. As he makes his way south, the washcloth falls away and his fingers drift between my legs. I lift my right knee and nail him hard in the sack.

Don't touch.

He falls hard, whacking his forehead on the shower floor ledge. His hands cup his baby-makers as he rolls back and forth, groaning in agony. I close my eyes and let the falling water spill over my face. When I open them, he's gone.

I shrug my shoulders and hum Humpty Dumpty while I wait for his return.

Steam fills the space. I can't sense the heat of the scolding liquid, but my reddening flesh tells me Griffin turned the faucet to Satan's basement setting.

No noise comes from his gaping mouth when he returns to the shower. My lack of response to his attempt to boil me renders him speechless. He stands in a towel before my lobster-colored skin, shaking his head.

He takes the cloth from my mouth. "Benny was right. There is something wrong with you. Can you feel anything?"

I tighten my lips. My heart pounds in my chest, responding negatively to the punishment Griffin unleashed on me. He stops the water, unhooks me, and drags me through the galley-style kitchen he had me in and into the room with the ladder.

It's a massive space with multiple closed doors. Wires dangle from the ceiling, secured with rusty eye hooks. Griffin removes a padlock from a wall cabinet and secures my cuffs to one of the dangling lines.

He takes both keys and curls them in his palm. "Breaking you will be hard, but not impossible."

I laugh at him, and he punches me in the stomach. Tears race through my lashes as he lands one blow after another to my abdomen. With every strike, my cackling grows louder, echoing through the hollow chamber.

His fist appears in the corner of my left eye right before it slams into my temple. Stars dance around me and the room blurs.

He circles me a few times, his eyes combing over my body before he stops and leans in close. "You will be worth even more than the rest, especially with your unique ability. The best part is, you're mine." He smiles out of the corner of his mouth, turns away from me, and climbs the ladder to freedom.

I raise my head, smirking as he disappears through the opening and the room turns black, blinding me to my surroundings.

"And you sir... are mine."

Chapter Two
Jenny

Light from a previously closed door pierces the darkness. I can't see out of my left eye, compliments of Griffin's fist. A gaunt woman, possibly around the same age as me, steps through the doorway and approaches me with a tray. She places it on the ground by my feet and removes the metal cover revealing my breakfast—runny scrambled eggs and undercooked bacon.

I curl my lip.

She straightens her wrinkled white nightgown, stands erect, and shifts a lock of her dirty blonde hair away from her face. A loose strand floats to the floor and lands on my disappointing first meal.

Fucking disgusting.

"I'm Jenny. While you are here, you will do exactly what I say, when I say it." She squats down and stabs the eggs several times with a fork. "Open your mouth."

The hair isn't a part of this bite, so I comply.

She stuffs the slimy eggs in my mouth.

I can't chew. Their texture, consistency, and powdery taste repulse my picky palate. When she bends over to retrieve another forkful, I spit the food onto her head.

"Fucking bitch." She shakes the mess from her snarled locks. "I'm only going to warn you once. If you do that again, I'm going to beat the shit out of you. I'm Benny's favorite, and if you disrespect me, I can punish you any way I like."

Punish me? Benny's favorite? Oh, we are going to get along swimmingly.

Not.

My sardonic grin enrages her.

She seizes a piece of bacon and jams the entire slice into my mouth. I chew it until it is in tiny pieces, cup it in my tongue, and launch it from my lips with a burst of air—crumbled meat litters her face and the front of her clothes.

Jenny's mouth gapes open. She picks up the plastic tray and strikes me in the head with it several times, screaming incoherent expletives. I tip my head back and laugh at her. Bacon bits coat my teeth as I grin.

She tosses the tray aside, balls her fists, and charges me.

Dumb bitch.

I grip the heavy gauge wire above my head, throw my legs in the air, and wrap them around her neck. Her face crushes between my thighs and reddens as she gasps for air, and I swing her around. My legs bleed beneath her sharp fingernails, digging frantically into my flesh.

Benny and Griffin charge into the room. They each grab one of my legs, pry them apart, and pull Jenny from in between them. She falls to the ground, and Benny drops to her side.

Party poopers.

Benny cradles Jenny in his arms, strokes her hair, and yells at Griffin. "Kill her."

"I think you forgot how hard Jenny was to break." Griffin places his hands on his hips and scowls.

"That was different." Benny frowns.

"Take Jenny to her room. I'll handle her." Griffin points at me with his thumb.

Handle me? They suck at it so far.

Benny helps Jenny to her feet and escorts her out of the room. Griffin closes the door behind them and turns to me. He reaches into his back pocket, unfolds the rental agreement that was sitting on the seat of my car, and reads. "Willow Stantonbury, P.O. Box 1114, Virginia Beach, VA." He releases the paper. It floats in slow motion to the floor. "I called the post office in Virginia Beach, and you know what they told me? There is no box 1114." He takes an ink pad out of his side pocket and seizes my wrist. "Soon, I'll know everything about you, Willow."

I allow him to press my pointer into the pad and roll it on a blank index card. He walks away from me but stops after glancing at the paper in his grasp. My knuckles snap when he snatches my hand and inspects the pads of my fingers. "Sneaky girl. Why would you sand off your fingerprints?"

I say nothing. It won't be long before they uncover the truth, but I'm not going to ruin the surprise.

He tightens his grip on my hand. "What are you hiding?"

I tilt my head and scan his inquisitive face, ignoring the question.

"Fine. I don't have a problem letting you hang here in the dark for a few days." Griffin raises his eyebrows. "Last chance to say something, anything."

I whisper inaudibly to myself, so he can't hear, forcing him to move closer. He leans in, turning his ear to my mouth. The air from his breath shifts the hair on my cheek as he exhales. I stick my tongue in his ear, and he jerks away from me.

"Gross." He uses his shirt to clean my saliva from his ear canal and furrows his brow.

I smack my lips together assessing the taste of his ear wax. A sudden slap tingles my face. I shake it off and glare at Griffin with a sinister smile.

"You want to keep playing games with me, that's fine. But what you need to understand is, I've been doing this for a couple of years, and I always get what I want." He turns on his heels, raises his head high, and strolls to the exit.

The door slams behind him when he leaves, and the room darkens within seconds. I imagine he's watching me on the not-so-subtle camera above the door. The only thing he may see in the dark is my bright white teeth, grinning at him like the Cheshire cat in Alice in Wonderland.

'No one does [play fair] if they think they can get away with it.'
—Cheshire cat.

Two days.

That's how long I've been hanging here with nothing to eat or drink. I don't have hunger pains, but the growling in my stomach is constant. My chapped lips stick together from dehydration, and the last time I went to the bathroom was yesterday.

What a pretty pile of poo and piss I have left for them.

If I don't get a drink by tomorrow, I may die. I'm not afraid to meet my maker. Everyone has to die sometime. We are born one day and then buried another. My final resting place may not be up to me. I could end up at the bottom of the ocean, buried in the ground, or on someone's mantle in a vase, like a piece of art. How ironic would that be?

The door opens and Jenny steps inside wearing a T-shirt and sweatpants.

She's a glutton for punishment.

She walks over to the wall, opens a door, and drags out a hose. A smile tugs at the corner of her mouth as she opens the valve and blasts my dangling frame with cold water.

I open my mouth and welcome the moisture.

Her eyes darken, and she approaches me with a fierce stare. The pressure washer rolls across the floor as she circles my body and continues bombarding it with liquid punishment.

I shake my hair and smile. She grimaces and aims it at my face. I shape my mouth into a circle like a clown at a carnival water gun game trying to win a prize.

"Do you think this is a game?" She holds the hose a few feet from my face.

I chuckle, and the hose sprayer strikes my face without warning, busting my lip open. Blood splatters onto the floor, and I glare at her.

Our time will come. I won't always be in restraints.

"Stop!" Griffin's voice startles Jenny as he enters the room with Benny on his heels.

She releases the nozzle and drops to her hands and knees. Griffin stands over her and seizes her by the hair. "Lick my shoes, dirty whore."

Benny looks away as she laps up their filth—dirt, grit, and all, then dries them with the hem of her shirt.

I roll my eyes and Griffin's eyes darken. "Benny, what time do the buyers arrive?" He places his palm on Jenny's face as she starts to stand and pushes her away from him.

Benny glances at his watch. "About an hour." He reaches his hand out to help Jenny off the floor.

"Good. I want them to see what is coming soon." He nods towards the open door, signaling for Benny and Jenny to leave the room.

Once they are out of sight, Griffin lifts the hose from the ground and sprays me from head to toe. He drags an industrial-sized fan from the utility closet and aims it right at me. Goosebumps pop up all over my skin as he cranks it high, hardening my nipples.

"The buyers love hard nipples…" He grins and grasps my right breast from the side. "…and so do I." My nipple disappears into his mouth. He sucks it like a gourmet lollipop, and moans seductively. "You taste so fucking good."

He squeezes my breast one last time before releasing it and walking away. The door bounces off the wall as Griffin whips it open, then slams it shut.

I glance at the eye hook securing the wire to the ceiling when the camera indicator light turns from green to red.

Righty tighty, lefty loosey.

I run on my tippy toes, counterclockwise. As soon as I gain momentum, I raise my feet and swing in a circle like Tarzan on a vine. The eye hook shifts as it slowly unscrews from the ceiling. I stop at once when the hatch opens and Benny climbs down.

In one way and out another. There are two ways in and out of this place.

Good to know.

He stops in front of me and swipes his face with his trembling palm. "I don't like you, and I don't like what you did to my girl. The only reason you're still alive is because of Griffin. Remember that, the next time you do something stupid."

I grin when he turns his back on me. "She likes the taste of his shoes. I bet she loves his cock even more." I make slurping noises.

Benny spins around, lunges for me, and grips my throat, cutting off my airway. "Watch your fucking mouth. We share her, but she is mine to control." He pushes my face back.

"I bet they fuck when you're not around." I hump the air and moan with a smile. "I bet she screams his name. *'Oh, Griffin. Fuck me, baby. Fuck me like Benny can't.'* They're probably fucking right now."

"Fuck you!" Benny punches my face with a weak strike.

Blood drools from my lips onto the floor. Another blow lands on my already bruised left eye.

Try and sell me now, bitches.

Griffin speeds down the ladder and drags Benny away from me by his shirt, tearing it at the neck. "What the fuck? We have buyers arriving any minute and you are fucking up the merchandise, Benny!"

"She talked. She said you fuck Jenny when I'm not here, and she likes sucking your dick." Benny's eyes narrow. "Is that true?"

"Seriously, Benny? I don't break my own rules. I don't fuck with Jenny until you've finished with her for the night. You know that. It's always been that way. Besides, I have Audrey right now, and we just brought in the new girl. We can start working on her soon. I know Jenny is your favorite."

"And what about her?" Benny nods in my direction. "When are you going to start working on her?"

"Soon." Griffin stares into my eyes, and I flutter my lashes.

"Fine." Benny crosses his arms.

"Make sure the other two are ready for sale—use the new dresses we bought last week."

"Whatever." Benny waves over his shoulder and walks out of the room.

Griffin glares at me. "You have only been here a few days and are already causing trouble. Your death would be regrettable, but I'll do what I must to protect my business."

Men's voices breach the silence above us. Shadows move and darken the hatch opening. The buyers have arrived.

Griffin watches as an alligator loafer steps on the first rung and makes its way down. He turns my head to face him. "You better behave."

I flub my lips, making raspberry noises, and roll my eyes, annoyed with his rules.

He balls his fist. "Don't test me."

I stare at his ass as he strolls away and shakes the hand of the first buyer. He's an older man with steel gray hair, a three-piece suit, and too much jewelry. Griffin steers him around me, but the buyer is curious. He stops and backs up to face me.

"What's her story?" The walking jewelry display rotates the gold Figaro bracelet on his wrist.

"She's new and needs a lot of work." Griffin grips the man's shoulder and turns him towards the open door.

The buyer glances over his shoulder before they enter the room. I run my tongue over my bottom lip and smile at him. He turns back to Griffin. "How much?"

"Mr. Barnes, she's not for sale. Not yet anyway."

The old man adjusts his tie. "What's her name?"

"Willow."

The old man removes a notepad from his inside pocket and scratches down my name with his left hand. "Let me know when she's ready. I want her." He passes the paper to Griffin.

"It will be a while. Perhaps you could pick another girl for now."

"No. I want her." The man puts his notepad back in his pocket and walks to the hatch exit. "Call me when she's ready." He climbs up the ladder, hesitating only when I smile at him, and then keeps going.

Griffin leaves the room and returns with duct tape and a piece of fabric. "If I lose any more money because of you, we are going to have problems." He presses the tape hard against my lips and tightens the fabric around my eyes so tight it shifts my eyeballs back.

His footsteps fade away and a door closes. I may not be able to see or speak, but I can still hear, and unfortunately, smell.

Benny's high-pitched voice grows louder as he leads the next person down. Musky cologne fills my sinuses, drying my throat when I inhale. The air thickens with sweaty body odor as Benny and the buyer stop in front of me.

"Why is she not in with the rest?" The buyer's loud voice is just as irritating as his smell. He steps closer, overpowering the air between us with his scent.

Benny clears his throat. "She's new, and we are still working on breaking her."

I grind the air in front of me and moan.

Benny grabs my hair and shakes my head. "Fucking stop."

"That will be enough of that." The man issues a stern warning to Benny. "Reserve her for me, would you?" A slight touch grazes the space between my breasts.

"I'm sorry, Mr. Dietrich, she's unavailable."

"Get your brother out here." The buyer raises his voice.

"Griffin will tell you the same thing."

Soft hands caress my abdomen. "Take off her blindfold and gag. I want to see her eyes and teeth."

"I can't do—"

"Now!" The man shouts, interrupting Benny.

I bite down on my gag with a devilish grin.

Benny's unkept nails scrape my forehead as he yanks the material away from my eyes. The man picks the corner of the tape with his well-manicured nails and peels it from my lips. He caresses the bottom one with his thumb, and my tongue comes out to greet it. His eyes are green like mine and the hair on his head is as orange as the fruit itself.

Jenny enters dressed in a cocktail dress with her hair pinned back. She walks with a supermodel stride, one foot in front of the other, swinging her hips as she passes a glass of champagne to Dietrich. "Welcome, Mr. Dietrich."

"Thank you, young lady." He takes a sip and passes it back.

Griffin enters, rubbing his palms together. "Ready to see the merchandise?"

"Have either of you had her yet?" Dietrich turns my body and smiles at my ass.

"No." Benny eyes Griffin.

Dietrich strokes my left nipple with his fingertip. "Good. Keep it that way."

17

"Mr. Dietrich, that's not how we do business," Griffin says over his shoulder as he exits the room.

I whimper and furrow my brow at Dietrich. "Please don't let Benny touch me. He has dicken pox. I don't want to catch them."

"Lying fucking cunt." Benny balls his fist and charges me.

Dietrich wedges his body between Benny and me, placing his hand on Benny's chest. "What the fuck is dicken pox?"

"She's a liar. I don't know what she's even talking about."

Dietrich turns away from Benny and gazes into my eyes. "Explain."

"They look like chicken pox, but they are all over his cock. It's probably herpes," I fake cry.

"You liar." Benny's fist just misses my face as he swings. Deitrich catches his wrist and tosses it away. "Don't you dare."

"She's full of shit. Jenny, tell him."

Dietrich raises his hand in front of Jenny's face, silencing her. "Prove it."

"What's going on?" Griffin enters carrying a piece of paper and pen.

Benny takes long strides and stops before Griffin. "Willow told Mr. Dietrich I have something wrong with my dick. Now he wants proof that I don't."

Griffin moves Benny out of his line of sight. "I don't think proving it is necessary. I can vouch for my brother."

Dietrich unbuttons his jacket and moves it aside, revealing a 9 mm handgun. "Show me."

I raise my right eyebrow and smirk at Benny. My head sways on my shoulders as I hum.

Na na na na na na.

"You knock it off." Griffin points at me and stares at Benny. "Benny, do what he says."

"What? Here? Now?" Benny's eyes dart around the room.

"Yes, Benny dammit. Right now. Drop your fucking pants."

Benny grabs his belt and pulls the leather end from its buckle. He unbuttons his jeans, unzips them, and yanks them down with his underwear.

I smile broadly. Just as I suspected. He and his brother are opposites not only in size and build but in manhood as well.

Benny's eyes set on mine, and I blow him a kiss.

Dietrich chuckles and glances at me. "You little liar." He turns to Griffin. "Put my name in for when she's ready."

Dietrich walks away and climbs up the ladder.

Griffin glowers at me.

A lesser woman would feel threatened, but I'm not concerned.

I shrug my shoulders.

Losing money isn't their only problem. Sometimes you must play with your prey before you kill it.

Griffin marches to the ladder and climbs out of sight.

Jenny speed-walks towards me and tosses the unfinished champagne onto my face. "You'll regret this."

I lap the liquid from my lips and grin. I have no regrets, but Griffin and Benny will.

Jenny storms away as Benny buttons his pants. He fumbles with his belt buckle and turns his back on me, huffing under his breath.

What a weak, defeated, and spineless pussy. He needs to jump off a building and get it over with.

Perhaps he needs someone to push him.

"Eenie weeny tiny peenie," I sing with a smile.

Benny quickly unbuckles his belt and yanks it from the loops of his pants. He turns to me slowly, swinging the belt buckle side down, with a sinister smile. The first swing misses me entirely.

Fucking idiot can't even hit a stationary target.

He moves closer and lashes me repeatedly as he screams. I cackle and press him further. "My pussy is bigger than your cock."

Benny tosses the belt aside and charges me.

My body shifts around like a punching bag.

With every strike, I laugh harder.

Griffin's boots squeak as he climbs quickly down the ladder. He grabs Benny around the waist and drags him away. Griffin pauses in the doorway, with his hand on the handle. He stares at me with rage in his eyes, and my stomach quivers.

I'm not afraid, just giddy that I'm wearing on him.

The slamming door echoes around the room, and the lights go out at once. They have zero sense of humor.

I have a method to my madness. People hunt for a variety of reasons, but the majority do it for the same reason as me.

To eat.

Chapter Three
Ari

No one enters the hanging room for hours. After losing two sales to me, I imagine they rerouted their buyers through the other entrance.

Shouting and a loud bang come from the only door with light beneath it.

"Fuck this whole day." Benny stomps in and walks to the storage closet.

He yanks the black hose from its wheel, unraveling it in a heap. The faucet handle screeches as he turns it. He sprays the front side of his jeans. A yellowish-brown substance with a chili-like texture washes down the floor drain. He turns off the water right as Griffin enters carrying an unconscious brown-haired girl over his shoulder. He secures her to the wire hanging across from me. Her red sugar-skull-covered sundress does little to hide her backside that's also covered in the same substance as Benny's pants.

Benny wipes moisture from his eyes and tosses the hose back into the closet.

Griffin rolls his eyes. "Put it away correctly."

"I'm not doing shit. I need a fucking shower." He walks around Griffin and disappears.

Griffin glances at my smiling face and grimaces. "I'll be back for you shortly."

I gawk at his backside and the way it swaggers as he too, leaves the room.

"Thank God. I thought they'd never leave." The girl hanging across from me raises her head revealing her swollen face and smiles.

I don't know how or why she is so happy with her current situation. Perhaps she's one of those optimists who thinks because she's still alive, there is hope.

Stupid girl. There are worse things than death.

I twist myself around, turning my back on her as she continues talking.

"What did you do to get strung up?"

Great. She's a talker.

"I shit on Benny when he tried to fuck my ass with his tiny dick." She snorts and chuckles. "He wanted to act nasty, so I gave him nasty."

A very funny and entertaining talker.

"I've never been so happy that the tacos I ate didn't agree with me. Granted, now I smell like sour garbage, and my ass crack is chaffing from the shit that's still in it, but it was so worth it."

I rotate around to face her, intrigued.

"I would do it again, just to watch that little weasel squirm." Her face goes blank and her eyes empty. It was as though her spirit left her body and went for a walk.

After several seconds of silence, she slowly turns her head to look at me, and a joker-like smile spreads across her face.

She's back.

I like her. Anyone who causes them displeasure benefits me.

"I'm Ari. What's your name?" She tilts her head and furrows her brow.

The door whips open and Jenny comes in with food. "Are you talking? There's no talking."

"Nope." Ari whistles out of tune.

Jenny removes a steaming beverage from the tray and throws it on Ari. "Liar."

Ari lets out a pained scream that morphs into a laugh. "Fuck you, Jenny. I'll fucking kill you, then shit on your corpse."

Temper, temper. Love it.

Jenny takes a glass of orange juice and chucks it; glass and all, striking Ari in the mouth. Blood drips from Ari's lips onto her now chipped tooth. I produce a throaty laugh, and Jenny turns her angry baby-blue eyes on me. "What the fuck are you laughing at?"

"She's laughing at you; you sad weak little bitch." Ari cackles.

I join her and Jenny's face drops. The redder her face gets, the more we laugh.

Tears blur my vision as I'm wracked with mirth. An ammonia smell rises in the air as yellow liquid dribbles from Ari. I nearly lose it altogether at the disgust on Jenny's face as she dumps all our food on the ground and runs from the room.

Griffin steps into the room and glares at us, making us laugh harder. Ari shoots snot from her nose.

He storms into the utility room, fights to untangle the hose Benny never fixed, and blasts Ari with it. Droplets of water bounce off her and land on me as the high-powered setting lashes her bare legs while she cries out. Her skin reddens with angry welts as he douses her repeatedly. When her head drops, and she falls silent, he stops the water and walks away, dragging the hose behind him.

Ari lifts her head and smiles at me.

Fuck. She's not finished yet.

Her mouth opens wide, and she belts out the loudest, most obnoxious laugh I have ever heard. Griffin storms over to her without a word, removes his leather belt, and strikes Ari over and over as she screams.

Benny races into the room, and Jenny is quick to follow. He throws his arm against her chest as she nearly passes him. "Stay." He removes his belt and joins Griffin.

Jenny crosses her arms and smiles at me.

By the time the men finally grow tired, wavy crimson lines and bruises paint every inch of Ari. Blood trickles from her brutalized skin adding to the collection of bodily matter partially obstructing the floor drain.

Benny drops his weapon and rests his palms on his knees, panting heavily. Griffin takes the hose, turns it on the shower setting, and rinses Ari's motionless body.

The pain was too much—the beating too great.

Griffin winds the hose, puts it away, and walks out. Benny follows and Jenny shuffles behind him with a satisfied smile. They turn off the lights and close the door, but I can still see Ari's shape in the sliver of light coming from under it.

Quiet words stagger from Ari's lips. "I'm going to kill them."

She's not the only one.

But cats like to toy with their food before they eat.

Meow.

She takes several shallow breaths. "I'm going to find the chemicals I need, and then I'm going to blow this fucking hole out of the ground."

That sounds like a fantastic idea to me. I tilt my head. "Do you know how?"

"Of course I do. I'm a fucking chemist."

A chemist? How lovely. Perhaps we can become good friends during my stay. I need to learn what she's capable of.

"Ari, what kind of chemist are you?"

No response.

"Ari?"

Silence.

She's passed out.

It's fine. It will give me time to think. If she knows explosives and can do what she says, I need her alive. The only way that may happen is if we start cooperating or make them think we are.

After several minutes of quiet and soothing darkness, the light comes back on.

Fluorescent lights buzz over our heads. My eyes follow a fly as it swoops around the room and lands on Ari's eyebrow. It assesses her face for a few minutes, then flies away. The indicator light on the camera flickers back to red, and I tip-toe counterclockwise until I reach Ari.

"Ari?"

She doesn't move.

I stretch my foot forward and poke her with my big toe. Her eyes flutter, then open, but she doesn't have the strength to lift her head.

"Ari, can you do what you said?" I glance at the red dot above the door.

She groans and licks a dried clump of blood from her lip. "One of my cousins found a journal I created with different bombs and tried to make his own. He didn't blow anything up but did succeed in burning down the family garage. Fucking moron."

I can use her expertise to carry out my plan.

"What kind of chemicals do you need?"

No answer.

"Ari?"

She must be out again. I swing in a smaller circle, so I don't strike Ari. I prepare to make another rotation when the green light on the camera comes back on, stopping me.

The light above us flickers off, and the camera indicator light switches to red.

It must be a phone application they are using for surveillance. The indicator light changes only when they open it to check their cameras.

"What do you do?" Ari's voice breaches the darkness.

I walk on my tiptoes, closing the distance between us. "I'm an artist."

I can't tell her everything I do; in case the brothers are listening.

"What kind of artist?"

"A killer one." I grin in the dark.

There's a long awkward pause between us. I won't elaborate—keeping my answers short and the whole truth locked away inside me.

She huffs at my insufficient answer. "No, I mean drawing, painting, sculptures, and stuff."

Boy, she's persistent.

"I prefer painting on canvas."

"Do you like oil-based or watercolor?"

I don't answer. You can't buy the paint I use at any arts and crafts store.

The light turns back on, and I make no effort to return to my spot. A small amount of tacky blood creates a partial circle between Ari and me. Using my toes, I make the circle whole, add eyes, a smiling mouth, and boop a tiny nose in its center.

Have a nice day.

Ari smiles at the drawing right before her eyes close.

I move back to my own space and think about how much vacation time I have left. Being a security consultant has its benefits. I get to travel a lot, rent luxury cars, stay at fancy hotels, and eat delicious food for free. But when it's time for a break, I can take months off, and my employer doesn't even bat an eyelash. That's the benefit of being an independent contractor. I can choose whether I want to take a job or not.

The car I rented for my little hiatus was due back yesterday. Griffin took the paperwork from the car, but my guess is, he never checked the trunk. Someone will notice it sitting on the side of the road, day after day. It won't be long now.

Ari moans across from me and mumbles about her aching shoulders. She may be tough, but most people who can feel pain can't withstand this amount of abuse for long. Did they take her from the side of the road like me, or kidnap her from some random location? What is their selection process?

I close my eyes and picture my surroundings—a massive room with one exit, bathroom, kitchen area, with a bed. That's all I have so far. Griffin, Benny, and Jenny must have a room, and the other girls as well. One of them has another way out.

I need to find it.

Chapter Four
The Tour

After several hours of silence, the door handle jiggles, and incomprehensible whispers come from the other side of the partition. Benny pokes his head inside and glances at me. His hair is wet from a recent shower. He turns back to the open doorway and murmurs something to someone over his shoulder.

It must be Jenny. He doesn't act secretive around anyone but her. He slides sideways into the room, strolls over to Ari, and yanks her head back.

She spits in his face. "Pussy."

He punches her in the stomach, knocking the air from her lungs. She gasps multiple times.

When our eyes meet, I shake my head. She needs to cooperate, or we will never get out of this room.

Benny unhooks her cuffs from the ceiling, and she drops to the floor in a heap. "Get up."

Ari staggers to her feet and collapses back down. Benny rolls his eyes at her weakened state. He grips her upper arm, half lifting and half dragging her out of the room.

He returns without Ari a few minutes later and reaches for my shackles.

"No." Griffin appears behind him.

Benny wipes his palms on his pants. "She's not going with the rest?"

Griffin's eyes scan my body as he rubs his chin. "No. I'll take her myself."

"Since when? I always take the girls to the holding room before we prepare this room for the banquet."

Griffin huffs through his nose. "Like you said, this one's different." He stops beside me.

Benny throws his hands up in the air and stalks into the next room. "Whatever."

Griffin shifts his weight from one foot to the other, crosses his arms, and glares at me. "You know, I don't want to kill you…" He hooks his thumbs over the edge of his belt and stares at the floor. "…but if you cause me any grief whatsoever, I won't hesitate to snap your neck. Understand?"

I raise my left brow and nod.

He reaches over my head, his chest bumping into mine, and detaches me from the wire. I release a staggered breath and close my eyes. When I open them, he's staring at my lips. I slide my tongue over my smile, a slow tease from left to right.

"Knock it off." He rotates me away from him and uses his palm on my upper back to guide me forward.

I drop my arms to my side, letting the blood rush back to my fingertips, and move slowly towards the door. Benny stands in front of me, blocking the entrance. He has an odd odor to him, almost like... he ate too much garlic pizza. The smell permeates the air, seeping from his pores. His clothes remind me of what the boys in gym class used to throw on in high school—wrinkled elastic shorts and an old vintage rock t-shirt.

"You better not try anything, or I will cut up that pretty face of yours." Benny touches my cheek.

I bite his pointer finger hard and shake my head back and forth like a dog thrashing its favorite toy.

Griffin grabs me around the throat, cutting off my airway. I let go, but he doesn't. The room darkens and my legs fail me, but Griffin doesn't let go.

His blurring face comes within inches of mine. "Big mistake."

I smile, just a little, and succumb to the darkness.

I wake up in a different room, tied spreadeagle and still naked. It's a tiny space, no more than one hundred square feet. The walls are bare—devoid of windows and any source of charm. A small cabinet hangs above the metal headboard, and a chair leans against the wall beside it.

Griffin stands across from me in the doorway with a subtle smile lingering in the corner of his mouth.

He has plans for me.

I gaze at his bare feet. His toes are long and lean, with sparse amounts of hair on top. The frayed bottoms of the faded ripped jeans he is wearing buckle slightly at his ankles. His white underwear band peeks out of the top.

I want to grab the elastic, pull it away from his bony hips, and release it.

Snap.

He climbs on the bed and places one foot on either side of my chest, straddling me.

From my vantage point, he looks like a giant—tall, godly, and powerful. I want to reach up, rip his zipper open, and eat his cock.

His head tilts as a twisted smile spreads across his face.

I reciprocate with a smile of my own. If I had to pee right now, I would.

He unbuttons his jeans and unzips them very slowly.

My heart skips in my chest. With every click of the zipper, my pulse elevates a little higher.

His hand skims the front of his abdomen before disappearing inside his underwear.

My pussy lips twitch. I swallow hard, anticipating what's to come. His massive cock springs from his underwear, and he points it at me. I stare at the end of its perfect, round tip, shaped like a delicious mushroom. I would trim it off delicately and sauté it in olive oil with a bit of garlic.

Warm liquid strikes me in the face. I shake my head back and forth, trying to avoid getting his piss in my mouth. Mother fucker.

I want to scream. I want to tell him I plan on cooking his cock for dinner while enjoying a glass of Merlot. But I won't because that's what he wants. He wants to punish me for my behavior. I close my eyes and take a slow, deep breath.

Don't react, don't react, don't react.

I open my eyes when the cabinet above me creaks open. Flakes of particleboard float down and land on my face and chest.

Griffin removes a gas mask and secures it to his face. My pussy drips with excitement.

I love fucking masked men. It's my favorite fantasy.

He pulls his jeans and underwear off and tosses them on the chair.

My breath quickens. I can feel my hunger for him becoming insatiable. His massive veiny cock dangles above me, and I rock my pelvis towards him.

His eyes smile through the circles in the mask.

My pussy lips swell. They need to depressurize, and he needs to be the one to do it. I moan and clench my ass cheeks together lifting my hips upward, waiting for him— needing him. He reaches into the cabinet above me and pulls out a canister.

My, oh my. What do we have here? Is this part of the game?

He tilts his head and slides his right thumb into the center of the ring on the canister.

I stop humping the air.

He wouldn't dare.

Click.

Son of a bitch.

Gas fills the room. I hold my breath for as long as possible, but eventually, I gasp for air, filling my lungs with noxious gas. My eyes water without control and liquid pours from my nostrils.

I've never felt so vulnerable. I'm completely at his mercy, somewhere I never wanted to be.

The weight of Griffin's body drops onto me, crushing my chest. He presses himself inside me, wraps his hand around my throat, and squeezes. My body shifts back and forth as he rams it repeatedly.

I'm suffocating. The room is cloudy, and black spots speckle my blurry vision. I can't keep my eyes open. Between the gas and Griffin's grip on my neck, I'm losing strength. I can feel my body growing weaker by the second.

He's killing me.

He's killing me as he fucks me.

I'd never cared before if I lived or died, but going out this way was not what I envisioned.

It's too soon and not part of the plan. If I don't die, I'll never have sex with a masked man again.

The tension in my body relaxes. It has no more strength to thrash about or energy to try and break free. My body is giving up.

I'm giving up.

His grip, and the gases, rob me of breathable air and the ability to cough. I squint my eyes, trying to focus, but their constant watering hinders my ability to see anything clearly.

Griffin releases my throat as his pace slows. He rocks into me one last time, holds his cock deep inside me, and moans.

His cum fills my insides, nauseating me.

This isn't what I expected.

I thought I could enjoy a bit of rough sex, which I love, before killing him but this was not what I had in mind. When it comes to his brother, he doesn't care if I die. All that mattered to him was punishing me for hurting Benny and fucking me was just a bonus. Money making may be the goal for their business, but family matters more to him. Benny matters more.

How lovely.

I will use this to my advantage. But first, I need to find a way to make me too valuable to kill.

Griffin's heaving chest presses into mine with every heavy breath he takes.

His cock slides out of me as it softens and rests against my taint.

I squint my eyes and try to focus on the chair beside the bed but they're still too blurry—too watery.

Griffin shifts his knees forward and sits on my lower abdomen.

I won't look at him despite feeling his eyes on me through the mask. He turns my head to face him, and I let it fall back to the side.

He dismounts me and flicks a switch on the wall. A fan draws the smoke from the room, and he waits beside the bed for the air to clear.

I smile at him. Boogers stretch across my lips like sticky taffy, so I blow a bubble.

Pop.

He grabs my snot-covered face with both hands, and the mouthpiece of the mask strikes my lip as he hovers less than an inch from me. "You will learn to behave. You will not touch or hurt my brother ever again. You are not even to speak to him unless spoken to."

Oh, Darth Vader, you have no idea what I have in store for your precious brother.

He releases my face and pulls his jeans off the chair. The sound of his zipper going up is louder than it should be. Everything seems louder—his footsteps, the doorknob turning, him leaving the room.

The door shifts, and Benny peeks inside. "You gassed her?" He enters with his black t-shirt covering his nose and mouth.

"Yes." Griffin's voice carries from the next room.

"What was it like?"

Griffin comes back in and places the mask inside the cabinet. He unhooks me from the bed's four corners and sits me upright. "You understand the rules?"

Of course, I do. It doesn't mean I'll follow them.

I nod to appear compliant.

He smiles at Benny and pulls me to my feet. "It was productive. She'll behave." His eyes squint and darken. "Won't you?"

I nod.

For now, I will play along. But soon; soon they will scream my name, and it won't be from pleasure.

Benny stops beside me and grabs me by the pubic hair. "I have to take antibiotics because of you."

Griffin squeezes Benny's wrist, forcing him to release me, and pokes him hard in the chest with his fingers. "Don't fucking touch her. You didn't want her, remember? She's mine and mine alone. No one touches her but me, ever."

Ooh wee. Possessive much?

"Alright, alright Griff. Geez, you don't have to be so aggressive about it."

I smile at Benny and Griffin catches me. "Look at me." He points to his face. "Only me. Understand?"

I nod and continue to smile. He breathes heavily through his nostrils. "Let's get you cleaned up and dressed."

We pass a floor-length mirror, and I catch a glimpse of myself. Blood stains my inner thighs, and superficial bite marks litter my abdomen.

This isn't me. It can't be. My body has always been perfect. I focus on my face, touching it to make sure it's real. Snot and tears dry to a crust that cracks when I move my jaw. I run my fingers over the textured crescent-shaped mark on my breast.

When did he bite me? It must have been when I passed out from him choking me after I bit Benny.

Blood pounds in my head.

He's scarred and battered my perfect skin. I swallow hard, grit my teeth, and hold my tongue. I'm not giving him the satisfaction of knowing how angry I am.

He smiles out of the corner of his mouth and holds my throat tenderly from behind. "Beautiful girl…" His thumb rests on the carotid artery of my neck as he stares at our reflection. "…you may not be able to feel what I can do to you…" When I look away from the mirror, he snatches my chin and turns me back. "…but you can see it."

His hand slides around my waist and he digs his nails deep into my stomach. My eyes widen as he rakes them from front to back, leaving four angry bleeding lines of torn flesh. I glower at the streaks of blood as they race toward my upper thigh.

My face prickles. I close my eyes and shove aside the raging thoughts barreling through my mind. His time will come. And when it does, I will cut away all his usable meat while he's still alive and make an extravagant meal out of it. Not just for this, but for everything he has done.

He pulls me into the next room. It's painted red with a black tufted leather couch with antique gold nail heads, white stick lamps, a small round table, and two red velvet armchairs. Off to the side, another doorway leads to a similarly decorated bedroom.

We enter the bedroom, and he shoves me against the wall, holding me in place with a hand on my chest. "Stay."

He opens a wardrobe and paws through multiple articles of clothing.

My body slowly slides sideways. It wasn't on purpose. I think I'm just fucking exhausted.

Griffin grabs my shoulder and pushes me back upright. He removes a purple knee-length cocktail dress, tosses it on the bed, and pushes open another door. Inside is the shower where I first saw him naked.

My knees buckle, and I drop to the floor by his feet.

"Get up."

I stay on the floor, ignoring him.

He lifts me under the armpits, and I dangle there like an uncooperative child. I'm not going to make this easier for him. Not after what he's done to me.

"You're pissing me off." He walks backward, scraping my bare ass as he drags me across the floor and into the bathroom, where he drops me.

He removes his jeans and stuffs them inside a hamper.

I roll onto my stomach and rest my face on the cold concrete. My finger staggers across the floor's surface drawing imaginary pictures.

Griffin snatches me by the hair and lifts me, but I won't stand. "Use your fucking legs." He growls, growing frustrated with my antics.

When he lets me go, I curl into a ball and close my eyes.

He walks away, turns the water on, and stands behind me. "Last chance. Get up, or else."

I turn my head and glare at him with a devious smile.

He kicks my back, and I shift towards the shower. "Move. Right now!" he shouts.

I crawl under the water and watch it circle the drain.

Griffin grabs a sponge on a stick, and dribbles coconut-smelling body wash on it. His balls shift around as he cleanses my bodily fluids from them. He kneels before me, forces me into a sitting position, and presses his forearm into my throat, holding me against the shower wall. "Don't move."

My skin reddens as he scrubs it hard, glaring into my eyes as he washes me. He squirts soap into his hand and strokes my inner thighs, cleaning his fluids off my skin.

His cock grows, and I can see the glimmer of his arousal in his expanding pupils. He grabs my hair, flips me onto my stomach in front of him, and scrubs my back beneath the falling water. His hand encapsulates my right ass cheek right before he squeezes it tenderly.

What the fuck is going on?

Pressure enters my anus, and I inch myself forward. No one has ever done this to me. I have rules. Assholes are for exiting shit only.

Period.

He pushes his finger deeper inside and moans. "So, tight. I would be willing to bet, no one has ever fucked you here before. Have they?" He climbs onto my back and kneads my cheeks like he's prepping dough for baking.

No, no, no. This can't happen.

I buck my body under him, push off the back shower wall with my toes, and launch myself onto the concrete floor. He dives onto my spine, crushing me against the hard surface, and knocking the wind out of me.

His breath warms my neck as he speaks softly in my ear. "Where do you think you're going?"

I try to lift my head, but he presses it against the floor with his palm, crushing my jaw against the unforgiving floor.

He grinds his hardening cock against my ass and smells my hair. "I love how you smell—so clean, so pure."

My exterior is the only part of me that's clean and pure. Everything else is rotten to the core.

I gasp for air when he pushes his arms straight, taking the weight off my back, and hovers over me in a plank position—his dick still touching my backside.

"If I had more time, I'd fuck that ass right here and now." He huffs and stands up, lifting me to my feet.

He walks me forward, stops before the partially fogged mirror, and slides his fingers up and down the lines on my abdomen, like the strings of a guitar.

Fucking asshole.

I tilt my head forward then drive it back into his face. His nose crunches as it breaks. He howls and throws me straight into the mirror, shattering its glass. My distorted, hunched-over image shifts across the broken remnants on the floor. He grabs me by the shoulders, forces my body flat, and sits on my back—droplets of his blood splatter onto my spine, and shards of glass dig into my abdomen.

Benny runs into the room, hearing the commotion.

Griffin raises the bloody hand covering his nose over my head and points to the door. "Out."

Blood falls from his pointing finger and dots the side of my face like freckles.

Benny cuts me a hateful glance before leaving the room and closing the door behind him.

"You must be a slow learner." He lays the full weight of his body on me—fragments of glass cut deeper into my bare skin.

It's not about slow learning, Griffy.

It's about wearing you down, strumming your last nerve, and discovering all your weaknesses.

"Did you like being gassed?" He whispers in my ear.

My bloodshot eyeball looks back at me in the reflection of a shard of glass by my face. I didn't mind the gas. It sucked, but at least it didn't scar my body. That was all Griffin.

"Answer me." He snarls.

Blood, from a piece of glass in my arm, smears the floor to my right. I take my finger and spell out my response.

'Fuck You.'

"Fucking cunt," Griffin shouts.

The floor suddenly disappears, and my body sails through the air, smashing into the cement wall. I slide sideways, and the room darkens.

Griffin storms towards me, tiptoeing around the bits of glass on the floor, blood still dripping from his nose, and yanks me up by the ears. He pulls my face even with his. "Say something."

I smile a big, toothy smile through my bloody pearly whites.

He hates that I won't speak to him—won't beg for him to stop.

I don't beg.

I'm not a fucking dog.

The blood-soaked hair in his nose shifts inside his flaring nostrils.

I can feel his rage and anger. He wants to kill me. If I were him, I'd want to kill me too.

But that's the difference between us. He needs me alive, despite all his threats and promises to kill me.

My fingernail glides smoothly down his abdomen and stops between his legs. I drag my nail across his hairless balls and smirk. A few slices with a scalpel, and I could take his balls out and rotate them in my palm like a set of Chinese Baoding Balls.

He grips my wrist and twists it. "Scream for me."

I glare at him as the pressure builds in my wrist. He continues to rotate it unnaturally despite my growing smile.

A wild cackle breaks from my throat, and Griffin throws me to the ground. "Stubborn bitch."

He kicks my legs and stomach. "Beg me to stop."

The anger inside me grows, heating the blood surging through my veins.

I could kill him now. One vicious bite on his neck—tearing his carotid artery with my teeth. But it's too soon.

Too easy.

Too merciful.

My body moves farther away from him as he continues to kick me. I chuckle at the way his dick swings and slaps the side of his muscular leg every time he strikes me.

"Fuck." Griffin yelps and jerks his knee toward the ceiling.

He grabs his foot, rotates it so the bottom faces him, and pulls a sliver of glass from his heel.

I laugh as blood trickles from his foot onto the floor.

His eyes narrow to slits as he glares at me. I cover my head but not in time to avoid the blow. Griffin's open palm slaps me hard in the ear taking my hearing at once. It rings noisily as he picks me up by my hair and strikes me again, this time in the eye, making it water.

"Griffin, stop!" Benny yells, entering the room with Jenny.

Griffin glares at him. "She broke my fucking nose."

"I get it. But we can't sell her if she's dead."

Griffin clasps his hands behind his head, his eyes wild and jaw clenching as he walks away from me and paces the room.

He swipes his face with his hand and blood splats on the floor with a sharp flick of his wrist.

I smile up at Griffin's reddening face and carelessly crawl over particles of glass to the bloody droplets he's provided me. The tip of my finger warms as I dip it into multiple crimson dots.

Benny narrows his eyes at me as I draw a circle and suck the metallic juice from my pointer.

I dab a bloody cut on my leg and add two eyes, a nose, and a mouth to the circular shape with a defiant smile on my face.

Jenny's eyes dart to Griffin, waiting for him to do something about my behavior.

He won't even look at me. His eyes fixated on the bloody happy face.

Benny scuffs my artwork with his shoe, smearing it and breaking Griffin's focus. He glances at Benny and walks away without a word.

When Jenny turns to leave, Benny grabs her arm. "Clean her up the best you can and help her get dressed."

Jenny's eyes dart from me to Benny. "But she's not in any shape to—"

Benny snatches her harshly by the back of the neck and forces her to the floor. "Do as I say." His sharp words silence her at once and bring tears to her eyes.

She grabs his knee with shaking hands, keeping her eyes on the floor. "I'm sorry."

He glares down at her and yanks his leg from her grasp. "Don't be sorry. Just do as you're told." Towels land in her lap as he throws them at her on his way out of the room.

She lifts my skull, sets it on her lap, and wipes the blood from my cheeks. I force my swelling eye open far enough to see her through my lashes.

When she sees me watching her, she drops the cloth, grabs my hair with both hands, and shakes my head violently. "You're fucking up the routine. I hate you. I hate you. I hate you. Just do what they say, or fucking die already."

Moisture lands in my eye as she spits on me.

She's a victim too, but it doesn't matter now. I've had enough. No one spits on me.

No one.

Chapter Five
Buyer Beware

After cleaning me up, helping me with my dress, and half carrying me to Griffin's room, Jenny leaves me with a bag of frozen peas to reduce the swelling around my eye.

I could have walked there without her help, but I have no intention of making things easy for her going forward.

An unfamiliar face enters and stops abruptly when she sees me. I don't know how I look, but judging by the solemn look on her face, it must be bad.

"I'm Audrey," she says quietly, sitting beside me on Griffin's bed, and unzipping a makeup bag.

Her black cocktail dress shifts above her discolored knees, and she yanks the hem back down. "You need to stop fighting them." Cool and creamy cover-up smears across my forehead. "If you do as they say, they won't hurt you. You can eat, drink, and even talk to the other girls. If not, they will starve you and beat you, until there's nothing left."

I seize her pale wrist and examine the cigarette burns on her forearm.

She pulls away from me and continues spreading concealer on my skin with tremoring hands. "They're not from them." Her eyes refuse to look into mine. "I don't know how long I was here before I learned my lesson." Her voice quivers. "Christmas came and went, that much I know. I was a fighter like you, Willow. Trust me when I tell you, it's not worth it."

Her eyes dart over mine but don't linger. I remain quiet as she swipes an emerald-green shadow on my lids. Bruises and scrapes cover both her kneecaps. I touch dried blood on one of them and her legs snap together quickly like an alligator's jaw.

She stops moving and holds her breath, frozen in fear by my subtle touch, and drops the shadow brush to the floor. Her hands caress her knees as she stares at the makeup applicator.

I bet on the surface, before these brothers dragged her into the depths of hell, she was once a beautiful and vibrant woman. A perfect rose with skin-like soft petals. Now, she's drained of life—tortured between the pages of someone else's story. Her life's no longer her own.

I lean forward, pick the shadow brush up, and rest it beside her on the bed.

She takes it, swallows hard, and continues talking. "Your eyes are beautiful. I wish I had pretty eyes. Instead, I got stuck with shit brown." She rotates the mascara rod in its container several times and brushes it on my lashes. "I should be leaving today. One of the buyers expressed interest last time we had a banquet." She clenches her jaw and spreads lipstick on my lips. "I know this situation isn't ideal…" She exhales a heavy sigh. "…but if you ever want to feel the warm sunshine on your face again, you'll learn to cooperate." She stuffs the makeup back in the bag and brushes her strawberry blonde hair over her shoulder. "There. It's not my best work, but it's the best I can do. Now let me do something about your hair."

She combs my hair over my left shoulder, twisting it as she goes to hold it together. The bed shifts up as she stands and extends her still-shaking hand out to me. It shudders involuntarily in my grasp as she pulls me to a standing position.

My legs quiver, and I nearly fall. She catches me in her arms, and our eyes lock for the first time. A lump develops in my throat. I stare deep into the eyes of this broken thing in front of me and know what I need to do.

She turns her head, breaking eye contact, and helps steady me when I stand.

I need to eat.

I need to drink.

I need to kill a motherfucker.

We move slowly from the room and enter the large space where Ari and I hung from the ceiling earlier.

This is what Benny meant by preparing the room for a banquet. They have transformed the place into a party hall.

Lights dangle from the wires and white linen cloths cover six round tables—candles flicker in their centers. A long buffet rests against the far walls with multiple wine bottles chilling in a bucket. They even covered the drain hole with a round gold-colored area rug.

Audrey leaves me at an empty table, and takes a seat alone at another, folding her hands in her lap.

I drum my fingers on the crisp white canvas and wish I had a paintbrush. My bare heels scrape back and forth on the textured floor, exfoliating them.

Jenny enters in a body-hugging gold, knee-length dress, and Ari hustles in behind her wearing a candy apple red one. Her eyes pan across the room. She waves when she sees me, pushes Jenny to the side, and sits at my table.

Griffin enters and walks briskly to us. "Get up," he orders, coming up behind Ari wearing a steel gray suit, white button-up, and baby blue tie.

She stares up at him and grimaces. "Why?"

He grabs her forearm and yanks her to a stand. "Go to an empty table."

Ari crosses her arms when he lets go of her and plops in a seat at the table to my right.

Griffin unbuttons the bottom of his jacket and sits beside me. Despite his attempt to hide my assault on him with some cover-up, bruising still darkens the skin under his eyes.

I can feel my face brighten, and even though my mouth isn't smiling my eyes are.

Griffin crushes my upper thigh in his grasp but says nothing.

I get the message. He's not finished with me yet. If it weren't for Benny interrupting his assault, he may have killed me.

I rest my palm on his white knuckles and wink at him.

He slides his hand from beneath mine, grabs my wrist, and slams my hand into my lap. "Keep your hands to yourself, psycho."

Psycho? Well, that is just downright rude even if it is true.

Two more girls—twins wearing white A-line halter dresses enter the room. They sit at separate empty tables and smile softly at each other. Their ebony skin glistens in the candlelight. I imagine Griffin and Benny use their love for one another to control them.

Benny stops behind Griffin's chair, wearing a similar suit to his brother, and leans down. "You shouldn't have her out here."

Griffin tips his head back and smiles at him. "What's the matter, brother? Afraid I'll start a bidding war and rake in a bunch of cash you can't have?"

Benny stands tall and leers at him. "Don't say I didn't warn you."

I take my fingers and shape them into a 'V' in front of my open mouth and plunge my tongue between them, wiggling it at Benny.

Benny shakes his head and storms away. I drop my hand away from my face and rest it on the table before Griffin catches me.

There are six of us, but only three are available for sale.

I glance at Ari. Her mouth dangles open and drool drops down on the table. I continue staring at her, hoping she would sense me looking at her, but her eyes are blank and locked on nothing across the room.

She blinks several times and smiles at me.

I can't tell whether she's doing it for attention, or she has a problem.

Griffin nods at Benny. He unlocks a metal panel on the wall and presses a red button.

The hatch above us clicks open, and men descend the steps one at a time. The old man, Mr. Barnes, and Mr. Dietrich, the redhead, approach my table. Dietrich smiles as he sits beside me.

Griffin interlaces his fingers and furrows his brow as Mr. Barnes sits in the empty seat across from me. I'm not ready or for sale. The two men know this but sit at my table anyway. Other men of various ages and sizes sit at the available tables. The twins draw more men than chairs available, so the extras lean against the wall.

I scan the room, counting as I go. Twenty men fill the seats at the tables and four more lean against the wall. Two dozen buyers, ready to piss away a small fortune to take one of us home and use us as they see fit.

Fucking predators.

A young buyer, around twenty, with terribly bleached hair and an even worse spray tan, scurries between tables when he spots me from afar. His hunter-green suit needs to be set on fire. He stuffs his pudgy short fingers into his pants pockets and raises his eyebrows. "Who do we have here?"

"She's not for sale," Griffin says, more to the other men at the table than the California boy speaking to him.

"Then why is she here? Why are they sitting at her table?"

"That's a great question, Mr.?"

"Fields. Matthew Fields." He extends his hand to Griffin, who ignores it.

"The Powerball winner. I heard you were coming."

Great, an immature man-child with a lot of money.

He sits beside Griffin. "Well, let's see what's coming soon then." He shakes his napkin and rests it on his wide lap.

Griffin rubs his forehead. "First, we eat."

"I'm not hungry. Let's get to it," the newbie announces.

Griffin pounds his fist on the table, making the silverware and Matthew jump. "I know this is your first time, but if you continue testing me it will be your last."

"Well, Griffin…" Matthew's tone comes out sarcastic and cocky. "…I thought we were here to buy girls, not participate in cocktail hour, but it's your show."

Griffin sighs heavily through his nostrils, staring at him with murder in his eyes.

I don't blame him. I want to kill him just for the outfit he's wearing. He looks like an oversized leprechaun that ate his pot of gold.

Griffin nods at his brother, who then whispers to Jenny. She stands, adjusts her dress, and taps on a metal door. Three men, wearing all-white attire, enter and gather platters and plates from the buffet. One drops a dinner plate in front of each person at every table, while the other two carry slices of roast beef or chicken around the room and serve the men. They return to the buffet, pick up loaded baked potatoes and pre-dressed salads and return to the tables. Ladies get salad and salad alone. I wrinkle my nose and push the pile of greens away from me. I'm starving, but a bundle of rabbit food is not what I desire.

The servers pour wine for the men and water for the women. Mr. Dietrich selects a rare piece of beef.

My mouth waters. I want to roll it into a tube, dip it in au jus and suck it.

Griffin pushes my plate back in front of me. "Eat."

I take a sip of water and ignore him.

He seizes my left thigh and whispers in my ear. "Do you want more stripes?"

I unfurl my silverware.

Plastic. How classy.

Griffin and Dietrich unroll their shiny, high-end silverware.

Scraping comes from the table beside us. Ari scratches the tablecloth with her plastic fork, trying to scoop up a piece of lettuce she dropped.

I stab my greens hard, and a piece of fork tine snaps off and lands on Dietrich's plate. He picks it up and flicks it onto the floor without a word. I take a small bite of tomato with my three-pronged utensil.

My throat closes. The strong dressing gags me. I spit the partially chewed food into my napkin. Dietrich slices into his roast and scrapes the plate when he reaches the bottom. Every time he cuts, the screech of the knife against the plate gives me goosebumps.

Griffin leaves the table to speak with a late-entering buyer. They argue back and forth. The forty-something-year-old man with dark gray hair just turning lighter above his ears, sprays when he talks. A drop splatters in Griffin's eye, making me smile.

A scraping sound directs my attention to my plate.

Deitrich slides a fatty, juicy piece of meat onto my salad. "It's too red for me."

I grab the bloody piece with my bare hands, dunk it several times in his au jus, and stuff it in my mouth like a rabid animal. It is what I need—what I long for.

Griffin grips my throat from behind, pressing his fingers into my Adam's apple. "Spit it out. Now!" he shouts.

I can't breathe, and I can't swallow. I don't have a choice but to comply. The pile of pulverized meat rolls out of my mouth onto the tablecloth, staining it.

"Get up." Griffin sneers, lifting me under the armpits. "You're finished."

"Wait." Matthew holds his hand out to Griffin. "I want to see what's coming soon." He scans my body, his eyes stopping on my breasts.

Pervert.

Griffin glances around the quiet room.

Everyone's eyes are on our table. Matthew isn't the only one who wants to see what's coming soon.

Griffin frowns, grips the back of my dress, and rips it down. He turns me around, roughly grabs both shoulder straps, and tears my dress in half like a phonebook. It falls to the floor in a heap.

Dietrich leaps to his feet. His eyes lock on the bloody lines on my abdomen. "What happened?"

"We need to break her. You know the rules." Griffin smiles and runs his fingers down my arm.

"I told you not to take her. I wanted her as is. Now look what you've done to her."

"Well, you don't make the rules." Griffin's hand drops away from me, and he cracks his knuckles.

"How much?" Dietrich reaches inside his jacket and pulls out a black leather wallet.

"I told you, she's not ready yet."

"Doesn't matter. Name your price. I'll take her now, before you ruin her any further."

"No." Griffin's voice elevates, and his face reddens.

"Griffin, I won't take no for an answer. Now, name your price."

"It's not happening." Griffin picks up the remnants of my clothes and turns me away from the table.

Everyone gasps and stands. Dietrich disengages the safety from the gun now pointed at Griffin.

He can't kill him. He's mine. I won't allow it.

"You brought a gun in here? You know you can't bring a gun to banquets." Griffin glances at Benny.

"Open the hatch." Dietrich motions to Benny.

Benny walks slowly to the hatch button.

"Benny, don't you dare." Griffin stares at the barrel of the gun.

"Open the hatch and let us both out, or I will shoot you." Dietrich lifts the gun higher, aiming it at Griffin's face.

"Griffin, just let him have her. She's not worth it." Benny pleads.

"No. She's mine." His eyes are fierce and defiant.

Mine.

Dietrich's hands are steady. He's killed before. He's not afraid. He will kill Griffin.

The gun raises slightly.

I snatch Dietrich's fork off his plate and swing. Blood gushes from Dietrich's neck as he pulls the trigger—the bullet lodges in the wall next to Benny's head, an unfortunate miss.

I tilt my head and smile at Dietrich's wide-open eyes, yank the utensil from his artery, and sit in his chair. The undercooked beef drips blood down my hand as I roll it between my fingers, smear it around his plate, and stuff it into my mouth as he falls to the floor.

No one says a word—not even Griffin.

Blood pools around my chilled feet warming them. I scrunch my toes in the crimson and rock my head from side to side as I chew.

So…fucking…delicious.

I dip the next bite in au jus, curl my tongue around it, and roll it against the roof of my mouth. It's the best roast beef I have ever tasted.

My bloody teeth slide across Dietrich's fork, as he gurgles his last breath on the floor beside me.

Chapter Six
Reprieve

Silence.

If it were any quieter, you could hear the dust settling on the floor. I hold the final piece of beef in my mouth, close my eyes, and moan.

Jenny wedges herself between Griffin and me and grimaces. "You're not supposed to eat meat." She glances at Griffin, seizes one side of my plate with a trembling hand, and I hold the other.

She's trying to do what she thinks Griffin and Benny expect of her—stop me from breaking the rules.

I squeeze the fork in my grasp and glare at her. Of all the things she should be worried about right now, she's worried about what I'm eating. She has no idea how much danger she's in. Now is not the time to be their enforcer.

No one comes in between me and bloody red meat.

No one.

"Jenny…" Griffin grabs her left wrist, tilting the plate, and spilling some of the juices on the tablecloth. "…let it go."

Jenny glances at me one last time with pursed lips and releases the plate.

Griffin just saved her life. I would not have allowed her to deny me the best part. I cup the plate in both hands and tilt the bloody liquid into my mouth.

Jenny curls her upper lip and shakes her head. "Fucking disgusting."

I turn to her and swipe the drippings from my smiling lips.

"Everyone out," Griffin orders as he stands.

Benny weaves around a table and grabs Griffin's shoulder. "What are you doing? We need to sell the ready ones."

Griffin grabs Benny's hand and drops it off his shoulder. "You handle the sales."

"Get up." Griffin squeezes the back of my neck, lifts me to my feet, and shoves me in front of him, cracking my neck as it snaps backward. "Walk."

There's rustling behind us followed by a loud *thump*. We turn around to see Benny struggling to get to his feet. His shoes slide in the blood as he smears Dietrich's bodily fluids across the floor.

He grabs the table's edge, nearly tipping it over, staggers to a stand, and examines the stains. "Fuck. This is my favorite suit."

Ari points at Benny's butt and grins. "I think your hemorrhoid is bleeding."

"Fuck you!" Benny yells at Ari, then looks at me. "You stupid, bitch. This is your fault."

"Benny, the Bloody Butted Boy." Ari laughs obnoxiously and slaps her knee.

The entire room laughs as Benny covers his butt with his palm. "That's not funny."

"Silence!" Griffin shouts. "Anyone who has no plans to buy today, or soon, leave now. Everyone else, we will be with you shortly."

Of the twenty buyers who attended, only three stuck around—the immature lottery winner, Mr. Barnes, and the late arriving buyer.

Perfect. A man-child, a geriatric, and a mid-life crisis—the beginning of a terrible joke.

Griffin removes his blood-speckled suit jacket, places it beside Benny on the back of a chair and speaks in his ear. "When you're done with the sales, have the remaining girls help you clean up this mess."

He takes me by the arm, pulling me roughly through the kitchen and into the bathroom.

We stop in front of the newly replaced mirror.

Arterial spray from Dietrich casts red lines across my face and abdomen. My blood-coated right hand looks like I'm wearing only one glove.

Hee hee.

Griffin scans my battered body. His eyes take in every inch of me before stopping on my face. He removes his clothes slowly and walks me into the shower.

I have no cuffs, no restraints, nothing keeping me in this room.

He takes me by the throat and pushes me into the shower wall. "Why did you kill him?"

I don't answer.

His hand tightens, and my breathing shallows. "Why won't you speak to me? I know you can. Do you think by saving me, and killing him, I would take it easy on you?" He spins me around and stuffs his fingers inside me from behind. "I will rip your pussy to shreds with my bare hands." He removes his fingers and grips my labia tight, pulling them away from my body.

Oh fuck, I love this. It's like when I use clamps. He's turning me the fuck on. *Fucking squeeze them tighter and harder.* I need a release. I reach down and tighten his grip on me.

He yanks his hand from under mine and turns me back to him. "You like that, don't you?" His breath smells like roast beef. "I'm going to find a way to break you, and when I do, you'll be at my mercy."

I trace the outline of his lips with my fingers, then drag them over his six-pack down to his stiff cock and yank it several times, playing with my food.

He rests his forehead against mine and pulls my hand away. "You are not in charge here." My back flattens against the shower wall as he slams me against it, creating distance between us. "You are nothing but a new toy I'm playing with. And I'm not going to be gentle."

I smile to myself at his daring threats as he steps out of the shower and turns the water on.

Rust-colored water spins around the drain as I rub Dietrich's blood all over my skin like lotion.

Griffin grabs my hand, stuffs a washcloth in my palm, and squirts an excessive amount of body wash on it. "Wash."

Blobs of soap drop between my toes making them slippery. I wiggle them to clear it and start washing my neck.

He's staring at me, but I ignore him. I feel his eyes boring a hole in my face.

I let the washcloth fall from my hand and make no effort to pick it up. Griffin kneels, keeping his eyes on me as he retrieves it. His eyes lock on my pussy as he starts to stand. I grab his head and shove it harshly into me—grinding myself into him, nearly knocking him over.

He pulls his head away, stands abruptly, and squeezes my neck. "Do you think you're special?"

I nod.

Of course, I am. You dumb motherfucker.

"Well, you're not. When I get bored with you, I will pass you on to the next person, like an article of second-hand clothing." He steps out of the shower. "You will get nothing more from me."

No more masked man, Griffin? Bummer. I'll just take care of myself.

I slide down the shower wall until my ass hits the floor, then turn my body to face him as he dries himself. He's trying to ignore me, but I can see him watching me from the corner of his eye. I rotate my fingers around and around the outside of my vagina, twisting my pubic hair slightly, and stick my fingers inside—moaning loudly. Griffin turns away from me and pulls on his boxers, stuffing his still-hard cock inside.

Those blue balls are going to hurt later.

It's coming. I can feel my orgasm nearing the surface. My breath quickens as my inner thighs tingle—a sure sign I'm about to rupture. I close my eyes, but they spring back open as my fluids race to the finish line.

Griffin yanks my hand away, trying to stop me from getting what I want, but it's too late. My head launches backward, and my eyelashes flutter as I squirt onto the floor of the shower and cry out, ignoring Griffin's presence. "Oh, yes. Fuck me. That's what I'm talking about, baby. That's how it's done. Fuuuuck."

Griffin releases my hand and gawks at me.

I grip my pussy and tighten my thighs around my hand, panting heavily as I smile at the ceiling.

He seizes me by the hair on the top of my head, drags me out of the shower, and throws me to the floor. I flip onto my hands and knees, flexing and rotating my hips, panting heavily.

I got mine and there is nothing he can do about it.

The bathroom door slams open, and Benny hustles inside. "We have a problem." He stares at me as I continue humping the air. "What the fuck is she doing?"

"I don't fucking know, Benny. What's so important?"

"Maybe you should put her away first." Benny points at me.

Put me away? Like I'm an object and not a person.

"Benny, just spill it." Griffin rolls his eyes.

Benny's hands shake as he talks. "The buyers are gone." He glances at me, and I smile.

"How many did we sell?" Griffin's voice lowers.

"That's the thing…" Benny stares at a wad of loose hair on the floor.

Griffin snaps his fingers in Benny's face to get his attention. "How many?"

Benny hesitates and then finishes his sentence. "…none."

Griffin turns away from us, glances up at the ceiling, and then at the floor. "None? Seriously Benny, how did you fuck this up?" Griffin doesn't turn to face us.

Benny storms around Griffin and stands in front of him. "First of all, I didn't fuck this up, she did." He points at me, smiling on the floor behind Griffin. "And second, they're coming back."

"What the fuck do you mean, they're coming back?" Griffin furrows his brow and crosses his arms across his bare chest.

Benny steps away from Griffin and stops at my feet. "They want her."

I curl my legs under me, sit cross-legged, and raise my brows. I love it when people want me. Can't wait to hear this.

"All of them?" Griffin raises his eyebrows.

"Yeah. That's what I said. But they all pretty much said the same thing. They like her fight. She's not a type they'd typically think to ask for." Benny stares at my hands as I rub my inner thighs.

Not a type?

That must be how they choose who they take. Buyers make requests and Benny and Griffin do their best to find and kidnap what buyers are looking for—Ari, the smart sugar skull goth girl, the beautiful twin African goddesses— who wouldn't want them? As for Jenny, I don't know what the hell they were thinking of taking her. She had to have been someone Benny picked. I don't know much about her, but from what I've seen, she's a trifling bitch.

Griffin rubs his temple and leaves the room.

Benny puts his hands on his hips and glares at me. We stare at each other for what seems like forever, locked in a staring contest he will never win.

He blinks several times, and I smile at him. "You want to wrestle, Benny Boy?" I slap the floor with my palms on either side of my legs three times. "One, two, three, you're out."

I land on my side as he slaps me across the face. "Shut up."

Griffin comes back wearing a white t-shirt and a pair of blue pajama pants. "They can't have her. Call them back and have them pick someone else." He grimaces at my red face. "Did you hit her?"

Benny ignores his brother's question and blocks Griffin's view of me with his body. "Griffin, we can't pass up how much they are offering."

He walks away from Benny. "It doesn't matter. She's not for sale."

He plans to keep me all to himself. How sweet. I have so many plans for us.

Griffin lifts me by the arm, turns me around, and secures my hands behind my back with his. "No more touching yourself," he whispers in my ear.

If my hands are free, I will fuck myself whenever I want, and there's nothing he can do to stop me.

Griffin leads me from the bathroom into his tidy quarters and shoves me onto his neatly made bed. Benny follows us in.

I caress Griffin's fuzzy black comforter. The light above us buzzes and flickers every few seconds. All the surfaces of his room are free of dust and clutter.

"But Griffin, their offers are more than we have ever gotten for the other girls."

Griffin turns his head. "What's the highest?"

"Fifty thousand."

Griffin hesitates, then opens his top dresser drawer, and removes his socks. "No."

Benny's eyes widen. "But Griffin we—"

"I said no." He glares at Benny and pulls on his socks. "I decide on this one, remember?"

Benny puts his head down. "Will you at least think about it? I mean, look what she's already done. She killed one of our best customers and scared away most of the others."

Griffin walks towards Benny, backing him out into the hallway. "What she did was save my life."

Benny peers past Griffin and stares at me.

I smile wickedly at him.

He shakes his head. "She's costing us money."

Griffin backs up into the bedroom. "And according to you…" He swings the door around slowly. "…they'll be back." He closes the door in Benny's face.

Turning them on each other may be easier than I thought.

The second drawer of his dresser scrapes open, and he removes a bundle of half-inch yellow braided rope. He takes one of my ankles, ties it, bends over, and tosses the rope slack under the bed. He walks slowly around to the other side and ties the other end to my other ankle. If I move one leg, it pulls the other. He returns to the dresser and removes two more lengths of the same rope—one he secures around my waist, holding me upright against the headboard. He removes my handcuffs and uses the other rope to tie my wrists like my legs.

I pull my left hand towards my face to scratch my nose, and my right arm pulls towards the outside of the bed. I try to use my other hand and it's the same effect. I slide my right leg inward, and my left leg slides outward.

I am my own marionette.

"You cost me a lot of money today." He removes a knife from his bedside table and strokes the sharp blade with his thumb—his face expressionless and his demeanor calm. His eyes fixate on mine. "I don't like losing money." He glances at my upper thighs and then back at me. "There must be consequences. Don't you agree?"

I nod. He's not wrong. I have plans for him, but I will never share them. It will ruin the surprise.

"I'm glad you agree." He turns his back to me. His ass cheeks tighten under the fabric of his pants as he opens a cabinet on the wall, removes a large box, and pulls out a smiling, red devil mask. "This one is my favorite. I'm someone else when I wear it. And since your license and name came back as being fakes, I assume you know what I mean."

How patriotic—red mask, white shirt, blue pants. I don't know whether to sing The Star-Spangled Banner or Oh, Beautiful. I'd say the latter because Griffin is hot as fuck.

"If you are not Willow, then who are you?" He sits on the bed with his legs crossed between my bound legs.

I say nothing.

He places the blade on my upper right thigh and asks again. "Who are you, Jane Doe?" His voice lowers to a throaty growl.

I remain silent.

A slight breeze escapes the mouthpiece of the mask as he sighs. "Very well." The blade slices across my flesh, leaving a bloody line behind. My breath quickens, and I grit my teeth, stifling the anger building inside me. The only thing about me that I love, my perfectly unblemished body, is now gone.

He tilts his head and slices the other side. "Of the twenty buyers that came…" The blade rises from my skin then comes back down and slices me a third time. "…only three remained, earning you seventeen cuts." His voice rises and falls with every cut he makes as he counts.

There's sadness behind his eyes as he cuts me. They glisten with excess moisture with every stroke across my skin.

This bothers him—me not talking to him. He likes being in control, and by not speaking to him he feels as though he doesn't have it.

He's ruining my flawless body. I've always hated who I was on the inside—born with a propensity for violence and a thirst for blood.

I've never been normal.

My older sister, Amelia, was the normal one. She was smart, compassionate, and understanding. We were inseparable until we weren't. Meeting someone and falling in love changes you.

It changed us.

We grew further and further apart. I blame her boyfriend at the time. Thinking back on things, I wish I had killed him back then. Perhaps she would still be with me now.

A tear breaches the rim of my eye—the first time in a long time. I'm imperfect now, inside and out.

Griffin stops cutting and stares at the glistening droplet on my cheek. He swipes it and rubs it between his thumb and pointer. "You should have left when you had the chance, Jane Doe."

I look away from him.

He slices me again. "If you talk to me, I will stop cutting you." His voice muffles behind the mask.

I'm already ruined. I won't give him the satisfaction.

He continues slicing my thighs until he reaches his quota and tosses the knife to the floor. The muscles in my legs tense when he grabs them, one in each hand, and smears the blood up and down my limbs, painting them red. He rolls onto his back and rests his masked head on my crotch. "I'm going to find out who you are, Miss Doe. You can't hide from the devil."

My lips twitch from the pressure of his head resting on them, flipping my mood like a light switch, from anger to lust. I rock my pubis into him.

I want more.

I need more.

He sits up abruptly and straddles my chest. "You want this cock?" He pulls it out and drops it between my breasts. "Talk to me. Say just one word and I'll give it to you."

Tempting. I mean, who wouldn't want a hot devil-mask-wearing man to stuff their cock inside them? But I can't give in. I won't give him what he wants.

I close my eyes and pretend to sleep.

He may be the devil offering me his sinful temptation, but I am the devil he doesn't know, and I plan to keep it that way.

The weight on my chest lightens as he leans over, removes something from the side table drawer, and conceals it in his hand.

"You're a stubborn bitch. But at least now I know one way to cause you pain. It's just not physical. You care about your body—looks, complexion, blemishes..." The weight on my chest returns as he leans on me and runs his fingers over the wounds he just made. "...scars."

I squint at him. How dare he? I am going to cut off every appendage he owns, including his cock. The last thing he will see is my smiling face fucking his detached dick before he succumbs to his mortal wounds.

"I know what you are thinking." He taps the side of my head. "You want to hurt me, don't you?"

I nod. Hell, motherfucking, yes.

He smiles and climbs between my legs. "Good luck with that." He stabs the side of my neck with a needle. My eyes grow heavy, and the room darkens as he pulls his cock out of his pants and thrusts it inside of me.

His head drops onto my shoulder. "My turn," he whispers as I lose consciousness.

Chapter Seven
A Name is Just a Name

I'm alone when I wake up. My legs are free and bandaged, but my arms won't budge—ropes keep them still.

Audrey enters from the living room area. "I put triple antibiotic ointment on your cuts. It will help minimize scarring."

She twists her nightgown hem between her fingers and sighs as she sits. "Mr. Dietrich planned to buy me. I'm not sure if I should thank you for killing him or be mad. The truth is, at least here I know the rules—what to expect from them, and how not to get hurt. Mr. Dietrich could have been a nice guy, but what if he wasn't? Word is, one of the buyers beat a girl to death for putting the wrong creamer in his coffee. Jenny knows which one, but she won't tell us. Of course, she could just be full of shit."

"Where are they?" I look over her shoulder.

"Who? Griffin and Benny?"

I nod.

"They're in the kitchen making dinner. Sometimes they do that. I think it might be to celebrate a pending sale. I don't care why they do it, I'm simply happy to have a whole meal. It's a real treat."

I frown at her. "I doubt that."

"It's better than salad and water for dinner." She furrows her brows.

Griffin enters the room from the hallway. He stands beside Audrey and gazes down at my bandaged wounds. "Are you finished?"

Audrey lowers her head. "Yes, sir."

He lifts her chin with two fingers and nods towards the door. "Out."

She gathers her supplies, dropping the empty gauze wrappers in the trash on her way out.

Griffin closes the door behind her, leans against the dresser, and swipes his face. "Who are you?"

I ignore his question, and the air between us stales.

He removes a folded piece of paper from his back pocket. "Just spoke to my guy. He says you don't exist. How can that be, Jane Doe?"

The corner of my mouth shifts upward.

He crushes the paper into a ball and throws it at me, hitting me in the face with it. "Everyone exists. Everyone has a story—background, friends, family, social media, something. But you, you are no one and someone at the same time. The way you killed Dietrich without a second thought or hesitation tells me it's not your first time. So, what are you, Special Ops, CIA, or FBI? Only people who work for the government can live as ghosts."

Ghost? I am no ghost. I am a vengeful spirit.

I cross my legs and yawn, bored by his insistent questions.

"The food's ready," Benny yells through the doorway.

"We'll be right out." Griffin steps towards me. "How many people have you killed?"

I exhale through my nose. How many people I have killed isn't the right question. *Who I've killed* is what he should be asking.

His eyes pierce fiercely into mine, but I give him nothing.

He grabs a hunting knife from his hip, moves quickly towards me, and cuts my wrists free. "Get up."

I stand and place my hands in front of me, waiting for the cuffs.

Griffin rolls his eyes and points to the door. "Go."

I move at a snail's pace, taking in everything I can see. Where do the wires and pipes above me go? His hand rests on the small of my back, pushing me forward. He steers me to the room where they first held me, and pipes above me end on the far wall.

The small bistro table and two chairs in the kitchen don't provide enough room for all of us. They pulled the bed into the center and placed eight plastic trays with food on them on the mattress and put pillows on the floor—four on each side. Ari, Audrey, and the twins are on one side, and Benny and Jenny are on the other. Griffin pulls me to the seat next to Jenny and then sits on the other side of me.

Ari winks at me with her non-swollen eye.

She's still causing trouble.

A steaming bowl of stew sits on the tray, along with a slice of bread with butter and a cup of water. No wine.

Bummer.

Jenny elbows my upper arm when she takes her first bite of food. I ignore it. The crowded space doesn't leave much room, so it may not have been on purpose. The stew has large chunky vegetables like how I make it. I pick out a baby carrot and bite it.

Nope.

I spit it on my tray.

Jenny grimaces beside me, and Griffin gives me a side-eye. Across from me, Ari chuckles.

Jenny elbows me a second time, and I glare at her.

What do they expect? This shit has no fucking flavor. I take a bite of the bread but can't swallow.

Seriously, margarine? Yuck. I pull the chewed food from my mouth and slap it on my plate.

Jenny turns her body to face me and crinkles her face. "That's so disgusting."

The twins keep their heads down and focus on their dinner. Audrey takes a small bite of bread and chews slowly.

They don't dare speak.

Griffin tosses his napkin on his tray and grabs my upper arm. "What's your fucking problem? Those are fresh vegetables from my garden and the venison from a deer I shot yesterday."

I gag and stick out my tongue.

"It's got no flavor," Ari sneers. "Right, Willow?"

I nod and push the tray away.

"Her name isn't Willow." Jenny huffs at Ari and rolls her eyes.

Griffin stands up, wiping his mouth with a paper towel. "No flavor, huh? Well, Chef Doe, if you think you can do better…" he grips my bicep and pulls me to my feet. "…have at it."

My knee strikes the oven door as he pushes me into it. The loud bang bounces around the quiet room. Everyone stops eating and talking and stares at me.

I turn the oven to four hundred degrees, grab multiple containers of seasonings, and shake varying amounts into the pot of flavorless food. Griffin leans sideways with his palm against the fridge, watching me. I place my hand on the refrigerator handle, and he shifts out of the way.

In my head, I'm singing my favorite phrase with a country twang.

'Butter makes everything better.'

I hum to myself and add a couple of pats of butter to the stew. Griffin seizes my wrist when I grab the bread knife. I tilt my head at him, and he lets me go. His palm rests on the handle of the knife on his hip, ready to use it if I try anything.

The sawing sound of the knife through the crust of the bread arouses me. The way it breaches the crusty surface and plunges easily through the soft center reminds me of what it's like to cut through bone and reach the spongy marrow—the center, squishy like jam.

Griffin clears his throat, bringing me back to the room and the bread in front of me. I toss some seasonings and diced tomatoes onto the bread slices, drizzle them with olive oil, and slide them into the preheated oven.

I catch Ari smiling at me. She mouths, 'Thank you,' and I nod.

After five minutes, I pull the bread out, sprinkle it with mozzarella, and return it to the oven for five more minutes. I turn away from the stove, grab Ari's bowl from our makeshift table, and dump its contents in the trash. I ladle a serving in, rest the bread on top, and pass it to her.

Griffin takes the bowl from me.

Ari stands abruptly. "Hey, that's mine."

Benny reaches across the mattress, grabs her shoulder, and pushes her back to the floor. "Sit down."

Ari plops onto her pillow and crosses her arms.

Griffin tears a chunk of bread with his teeth and pulverizes it in his palate. He nods, raises his brow, and takes a massive bite of stew.

"Is it good?" Benny asks.

"It's fucking delicious." Griffin hands Ari her food.

She hesitates, then takes the bowl "Can I get a fresh one since you already ate half of it?"

"No." Griffin sucks butter and oil from his fingers.

Jenny, Benny, Audrey, and the twins line up like they're waiting in line at a soup kitchen. They take their seats and dive in—lips smacking, fingers licking, bowls scraping.

"This is good." Ari shovels bite after bite into her mouth with a smile.

"Do you have to be such a slob?" Jenny wrinkles her nose at the drippings on Ari's clothes.

Ari frowns and slides Jenny's tray away from her. "I'd rather be a slob than a frigid bitch."

Jenny grips the side of her tray and brings it back in front of her. "I'd rather be a bitch than a disgusting slob."

"Ladies." Griffin glares at Ari and then Jenny as he sits beside me and sets a bowl on my tray.

Audrey wipes her lips. "Willow, where did you learn to cook?"

"Her name's not Willow." Griffin glares at her and glances at the other girls. "Call her Jane." His eyes dart to mine with a penetrating fierceness. "That's the name you give to people without identification, dead or alive."

"I'm sorry." Audrey drops her head.

Benny lifts his bowl and slurps it. "Griff, you should let her cook all the time."

"I don't think that's a good idea." Jenny peels off a piece of crust, dips it into her bowl, and stuffs it into her yap.

"So, Willow, what's your secret?" Ari pats her lips with a white paper napkin.

There are so many, so I'm not sure which secret she's referring to—the food, my past, or my plans.

Benny's face tightens, and a vein in his forehead protrudes as anger builds inside him. He balls his fist, reaches across the makeshift table, and punches Ari in the side of the head.

She falls onto Audrey's lap. Audrey holds her against her thighs. "Please, Ari, stop. He's going to kill you." Ari opens her mouth, and Audrey presses her palm across her lips. "Don't."

Ari nods, and Audrey removes her hand so Ari can sit upright.

Griffin stands and places his hand on Benny's chest as he prepares to strike Ari a second time. "Enough, Benny." Griffin strolls around the footboard and stands over Ari. "Ari, not another word."

Testing Benny is one thing, but Griffin is another. Ari, however, can't help herself.

"She's Willow to me." Ari rolls her eyes and scoops a spoonful of stew.

Jesus, Ari.

Griffin shakes his head and nods to Benny, permitting him to continue. Benny snatches Ari by the neck and drags her across the mattress. Food and trays crash onto the floor, spilling food across the clean concrete. He slams her headfirst into the side of the stove and opens the door. "What's her name?"

Don't do it, Ari.

She rubs the lump on her head. "Willow."

Fuck.

Benny seizes Ari's right wrist and presses her palm onto the hot grates.

Her eyes widen and her mouth drops open as a blood-curdling, ear-piercing scream escapes her lips. Tears stream down her reddening face.

"Are you stupid?" Benny shouts over her screams.

The putrid sweet scent of burning flesh fills the air as he burns her other hand. The twins hold each other and whimper quietly. Audrey covers her eyes. Jenny watches the show with a satisfied smile.

I launch upwards, and Griffin grabs me around the waist. He holds my arms tight as I buck against his grip, desperate to put an end to Ari's agony. I stare over my shoulder into Griffin's eyes and then back to Ari's. The pain in her face rips my heart out.

I can't allow this.

My insides burn with red-hot anger as Ari's face morphs into my sister's before my eyes. I turn back to Griffin. He smiles with his eyes at Benny's angry face as he tortures Ari. This is the side of Benny he likes. The side of Benny that's not afraid to get his hands dirty.

"Anony," I blurt unexpectedly.

Griffin loosens his grip on me and turns me around to fully face him. "What did you say?"

Benny lets Ari go, and she falls to the floor.

I wiggle away from Griffin, drop to the floor, and place my hand on Ari's head. A smile twitches at the corner of her defiant mouth.

I shake my head. "Behave."

Griffin kneels beside us and yanks my head back by my hair. "What did you say?" His breath smells like garlic as he speaks through gritting teeth.

I huff and wet my lips with my tongue. "My name is Anony."

Griffin rubs the back of my head softly, smirks at Benny, and stands. He places his hands on his hips, glances at the blisters and weeping skin on Ari's palms, and turns to Audrey. "Take her to the holding room and treat her hands."

Audrey bends at the waist and helps Ari to her feet. She places her head under Ari's armpit and leads her from the room. The twins hold each other's hands on top of the mattress. My eyes fixate on their interlaced fingers, admiring their closeness and dedication to each other. I remember that closeness. Amelia and I shared it too.

Jenny laughs through her nose and nods at Benny's broad smile. He enjoyed that and so did she.

Griffin sits on the mattress across from me, rests his elbows on his knees, and interlaces his fingers against his face. "Audrey's a nurse. She'll take care of Ari."

I watch a dust bunny blow across the floor and stop under the bed, ignoring him.

One of the twins rubs a tiny scar on her left hand with her thumb. It's the only difference between the two.

She smiles at me. "Dinner was lovely. What changes did you make?"

"Who the hell cares." Jenny gathers the trays left on the mattress and stands.

Benny blocks Jenny's access to the sink. "That's enough, Jenny." She nods, and he moves so she can wash the trays.

"What's your name?" I ask the twin with the hand scar. She looks at Griffin. He nods, giving her permission.

"I'm Eve, and this is my sister Leah."

"Well, Eve…" I crank my head and stare at the back of Jenny's head. "…you can make anything taste good with the right amount of seasoning."

"Makes sense," Leah and Eve say in unison.

Jenny tosses the trays in the strainer and turns around. "Blah, blah blah. Why is she even out here after what she did to Dietrich? She should be in chains or dead."

My hands shake and my face prickles as the monster inside me tries to take over. The pressure in my head grows, and my ears start ringing.

Not yet. It's too soon.

Benny rests his hand on her arm when she reaches for the silverware still on the makeshift table. "Quiet, Jenny."

She yanks away from him. "No. I'm tired of this crap. Ever since she arrived it's been nothing but a shit show."

My heartbeat pounds in my chest. I close my eyes and take a deep breath—trying not to kill her.

Don't do it. Don't do it. Don't do it.

My face flushes, and my cheeks tingle.

The twin's eyes widen as they stare at me. They can see it. The rage inside me is visible and emanating outward from my body. They slide off their pillows, move backward away from us, and lean against the wall.

Griffin senses it too because he feels the same. Not only is she pushing his buttons for defying Benny, but she's pushing mine. He shakes his head at Jenny. "Jenny, not another fucking word."

Jenny purses her lips and bends over beside me. She grabs a red plastic cup from a tray that has fallen to the floor and dumps the remaining water on my head. "Cunt."

Fuck.

I can't stop myself. Before Jenny could blink, I grip her hair, force her to the floor beside me, and thrust a spoon toward her eye. I pause as it grazes her lashes, stopping millimeters from her eyeball. Everyone gasps.

The unmistakable scent of urine fills my nostrils as I push her head closer to the floor and whisper in her ear. "Just a quick push and flick of the wrist, and out it comes. I'd take it home and play with it like a ping-pong ball. Pop, pop, pop."

Something sharp presses against my neck. "She may lose an eye, but you'll lose your life." Griffin shifts the blade of a knife to the front of my throat.

I glare at Jenny with a menacing smile. "Until next time." I wink at her, drop the spoon, and untangle her hair from my grasp.

Benny ignores her when she crawls to him, disappointed in her disobedience. He stares at me and shakes his head. "Griff, she's too dangerous. We have to get rid of her. Now."

Griffin slides the knife back into the sheath on his hip. "That's not for you to decide."

I grin at the yellow puddle by Jenny's feet. "Scared the piss right out of you, didn't I?"

She closes her eyes and cries into her trembling hands.

Griffin shakes out a set of handcuffs and secures my hands in front of me. He leads me to the hanging room, yanks my arms up, and secures me without a word.

Benny enters, dragging Ari by her arms. The scent of melted flesh stales the air around her bandaged hands and quickly fills the room. He lifts Ari, attaches her to the wire across from me, and glares at Griffin and me. "She needs a fucking lesson." He points at me with one hand and covers his nose with the other.

I wiggle my nose. I've never liked the smell of cooked skin.

Griffin grabs me around the waist and swings me into his chest. "What kind of name is Anony?"

Benny comes up beside Griffin. "She's probably lying."

Griffin tilts his head and stares up at my face, scanning it before locking eyes with me. "Do you have a last name to go with it?"

"Yeah." I smile broadly at his baby blues. "It's Mous."

Benny drops his head and chuckles. "Told you."

"Anony Mous?" Griffin glances at Benny as he puts it together. "Anonymous. Cute." My head whips to the side as Griffin's hand connects with my smiling mouth, and I taste the copper tang of blood. "What's your fucking name?"

"Anony Mous," I grin through bloody teeth.

Benny shakes his head and walks away. He already knows how this conversation will end.

Griffin strikes me again, and again, and again. My manic cackle chases Benny as he exits the room, the door clicking closed behind him.

"Tell me your name!" Griffin roars, blood splattering across my would-be tormentor's face. "Answer me."

He takes my head in his hands, and I lift my eyes to meet his incensed gaze.

"It's Jane." I gift him a blood-soaked grin. "Jane Doe."

He releases me and throws his hands in the air. "Fuck!"

I cackle one last time before the room disappears as his fist hits my head, knocking me unconscious.

Chapter Eight
Company

I'm not alone.

Jenny hangs across the room, crying quietly. Benny warned her to stop, but she wouldn't listen.

There's a hacking cough beside me. I rotate and twist my body to face Ari. I didn't notice before, but they hung her so high her feet don't touch the ground.

I tiptoe over and push her leg. "Ari?"

She mumbles unintelligibly.

I turn my ear to her. "What?"

"She's passed out, stupid," Jenny says, smirking. "Thanks to you, she can barely open her mouth."

"Jenny, if you don't shut your mouth, I'm going to slice you open and release your guts onto the floor like a fucking piñata."

Her grin sours. "Ari will be a piñata shortly." She squints her eyes at me.

"What the fuck are you talking about?"

"That's how Griffin plans to get you to cooperate. He knows you have a soft spot for her."

She isn't wrong.

I was only eighteen when I lost my sister. I saw the signs—excessive makeup, excuses for the bruises, withdrawing from her family. After putting up with her boyfriend's abuse for almost two years, she finally left him. The next day he showed up at her job, pulled out a gun, and squeezed the trigger in front of a restaurant full of dinner guests. By the time I made it home from college, the police had already found him. Instead of putting him in prison for life, the judge decided his mental health played a part in his behavior and sentenced him to five years in a mental health facility. Her autopsy report revealed the extent of the abuse she hid from us—multiple broken ribs, a healing wrist fracture, and fragments of bone in her shoulders from repeated dislocations. Brown, green, and purple bruises tarnished her flesh in the autopsy photos.

I never went back to college. Riddled with guilt, I joined the Army and did four tours in some of the most hostile countries in the world—punishment for not protecting her and training for what's to come.

Griffin enters the room. A baseball bat staggers across the concrete behind him. He swings it onto his shoulder and stops in front of me. "Are you going to cooperate?"

I twist my body away from him.

"Ignoring me again. That's fine, Miss Doe. Let's see if you can ignore this."

I turn my head towards him as he strolls away from me and stands before Ari.

Griffin swings the bat, striking Ari in her upper thigh. She lifts her head and screams at him. "Fuck you."

Griffin rests the bat against her temple, removes it, and rests it again. A blow to this location will kill her.

"Stop!" I shout, stopping Griffin mid-swing.

He lowers the bat. "No more trouble. There will be no warm-up next time. Understand?"

I bow my head.

Griffin walks away from Ari and stops in front of me. He leans his palm on the bat handle and rocks it against the floor. "Answer me with words." The bat end staggers up my abdomen, stops at my chin, and lifts it.

"Yes." I glare at him with angry eyes.

He smiles and tilts his head. "Yes, what?"

"Yes, sir." I purr with a small smile.

"Good girl."

Benny enters, pulling the twins behind him. He launches Eve over to Griffin and she stumbles into him. "I'll go back and grab Audrey after I secure Leah."

Griffin pushes Eve away from his body, just enough to grab her by the arms, and jolts her. "Arms up."

She raises her hands so he can secure her to her wire, then disappears into the utility room. He reappears with multiple lengths of rope and drops one beneath each one of us. Griffin wraps the rope tight around my ankles and thighs, then slowly lifts each end to a ring on the wire. He feeds one side through and pulls hard. My heels draw up to my ass, bending my knees in front of me and gaping my legs open as he ties it. Soon, we all dangle above the ground like teardrop-shaped Christmas ornaments—a pyramid tie position. I've been in this position before during an alluring sexual game. Is that what this is, a game?

Benny secures Audrey and nods at Griffin. "Ready?"

Jenny whimpers at Benny as Griffin tightens her ropes. "Please, don't."

Griffin smiles at him when he stops by his side. "I'm ready."

Benny rests his hands on Jenny's knees. "Sorry, doll. You know we play this game when everyone hangs." He pushes her hard, and she swings towards the center of the room.

Griffin does the same to me, and then the twins, as Benny pushes Audrey. We swing around the room, none of us close enough to strike each other in our current folded state. Audrey moans and Eve stifles an outcry as her sister wails. I can't feel the pain, only the pressure and wind on my face.

The doctors told my parents when I was younger that I was an anomaly. People with my illness rarely live beyond three years of age and typically have mental or physical disabilities.

But I'm different.

I've always been different.

And I plan to defy the odds.

Benny raises his hand from the sidelines and smiles at Griffin. "On your mark…"

Oh, boy. Here we go.

Griffin kneels to the ready position. "…get set..." Griffin raises his ass in the set position and Benny's arm dangles slightly just before it drops in a chopping motion towards the floor. "…and go."

Griffin launches forward, weaving in and out of our swinging bodies, and comes out to the other side unscathed. He raises his hands to the ceiling in victory. They grab our ropes and swing us hard a second time for Benny's turn—the girls all scream as I swing silently.

Benny spits into his palms, rubs them together, and darts into the obstacle course.

Eve knocks him to the ground, and Ari swings into him whacking him in the head. I laugh as Benny struggles to get to his feet. His eyes widen as I swing towards him with a massive smile on my face. I tilt my knee downward, but he ducks, and I miss. My body spins in a partial circle and glides back towards him.

Benny hops left, then right, avoiding Audrey and Eve's swinging bodies as I barrel towards him.

Griffin seizes my legs and draws me against his chest, robbing me of my second attempt at nailing Benny. "Miss Doe, what did I say about behaving going forward? Now, you tried to hurt Benny on purpose. Apologize to him."

I produce a throaty laugh.

Griffin spins me around and nods to Benny. He charges me, swerves at the last second, and slams into Ari. Tears stream down her face as she howls.

Benny scrapes the floor with his feet, one then the other, like a bull does right before it charges.

"Stop," I yell at him.

Griffin holds my body still, so I face Benny. "Apologize."

I roll my eyes and bark my apology. "Sorry, Benjamin."

Benny's eyes lock on the gap between my legs. "Let me have her, Griffin. Just for one day." His hand slides across my tied calf.

Griffin grabs his fingers and peels them off me. "She's mine, and mine alone, remember?"

"Fuck, Griffin. I know what I said, but it's just one time."

"Maybe for your birthday." Griffin pushes me aside and heads for the door.

"My birthday? Griffin, that's like two months away." Benny jumps backward to miss my body as it swings back towards him.

"Patience, my brother."

Griffin shuts the door and Benny glares at me. "I will have you. My brother and I share everything. And when I finally do, I'm going to fuck you right in your ass."

I laugh. I've shit bigger than his cock.

"You better hope you secure me well, Benny-boy. Because if I get my hands on that tiny cock of yours, I'm going to cut it off, tie a string to the end of it and stuff it in Jenny's pussy like a fucking tampon."

Jenny's eyes widen. "Fucking hit her, Benny."

"He will not." Griffin's voice booms over the loudspeaker, making us all look up.

Benny looks at the green light on the camera. "Did you hear what she said?"

"I heard her. Come inside, we have urgent business to discuss."

Benny walks away from me and stops at Ari. He smiles at me and then punches her in the kidney.

My hands tighten into fists, cracking my knuckles.

Ari hums an unfamiliar tune with a forced smile, pretending the strike didn't hurt. Benny stuffs his hands in his pockets and leaves the room.

"I'm going to kill them all," I whisper to Ari when she looks at me.

Jenny gasps. "I'm telling them what you said."

I wiggle my floating frame until I can see her. "Go ahead. Be sure to let them know you'll be the first to go."

She purses her lips then yells, "Benny!"

No one comes.

"Benny!" She screeches even louder.

Nothing.

"Benny!"

"For the love of God; Jenny, shut up," Leah yells from across the room.

"What did you say to me?" Jenny turns to face her.

"She said shut up," Eve repeats her sister's sentiment.

Audrey sighs loudly. "Yes, please be quiet. I have a headache."

Jenny's eyes dart around the room, landing on each one of us. "You're all dead when I tell Benny how you've spoken to me."

"Willow, are you really going to kill her?" Ari nods at Jenny.

I grin and glare at Jenny. "Abso-fucking-lutely."

Ari starts laughing and I join in. She snorts, and Eve and Leah begin laughing as well.

"Stop laughing at me. How can you laugh at what she said?"

The door slams open, and Benny comes inside. He rushes over to Jenny and unhooks her with shaking hands.

"Benny, what's the matter?" Jenny places her hand on his shoulder.

"He's coming; we have to get ready."

"Who?"

"Femi."

Jenny's face drops. "The Egyptian?"

Benny nods his head.

"Benny, please tell Griffin not to put me up with the other girls this time, please."

"Jenny, you know the rules, everyone must hang for him."

They walk towards the door. Jenny falls to her knees and grabs his leg. "Benny, talk to Griffin. You have to protect me."

"I'm sorry, rules are rules." He yanks his limb away. "Now get up, we have work to do."

I turn to Audrey when they leave. "Does she think Femi is the one who killed one of us over creamer?"

"I wasn't sure until now. Jenny would never tell us. But judging by her reaction, I'd say that's a fair assumption. Benny and Griffin only heard about it from another buyer, at a different bunker. She also said she heard one of the sellers at the other bunker got the shit beat out of him by the Egyptian for being disrespectful."

"So, a buyer is spreading the rumor that the Egyptian killed this girl?" I raise my eyebrows.

"Yes." Audrey's voice elevates. "I mean, I think so."

I smile at the ceiling and chuckle. "How do they know she's dead? Maybe he just let her go."

"Oh, no. She has to be dead. I mean look what he did to the guy for disrespecting him."

I nod and offer my theory. "But the guy who the Egyptian allegedly beat up was a seller."

"So?" She furrows her brow.

"So, perhaps the rumors are just that, rumors—planted to scare us, to scare them." I nod to the door and camera.

"Why would someone do that?" Leah asks behind me.

"Build a reputation and..." I glance at each of the girls. "...build trust."

Ari snorts. "Sounds like a load of shit." She grunts and curls her lips. A loud airy fart echoes through the hollow space. "Sorry. Red meat gives me gas."

Everyone wiggles their noses as stale raunchy air fills the room. I huff and cough. "Good God, Ari. Can you save those bombs for them next time?"

Audrey blows air from her nostrils. "They'll be coming to prepare us for his arrival soon."

"Why didn't he attend the banquet?" Ari asks Audrey.

"He's the only buyer that comes when he's in town on business. Benny and Griffin work around his schedule. I think they're afraid of him. He's only been here one other time, but the other traffickers feed information to Benny and Griffin about him. I overheard Benny and Griffin talking about him after he came here the first time.

"How do they *prepare* us?" I turn back to Audrey.

"I'm in charge of doing hair and makeup. Femi wants us dressed in ancient Egyptian attire that barely covers a thing."

"So, like lingerie?" I raise my left eyebrow and smirk.

"Yes."

"Then what?" I focus on her mouth as she talks.

"Well, he walks around the room and makes his first selections. After he chooses who he wants to have dinner with, he asks a bunch of questions before making a final decision."

"So, you've seen him?"

"No. None of us have. I only heard about it from another girl who was here before."

"Is she the one who died?" Eve's voice elevates as she speaks.

"I don't know." Audrey shakes her head and stares at the ladder leading upward. "It all seems so hopeless."

Salty liquid drips from the girls' faces as they whimper.

If the Egyptian takes a few of them out of here, there will be fewer girls they can use against me. The atmosphere in the room grows solemn and depressing.

They're suffocating me with their sadness, and I can't take it.

"Listen up. No one in this room is going to die. I won't allow it. We need to be strong and vicious women, not a bunch of feeble, whining, weak, little girls."

One by one, my fellow prisoners lift their heads— blinking their shining eyes as they peer at me. I let them all see the certainty etched onto my face. Let them know that I stand with them.

Tears dry up as the women grab ahold of this last vestige of hope.

We can do this.

Well, at least I thought we could until Griffin stepped into the room, and their spirits deflated like a bunch of balloons.

Damn it.

He unhooks the twins and points to the open doorway. They disappear through the opening as Griffin unhooks Audrey. "Help Ari to her room. Do the best you can to get her ready. Put her in the outfit with the most coverage."

"I understand." She waits patiently beside Ari, staring at the floor while Griffin unhooks her.

Good grief. If only they didn't feel pain. Perhaps they wouldn't be so scared to take part in their own rescue.

Ari drops to the floor when he releases her. Audrey pulls her up and helps her walk from the room.

Griffin unties the rope holding my legs and rubs them softly as he sighs. "He won't be able to take you today since you are not ready. It's the rules, so you don't have to worry."

I smile broadly at him. "I'm not."

"I believe you." He grabs me around the waist and crushes me against his body as he growls a word of warning. "This is not Dietrich. This man comes with bodyguards and a gun of his own. If you try anything, they won't hesitate to kill you. Don't do anything stupid."

"I'll be good."

He sighs and unhooks me. "Somehow, I doubt that."

Griffin pulls me by my arm into his bedroom and shoves me onto the bed. "Stay." He walks away from me and locks the door when it closes behind him.

I rub the furry comforter against the side of my face, as I rest my heavy head. Egyptian men can be cruel and unforgiving, but not all of them.

I turn over, stare at the ceiling, and close my eyes, picturing the Egyptian in my mind—dark hair, bedroom eyes, smoldering chiseled body, with caramel-colored skin.

My pussy lips twitch. I cup them with my bound hands and press them into me. They tingle and moisten at the thought of Femi touching them. My fingers slide in and out with ease, lubricated by desire.

Provoking the Egyptian could lead to collateral damage from Griffin, and that's not an option. I must behave as Griffin expects.

I shall be a seductress, like Cleopatra.

I rub my pussy in a circular motion.

A temptress, like Jezebel.

My thighs tingle as my orgasm races to the surface.

I will be a femme fatale.

My hips buck toward the ceiling, and my juices squirt against my fingers, soaking them. "Oh, Femi."

I close my eyes and inhale the scent on my soiled fingers. "Mmm…that was a good one," I whisper to myself.

Chapter Nine
The Egyptian

Fuck this.

If my outfit had any less material, I'd be naked. Triangle pieces of linen cover my lady parts and nipples, while a tiny strip covers my crack. The rest of my attire is all beads—annoying, uncomfortable, fine-hair-pulling, beads.

I gaze at my reflection in a wall mirror as Audrey adjusts the gold crown on my head. I must admit, I look like a goddess, but that's not the point.

Audrey applies black and green makeup to my eyes, and gold, glittering lipstick to my mouth. "You are a beautiful woman." Audrey presses the mascara wand into its container, blowing out a solemn breath. "For your sake, I hope he doesn't pick you."

"I want him to pick me." I smile at her reflection.

Her eyes widen with surprise. "Why? You know what he's capable of."

"When he chooses me, you girls will be safe. I'm not ready, so he will have to wait. It will buy me time."

"Time for what?" She dots my face with powder.

"Time to kill them all."

She looks behind her, looking for them. "Come on, Jane. You shouldn't say such things."

I grab her hands and squeeze them. "Two things. First, when we are alone you call me Willow. And number two, I will kill them."

She looks at me, nods, and then removes my hand from hers. "It's time to go." She stands and knocks on the door.

It swings inward, and Griffin enters.

He says nothing. His mouth hangs open, like a fish waiting for a worm. Audrey puts her head down. "How does she look?"

"Out." His order comes out quietly.

"I'm sorry. Is there something I did wrong? Whatever it is, I can fix it." She bites her nail and grimaces.

He pushes her out the door and locks it. I tingle between my legs and air catches in my lungs as he moves swiftly towards me. I back away from him, but he seizes me around the waist, pulls me into him, and holds my hands behind my back. "I don't know what it is about you, but I can't get you out of my head."

"I think about you too." I gaze into his baby blues.

"About fucking me or killing me?"

"Both." I lean forward and suck his bottom lip into my mouth.

He grasps both of my ass cheeks with both his hands and lifts me from the floor. I drop harshly onto the bed, as he slides down his boxers.

That's right, foolish boy. Let your guard down and fall into my trap.

He rolls my bead dress up, wraps one hand around my throat, and presses two fingers inside me while I moan. I grip his fine hair and shove his head down to my pussy. He hesitates and stares at me with lust in his eyes as I pant and rub my breasts. His tongue slides in and out of me, tasting its juices. He bites my inner thighs, one then the other, then digs his nails into my hips and dives on top of me. A pillow lands on my face, and he presses it down hard, suffocating me as he rams his cock into me.

I grab the pillowcase fabric and pull it hard away from my face, but he presses harder.

His voice mumbles through the pillow. "Wrap your arms and legs around me and I'll let you breathe."

I release the pillow, dig my nails into his shoulders, and press my heels into his lower back.

He pulls the pillow away and pants in my face. "Kiss me."

I turn my head away from him. Kissing is personal and not meant for situations like this.

He slams me hard and holds his cock deep inside me. "Do it, or I'll suffocate you until you pass out and finish that way."

I stretch my neck so my face can reach his and peck his lips.

"No." He grabs my head. "Like this." He stuffs his tongue into my mouth, swirls it around, and yanks his head away.

I close my eyes and picture my boyfriend. "Faster."

Griffin moves faster.

"Deeper," I beg, pinching my eyes closed tighter.

The headboard of his bed bangs against the wall as he fucks me hard. I shove my tongue into his mouth and press the full weight of his body into mine. He rocks his cock into me, and I lift my hips to meet his pace.

"Let me taste your pleasure," he pants through winded breaths.

"It's coming."

He pushes off my abdomen and dives between my legs. I yell out as I burst inside his mouth. His tongue glides over my abdomen as he makes his way eye-to-eye with me. "You're fucking mine."

His ass crushes my breasts as he sits on them and jerks his load onto my face. I turn my head fast, but a blob of semen lands heavy on my eyelashes weighing them down. I keep my eyes closed not wanting his fluids to enter and contaminate my eyeball.

Angry thoughts barrel through my head as he uses the pillowcase to wipe his goop from my face. I need to restrain myself, but my eyelashes keep sticking together, and it's pissing me off.

Fuck it.

I glare into his satisfied eyes and sweating face. "I'm going to kill you."

He huffs out a laugh and kisses me hard on the forehead. "I'll risk it."

I narrow my eyes and push him away from me with both hands, but he doesn't budge. "Fuck you."

He smiles, rolls off the bed, and picks up his underwear. "You just did.'

I shake my hair away from my face, lean on my elbows, and grin. "Foolish boy. Don't you know I'm a man-eater?"

"I'll let you eat my cock any day of the week, beautiful. Just say the word."

I moan. "You should let us all go before I take you up on that offer."

"Why would I do that?" He pulls on his underwear.

I scan his tattooed flesh and smile. "Because then no one else has to die."

"You're crazy. Do you know that?"

"You're the only one that doesn't realize how crazy."

"Fuck you, Jane. Get up." He grabs my wrist and pulls me to a stand.

"My name isn't Jane." I run my fingers from his left shoulder down his arm.

He brushes my hand away from him. "I don't care what your name is at this point."

"You will." I stick my pointer finger in my mouth and scrape my bottom tooth with my fingernail, making an annoying sound.

"Griffin." Benny's knuckles strike the door.

"Yeah." Griffin pulls his t-shirt over his head and unlocks the door.

"He's here." Benny's eyes lock on my barely covered flesh.

I move my feet apart, gapping my legs open, and lick my top lip with my tongue. "Wish you were here, don't you Benny boy." I grab my pussy.

"Knock it off." Griffin seizes my forearm and holds it tight.

"Come on Griff just one time." Benny adjusts his tiny pecker.

"We'll be right out." He moves Benny into the hall and closes the door.

"He's not a man." I gaze at Griffin with sultry eyes.

"That's my brother, and you will respect him in my presence, understand?" He crushes my arm in his grasp.

"Yes, sir." I salute him like a good soldier with my free hand.

"Good girl. Now, go into the bathroom and wash that pussy."

I enter the bathroom and gawk at my face. Makeup smears across my eyes, blackening my lids with mascara—cover-up no longer hides my bruises, and my lipstick shimmers all around my mouth completely displaced from my lips. I touch up my face the best I can under the circumstances.

When I exit the bathroom, Griffin is waiting in the chair dressed in an all-white formal suit. He drops a pair of gold gladiator sandals between his feet and summons me to come to him with a hooked finger. "Put these on."

I steady myself on his broad shoulders and rest my foot between his legs on the chair cushion.

I could kick him now and ruin his day, but I won't. He feeds my feet into the sandals, wraps the straps up my calves, and ties them. I gyrate my pelvis on his head and moan.

"Mmm. While you're down there, why don't you lick my pussy."

"Quit it." He stands and roughly grasps my upper arm. "Time to go."

They're beautiful. We're beautiful. All of us wear different variations and periods of Egyptian dresses. In the center of the room is a single, gold-cloth-covered table with four chairs. I picture us, all of us, standing in a great hall with the Egyptian at my feet. I'm Nefertiti reborn, and my girls are slaves to no one.

Griffin attaches me to the wire with the loose hook. He nods to Benny who grimaces then slams the red button on the wall with his palm. Three men descend the ladder, but the shadows of two more silhouettes shift just outside the opening. One of them has a commanding presence. The men flanking him stand stiffly beside him, waiting for their orders—eyes assessing the room.

Femi.

Griffin extends his hand, and the guards grip the guns secured to their hips. Femi gives them each a nod, indicating all is well. They take a step back and Femi shakes Griffin's hand. Benny offers his hand too, but the Egyptian ignores it. Even he knows Benny is nothing more than an errand boy.

I raise my eyebrows as Femi moves from the shadows into the light.

Mmm. Isn't he sexy?

His shining black hair and perfectly tanned skin glisten under the fluorescent lighting. He rests his phone face down on the table and removes his dark gray jacket, revealing a steel gray undershirt. Benny reaches for the jacket. The Egyptian glares at him, and he retreats to his place beside Griffin.

"All new?" Femi folds his jacket over his chair, rolls up his sleeves, and glances at Griffin.

"All except for Jenny. They are all ready to go except for one."

"I have no use for Jenny. I'm not sure why you keep presenting her, or anyone else who's not new to me. Send her out."

Griffin nods to Benny, then turns his attention back to Femi. "I just want you to see all the options in case you change your mind about what you want."

Femi furrows his brow. "I know what I want." He glares at Jenny as Benny unhooks her and pats her on the ass on her way out of the room. "And it's not her. I don't like the way she smells."

Benny wrinkles his nose. "Smells? Jenny doesn't smell."

Femi raises his brow and turns his back on Benny. "Tell me who we have here?" He stops in front of Audrey and glances at Griffin.

"This young lady is Audrey. An unmarried twenty-three-year-old nurse, with no children, no siblings, and both parents deceased. Besides her job, no one will come looking for her. She will fade into the cold missing person cases without a problem."

"She looks familiar. Have I seen her?" Femi swings his hands behind his back and holds them there.

"Yes, last month when you picked the Hispanic girl."

Femi stares at Audrey's lips. "Open your mouth."

Audrey's eyes water. She swallows hard and opens her mouth.

Griffin backhands her in the face. "Smile."

Audrey's teeth are nearly perfect except for one front top tooth that tilts slightly. Femi grips her legs, and she tightens them together.

Griffin raises his hand to strike her again, but Femi shakes his head, stopping him.

He rests his hands gently on Audrey's thighs and gazes into her eyes. "I'm not going to hurt you."

Audrey hesitates and then relaxes her legs.

She turns her head away from him and pinches her eyes closed as he opens her legs and inhales the scent of her pussy. He lifts his head and looks at Griffin. "Take her down."

Audrey's eyes spring open, and she sobs quietly.

Femi has made his first choice.

As soon as her hands were free from restraints, she races to the ladder. Femi's bodyguards seize her arms and force her into her seat.

Femi pushes his sleeves further up his arm, revealing an Eye of Horice tattoo on his wrist. He places his hands behind his back and strolls over to the twins.

"Twins, how lovely." He glances at Benny and Griffin then looks at the girls. "Open your mouths and smile."

Benny straightens his sleeves and then rattles off their information. "These two are twenty-one, come from Virginia, and fresh out of college. They speak English, Spanish, and French. You will find that they have minimal scarring, thanks to their obedience and age."

"Selling as a pair, or can they be split?" Femi pries Leah's legs open and sniffs her slowly.

Benny glances at Griffin who nods. "Whatever you like."

He walks away from Leah, opens Eve's legs, and sniffs multiple times. "Interesting. Even their scent is the same. It's just not for me." Femi waves his hand dismissively and moves away.

When Benny unhooks them, they hug each other and sob. He forces his hands between them, pushing them apart before leading them from the room.

My turn.

Femi rolls the beads on my dress under his palm, examining the many cuts on them. "And this one?" He glares at Griffin.

"She's not ready."

"I can see that." Femi runs his fingers over each leg mark. His eyes grow darker as he counts them to himself. "Seventeen cuts. Is that how many times you've punished her so far?"

"No. It's how many potential customers I lost due to her combative and violent behavior."

"Violent?" Femi raises his eyebrows and removes his hand from me.

Benny stops beside me. "She killed Mr. Dietrich."

Femi's head whips back to me. "She killed Dietrich. How?"

"She stabbed him in the neck with a fork."

I smile at Femi, and he smiles back.

"A fork. How clever." He snatches my legs firmly and yanks them swiftly apart but doesn't smell me. There's no need. The smell of sex emanates from my body all on its own. "You've defiled her recently. I can smell it from here." His eyes soften and lock on mine.

"Yes. Right before you arrived." Griffin shifts his weight from one foot to the other.

Femi rests his head against my abdomen, and my breaths quicken. "Put her at my table."

Griffin raises his head and steps towards us. "Sir, she's not available yet."

Femi's head jerks to the right, and his raging eyes burn a hole through Griffin's face. "I don't care if she's available or not, put her at my table."

Griffin glances at Femi's bodyguards and nods to Benny. As soon as he's close enough, I high-kick him in the chin like a Rockette.

"Fucking bitch," Benny shouts and punches me in the stomach.

I laugh at him. He swings at me again, this time striking my rib. I laugh harder. Ari giggles behind me. "She can't feel pain, moron."

Femi stands between us, so he can't hit me again. "If she can't feel pain, then you're doing nothing but giving her what she wants."

"And what do you think she wants, besides getting her ass kicked?" Benny opens and closes his fists several times.

Femi's palm slides down my lower back and grips my ass cheek. "Attention."

I smile at him.

He turns to Benny. "She wants attention. It doesn't have to be positive or negative. It's still attention. And when you give it to her, she's getting what she wants." He curls his pointer finger at one of his bodyguards who promptly reports to his side. "Give me your blade."

The guard slides a six-inch blade, from a brown leather sheath on his hip, and passes it to his boss. "Everything with someone like her needs structure and balance. The scales need to stay level, or it messes with her internally." Femi tilts his head and slices an eighteenth slash mark across my thigh, making my rows even.

I do not move or cry. He's done me a favor, and I'll repay his kindness later. I can't stand odd numbers.

He hands the blade back to his guard and turns to me. "I'm going to unhook you now. If you try to hurt me, the gentlemen by the table over there have my permission to shoot you in that pretty face of yours. Understand?" He winks at me.

"I do." I wink back.

Benny rolls his eyes. "This is all a game to her."

I rest my arms on Femi's shoulders as he detaches me from the ceiling. "A game she doesn't want you to be a part of right Benny?" He holds me against his chest and strokes my hair as I gaze into his bedroom eyes.

"It's not just me." Benny straightens his tie.

"What is your name, beautiful girl?"

"Today?"

Femi smirks and tilts his head. "Yes."

"Anony."

"Anony, how intriguing." He looks at Griffin. "And your last?"

"Mous."

"Anonymous. Oh, you're funny. Griffin, she's funny. What do you know about her?"

"That's another reason she's not for sale. I don't know her name. I've been calling her Jane Doe. Her fingerprints should be close to the surface in a few weeks, and then I can run them again."

Femi grips my fingers and examines them closely. "Sanding with something abrasive lately?"

I nod.

"My, oh my, aren't we mysterious? Take a seat at my table."

I sit beside Audrey and squeeze her trembling knee. Femi looks at Ari briefly and waves over his shoulder. "I have made my selections."

Ari huffs, disappointed she wasn't picked.

Jenny enters with a tray holding a bottle of wine and a single glass. She places it before Femi as he sits beside me. He swirls it in a circle, smells it, and takes a small sip.

I'd kill for a glass, but I need to behave.

He questions Audrey first. I follow a bead of condensation as it races down the wine bottle, lands on the tablecloth, and seeps into the starched cloth. I slide my fingers across the textured fabric and run my finger over the wet spot.

Griffin rests his palm on my shoulder. "Hands in your lap."

I place them face down on my thighs and blow out a quick breath. All this talk is boring me to death. I roll my head back and glance at the two bodyguards guarding the ladder to freedom. Griffin clears his throat, and I turn my head. He mouths the words, 'Don't you dare,' and I smile broadly.

I have no intention of leaving until my work here is complete.

Femi rests his hand on my knee. "So, Miss Anonymous, how many people have you killed besides Dietrich?"

"Total?"

"Of course."

I unfurl my fingers one at a time on one hand, then switch to the next and open them as well.

"Ten?"

I take his open hand, create a circle with my thumb and pointer, and slide it up and down his index finger.

"Eleven?"

I pucker my lips and blow him a kiss as I continue stroking his appendage.

"Liar. Get up." Griffin yanks me from my seat and onto the floor. "There's no more truth to that than her name being Willow."

Femi places his arms behind his back, glances at the floor then raises his head to face Griffin. "I thought you said you didn't know her name." He stands in front of me, blocking Griffin.

Griffin stares at a speck on the floor. "I don't know. Her identification is a fake."

There's a long awkward silence. Femi's eyes drill through Griffin, waiting for him to make eye contact.

This is magical. The way Griffin cowers to the Egyptian brings a pleasant smile to my face.

A devious smile spreads across Femi's face as he lifts his head slowly and looks at me with lust in his eyes.

"It doesn't matter. Audrey, you can go. I have made my decision." He extends his hand to me while maintaining eye contact. "I choose Willow."

He pushes me away from him. "I'm not afraid of you."

"Cluck, cluck, cluck. Benny's so fuck, fuck, fucked," I sing in a high voice.

Griffin grips me around the throat and squeezes. "What did I say about messing with my brother?" He releases me. "Apologize."

"Sorry, Benjamin." I glance over my shoulder and wink at Femi who shakes his head and disappears through the hatch opening.

Until we meet again, you hot, sexy fuck, I'll be waiting.

Chapter Ten
Griffin

Griffin tosses me on his bed and paces back and forth. His face grows redder by the second. I cross my legs at the foot of the bed and watch the tantrum unfold.

"Fuck, woman you are driving me crazy. Why can't you just behave?"

I furrow my brow at him. "I did behave."

"The fuck you did. You kicked my brother in the face, lied, and acted like you wanted to fuck Femi right there in front of everyone."

"I don't lie, number one." I stand and stroll over to him. "And I did want to fuck Femi. He's very alluring, don't you think?" I stroke the bulge between his legs through his suit.

"Get off me." He shoves me backward, and I land hard on my ass.

I let my legs fall to the sides and lay my spine on the cold concrete. "Lighten up Griffin. You should enjoy the time you have left with me before you're gone."

"You mean before you're gone?"

"That too."

He storms towards me and straddles my abdomen. "You better stop testing me, or I will kill you here and now."

His weight makes it difficult to breathe, but I can't help but smile. He's getting more and more frustrated with me every day.

I take his hands and slip them around my throat. "Go ahead. Choke me now. Kill me now. If you don't, I will kill you all."

His grip tightens around my neck, cutting off my airway. A vessel in my right eye pops, and spots dance in my field of vision. "Don't tempt me."

Oh, Griffin, that's all I've done since I arrived here.

I wink at him, and he growls without using words. His rage, twisting and reddening his face, making him look less like himself and more like the devil.

I slap his arms, indicating I'm tapping out, but he doesn't feel my touch. The adrenaline flooding his veins numbs him.

I'm fading, and I'm fine with it. If he doesn't take me out, the killing will never stop.

I will never stop.

Benny enters from the living area and grabs Griffin around the waist. "Griffin stop. If she dies, Femi will fucking kill us."

Griffin lets me go, stands, and pushes Benny onto the floor. "Don't fucking touch me. You should never have made that deal without speaking to me first."

"I always manage the deals, Griffin. And considering he just paid triple for someone who may kill him, you should be fucking thanking me."

"I told you she wasn't for sale!"

"She's too dangerous to keep and you know it. I think you need to take a step back. Let her stay with Jenny and me in our quarters for a few days, just until you can clear your head."

Griffin presses his palms against his hips and stares at the ceiling. "Maybe you're right. Fuck, I need a vacation."

No, he's not right. I need Griffin right where I've got him.

"Why don't we go to the hunting cabin for the weekend? Jenny can oversee the girls while we are gone."

Griffin shakes his head. "We can't trust her."

You're damn right you can't.

"Come on. She wants to hurt us, not the girls."

I clear my throat to stifle my laugh.

Griffin sighs through his nose and looks at Benny. "Tomorrow, I'll move the bed from the galley into your room. You need to make sure she's secure, wrists and ankles every evening."

Benny nods. "Yeah, I know. Want me to send in Audrey to take care of her wound?"

"No. I can do it."

Benny flubs his lips and steps into the hallway.

I glance down at my eighteenth blemish and pick at it with my finger.

Griffin pulls me off the floor by my upper arm and steers me into the bathroom. "Sit here." He leans me against the wall, pushes me down until I reach the floor, and leaves the room.

I lean my head against the perfect white wall beside me. My hand twitches. It misses painting masterpieces. I turn myself to face the canvas and pull my wound open wider. The textured surface vibrates my blood-coated fingers as I swipe them in an upward motion. I paint myself a tree on the bathroom wall. The gnarled trunk rises out of the bathroom floor, splitting into many bare branches. I smear blood on my palm and swirl it several times in a circle, creating a beautiful blood moon just beneath a low-lying branch.

Griffin hoists me off my feet, tearing me away from my masterpiece before I can initial it. "What the hell are you doing?"

"I miss trees."

He gawks at the four-foot-high artwork I created in his short absence.

I'm dizzy. My head wobbles on my shoulders and I drop to my hands and knees. Griffin reaches for me as I fall to the side and the room slowly fades away.

Griffin bites the end of the thread he used to sew me up. He rubs my leg gently as I shake my head and my eyes refocus. I rub the fuzzy comforter under my palm and close my eyes.

"He cut you deep. You lost too much blood."

That's not the only reason. Everything about being here is zapping my strength—fighting with them physically and mentally, not eating my normal diet, the abuse, the lack of routine.

I'm fucking exhausted.

I pop my eyes open. "Maybe you can give me some of yours." I smile at him.

"Some of my what?" He furrows his brow and stands.

"Blood."

He hesitates with his back to me, then looks over his shoulder. "You don't scare me." He continues to his dresser and paws through the clothes in the top drawer.

"The thought of me having you for dinner doesn't frighten you?"

He spins around, dives over the footboard, leaps onto my midsection, and presses me by the throat into the mattress. "Stop. Just fucking stop—the games, the threats, your psychological warfare." He loosens his grip on my throat and swipes his face with his palm.

I bat my eyelashes and smile. "Don't knock it until you've tried it."

He glares at me. "Tried what?"

"Eating a person." I sit up on my elbows and tilt my head with a sinister grin.

He seizes both of my breasts and squeezes them hard. "Shut the fuck up."

"Griffin, what the fuck is this?" Benny shouts from the bathroom.

Griffin stares at the ceiling and yells, "I didn't have time to clean it yet."

Benny walks into the room wearing white boxer shorts with red polka dots. His bony chest caves in and out as he breathes heavily. "Whose blood is that?"

Griffin climbs off me and returns to the dresser. "Hers."

"You let her draw on our bathroom wall with blood?"

"Of course not." Griffin rubs his forehead. "Benny, go take your shower. The steam will moisten it, and when you're done, I will spray it with bleach and clean it."

"Oh, my God what the hell is that?" Jenny's voice echoes in the bathroom.

Griffin scratches the back of his head. "Benny, you can explain it to her. I'm fucking tired."

He strolls over to the bathroom door, places his palm on Benny's hairless chest, and guides him out of the doorway.

He's tired.

I'm making him tired.

"I have to pee." I sit up and place my feet on the floor.

Griffin rolls his eyes. "Well, they're showering at the moment, so you'll have to wait."

I flop back on the bed and open and close my legs. "I could just piss right here and now."

"Don't be a child." Griffin grabs my knees and holds them together. "Lie down and turn on your side."

I rotate away from him, and he positions himself behind my back. He wraps his right arm around my waist and draws me into him. "I hate you."

I rotate my ass into his cock. "You want to hate fuck me now, don't you?"

He grabs me by the shoulder and forces me onto my back. "You are fucking crazy. The way you speak to me, don't speak to me, save me, then threaten to kill me." He yanks my head back by my hair, cracking my neck. "You're driving me mad."

'We're all mad here. I'm mad. You're mad.'
—Cheshire Cat

The shower shuts off in the next room, and Griffin lets my head go. He presses his forehead between my breasts, warming them with his breath. His thumb fiddles with one of the dress beads on my arm.

I suck my pointer finger and stick it in his ear.

"God damn it." He uses the edge of the comforter to dry his ear then stands.

I grin and sniff the wax on my finger. "You should clean your ears."

He clenches his fists, walks over to the bathroom, and places his ear against the door. "They're finished. Come on."

Griffin enters the bathroom first and stops. Dirty towels litter the floor by the shower. "Fucking, Benny. He's such a slob." Griffin scoops them off the floor and drops them in the hamper.

He takes me by the wrist and swings me in front of him. I bounce off his chest, and he steadies me with his hands. His fingers caress my shoulders on both sides.

I smile at his twisted red face. He curls his fingers around the beads on my arms and breaks them with a violent yank. Beads bounce as my sparse attire falls to the floor. I thought he might take me. I can see it in his sultry eyes that he wants me. But he forces me to the floor of the shower and walks away. Seconds later, water drops onto my head, startling me.

Griffin returns naked, carrying a spray bottle and scrubbing brush. His ass jiggles slightly as he scrubs the wall. The falling water distorts his face when he looks over his shoulder to check on me. I wave my fingers forward and back, calling him to me. He shakes his head and continues scrubbing.

"You'll never let me go. I am a mystery you can't solve, a problem you can't fix, a woman you can't break."

He lets the cleaning brush fall to the floor. His bowlegs mosey towards me—his cock sways left to right, and his balls vibrate with every step. I watch them, my eyes swinging with their movement, like Newton's Cradle.

Click, click, click—back and forth they swing.

His knees crack as he squats in front of me, interrupting the shower stream. "I will find out who you are." He strokes my left cheek with his thumb. "And I don't need to break you, I just need to keep breaking Ari and the other girls. That is your weakness Miss Doe, and I intend to use it."

He steps back out of the shower to continue cleaning the wall. "And as for letting you go…" He keeps scrubbing without looking at me. "…when Femi returns, I'll pass you off to him with a smile on my face, and never think about you again."

He thinks he's going to live that long. What an arrogant prick. He will be the last to die.

"Not if I kill you first."

He sets the cleaner on the sink and rinses the scrub brush. His words are barely audible over the falling water of the sink and shower. "Just because you killed Dietrich to protect me, or yourself, doesn't make you a killer."

He doesn't believe me. I imagine he finds it hard to believe that I, as a woman, could ever be a killer.

Denial.

It's the only thing that explains his unwillingness to see the truth.

He steps into the shower, towering over me—so fucking sexy.

It's too bad it won't save him.

'Imagination is the only weapon in the war with reality.'
—Cheshire Cat

Chapter Eleven
Benny

After cleaning up both me and the bloody wall, Griffin hands me a pair of his sweatpants and a long-sleeved shirt to wear. We walk through a secondary doorway, off the bathroom, leading to Benny and Jenny's room.

The layout of the bunker comes together in my head as I try and create an idea of how it may look from above. The hanging room, containing the exit, sits at the center. From there, the galley, the men's bedrooms, and the bathroom radiate outward like the spokes of a wheel. The other door we didn't go through off the galley must be the holding room for the other girls. So, where is the secondary exit?

The bed from the galley is already inside, facing off against a queen-sized bed on the opposite wall. Griffin binds my wrists with rope and secures me to the brass headboard. "I'm leaving your legs free." He gives me a death stare. "Don't kick Benny."

"Okay." I grin.

He said not to kick Benny, but he didn't say I couldn't do anything else or kick Jenny.

Benny enters carrying a glass of water. He sets it on the bedside table, rolls his eyes, and crosses his arms. "Why isn't she wearing a nightgown or naked like the rest?"

Griffin doesn't answer, but I know the reason. He doesn't trust Benny with me. Benny wants what he can't have, and the longer Griffin keeps him from what he wants, the more desperate he will become.

"I don't know why you're coddling her, Griffin. Just strap the bitch down naked as per protocol."

Griffin exhales noisily before walking away and closing the door without a word.

Jenny opens the door and enters wearing a sheer, floor-length white nightgown. "How come she's wearing that?" Her bare foot taps quietly on the floor as Benny ignores the question.

As if she has any say in what I'm wearing.

Her eyes roll so far into her head, that I can no longer see their color. "Hello?"

Benny's brow furrows and his face reddens. "I don't fucking know Jenny, get in bed," he yells, startling her.

There's a long awkward silence. Words hang in the air like a fart in the shower, but neither one of them speaks.

I know why, and Benny does too. Griffin doesn't want me nude around his lusty brother—too much temptation.

Jenny climbs onto the mattress on the wall side, and Benny slides in beside her. He flicks off the table light and the room darkens, except for a sliver of light shining under the bathroom door.

My eyes adjust slowly to my surroundings. I turn my head and stare at Jenny and Benny across from me. They're lying in the dark, unable to sleep. I guess we all are, technically. I can't see their faces, but I sense Benny's open eyes on me, and Jenny's are likely on him.

You don't need sight to feel someone watching you. It indescribably grips you. Some feel their skin crawl, others—their faces prickle. With me, it's a tense feeling in my stomach. Not quite a knot, more like a twitch that starts but doesn't complete its twitching. I imagine trying to sleep in a room with a killer might be difficult, but they have nothing to fear from me.

Not yet.

Images of my sister flash in my head. She had such a beautiful smile. It emanated light, love, and happiness to

everyone around her, especially me. She grounded me—
kept me out of trouble and on the right path.

The tension in my abdomen slowly subsides and the
air in the room shifts—unspoken words slipping into the
void as the others fall into uneasy slumber. Jenny's breath
vibrates out of her mouth every time she exhales. She's a
mouth breather.

Great.

Benny snorts beside her. He snores louder than an old fat
guy with undiagnosed sleep apnea. Good grief. I could sleep
better in the hanging room. Between the two of them, I feel
like I'm in a sawmill—preparing wood for shipping.

Benny gasps a few times and then sits up and tosses his
blankets onto Jenny. He creeps into the bathroom and
returns a few minutes later but doesn't get into bed. My
stomach flutters as I sense him staring at me in the dark. A
drawer scrapes open near me.

A musty odor fills my nostrils, and the mattress shifts
when he leans against it. I gasp, intending to scream, but he
quickly seals my mouth with tape, silencing me. His hands
grip my ankles, and I kick my legs trying to free them from
his clammy paws.

"Benny, what are you doing?" Jenny turns on the light,
blinding me.

"Turn the fucking light off Jenny." He sits on my legs
pinning them to the bed.

The light clicks off, and Benny tightens a rope around
my ankles, holding them together. I buck the center of my
body, bouncing it off the mattress and rocking the
headboard against the wall.

Benny's forearm pushes against my throat, cutting off
my airway. "Stop, fucking moving."

"You can't have sex with her. The Egyptian and Griffin
forbid it, remember?" Jenny murmurs.

"Shut up and go back to bed," Benny says with a sharp tongue.

His dry fingers slide across my stomach, under my elastic waistband, and into my vagina. "How's that feel, bitch?"

His fingers are rough and cold. The pressure increases as he adds another finger and moans quietly.

He takes one finger out and presses it into my other hole. "Two in the pinky and one in the stinky."

How I wish I had to shit right now.

"Jenny, grab our toy."

Their bed creaks as she stands. "Benny, you can't do that to her. It's the same as fucking her, in their eyes."

"I'm not. You are."

"What?"

"You heard me. Get over here and fuck her with it while I watch."

A drawer in the nightstand scrapes open and the silhouette of a dildo jiggles in Jenny's hand. White teeth stretch into a smile on her face as Benny pulls my pants down.

Fucking bitch is enjoying this.

She pushes me onto my side, leans into me, and forces the silicone stick between my tightly bound legs and inside my pussy. A container squirts as Benny adds some sort of lubricant to his hands. Even in the dark, I can hear him struggling. The friction he's creating could start a fire with his matchstick-sized cock. Someone needs a little blue pill or a cock doctor.

"Harder, Jenny." Benny pants.

She moves it in and out harder, without picking up speed.

"Faster, stupid. Like this." He takes the dildo from her and jams it in and out of me rapidly.

Something inside me snaps like a rubber band.

She yanks it away from him and moves it in and out fast and hard, like she's shaking a can of spray paint. "Benny, I think she's bleeding."

"So, what? Keep going, I'm almost there." Benny's voice staggers as he strokes his dick harder.

"Maybe we should try something else."

"Just shut up. I'm almost done."

Jenny pulls the dildo out of me. "Turn her onto her stomach."

Benny flips me over, tightening my wrist bindings and twisting my back unnaturally. The pillow under my face presses into my nose making it difficult to breathe. I turn my head and glare at Jenny.

She gives me a smug smile and there's pressure in my anus as Jenny violates me with the artificial cock.

If I had any doubts about killing Jenny before, they just dissolved.

My stomach tightens and bile races into my esophagus.

Benny's breaths pick up speed. "Yes, that's it. It's coming."

It sure is.

My mouth waters excessively as vomit makes its way to my mouth.

Jenny moves it in and out faster and harder. Benny straddles my legs while she assaults me. Moisture lands on my ass cheeks as Benny squirts onto them.

"Fuuuuuuuuuuck." Benny bucks up and down on my legs panting heavily.

"I knew you'd like that." She lets the dildo go, and it slides out of me on its own.

Sour liquid launches from my nose, unable to escape my mouth.

Jenny flicks the light on and stares down at the dots of vomit on her nightgown. Her lip curls. "You are a disgusting cunt." She raises her hand, meaning to hit me.

"Enough, Jenny." Benny scoots off me and picks up his underwear. "Clean her up and fix her pants. I'm going to take a quick shower."

"What about the blood on the sheets?"

"I'll take her to the bathroom for her shower before breakfast, and you can put fresh ones on."

"What if she tells Griffin?" Jenny's face pales.

"She won't."

He leans down and whispers in my ear. "If you open your mouth, I will bring Ari in here and do the same to her, or worse."

I thrash my head back. An audible crunch confirms I hit my target, his nose. I told Griffin I wouldn't kick him. He didn't say anything about headbutting.

Benny grabs his bleeding nose and swears quietly into his hand as he stands. "Fucking bitch."

Multiple tissues slide out of a box on the nightstand. Jenny pushes them into Benny's nose and glares at me. "You whore. Why did you do that?"

Seriously? Maybe she is just that dumb. I can't wait to kill her stupid ass.

Benny disappears through the bathroom door as Jenny rolls me onto my back and punches me in the abdomen. "You think you're so tough. You're nothing but a tied-up animal waiting for slaughter." She punches my stomach a second time. "When the Egyptian comes for you, I'll be the first one to celebrate. Not only because you're gone and we can get back to our normal routine, but also because I know it won't be long before he kills your ass."

I smile with my eyes, and she slaps me across the face. I laugh through my throat, and she smacks me again.

She raises her head high and walks over to the dresser with a smug look on her face.

Benny enters as Jenny pulls a fresh linen gown over her head. "Maybe you should take a quick shower, so you don't smell like vomit."

Jenny smells herself. "I don't smell anything."

He peels the tape from my lips, turns towards Jenny, and sniffs. "Huh, I guess not."

"You both must be used to smelling like shit because you both fucking reek."

Jenny slaps me across the face.

I burn holes in her face with my eyes.

Benny grabs her arm as she raises it to hit me again. "Jenny, that's enough for one night. Save your energy for tomorrow."

Benny lifts a blanket from the foot of the bed, unfolds it, and covers me up to my neck. As he speaks, his foul breath suffocates me with the smell of unbrushed teeth and old greasy food. "You touch me again, and I'll make sure you never leave this place."

I grit my teeth. "You're the one who will never leave."

His fists ball and his body sways left to right as he rocks on his heels. He wants to hurt me more but knows he can't. After staring at me for several seconds, he turns away from me. His mattress creaks as he perches on the edge of it, elbows braced on his knees. Air blows hard through his lips, striking me in the face with its stale scent.

"Benny," I whisper.

"What?" His voice comes out breathy and irritated as he leans over and turns off the light.

"Brush your fucking teeth, you nasty ass mother fucker."

"Fuck you," he hisses and swings his legs onto the bed.

I breach the silence after several minutes of quiet. "Benny?"

He sighs heavily. "Shut the fuck up and go to bed."

"Benny?"

"I'm not telling you again. Shut up." His voice elevates.

"Benny?"

"For fucks sake, Jane, what?" Benny utters in a frustrated tone.

"Benny, Benny, Bo, Benny, little dick and ho Jenny, beep bop bo beep, beep; you're a creep." I sing cheerfully.

Jenny sits up behind Benny. "For the love of God, shut her up."

"Dead, dead so dead, you're going to lose your heads, beep bop boo bop dead, so dead," I continue singing.

Blankets fly in the air as Benny throws himself out of bed and charges to my side. He grabs the roll of tape from the bedside table, picks the edge of it aggressively, rips an enormous piece off the roll, and slaps it across my mouth. The tape falls to the floor and rolls away as he flops back into bed and sighs.

"That ought to shut her up," he says to Jenny.

No one is sleeping tonight if I can help it. I start humming loudly in tune with the song I was just singing. A pillow slaps the side of my face, making me smile. What more can they do to me?

Benny reaches over the edge of the bed, grabs the pillow, and holds it over his ears as I continue humming.

Chapter Twelve
The Silent Treatment

Before I even open my eyes, I know that I'm alone. I only slept for a couple of hours, and my throat aches from all the humming, but it was worth it to irritate the shit out of Jenny and Benny.

Griffin should have never trusted them. They made me bleed, now I must do the same. The bathroom door creaks open. Benny enters the bedroom naked, water dripping all over the floor. He dries his scrawny, disturbingly pimply ass, and pulls on blue and white striped boxers. Jenny enters wrapped in a plush white towel, with her head held high, and a smile stretched across her face. She drops the dildo into the top dresser drawer and removes a pair of pink underwear.

Someone got some false cock in the shower I see.

She turns her back to me as she dresses. A small birthmark on her bony left hip disappears as she covers it with her underwear. After pulling on a pair of sweats, she stands by the bed and waits for Benny to finish detaching me from the headboard so she can change the sheets.

Benny rips the tape from my yackety yap, helps me stand, and guides me into the shower room. He removes my clothing, turns on the shower, and shoves me toward the falling water. "Get in."

I don't move.

He grits his teeth. "Get in the fucking shower, bitch."

I've had enough of his bullshit. These mother fuckers aren't getting away with what they did to me. I refuse to comply.

My head snaps back, yanked by my hair, and Benny whispers in my face. "If you don't get in the fucking shower now, tonight I will fuck you with my revolver while playing Russian roulette."

I mutter inaudibly.

He turns his head to my lips. "What the fuck did you say?"

I latch on to his ear with my mouth, bite down on his lobe, and rip it away from his greasy head. Metallic liquid coats my palate. His screams echo throughout the hollow space. I smile at him while holding his flesh between my teeth. Blood drains between Benny's fingers and splatters on the floor as he holds his left ear.

I laugh aloud, reveling in his agony even as he punches me in the temple—sending the room spinning and the edges of my vision blurring.

Griffin's blurry silhouette rushes into the room and stops in front of Benny. "What happened?"

"She bit off my fucking ear," Benny cries.

I grin at Benny as his tear-covered face comes into focus. Something strikes my lower back, shifting me towards them. Griffin's eyes widen as blood pools under me. He reaches over my body, grabbing Jenny's hand before she can stab me a second time.

Who would have thought *Jenny*, of all people, would fucking stab me?

Bitch.

I roll onto my back, feeling my warm blood pooling beneath me.

Griffin wrestles the compact tactical folding knife away from Jenny and punches her in the face, knocking her out.

Benny crawls to her side as the black-bladed weapon drops to the ground between Jenny and me. "What the fuck Griff? She was just trying to protect me." He lifts her head, cradles it in his lap, and strokes her expressionless face. "Jenny?" He taps her face with his palm.

Griffin snatches a towel off the rail, pulls me onto my side, and presses it against the hole in my back. "Fuck. She needs a doctor." His eyes lock on the smeared, dried blood on my buttocks. He furrows his brow. "Did she get her period last night?"

"Fuck her, Griffin. Let her fucking die," Benny barks at him.

Griffin raises his brows and balls his fist. "Do you know what the fucking Egyptian is going to do to us if she dies?"

"Who cares, Griff? We can find him someone else. Besides, you were never planning to let him have her anyway, right?" Benny shrugs his shoulder. "Shit happens."

"Shit happens? Seriously, Benny. He already paid us, and your stupid bitch just damaged his property."

Benny stares at the blood-soaked towel Griffin holds against my back. "Have Audrey patch her up."

"This isn't just a patch-up, dumb ass." Griffin brushes the hair from my face with his fingertips as stars dance before my eyes.

I'm tired. Between lack of sleep, proper nourishment, and my injuries, I don't have the energy to keep my eyes open. I let my head fall to the side, shifting the chunk of meat in my mouth. Jenny's eyes open slowly and stare into mine. I push Benny's earlobe between my lips with my tongue, draw in the largest breath I can with what little energy I have left, and launch it at her. It hits her in the nose and bounces onto the floor between us. I smile briefly at her shocked stare, then my eyelids flutter closed.

Griffin sits in a folding chair beside me, biting his nails when I regain consciousness. His eyes dart from me to a woman standing over me. His goatee looks unkempt and scraggly. He must have combed his fingers through it too many times in the wrong direction.

I run my unrestrained hands up and down my thighs, trying to remember what happened.

The blonde-haired woman removes rubber gloves and hands him two plastic bottles. "This one's for pain, and this one will prevent infection." She straightens her navy blue blazer and pats the back of her head with her right hand, checking the tightness of her pinned-back hair.

Griffin stares at the medications for several seconds before handing one back to her.

"She can't feel pain, so she won't need these."

She takes the bottle from him. "Really? Interesting. Well, that explains why my employer wants her so bad," she says with a soft smile and a wink in my direction.

I wiggle my fingers at her.

"When is he coming?" Griffin stands from the chair, sits on the bed, and fixes his eyes on the stove. His knees bounce up and down, shaking the mattress as he talks.

"I informed him that besides the one-inch scar and associated blood loss, there didn't appear to be any internal damage. I couldn't be sure without imaging. But judging by the size of the knife she used, I'd say it was doubtful."

"What did he say?" His legs stop moving as he glances at her.

"He didn't say anything; he just hung up."

"So, he didn't say when he's coming?"

"No." The woman picks up a leather bag from the floor and raises her brows. "I'd suggest making sure nothing else happens to her."

Heels click across the floor as she exits through the hanging room door and speaks to someone in a low voice.

Griffin stands and leans against the stove across from me. "Why?"

I ignore his question and stare at some peeling paint on the galley room ceiling.

"Did something happen?"

Something happened alright, but I'm not saying a word. He needs to interrogate Benny, not me. He left me with them. This is his fault, not mine.

The hatch door clanks closed, and Benny steps into the room a few seconds later.

"Benny, what the fuck happened last night?"

"What did she say? Whatever she says, you can't believe her, she's a fucking liar. Nothing happened."

Griffin crosses his arms and glances at me. "Is he telling the truth?"

"Why are you asking her, Griffin? I'm your brother."

He steps to within a foot of Benny. "Let her answer." Griffin tilts his head down. "Did Benny hurt you?"

I shake my head. It's not technically a lie. It was mainly Jenny. He just beat his shit off on me.

"See. I told you nothing happened." Benny turns his back and opens the fridge.

Griffin wipes a bead of sweat from his forehead. "But according to you, she's a liar."

Benny hesitates, his hand resting on the cap of an unopened beer. "What did the Egyptian say?" He pops the cap and passes the beer to Griffin.

Griffin takes several gulps from the bottle and sets it on the counter between them. "Nothing."

"Nothing?" Benny takes a few sips of his beer and rotates the bottle in his grasp.

Griffin crosses his arms and glares at him. "Yeah Benny, nothing. He just fucking hung up." He chugs down his entire beer and drops the bottle into the trash.

"That's bad right?" Benny purses his lips.

"I can't deal with your stupidity right now. Get out." Griffin orders, grabbing another beer from the fridge.

"What about Jenny?"

"Jenny is mine until further notice."

"But she was just—"

"I don't give a shit. Now get out."

Benny slams his bottle on the counter and stalks out of the room.

Griffin's knees crack as he squats down to my level. "Why would you break our deal and risk me hurting the other girls?" He strokes my bare chest with his fingers and grips my breast.

I stay mute.

"Fine. Don't talk." He stands, walks quickly to the door behind me, and whips it open.

Screaming pierces the walls of the room where the other girls bunk. Griffin comes back through the doorway with blood dripping from his hand. He drops a chunk of something bloody on my face. "An ear for an ear."

My breath quickens and my face tingles. The piece of flesh is white. So, it must be Ari's or Audrey's. Anger races through my veins, stopping in my head and threatening to rupture through the top like a long-dormant volcano.

Deep breath in, slowly release. Deep breath in, staggered release. Deep breath in, don't let him win.

He lifts me by the neck, but I can't support myself. My legs shake, then fail, and I fall hard to the floor.

"Jesus Christ," Griffin shouts, rocking the stove back and forth above me with his palms. "I'm going to pick you up. Don't fight me, okay?"

Fight him? I barely have the energy to breathe. I am completely vulnerable and at his mercy.

He slides his bare arms under me and lifts me from the cement. I reach for his face, and he flinches. I reach again, this time moving slower, and he lets me touch his lips. He stops walking and gazes into my eyes.

I tug his bottom lip down slightly and smile. Fall for me you foolish boy, so I can rip your heart out and eat you for breakfast.

He shakes off my touching hand and continues into the gas chamber room. We stop at the foot of the bed where Jenny's naked, bound, and gagged. He sits me in a chair beside the bed and ties my hands to its arms and ankles to the legs with rope. The cabinet above the bed creaks open and he removes two masks. He fits one over my head and secures it to my face. Jenny shakes her head back and forth, screaming as Griffin puts his mask on, grabs a canister of gas, and pulls the pin.

The room clouds quickly but doesn't impair all my vision. Snot and tears plaster Jenny's face as she coughs uncontrollably. Griffin removes his belt, flips her onto her stomach, and strikes her several times in the back with it. With every lash, her chest presses into the mattress. His left hand reaches under her throat and grips it firmly as he pulls out his massive cock and pushes it inside her.

Jenny wails and her eyes widen with every thrust Griffin delivers.

He drops onto her back and grinds his cock deep into her then pulls it out, rests his ear against her spine, and stares at me through the mask-eye windows. He positions the head of his penis on the outside of her anus just touching its opening. She thrashes about screaming as she tries to avoid what's coming.

He knows. The doctor must have done an exam and told him. Griffin knows what she did to me, and he's punishing her.

He's not entering her, just lingering.

He's waiting for me—waiting for me to give him permission, waiting for me to authorize the torture he's about to unleash, authorize my revenge through him.

I nod because fuck that bitch and what she did to me.

125

He stuffs his dick into her ass dry. She screeches and uses her toes to push herself towards the headboard trying to get away, but he seizes her around the abdomen and thrusts into her farther. Tears flood her face as he moves rhythmically in and out of her. Nothing comes out of her mouth when she opens it now. All the screaming, crying, and fighting against Griffin has drained her. She closes her eyes and surrenders to his assault. It's quiet now, except for an occasional cough, as he thrusts into her over and over. The sound of the head of the bed rocking and striking the wall is all I can hear now.

Bang, bang, bang.

Griffin's breaths quicken right before he takes a deep breath, pulls his cock out, and releases his load on Jenny's backside much like Benny did to me. The door vibrates and Benny's muffled inaudible voice carries through it. Griffin stands and flicks on the fan but doesn't answer the door.

The room clears of its haze, and I have a clearer view of Jenny now. Snot and tears cover her face as she squints at me. Griffin removes my mask, then his, and unlocks the door.

Benny's eyes turn to saucers as he enters, grabs the sheet beneath Jenny, and examines the blood spots. "Griffin, what the fuck did you do?"

Griffin hikes up his jeans, buttons them, and pulls his shirt over his head. "You may not have hurt Jane, but Jenny did."

Benny's eyes jump from me to Griffin and back to Jenny. This is his fault, and he knows it.

"Did you think I wouldn't find out," Griffin growls as he snatches Benny's sweatshirt collar and yanks him within inches of his face. "This is on you." He points at Jenny's bloody ass.

Jenny sniffs the snot into her nose and furrows her brow at me.

I mouth the words, 'You're dead.'

She screams and bucks on the bed like a wild mare. Griffin unties me and lifts me by the arm. "As for you, you're staying with me tonight."

"But Griffin, we agreed you'd take a break for a few days."

"Do you think I'm going to trust you after what you did? The Egyptian is not someone to fuck with, and you and that dipshit on the bed have already pissed him off. Besides, we have that thing this weekend. That will be plenty of time."

"Are you serious? We can't leave them alone down here after all of this."

"The expo is non-refundable. Besides, it's only two full days."

"Griffin, can we talk about this?"

Griffin steers me in front of him and guides me through the doorway.

Gone for two days.

Oh, the things I can do with such a large window of opportunity. My stomach shakes with giddiness.

I stop walking and turn to Griffin. "Can I cook while you're gone?"

"Why, so you can poison Jenny?"

"I love cooking. I wouldn't waste a good meal on her. She can be a part of it." I smile up at his untrusting face.

"Oh, so you would just put aside the fact that she stabbed you. Do you think I'm stupid?"

He tries to move me forward, but I plant my feet firmly. "I promise that after your return, you won't hear me argue or fight with Jenny ever again."

"We shall see." Griffin strikes the back of my knee with the front of his, buckling it and forcing me to move into his room.

I lie on the bed and raise my arms so he can attach me to the headboard.

He shakes his head and swirls his finger in a circle. "Roll over."

I turn onto my stomach, and he picks at the tape over the wound on my back and rips it away slowly. "This shouldn't scar too badly."

He smears ointment over my stitches and applies a fresh bandage.

I stay quiet. In my head, my plan is already in action. There are so many more reasons to kill him now; revenge is just one of them. I must send a message— burn their whole operation to the ground.

Griffin rises, shifting the bed upward, and drops my soiled bandage in the trash. "I'm sorry Jenny hurt you," he says more to the door he's staring at than to me. "It won't happen again."

I roll over as he continues through the door and closes it softly, leaving me unrestrained.

No, it won't happen again.

Never, ever, ever, again.

Chapter Thirteen
The Trunk

I don't know what time of day it is anymore. They could be feeding us breakfast at dinnertime, and dinner at breakfast for all I know. When you're stuck underground, with no sense of time, it can get a bit disorienting.

Griffin strolls into the room with his hands in his pockets and sits in the chair at the foot of the bed. "The twins are gone."

"What?"

"The rich kid got them. I guess he didn't want to wait for you."

It's two fewer girls to worry about. I should be happy, but all I feel is concern for their safety. A rich, immature prick who thinks he's untouchable can be dangerous. I'll free them later.

"Today, we celebrate," he smiles and slides on his brown leather boots. "Tomorrow, we hunt for their replacements."

"Replacements?"

"What, did you think we would wait until we got rid of all of you? If that were the case Jenny wouldn't be here either."

"I thought Jenny was Benny's and that's why she's still here."

"Trust me, if someone wants Jenny badly enough, and there is a suitable replacement that comes in for Benny, he will let her go. She's expendable, like the rest."

He takes me under the armpit and lifts me to my feet. We stand there, chests touching, sharing each other's air space.

He wants to kiss me.

His tongue licks his lips before he chews the bottom one. "Tempting, but I'm not breaking the agreement with the Egyptian."

"Didn't you already?" I say with a smile.

He turns me away from him and sighs as he pushes me forward. "That was Jenny."

I stop walking, and he runs into me as I turn around. "So, he plans to kill her?"

"I don't fucking know. Just walk." He twists me and pokes my shoulder with his fingers.

I stumble into the galley where Audrey, Ari, and Jenny are already waiting on the bed. I take a seat beside Ari and nudge her knee with mine. She turns to look at me, and that's when I see it. Griffin took her ear lobe, but he took something else.

Her.

It's written all over her face—the redness in her eyes, irritated nostrils, and uncharacteristically quiet demeanor. He took her to the gas chamber.

I take her hand in mine, and she stares at it. "It won't be long now," I whisper.

She slides her hand away from mine. A solemn gaze replaces her once determined demeanor as though time has already run out for her, and I am too late. I can't fault her for being angry. They did this to her because of me.

I clench my fist and rest my head on her shoulder. "I promise they will pay. All of them, even Jenny," I murmur.

Ari shrugs me off, sticks her nose in the air, and gawks at the flickering light fixture above us.

Jenny's bloody toenails catch my attention. They folded and tore while she was trying to get away from Griffin's brutal thrusts. My eyes shift to her hands. She picks at the skin on the edge of her chewed-off thumbnail. I smile with my eyes at her bloodless face.

She glares at me with puffy eyes, leans forward, and clenches her teeth. "You know I can hear you."

"I don't give a shit, Jenny."

She tilts her head down, severing eye contact. Not much fight in her, compared to most days. She fidgets with the fabric of her gown, rubbing it between her fingers.

Ari smirks. A small sign of hope that she will be herself again one day.

Jenny's body tenses when Griffin steps through the doorway carrying a small flatscreen television and places it on the counter by the stove. I shoot her a crooked smile as a single tear escapes her eyelid, lands on her lap, and seeps into her cotton attire. She jolts in her seat as he walks by her and into the hanging room. He returns dragging an orange outdoor extension cord through the doorway.

Benny steps over the cord, entering with two large pizzas. He keeps an eye on me as he sets the pizzas on the mattress behind us and removes a remote from his pocket. Jenny reaches for him when he makes eye contact with her, but he does not engage.

The television flickers and loads different network options. We get an hour. Too short for a movie but long enough for a show.

"At seven a sitcom comes on the local channel and runs until eight." Griffin glances at his watch. "Three minutes."

Jenny flips the pizza boxes open behind us. One is pepperoni and the other is just cheese. Something touches the side of my face, and I turn to see Griffin offering me a paper plate and a smile.

Money must put him in a good mood.

I nod and accept the plate. Jenny drops a piece of pepperoni on it, and I shake it back into the box. I can serve myself.

"You get what you get, you picky bitch," she hisses and throws the slice back on my plate.

131

I jerk the plate in the air, tossing the unwanted piece topside down onto the comforter, and grab a piece of cheese.

She grips my wrist and shakes it out of my hand. "Let go."

I tilt my chin to my chest and give her a death glare. "I don't like that fake meat bullshit." I peel her fingers off me.

"Ladies." Griffin reaches over us. He takes two slices of cheese and sets them on my plate, then grabs two slices of pepperoni and puts them on Jenny's.

He glares at Jenny. "Don't start trouble."

She puts her head down at once. "I'm sorry." A tear shimmers in the corner of her eye.

"It's time," Benny announces, taking a seat on the floor by the foot of the bed. Jenny bores a hole in the side of Benny's face with her eyes, but he doesn't look at her. Another tear joins the one trapped on her lid, and they cascade over her cheek. A staggered breath escapes her lips as she tries to hold herself together and not let his rejection bother her.

Griffin leans against the stove and takes a bite of pepperoni.

The show theme music plays and the audience claps.

For a moment, we all felt like we were home on a Friday night—pizza and a show, vegging out. But all good things must end.

A breaking news report interrupts our regular programming.

Benny grabs the remote. "Fuck this, bullshit."

"No. Let's hear it. It could be important," Griffin insists.

As soon as my rental appears on the screen, I knew it was important.

Griffin and Benny glance at each other and then look at me as the news anchor reports.

Early this morning a concerned jogger called in a report of an unusual odor coming from a disabled vehicle on the side of the road. When the police arrived to investigate, what they found in the trunk was more than they bargained for. The body of a white male was found tied up inside. The authorities are currently investigating the matter as a homicide. More on this story as it develops...

Griffin and Benny stare at me with wide eyes.

I smile at them and shrug my shoulders. "Twelve."

I mean, what else am I going to say? It's not my fault the dude baked to death in my trunk. That wasn't part of the plan. I mean the guy was going to die either way, but cooking in my rental car wasn't how I imagined it.

Griffin steps toward me. "Who was in the trunk?"

"A friend of yours." I grin.

He slaps me hard across the face. "Benny, take the others back to their rooms."

Benny doesn't move. His mouth holds an unchewed piece of pizza. It tumbles onto his paper plate, rolls across its surface, and lands on the floor. "I told you something wasn't right. Now we find out there was a body in her trunk the whole fucking time?" He slams his paper plate into the trash can, knocking it over.

Griffin steps toward him and forces a smile through tight lips. "You were supposed to clear the car."

Benny grips his scalp with both hands. "I did. Just not the trunk."

"You fucked up." Griffin paces the room.

"No, you fucked up," Benny yells. "I told you something wasn't right, and you wouldn't listen. This is on you."

"Me?" Griffin points at himself and then back to Benny "You had one job, and you couldn't even do that right."

"No. I warned you. Now they are going to come down on us for this." Benny wipes the liquid dribbling from his eyes.

"Shut up, shut up, shut up," Griffin shouts. "Just take care of the girls so I can talk to Jane."

Benny takes Ari and Audrey by the arms, pulling them off the mattress. Ari yanks her arm away from Benny, folds at the waist, and whispers in my ear. "Make them pay, Willow. Make them all pay."

I kiss her cheek tenderly. "I will."

She yelps as Benny grabs her bloody ear and turns to Jenny. "Take Audrey to the holding room." He glares at Ari. "And you, you're going to the hanging room."

Griffin pushes the door closed behind Benny and towers over me. He clenches his hands by his sides, his knuckles blanched with some internal strain. "So, you're a killer?" He glances at the ceiling and then back to me with inquiring angry eyes.

"Well, technically heat killed your friend in the trunk."

"I don't have any fucking friends, Jane. So, whose body is in the trunk."

"Question has been asked and answered."

He yanks my head back and spits in my face when he talks. "Do you think we are afraid of you?"

"You should be." I grin from ear to ear.

He draws his fist back. "I'm afraid of no one."

The blow from his hand strikes me in the ear, knocking me sideways onto the mattress. It rings at first then stops suddenly. I can't hear out of it.

The blood in my face disappears along with my ability to focus.

His voice mumbles into my opposite ear, but I can't decipher what he's saying.

He grabs my hand, holding my pointer finger tight in his grasp, and makes a small incision with a paring knife. Blood puddles on my fingertip, and he places a piece of white paper against it. He squeezes a piece of my hair between two fingers and plucks it from my scalp.

Perhaps he thought I was too out of it to know what he was doing—the plastic bag, a piece of my hair, a small sample of my blood. He's collecting DNA.

He overtightens the cuffs around my wrists, pinching the skin. His hands wrap around my ankles and yank me harshly off the bed. Air launches from my lungs, taking my breath away as my back hits the floor, and he pulls me from the galley into the hanging room.

Ari dangles from my usual wire—punishment for encouraging me to go after them and for calling me Willow.

Griffin's tightly tied boots stop in front of my face. I close my eyes, waiting for him to stomp me in the head, but it doesn't happen. He lifts me by the cuffs around my wrists and clips me to a wire.

His eyes, full of fire and anger, pierce into mine.

My head bobbles and drops. I can't hold it up any longer. He lifts my chin. "Who's in the trunk?"

I manifest all the energy I have left in me and direct it to my face. "Spoiled meat." I chuckle and close my eyes.

The red light on the camera is on when I wake up. I take a deep breath and try to run a rotation to loosen the fresh bolt, but my legs are like weak noodles cooked beyond al dente. They don't work.

I shake the fog from my head. The ear Griffin struck throbs in rhythm with my heartbeat.

Ari's voice muffles into my damaged canal. "He beat your legs pretty good when you passed out."

I turn my good ear toward her. "I'm going to make them pay."

"I know. I want to help."

"I don't think you want to be a part of what's coming." I raise my eyebrows. "It's going to be pretty gruesome."

She chuckles and smiles at me. "I have a strong stomach."

I shake my head. "I don't want you to get hurt if something doesn't work out, or the plan falls apart."

She wrinkles her nose and furrows her brow. "Listen, I once stuck my hand in a fire ant mound on a dare. I'm not worried about getting hurt."

It all makes sense now. The excessive farting, the back talking, the risky behaviors.

She longs for attention—to be wanted.

To be needed.

I'm beginning to wonder if she's the one who burned down the family garage.

Ari clears her throat. "Well? Am I in, or not?"

I laugh with a malicious cackle. "Alright, you're in."

She smiles broadly. "Awesome. When do we start?"

The door opens and Jenny shuffles inside with a tray.

Staggered air escapes my nose as I laugh through my nostrils and smile at Ari. "Right now."

Chapter Fourteen
Play Nice

"You two will have to split a peanut butter and jelly sandwich. We only had enough bread left for one." She drops the tray on the ground.

"Thank you so much, Jenny," I say enthusiastically.

Ari squints her eyes and draws her head back, confused by my sudden kindness.

Jenny takes a few steps back and glares at me. "Why are you being nice?"

I take a deep breath in, hold it for a second, and then exhale as I answer. "I don't know, Jenny, maybe I took too many blows to the head, and I'm tired of all the fighting. Aren't you?" I say with raised eyebrows at Ari.

Ari's eyes light up. "I am. I think we should make an honest effort to just get along."

"You two are up to something." Jenny takes another step back.

I change my voice to that of a retail sales associate greeting a new customer. "Well, we are all going to be stuck together for a couple of days while the boys are away. I just hate to see us fighting amongst ourselves the whole time they are gone." I pitch my bullshit to her like a top-notch salesperson working on commission. "We should take this opportunity to bond over our mutual traumas." I produce a genuine smile and raise my eyebrows, holding them there while I blink several times for dramatic effect.

Jenny moves a few steps closer to me and tilts her head. "Who's in the trunk? I mean, you killed the person, so obviously he did something to you. Who was it?"

"A friend of theirs." I nod towards the still open door where a shadow shifts. "And I didn't kill him, the heat did."

She picks up half of the sandwich and gives me a bite. "But you tied him up, stuffed him in your truck, and took him. Why? I mean you had to have a reason. What was it?" She tilts her head, glances at the doorway, and looks back at me—eyebrows raised, and face twisted with genuine curiosity.

She's playing nice to collect information for them. How dumb do they think I am? Still, I'll play along.

I lick peanut butter off my teeth as Jenny offers the other half of the sandwich to Ari. "Well, Jenny, sometimes things happen in life that cause you to do things you wouldn't normally do—behave in ways that are outside of what's considered 'normal'."

"I don't understand what you're talking about." Jenny turns to Ari. "Do you know what she means?"

"She means when something happens to people, some will fold—turn to alcohol, drugs, become depressed, or withdraw from the world. They carry it on their shoulders like a painful backpack for the rest of their journey through life. While other people choose to go a different way. They make it their life's mission to right the wrong that's been done to them—they work out and get a perfect body, go to school, get a killer job making serious money, or take a job in a position of power to use to their advantage. Some people will kill to right their wrongs or pay someone else to do it."

Holy shit, she's good.

Jenny turns to face me and squints. "So, like people who are victims of a crime turn around and become police officers?"

"Well, yes, if you go the legal route like a normal person." I smile.

She frowns and rubs the fabric on her neckline. "And you're not a normal person."

"Now she's getting it," Ari announces.

Benny appears from the shadows. "Jenny, stop talking to them." He picks up the tray with a furrowed brow and shoves it into her chest. "They're done for now."

A bead of sweat rolls down his temple as he watches Jenny leave the room. He's nervous or afraid. Perhaps it's both. He did fuck up by not checking my trunk.

He paces back and forth in front of me. "Tell me who's in the trunk."

"I already did."

He's so dumb. They have no idea who I am, and I'm loving it. Everything inside me wants to blurt it all out, but I must contain myself. If I reveal my secret now, it will change how everything plays out going forward. I feel like the person standing beside the red button that everyone says not to push. My hands twitch, eager to slap the button anyway and destroy their world.

Benny bites his nails and combs his fingers through his slippery hair. What a worrywart. I should put him out of his misery early, but order is important.

"You love her, don't you, Benny?" I nod at Jenny standing in the doorway.

He stops pacing and glares at me. "I don't love anyone."

Jenny puts her head down and stares at the floor.

He hurt her feelings. She does everything for him, and they share a closeness. Despite being here against her will, she can't help how she feels about him.

"Benny and Jenny sitting in a tree…" I sing to him then look at her as she raises her head. "K-I-S-S-I-N-G."

Jenny covers her eyes and runs straight into Griffin, who just came around the corner into the room. He pushes her bawling frame away from him, and she disappears into the galley.

I laugh with a sinister grin at Benny and continue to sing. "First comes love, then comes marriage…"

"That's enough." Griffin stands between Benny and me. "You want to die, don't you?"

"We all have to die sometime. Some sooner than others." I glance at Jenny as she peers through the doorway watching us. "But I don't plan on dying until I get my revenge for what you've done." I turn back to Griffin and smile. "You and I have unfinished business."

Griffin grabs my legs and squeezes them against his chest. "You won't have the opportunity to do anything if I decide to let Femi take possession of you."

He's bluffing. He doesn't want to let me go any more than Benny wanted to ever let Jenny go, long ago. We have an attachment he doesn't understand yet, but he will soon enough.

"Femi's a pussycat." I rotate my hips in a circle. "Meeeeeooooowwwww."

Griffin shakes his head and stares into my eyes. "I hope he kills you."

"He needs me, wants me, has to have me. He's coming to collect very soon. How does that make you feel, Griffy?"

He rocks his jaw from side to side. "Relieved."

"I'll miss you when you're gone." I smile. Griffin opens his mouth to speak but he thinks better of it. He turns and marches from the room with Benny close on his heels.

"How did I do?" Ari asks once the door clicks closed.

"Perfect."

"So, we are being nice to Jenny so she'll let her guard down and then you can take her out?"

I glance at the green light on the surveillance camera. "No, Ari, we are all in this together, Jenny included."

She nods and rotates away from me.

In my head, the song I sang to Benny and Jenny is stuck on a loop like the Wheels on the Bus going round and round song.

The wheels on the bus go round and round, round and round, round, and round…

Fuck.

Now that one's stuck there. I need to think of something else.

I close my eyes and think back to my younger years. My sister and I would have picnics under the maple tree in our front yard. Sometimes we'd play tag, but I preferred to play hide and go seek with the neighborhood boys. One day, the boy who lived next door found me hiding in a shed. He pinned me against the wall and kissed me hard on the mouth. I grabbed a scrap piece of wood from a workbench and cracked him over the head with it. He ran from the shed. I could have let him go, but what fun would that be? I chased him down and tackled him on the sidewalk. He screamed and cried for his mommy as I bounced his forehead off the cracked cement.

My sister saved his life that day by pulling me off him. I had no intention of stopping. I was only eight at the time, so I didn't get in much trouble. Just a good scolding from my mother.

I miss my sister. The way she used to talk to me—it made me feel *normal.* She didn't treat me any differently or look at me with disdain. My other family members, neighbors, and friends saw me as an outcast, a freak. When boys show violent behaviors and tendencies, it's brushed off as boys being boys. But when it's a girl, oh, the horror. She needs help—counseling, medications, an exorcism, Jesus, *something.*

It's not like I ever hurt animals. Perhaps it all started in kindergarten. A bully named Timothy Beckhorne pulled my hair, called me a green-eyed monster, and said I had chicken legs. I put up with his nonsense for almost a month before I decided I'd had enough and told my teacher. Do you know what she said to me? She said it was because 'he liked me.'

Liked me? Seriously. Even at five years old I knew that it wasn't okay for anyone to hit me or call me names.

My way of thinking was different. If a boy knew ahead of time that treating me this way would result in several broken bones, do you think he would do it ever again?

I bet little Timmy still thinks about the day I pushed him off the playground castle structure.

The look on his face was priceless. It changed from surprise to all-out screaming in seconds. His uvula vibrated in his wide-open mouth—the pointed bone, resembling a sharpened tusk, sticking out of the skin on his leg. From what I hear, he still walks with a limp.

That day changed something inside me. My parents grounded me, but my sister came into my room that evening, hugged me, and asked me if I was okay. She told me that if I didn't stand up to my bullies, they would never stop. The only thing she made me promise was not to kill anyone, which I did.

But her death gave me a reason and voided our verbal agreement.

I joined the military to strengthen myself and improve on ways to kill. My body count currently stands at twelve—three are from my time in the service. Two were our enemies, trying to kill us, and the last was a soldier accused of multiple sexual assaults.

My eyes settle on Ari's bruised face as soon-to-be unlucky number thirteen marches through the door holding her head high.

"I'm just letting you girls know that they are leaving you in here for the night."

"And tomorrow?" I ask.

Jenny swings her hands in front of her, holds them against her stomach, and stops a few feet in front of me, maintaining a safe distance between us "Tomorrow, Ari will be taken down, but you will stay here where you're secure."

"But I thought Willow was cooking?" Ari grimaces.

"I'm cooking, and her name isn't Willow."

Ari curls her lips. "Gee, I can't wait." She makes gagging noises.

I produce a fake smile. "I understand."

The door closes behind Jenny, and I glance at Ari who's wrinkling her nose.

Fuck.

Cooking was the only excuse we had to convince Jenny to let me go.

If I can't get free, I won't be able to carry out the plan. The green light flickers to red above the door.

Ari moans. "Well, there goes my appetite—Jenny can't cook for shit."

"Once you're free tomorrow, I need you to whine and complain. Get Audrey in on it too. Both of you tag team her."

A wicked smile spreads across her face. "You got it."

What a good girl she is. Perhaps if she makes it out of this, I will take her under my wing.

I have yet to confirm the location of the secondary exit. All I know at this point is where it isn't.

"Ari, what rooms have you been in?"

"Besides this one, Benny's, the bathroom, kitchen, gas chamber, and the holding room."

"The holding room. I haven't been there yet. Tell me about it."

"Well, it's just a room with two bunk beds on one side of the room and a full on the other. That's where the twins, Audrey, and I usually stay. Sometimes they would come and grab one of us but bring us back later."

There has to be more. I'm missing something. "What else can you tell me about the room? How many doors?"

"Just one way in and one way out. Why?"

"Because there is another entrance somewhere, and I'm trying to figure out where it is."

I scan the walls. Each door in here has a purpose and already has an exit, so it's not in here.

Ari stares at the blank wall beside me. "Maybe it's behind like a false wall or something. I knew this girl once whose parents had this big library in their house and one of the bookcases swung inward and led to their basement. I always thought it was cool."

I close my eyes and picture each room I've been in inside my head—the gas chamber, Griffin's room, Benny's, the bathroom, and the galley.

"The kitchen."

Ari blinks several times, her spirit returning from memory lane. "What about it?"

"Think about it. It's the only room where they keep us the least. When we are in there it's only with them or in restraints. Why would they do that if they didn't want us snooping around the room?"

Pounding on the hatch startles us both. We stop talking and glance at the locked portal at the top of the ladder.

Someone's here.

Ari's wide eyes fixate on mine as Griffin throws the door open and marches into the room with Benny. They each rip a length of tape from a roll and secure it across our lips. The hatch rattles a second time as someone hammers it with their fist.

The door echoes with a loud bang for the third time, and Griffin and Benny quickly leave.

I turn my ear towards the door, close my eyes, and listen intently.

Nothing.

After several tense minutes, Griffin barrels into the room—his face stormy with rage as he punches me in the gut. The air in my lungs rushes out. "You are more trouble than you're fucking worth." He rips the tape off my mouth. "Who's in the trunk?"

"I already told you." I smile at him.

Benny takes the tape off Ari's mouth, and she gasps. "Was that the police?"

"No." Griffin sighs and rubs his chin. "One of my employees who works at the doomsday shop and cooks for the banquets."

I tilt my head. "So, the police came to your shop. Did they tell you who's in the trunk?"

"They have to locate his family first before releasing a name." His eyes darken. "Why don't you just tell me, and get it over with?"

"I'm sorry. You're both going to have to wait." I close my eyes and twist away from them. "Perhaps you should've kept driving instead of kidnapping someone so close to your shop."

Griffin sighs noisily through his nostrils, turns me back to face him, and growls. "You're a piece of shit."

I blink several times and smile. "Why, thank you," I say to his back as he turns away from me, marches to the door, and slams it closed behind him.

Chapter Fifteen
Eating with Jenny

I'm a little offended that Griffin didn't say goodbye before he and Benny left on their road trip. It's fine. I understand.

I run on my tiptoes and swing in a circle. The hook on the ceiling shifts to the left. It wiggles back and forth when I jiggle the wire. This one loosens faster than my original wire. I grip the metallic string, run, and float in a circle a few more times.

Almost there.

I do one more rotation and check it again. It's one yank away from coming down.

Perfect.

I step one foot forward and stop when the door opens.

Jenny carries in a tray and sets it down—white toast, two sausage links, and an orange. She smiles proudly down at her breakfast masterpiece. "Looks good, doesn't it?"

"Oh, sure. I'm so excited—like an inmate on death row, and this exact meal was my dying wish," I say in a sarcastic tone.

"Don't be dramatic." She rests a piece of sausage before my lips. "Just fucking try it."

I turn my head. "Sausage gives me heartburn and a stomach ache. So, unless you want me to shit on the floor, you need to give me something else."

She rolls her eyes and grabs a half-piece of toast. When I open my mouth, she stuffs the entire thing inside. I fold the soft slice in half with my tongue and bite down.

Butter oozes out and coats my palate. I push the soggy bread out through my lips and onto the floor.

She can't even make toast the right way.

"What the fuck, Jane." She spreads her arms open, palms up.

"My name isn't Jane." I roll my eyes.

"Well, it isn't Willow either, so I guess I'll just call you Stubborn Bitch. Or just Bitch for short."

This stubborn bitch is about to kick your ass.

She peels off a chunk of orange and holds that up to me instead. I accept it with a nod and a smile. I love fresh fruit.

She huffs and picks up another slice. "You're so annoying."

I open my mouth, and she plunges another wedge of orange inside. "Can I have some coffee?"

She sighs and rubs the sleeve of her shirt. "I don't know how to make coffee."

"Seriously?" I raise my eyebrows. Such a simple task and she has no idea how to do it. "Let me out, and I can show you."

"Yeah, right. That will never happen." She drops the next piece of fruit onto the floor, picks it up, blows off the dirt, and tries serving it to me.

I turn my head and roll my lips tightly into my mouth. "I don't do the five-second rule."

She drops the contaminated piece onto the tray, grabs a fresh one, and shoves it in my mouth. Her eyes grow fierce as she takes a sausage link and crushes it into my face, missing my mouth entirely. "I can't fucking stand you. Why can't you just cooperate like the rest?"

"Because I'm a stubborn bitch remember?"

Her hair grazes my face as she whips her head around, turning on her heels. "You got that right." Her bare feet slap against the floor as she storms away.

Such a touchy woman.

My stomach growls, the beast inside understandably ravenous. Coffee would have helped dampen my appetite, but she'd rather let us all have headaches than let me show her how to make it.

Audrey shuffles into the room, carrying a fresh dressing for my back. She turns me slowly and a tiny fleck of stone drops from the ceiling, landing at her feet. Her eyes drift to the ceiling, dart to me, and then back to the floor.

She ignores the obvious and tends to my back instead.

The dressing pulls the fine hairs on my back as she peels it away from my skin. "This looks good. I think we should leave it uncovered, and let it air out a bit."

She steps in front of me but doesn't look at me when she talks. I thrust my neck forward and widen my eyes, locking in on her face.

"What?" she asks with a confused look on her face.

I nod for her to come closer, and she leans in as I whisper. "Did Ari speak to you?"

"She did." She steps away from me and stuffs my soiled bandages in her pocket.

"And are you in?"

She looks away from me and stares at the doorway where Jenny stands, waiting for her. "Willow, you're going to get us killed," she says just above a whisper and turns me around to face her.

"I'd rather die fighting, wouldn't you?"

Audrey stares at the ladder leading to the surface. A tear races down her left cheek as she fixates on the hatch door. She sniffles and wipes her nose with her gown sleeve. "Do you think you can get us out of here?"

Has she learned anything in my short time here? I can do anything, kill anyone, save everyone.

"Yes."

Jenny clears her throat.

Audrey reaches up, hugs me, and murmurs. "I'll talk to Jenny." She walks away and disappears as Jenny closes the door.

The surface of my big toenail dulls as I use it to flick a piece of ceiling away from me. Another piece drops and lands on my shoulder and I blow it off with a quick burst of air from my lips.

Damn.

If I keep swinging here, it's going to come down sooner than I want it to. After several minutes, arguing filters through the adjacent room, like sweet music to my ears. The girls are bitching to Jenny about the quality of the food she's serving them.

Jenny stomps into the room, glaring at me. "If I let you down to make us breakfast and coffee, I need your word that you will come right back in here without a fight."

"You have my word." I grin at Audrey standing across the room.

Jenny unhooks me from the wire but doesn't remove the cuffs. "Those stay on," she says pointing at my restraints.

I'm okay with that. Dinner is when I plan to shine. I enter the galley and Ari uses her eyes to point to something on the floor to my left. A thin semi-circular scrape marks the floor. It's faded but still noticeable. The rubber boot tray that usually covers it hangs over the sink, freshly cleaned. That's why I haven't seen it before.

"What do you need?" Jenny says with a huffy tone, drawing my attention away from the false wall.

I give her a list of items we will need for pancakes and walk her through the process. Ari fills the coffee pot, puts the coffee grounds in as instructed, and sits down.

A pineapple rests on the counter, and I eye it. "Cut that up for us and we can spread a little on our pancakes."

Jenny shakes her head. "I don't know how to cut a pineapple, and I'm not giving a knife to a killer."

"Listen, Jenny, I give you my word. I will cut it, dice it, and hand the knife right back to you without a fight. I'll be on my best behavior. I'm just trying to make us the best breakfast I can, with what we have to work with."

Ari and Audrey wait on the bed with their eyes on Jenny. She reluctantly removes the key from her apron pocket and unlocks my cuffs. She passes the knife to me, the blade end first, hesitates, closes her eyes, and then lets it go.

I turn away from her with a slight smile on my face. She thought I was going to kill her.

Not yet, Jenny. Not yet.

I get to work slicing the spiky fruit. The tension in the air is thicker than the pineapple's protective layer. I smile to myself, sensing Jenny's eyes planted on the back of my head—watching me suspiciously.

Sweet-scented juice sprays in the air—intoxicating to my heightened senses. My hand practically vibrates as I slice the fruit into bite-size pieces, toss them into the pan, and sauté them with a little butter and brown sugar.

I wish it was meat.

Steam billows from the pancakes as I scoop a serving of pineapple on top and drizzle maple syrup over them. I watch Jenny, my head on a predatory tilt, as she accepts a plate from my outstretched hand and perches on the bed.

She drags her wary gaze off me for a single moment, to cut up a piece of pancake and fork it into her mouth. "Oh my God, that's good."

I point the knife towards her, a wicked grin curling my lip. "Told you."

She sets her plate down and holds her hand out. "Give me the knife, now."

Ari and Audrey pin their eyes on me, every muscle in their bodies coiled like an overloaded spring.

I wipe my thumb along the edge of the blade, gathering the remnants of pineapple juice, and lick it off. Her palm shakes before me, waiting for the knife. I flip the blade around and pass it to her, handle first, for safety.

Sorry ladies, it's not time yet. I need Jenny to trust me.

Jenny gives everyone a plate, including me, and we eat like four women on a brunch date. Audrey and Ari make small talk with each other as Jenny watches me over her cup of coffee. This is the most I've eaten since arriving here, and I'm not wasting a single bite.

After breakfast, Jenny grabs the handcuffs and places them back on my wrists.

"Come on, Jenny," Ari objects.

"I shouldn't have let her out of them for breakfast. If she behaves herself, maybe I'll let her make dinner."

"What about lunch," Audrey asks.

"I can manage lunch; it's just grilled cheese."

"Just a thin layer of butter," I say to her.

"I know how to make grilled cheese," she insists, yanking me by the cuffs until we are in the hanging room.

She hooks me onto a different wire and stuffs her hands into her apron. "You know before I came here my life was boring. My husband barely acknowledged my existence in my own house. I can't have children so that didn't help. I know my situation is not ideal, being stuck down here, but Benny makes me feel alive and wanted. He sees me and that's something I never had on the surface."

Wow. She has no idea she has a serious illness. I feel bad for her. Okay, maybe not, but still, she should know.

"You know there is a term for your illness, right? It's called Stockholm syndrome."

Jenny gasps, appalled at my suggestion that she is in some way sick for the way she thinks and behaves.

She yanks her hand from her apron and pokes my sternum with her finger. "I don't have an illness or syndrome or whatever it is you're talking about. They didn't make me want to stay down here. I like being here. At least I have a purpose."

I stare at her finger, still lingering on my flesh, and narrow my eyes at her. "Your purpose is going to get you killed."

"Fuck you, Jane Doe. No one can touch me, or my Benny will kill them." She turns and storms out of the room, slamming the door behind her.

She's a lost cause. I'm not wasting my time or energy trying to convince her that she's a victim—she's just too far gone.

I need to pee. I haven't even been hanging for exceptionally long but that damn coffee ran right through me.

"Jenny," I yell.

No response.

"Jenny, I have to use the bathroom," I shout at the closed door.

Her muffled voice carries through the partition. "So go."

Fucking bitch.

Urine flows down my leg and creates a sizable puddle on the floor. I'm spitting in her food at dinner. I've already decided.

The door swings open and Jenny floats into the room with a smile, carrying a pile of clothes. She walks over to the utility closet and drags out the hose. This is what she wanted—for me to soil myself so she could have an excuse to blast me with water.

She stands before me, opens the valve to full blast, and showers me with liquid hatred.

My skin reddens as she turns the nozzle to the jet setting. She smiles at my red, angry skin.

I glare at her.

There's nothing more in the world that I want right now than to stab her in the face and rip the smile right off her smug yap.

She strolls to the back side of me and yanks my underwear to the floor.

I roll my eyes and stare at the ceiling. She's trying to humiliate me like Benny and Griffin do, and it's not working. "Jenny, is this necessary?"

"Just reminding you who's in charge."

She slides beige linen pants over my waist, unhooks me from the ceiling wire, and unlocks my cuffs. A matching shirt hits me in the face. The fabric strikes my eyeball, making it water. I wipe the liquid from my cheek and pull the shirt over my head.

"Give me your wrists," she orders.

I extend them and stare straight into her eyes, but she refuses to look at me as the cuffs click closed. "Why won't you look me in the eye, Jenny? Are you afraid to see yourself inside them? Inside me?" I tilt my head at her. "Everyone has darkness inside them, even you. But you already know that don't you? You have already used it on me. So, what makes you any better, any different, than me?"

She yanks my arms violently upward and attaches me to the wire. "I am nothing like you."

"Really? Before you came here, would you ever have done what you did to me to anyone?"

She hesitates with her hand still on my cuffs. "Of course not."

"Wouldn't you?" I smile at her. "What if your husband asked you to? Would you have?"

"Just shut up." She turns away from me.

"Of course, you wouldn't have. Because you know it was wrong, and you would go to jail. Being down here, with them, has made you one of them—made you a sexual predator.

She spins quickly around and strikes my face with her balled-up fist. "I am not a predator!"

I rock my jaw back and forth and smirk at her. "Perhaps if you showed your husband the attention and hatred you've shown me, he wouldn't have ignored you—couldn't have ignored you. You would've been his boss, his master, his worst nightmare. You would never have been vulnerable, never been a victim."

"I am not a victim, you are. I want to be here." She crosses her arms and raises her chin.

I smile broadly with a sinister face. "Ditto, Jenny. Ditto."

Her face drops just as fast as her arms. "You don't get it. When they took me, I was relieved."

I cackle at the ceiling. "You took the words right out of my mouth."

She throws her hands at the ceiling, hitting my defective wire with her palm. It sails to the right as she growls, "I can't stand talking to you. You're fucking crazy and don't make any sense."

She stomps away from me and through the door, slamming it behind her.

The wire swings before me like the pendulum on a grandfather clock. I follow it with my eyes.

Tick tock. Tick tock.

Her time is running out.

Tick tock. Tick tock.

The countdown to Jenny's demise has begun, and time waits for no one.

Tick tock. Tick tock.

The wire swings slower and slower.

Tick.

Tock.

Chapter Sixteen
Dinner and a Show

It's been hours and no one has come for me. Dinnertime must be close. If Jenny doesn't let me cook, I'll have to improvise and change my plans.

Ari and Jenny's muffled voices rise and fall as they argue on the other side of the door. Ari's pleading my case as planned. The door flies open, slamming against the wall. Audrey's bare feet slap against the ground as she approaches me.

"I don't care what you say, Jenny, Willow's cooking. Your food tastes like garbage," she yells over her shoulder.

"Don't you dare let her go," Jenny warns, marching towards us and stepping in front of Audrey. "She's dangerous."

"If she was so dangerous, why didn't she stab you at breakfast when she had the chance?" Ari asks, wedging herself between Jenny and me. "Let Audrey take her down so she can cook for us. After dinner, we'll hang her back up."

"You two are not in charge here." Jenny's face reddens, eyes darting from Ari to Audrey. "I'm in charge." Jenny sidesteps away from Ari and stands in front of me.

"And you can stay in charge. We just want a decent meal." Audrey swerves around Jenny, reaches up, and unhooks me.

Jenny glances at the red camera light above the door and grimaces.

No one is watching. Even if the guys knew a hostile takeover had started, they couldn't make it back in time to save her.

Ari, Audrey, and I walk away from her and head to the galley.

Jenny joins us after a few minutes and stands beside me as I stare into the fridge. "No tricks. You make dinner, we eat, and you go back. Understand?"

"You're the boss," I say with a tight smile.

She rolls her eyes and sits on the bed in between Audrey and Ari. I have all the supplies I need for a steak stir fry and stew.

"Whatcha making," Ari asks from behind me.

"I am making us stir fry and making the boys a pot of stew."

The mattress springs bounce as Ari jumps up, leans on the counter beside me, and whispers, "Are you going to poison it?"

I snap my head to the right, appalled she would ask me such a thing. "Of course not."

"Can I have stew instead of stir fry?"

I soften my eyes and smile at her like a mother would a begging child. "No, Ari. The stew needs to cook for several hours to be any good."

The bed sinks as she flops back down. "Fine."

I shake my head and return my attention to the stove. After thinly slicing two pounds of round steak and coating them with multiple seasonings, I swirl olive oil into a neat spiral in the pan, add garlic and two pats of salted butter, and toss the meat in.

Mmm, butter.

Onion vapors make my eyes water as I chop them into one-inch strips and set them aside. I drop a handful of pre-shredded carrots and frozen green peppers into the pan and the sizzling intensifies.

Steam billows from the frying pan. Once the vegetables in the pan cut easily with a rubber spatula like a tender cooked tongue, I add the meat and onion and turn it down low to simmer.

It doesn't smell quite the same as my usual meat of choice, but it still makes my mouth water.

I remove a crock pot from under the cupboard, set it on the stove, and plug it in.

"There isn't any meat left, dummy," Jenny chuckles from behind me.

"Haven't you ever heard of vegetable stew?" Ari scoffs at her.

"Trust me, Jenny, no matter what I put in this pot, the boys are going to love it. If you add enough ingredients to anything, it will taste good. The key is an equal balance of sweet, salty, and spicy."

She murmurs inaudible words under her breath.

I make a large saucepan of rice to serve with the stir fry and continue preparing vegetables for the stew—onions, carrots, potatoes, celery, mushrooms, and a can of Italian diced tomatoes. Beef stock will be my base.

I stir the frying pan and scoop out a piece of meat to check it.

Medium. Not as tasty as rare, but acceptable and tender, nonetheless. I drop four plates on the counter, scoop a heap of rice into the center of each, and drop a few spoonfuls of stir fry on top. Jenny stands, grabs her plate first, and flops back into her seat between the girls.

Greedy bitch.

I pass Ari and Audrey their plates and then take a seat on the floor in front of them. Their eyes widen as they dive into their meal. Ari smacks her lips, and Audrey shovels a massive forkful into her mouth. Jenny stays expressionless. She doesn't want me to know she likes it.

I skid my butt across the floor, moving closer to Jenny. "Do you like it?"

She raises her eyebrows. "It's okay."

"Not bad for a last meal, right?"

"Wha—"

She didn't get the whole word out. I guess when someone jams a chopping knife into your chest you become lost for words—the knife gliding in with ease thanks to Griffin's meticulous upkeep.

Audrey and Ari leap away from us.

I stare into Jenny's wide-open eyes—the shock, the horror, the betrayal, the nerve. It's all wrapped up in a neat little blood-stained bow.

"I know what you're thinking." I tilt my head and study her paling face. "Why now? Why didn't I kill you at breakfast? Because no one's last meal should be breakfast, Jenny, and timing is everything."

Her plate slowly slides out of her hand. I grab it and set it on our makeshift table. She tips her head forward, and I rest mine against it with a devilish grin. "You should never have wished me dead."

Blood gurgles from her mouth and lands on my hand and lap. I rest my bloody palm on her cheek. "Now we are even." I inhale the metallic, heavenly scent of her fresh blood and yank the blade from her torn flesh with a twisted smile.

Her useless tears and pleading eyes mean nothing to me. No one can save you, Jenny.

No one.

She topples over and lands on the ground beside me.

Such a tragedy. Perhaps in another life, we could have been friends. This place changed her—made her crazy. But she had a choice, and she chose them.

I rest her head on my lap and comb her hair with my stained fingers. Audrey cries on the floor across from me. If I'm being honest, I forgot the girls were even here—trapped in a daydream filled with memories of what could have been if Jenny chose to be one of us instead.

Jenny's eyes dilate and her jaw opens. I seize her chin and move it like a ventriloquist's dummy. "I'm in charge, not you," her corpse says.

I chuckle and shove her head off my lap. It bounces once like a deflated basketball.

"What have you done?" Audrey whimpers.

Ari reaches for me. I grab her hand, and she pulls me from the floor. "What needed to be done."

Audrey covers her mouth, filtering her breaths as they stagger out. Ari places her arm around her shoulder and stares at Jenny's lifeless body. "Rest in peace, bitch."

I swipe Jenny's plate from the mattress, take several bites, and sigh. "One down…"

"…and two to go," Ari murmurs, finishing my sentence.

I scrape the last of Jenny's stir fry into my mouth and then scan the floor on the other side of the room. The wall by the hanging room entrance appears normal, except for the slight scratch in the shape of an upside-down half circle on the floor. I push the left side of the wall hard, and it pops open. It's an identical room to the hanging room, but half the size and no wires hanging from the ceiling—four crisp white walls, a gray-painted cement floor, and a ladder going up to a closed hatch.

It's perfect.

I lean a jug of water against the doorway to hold it open. Ari and Audrey are face to face, mumbling to each other while holding hands. I lift Jenny under her armpits, drag her into the clean space, and drop her onto the floor. A red smear stains the floor of the galley.

I step over the mess, open a cabinet in the galley, grab cleaning supplies, and set them on the counter beside Ari. "Girls, I need you to clean up this mess—strip the bed, clean the floor, cabinets everything."

Ari swipes her hair away from her face with shaking hands. "What are you going to do?"

I grab her arms and squeeze them gently. "Don't worry about what I'm doing. Just get this mess cleaned up."

She nods her head and grabs a bottle of cleaning spray.

Audrey hasn't moved. She's frozen in time and space, with her mouth hanging open. I take hold of her shirt and pull her to me. "Audrey, listen to me. I know this is a lot to take in right now, but I need you to be strong and trust me. Can you do that?"

Her eyes flit to the blood on the floor. I grab her face with both hands. "Audrey, look at me."

Her gaze rises to meet mine, tears spilling down her cheeks. "I...I...can't move."

"You have to help Ari. I need you girls to clean out here. Just leave the stew on the stove."

"What are you going to do with her?" Audrey looks over my shoulder at Jenny's body in the next room.

I hold Audrey at arm's length. "I'm an artist, and my canvas awaits." I let her go and nod to Ari. She can manage things from here.

I remove a basting brush from the drawer and a roll of paper towels from the dispenser, enter the hidden room, and swing the door closed behind me.

The basting brush is nice for finer lines, but there's nothing like using your fingers to add a bit of sass and flare to a work of art. I'm not sure how long I've been painting, but it was long enough for my fingers to tingle and go numb. I barely have the strength left in them to scribble my signature in the bottom right-hand corner. The paper towel removes only the wet crimson from my hands—soap and water will do the rest.

I spin in a circle with a massive smile, and my arms stretched out like the woman from The Sound of Music. Except, it's not the hills that are alive.

It's me.

I am alive.

This masterpiece makes me sing, makes me dance, makes me feel…free.

It's the largest piece I have ever created, and it's breathtaking. A full account of our time here perfectly laid out in multiple murals of blood—me strapped to the bed, all of us in the hanging room, Jenny's untimely death. There's even a painting of what's to come.

Fingers drum the hidden door. I pull it open and Audrey steps inside. She gasps and her eyes roll back in her head right before she collapses, passing out on Jenny Lane.

Ari peeks around the corner and grimaces at Audrey's motionless body. "What did she do, faint?"

I nod. "I think this was too much for her."

Ari strolls around the room, admiring my artistry. "Is that us in the hanging room?"

"It is."

She steps over Audrey, stops a few feet from the message I scrawled on the wall, and reads it aloud.

'You should've kept driving.'
~Odeya

"Odeya? That's your real name?" Ari turns and looks at me.

"Odeya Willamina Parks."

"I like Willow better," she smiles.

"Yeah, me too. But my sister always called me Odie, so that's what my coworkers and friends call me."

She turns her attention back to the wall and smiles. "You're right, they should have kept driving."

"I may have never found them if they did."

Ari furrows her brow and squints at me. "What do you mean?"

Audrey stirs on the floor, moaning. Ari goes to her side.

"Take her to the holding room, and I'll meet you there when I'm finished," I announce, walking around them.

"Willow, what did you mean when you said you would never have found them?" Ari asks.

"Take care of Audrey and I'll explain later."

Ari lifts Audrey from the floor and helps her from the room. I scan the room one last time, before heading to the galley.

The galley sparkles with freshly cleaned surfaces and the strong scent of bleach. I walk around the room and examine every area—no blood. The crockpot blinks on the stove. I turn it to low, grab a filet knife from one of the drawers, and head to the holding room to check on the girls.

Ari stares at the knife in my hand when I enter. "What are you going to do?"

"Get rid of the body of course."

Audrey covers her mouth with her fist and gags several times. Ari quickly grabs a plastic trash can and thrusts it under Audrey's mouth, catching her vomit.

Ari wrinkles her nose and grimaces. "Gross."

I stare at the undigested vegetables running down the inside of the trashcan and curl my lip. Ari rolls her eyes, shoos me from the room, and closes the door.

I stand in the hallway listening to Audrey retch and heave. I'm glad I have a strong stomach.

Chopping Jenny up was my first thought but what a waste it would be. I grab several garbage bags from under the sink in the galley, and a roll of duct tape, and enter the hidden space. It's musty and warm inside. The girls did such a great job cleaning the kitchen, I don't want to make a mess. I rip each garbage bag down the sides, making them large rectangles, and tape them together on a clean spot on the floor. Jenny's body feels stiffer under my palms when I roll her onto the bags. I wrap the plastic around her, tape the edges, and drag her corpse to the gas chamber.

I use the filet knife to slice open the body bag and begin skinning Jenny like a freshly shot deer. The blade glides easily through her cold, clammy flesh. I peel and remove all of it, even her scalp. After chopping off a few more chunks, I hoist what's left of her onto the bed and secure the corpse's wrists and ankles spread eagle with yellow rope. The bed sinks as I stand on it and remove a gas mask from the cabinet. I secure it to Jenny's skull, climb off the bed, and stand at the foot of it.

Hmmm, something's missing.

I slap my forehead. What's missing is so obvious.

I exit the room and go to Jenny and Benny's room. The dresser drawer scrapes open. The dildo they used on me rests underneath Benny's boxers. I lift it to my nose and sniff it several times.

Smells like soap. At least they were hygienic about cleaning it.

I return to Jenny, lift her skinless buttocks, and shove the purple dildo into her squishy, decomposing anus.

Perfect.

What a wonderful display this would have made on Halloween. You know the kind. The ones they put together for walk-through haunted houses. A little light with a sheer red fabric covering the shade would light the room. Boys and girls would wander through, taking selfies with her corpse. I would jump out with a real knife in my hand, scare the shit out of them, and cackle like a lunatic. If only I had more time and October was closer.

I wad the trash bags on the floor up, carry them to the galley, and stuff them inside the garbage can. After dropping in a few last-minute ingredients, I set the twelve-hour timer on the crockpot. A small amount of blood bled through the body bag I made. I grab a towel and some cleaner and crawl on my hands and knees, scrubbing the floor from the hidden room to the gas chamber.

I can't wait for them to see their display. If I'm lucky, Benny will find Jenny first. If not, I have other plans for him. I take a quick shower and stuff my bloody clothes into the bottom of the hamper.

The outfit Griffin made me wear when I stayed the night with Jenny and Benny, sits neatly folded on his dresser. I pull the sweats on and shirt over my head and snoop around his room.

It's clean. There are no photos, no papers, the bed has fresh sheets, and the pillows are fluffy and inviting. I imagine it's the only duty he gave Jenny. He didn't seem to care too much for her. I don't blame him—she was an annoying whiny bitch.

I leave the room as it was and go check on the girls.

Audrey is sobbing in Ari's arms when I stroll into their room. "Ari, I need you to hook me back up."

She pats Audrey's hand and stands. "Are you sure?"

"Yes."

I walk into the hallway, and she joins me. We walk quietly to the hanging room. I grab a set of handcuffs from the wall cabinet, place them in Ari's palm, and stand by my wire.

Ari tightens the cuffs around my wrists and secures my hands above my head. "You'll be defenseless."

I wiggle my hands a little, and a flake of ceiling drops onto Ari's shoulder. She glances at it and smiles. "Oh, shit. You did it. It's ready to come down."

"Now you understand?" I grin.

"Abso-fucking-lutely," Ari says with a pearly smile.

Chapter Seventeen
Where are They?

I haven't heard the crockpot beep, so it's been less than twelve hours since I set the timer. I thought they'd be back by now.

Rain pings off the metal hatch above me. The boys never mentioned if they were returning morning or evening, but I imagine a two-day expo would end around dinner time.

I sniff the air.

Yes, there it is. The faint scent of cooking meat and vegetables has reached my nasal passages. When the hatch opens above me, the boys will smell the overwhelming odor of their awaiting meal. It will surely make their mouths water.

Ari enters with a yellow bowl in her hands. "I made you some oatmeal."

"Thanks."

"Want me to unhook you?"

"No, just feed me a couple bites and go. You need to lock yourselves in the room. Everything must appear normal."

"Willow, what did you mean by 'I may never have found them'?"

I take a deep breath and hold it. She wants answers, but I'm not prepared to tell her everything at this very moment.

Something that sounds like a pebble bouncing on metal hits the hatch above us, and we glance at the ceiling.

They're here. Or at least someone is.

Their boots or shoes are sliding back and forth on the lid like someone is butting a cigarette or scraping mud off their feet. I've never known Benny to smoke, Griffin neither. At least, I don't think so. I've never smelled it on them.

I made eye contact with Ari. "Go to your room," I whisper. "But don't lock yourselves in until you hear them for sure."

She tiptoes away and closes the hanging room door quietly behind her. The light on the camera flickers from red to green.

The hatch rattles as someone yanks on it multiple times. Something dull but hard strikes the hatch door. The butt of a gun maybe?

"Hey, Griffin, are you down there? It's Pete from the store."

The camera light flickers back to red.

Perhaps Pete's coming to let him know the identity of the person in my rental and that he's linked to Griffin and Benny.

Griffin's people refused to talk at all. I chose his one friend first since they don't talk anymore. A falling out, I guess. Despite their estrangement, his buddy wouldn't give him up no matter how much I tortured him.

Benny's friends, on the other hand, have zero sense of loyalty. They didn't hesitate to steer me to the guy who baked in my trunk.

Benny's best friend, Georgie.

He was a skittish little shit, just like Benny. But he still didn't offer up any information right away. It wasn't until I ripped all his toenails off that he decided to speak to me—blabbering like a traumatized schoolgirl.

Pounding comes from above. "Hello?"

Knock knock.

Who's there?

A killer.

A killer who?

A killer of abusive men.

Oh, and Jenny.

Pete will give up eventually when he realizes Griffin and Benny aren't back yet.

The light flicks back to green. I smile and wink at it. I imagine they are shaking their heads at me. I close my eyes and hum softly to myself.

The timer on the crockpot dings several hours later. They should be back soon. I should yell for Ari to take me to pee, but that's not what Jenny would have done. She would make me piss myself. So, that's what I'm doing.

Warm liquid runs down my leg, hits the floor, and keeps going. I didn't realize how much I had to go until now. I made a pond and the creek leading to it.

Ari opens the door and peeks inside. "I found something," she whispers. I shake my head 'no' and nod to the camera. She stays in the doorway where they can't see her. "I snooped in Benny's room. He's so gross he's got more porn under his bed than the Playboy Mansion. Anyways, inside the end table was a calendar. It had the expo dates and times written on it. Willow, it ended yesterday at three."

I furrow my brows. If it ended yesterday at three, and checkout from the hotel is ten or eleven the next day plus the drive back, they should be coming soon depending on what time it is now. I rotate away from the camera, so the guys can't see me talking.

"What time is it right now?"

"Noon," she whispers to my back.

"They'll be back any minute. Go stir the stew and click it on warm if it's shut itself off. Then lock yourselves in."

"Gotcha."

I twist back around when the door closes, and the light is red again. I'm tired but don't want to fall asleep. If my weight pulls too hard on the eye hook it's likely to fail before I want it to.

The door opens again and only Ari's eyes, nose, and the hand holding the door are visible. "I just want to let you know, that's the best stew I've ever had."

I raise my eyebrows. "Good to know. But Ari, I think you should save the rest for the guys."

"Oh, I know it was just for them, but I was curious, and it smelled so good."

Voices carry through the hatch door. My eyes dart to Ari. "Go."

She vanishes from sight and swings the door shut.

They're arguing. The rise and fall of their voices give them away, but I also hear something else. I turn my ear up and hold my breath, listening intently.

Crying.

They've taken someone else.

The hatch door whips open, and Benny descends first. He lifts his foot when he reaches the bottom, staring at my piss dripping from his shoe. His head twists slowly to face me and his eyes burn angry holes through me. He storms right to me without hesitation and punches me in the stomach. "That's for Georgie."

He returns to the ladder and grabs the bottom of a young girl's dress as she fights her way back to the surface. He yanks her hard and she falls into the room. This one appears young. She can't be more than eighteen. Her eyes are brown and round like a doe and her brown hair is straight and long like mine. It comes close to touching her buttocks. Benny hoists her up by her hair and tosses her at my feet.

"Look at her," he orders.

She gazes up at me with tear-filled eyes.

"If you give us any trouble, your body will look like this." He tears my sweatpants down and points at the crusty healing scars on my legs. "This is what happens when you misbehave."

"Down," Griffin shouts as bare feet with blue-painted toenails step onto the first ladder rung and work their way down. This one has long blonde hair and baby-blue eyes. She runs to the girl on the floor and hugs her. Griffin and Benny each grab one around the waist and pull them apart.

Eve and Leah's replacements.

Benny grips the back of the blonde's neck, forces her beneath one of the wires, cuffs her wrists together, and secures her hands above her head. Griffin drags the brown-haired girl across the floor like a caveman. She digs and scratches at the back of his hand making him bleed. He lifts her by her upper arms, shakes her violently until she stops fighting, and secures her to the wire beside her friend.

The blonde kicks Benny in the back of his knee as he walks away, buckling it. He stumbles and nearly falls on his face—his left hand landing in my piss puddle.

Benny staggers to his feet and shakes my bodily fluids from his palm. I giggle and he balls his fist and strikes me in the face. Blood pours from my lips, and I laugh at him through my bloody teeth as he wipes his hand on his pant leg.

Griffin smiles at me and punches the blonde in the stomach. Her body swings several feet backward. When she swings back to Griffin, he hits her again. She gasps, trying to catch her breath. Every time she came back towards him, he would hit her again.

Benny stops in front of her and grabs her legs, stopping her swaying. He draws his hand back and open hand slaps her across the face. His eyes darken and he glares at her. "Don't fucking kick me again."

"Gina," the brown-haired girl yells. "Don't fight them."

"Yes, Gina, don't fight. You wouldn't want to end up like Jane Doe here, would you?" Griffin scans my attire up and down. "Jenny gave you my clothes. I'm surprised she let you wear anything at all. She must be going soft."

"Oh, she's so tender. I worked hard on her while you were gone."

Griffin raises his eyebrows and glances at Benny. "Really? Did you hear that, Benny? Jane here has won over your girl."

"Somehow, I doubt that." He sniffs the air several times. "Something smells good. What is that, roast?"

"Stew," I smirk and flutter my eyelashes. "Made especially for you."

Benny nods his head and glances at Griffin. "Just for me."

"If Jenny made it, it probably tastes like flavorless ass." Griffin chuckles.

"I helped," I announce with a smile.

"I'll eat anything at this point," Benny says exiting the room.

Griffin crosses his arms and spreads his legs apart. "The guy who died in your trunk was Benny's friend. Why did you have him?"

"Because I'm a killer Griffy. It's what I do."

"My guy at the police station said he was missing his toenails." He places his hands on his hips. "Why did you do that to him?"

I gaze over Griffin's shoulder. Gina and her friend whisper back and forth. Her friend glances at the ceiling.

Smart girl. She sees I'm a few yanks away from escaping.

Her eyes follow a paint flake as it floats towards Griffin's head. She belts out an obnoxious scream to get Griffin's attention. He turns to her, strolls over, and slaps her across the face. "There'll be none of that."

I use my toe to tuck the flake beneath my feet.

He turns back to me just as Benny enters with a steaming bowl of stew. Juices trickle down his chin, and he swipes them with the back of his hand.

I smile broadly at him. "How is it?"

He finishes chewing the food in his mouth. "It's fucking delicious."

Inside, I'm screaming with laughter and peeing my pants. On the outside, I remain pan-faced and serious. "Well, you have Jenny to thank."

He nods his head and takes another huge bite. "I will, when I find her."

Griffin steps away from the girls and stops in front of Benny. "What do you mean when you find her?"

Benny ignores his question. He scoops a massive spoonful and holds it out to Griffin. "Griff, try a bite of this. This shit is slamming."

Yes, Griffin, please do try some.

Griffin waves off the food Benny offers him. "Put that down and find Jenny. She needs to meet the new girls."

Benny eats the bite he offered Griffin and nods. "Yeah, okay. Let me get some more food. I'm fucking starving."

Griffin rolls his eyes as he walks away. He stares at the new girls and points at me. "This is Jane Doe. Take a good look at her—the bruises, the scars, and the cuts." He takes his eyes off them and furrows his brow at me. "If you don't want to look like her, do as you're told."

"I'm Marley, and that's Gina," the brown-haired girl says quietly and nods to her friend.

Griffin grabs Marley by the face. "This isn't a social hour. You aren't friends. Do you understand?"

The girls' heads bobble up and down rapidly.

Benny enters holding a full bowl of stew. "Hey, Griffin. I can't find Jenny."

"What do you mean you can't find her? There are only a few places she's allowed to go. Did you check in the holding room, bathroom, your room, and mine?"

"Not the holding room. The door's locked, and you have the keys."

Griffin sighs through his nose and fishes the key out of his front jeans pocket. He drops it into Benny's palm. "When you find her, bring her to me. And Benny, leave the stew."

I smile as he passes his bowl to Griffin and leaves to search for Jenny. Griffin stirs it several times before taking a massive bite. He raises his eyebrows and nods his head several times. "Better than last time."

"Of course it is."

Benny runs into the room panting heavily. "She's not in there, and something's wrong with Audrey."

"What are you talking about?"

"Griffin, didn't you hear what I said? Jenny's not here."

Griffin cranks his neck at me. "Where the fuck is Jenny?"

I stare at his bowl and nod with a sinister smile. "She's cooking."

Chapter Eighteen
Where's Jenny?

Griffin's bowl falls in slow motion. The ceramic bowl shatters on impact—chunks of stew splatter on his pant leg and tumbles to the floor. His head swivels side to side atop his neck. "No."

"No, what?" Benny asks confused.

"No, no, no, no," Griffin repeats storming from the room with Benny on his heels.

It's time.

I may die, but it will be worth it.

Marley's bottom lip quivers. "You killed her, didn't you?"

I didn't have to answer.

Griffin reappears in the doorway looking rattled. He holds his hand over his mouth, partially covering his bloodless pale face. "Odeya. You're her sister, aren't you?"

I raise my chin, casting more light on my menacing grin. It wasn't by random chance that they found me on the side of the road. Benny's friend helped me get there. I just had to be patient, flaunting the goods beside the rental car I'd sabotaged until they happened to drive by. I wouldn't even be here if they hadn't stopped.

Benny's screams echo through the entire bunker. If anyone were on the surface, they would hear it too. Griffin glances at me, pushes off the door frame, and runs to his brother.

Inaudible yelling carries through the bunker and grows louder as the brothers make their way back to the hanging room. Within seconds, Benny barrels into the room and trips over his own feet trying to get to me. The knife in his hand skids across the ground. Griffin tackles Benny and holds him around the waist. The handle of the blade he dropped sits just out of reach. He fights against Griffin, trying frantically to reach the weapon. Griffin kicks it away from them and hugs Benny tighter. "You can't kill her," he whispers in a broken voice.

Benny wails at the ceiling. Tears plaster his face and glisten under the flickering fluorescent lights. "Let me go." He struggles in Griffin's arms.

"I can't. We will punish her, but first I need to make a deal with the Egyptian. Maybe I can give him all the girls we have in exchange for her. Then you can do whatever you want."

He doesn't want me now that he knows who I am. I smile at him when he looks at me—disgusted by my actions, shocked by my identity. He swallows hard, like a pill trapped sideways inside his throat. Benny sees it too and thrashes about wildly.

Griffin leans the whole weight of his body on him, pinning him to the floor. Benny growls and belts out a blood-curdling scream—his heart broken, and his mind fractured.

Griffin's eyes lock on the puddle of Jenny stew on the floor. He swallows hard and looks away.

After several solemn minutes, Benny relaxes in Griffin's arms.

He takes Benny's forehead and presses it against his. A tear races down Griffin's cheek.

It is the first time he has shown any sign of sadness since my arrival. Perhaps it's angry tears.

His hands comb Benny's hair, and he whispers quiet words to him. Benny nods, and Griffin lets him go. He crawls away as Griffin stands, picks up the knife on the floor, and secures it in his back pocket.

Benny rocks back and forth on his hands and knees. "Why did you do this?"

I stare intently at Griffin. "Are you going to tell him?"

"Tell me what?" Benny sits back on his heels.

Griffin rubs his forehead and paces between Benny and me. "Shut up, Odeya."

"Odeya? Griffin, you know her name. How?"

Griffin sighs and glares at me. "She wrote it on the wall by the secondary exit."

Oh, isn't this rich? He doesn't want Benny to know who I am. Well, I can't allow that. "Tell him the truth, Griffin. Tell him why I am here, or I will."

"What truth? What is she talking about?" Benny climbs shakily to his feet, swaying unsteadily and clutching at the wall for support.

Griffin says nothing. How do you tell your brother he was right from day one?

Benny leaves the room, presumably heading to the hidden room. Griffin waits, propped against the wall, his face taking on a green hue.

Benny wanders back into the hanging room moments later—eyes unfocused, breaths shallow, and barely moving the air.

He's going into shock. I think to myself.

His pain is so raw, so delicious, that it's arousing. A spark ignites between my legs, and my body sends juices to put out the fire.

Benny stumbles, catching himself at the last minute against the door frame, his listless eyes finally landing on his brother. "What the fuck did you do, Griffin?"

"Benny…" Griffin's quiet voice barely elevates above a whisper as he takes a few steps towards him.

"No. Don't Benny me. Tell me the truth."

Griffin hangs his head, refusing to speak.

I can't contain myself. He's kept this secret from his brother for far too long.

"Well, if he won't tell you, I will. Your brother murdered my sister. They were dating, but she broke up with his abusive ass. The next day he walked into the restaurant where she waitressed, put a gun to her head, and pulled the trigger."

Marley and Gina exchange frowning faces. Benny tightens his hands into fists, whitening his knuckles.

I narrow my eyes at Griffin. "He didn't do shit for time since his lawyer got him institutionalized with some bullshit insanity plea instead of putting him in prison for the rest of his life, where he belonged. So, I made it my mission after that to find him and kill everyone he knows, and everyone who knew how much he was hurting her."

Griffin covers his mouth with his hand and focuses on the floor, refusing to look at Benny or me.

I clench my teeth and glare at Griffin. "Look at me."

His head slowly rises and meets my gaze. "She loved you. No matter how many times she came home with bruises, she defended you. I think deep in her heart she thought she could change you and make you a better man."

Another tear escapes Griffin's lid. I believe he loved her too but didn't know how to show it without hurting her—possessing her, controlling her, killing her. She tried to understand why he acted the way he did, just like she did with me. The difference is, she was my sister, and I would never hurt her no matter how much she worked to curtail my behavior. But with Griffin, the more she pushed to change him, the more abusive he became.

I turn and look at Benny with fire in my eyes. "Your brother took everything from me. She was my heart and soul and the only person in my life who understood who I truly was inside."

Griffin staggers backward, bouncing his back against the wall. Words can't escape his lips. They're trapped in his throat—cut off by grief, by the mistakes of his past, and by me.

"You did this, Griffin. Jenny's death is on you. Your brother's pain is on you. What happens next is on you."

He pushes himself away from the wall and stalks towards me. "No. This is on you. You killed Jenny, not me. You came here for vengeance for your sister and that was your choice, not mine. So, what happens next is not on me, it's on you."

I cackle at the ceiling. "Oh, Griffin. You have no idea what you're talking about. Don't you see? You chose to pull the trigger and kill my sister." I glower at him and raise my voice. "I held back for her—kept my thoughts and desires to myself for her. Stayed out of trouble for her." I tilt my head and smile. "You are my catalyst. You killed the only person in the world who could stop me from being my true self. And now that I'm free, I'll never stop."

Benny wipes his face and stares at Griffin. "Is this true? The girl you killed was her sister?"

"Yes."

"You told me it was an accident. You said the gun just went off and that's why they put you in that facility."

"I'm sorry, Benny."

"*Sorry*?" He grabs Griffin's shirt, spitting as he talks. "You're fucking *sorry*? Jenny's dead because of you."

"So, you did love her?" I chuckle. "Well, don't worry—a part of her will always be with you."

"Shut up, Odeya," Griffin growls a warning.

I smile broadly. "In your heart, in your mind, and in your *belly*."

Griffin pushes Benny's hands off his chest, and strides forward, slapping me hard across the face. "I said shut up!" he screams.

"What do you mean in my belly?" Benny tips his head sideways.

Griffin rubs his temples. "Just ignore her Benny. She's just trying to upset you further."

I grimace at Griffin and tilt my head. "He has a right to know."

"There's nothing else to say. You killed Jenny. The end." Griffin glares at me.

Oh, he's in denial.

Tisk tisk. This is too good of a twist to keep to myself.

The corner of my mouth twitches upward with a slight grin. "Now, Griffin. Keeping secrets from your brother is what got us here in the first place. I think you should tell him."

"Tell me what?" Benny moves forward, standing between Griffin and me.

"There is nothing to tell." Griffin refuses to look Benny in the eye.

I can't hold it in anymore. I feel like I'm going to burst at the seams.

"Well, Benny, where Jenny lacked in personality she sure made up in flavor, don't you think?"

Griffin rubs his mouth with his palm as Benny turns to me slowly and squints his eyes. "You're a fucking *liar*. Even *you* wouldn't do that."

I laugh at the ceiling. "That wasn't beef stew. You ate two massive helpings of Jenny stew. Mmm. I bet it was delicious. I didn't get a chance to try any yet, but Ari said it was good, and well, you two both seemed to like it."

Benny's face drains of color and turns a lovely shade of green. His knees buckle, and he crashes to the floor retching and gagging. Bits and pieces of Jenny's meat and pulverized vegetables puddle onto the floor.

Griffin's punch has me swinging through the air, but he can't stop the joyful laugh that pours from my mouth. Tears stream down his wretched face.

I've succeeded in doing what I came here for.

I broke him.

I broke them both.

They thought they could hurt me—take everything from me—and turn me into an empty shell of a human. Instead, they unleashed me on the world.

Benny pants from his watering, contaminated mouth, watching Griffin land blow after blow to every inch of my body while I cackle. Vomit launches from my lips, striking Griffin first, then joining Benny's mess on the floor.

What more can they do? They can't kill me without offending the Egyptian. And I won't let him kill them—not when I've been so patient.

Flakes and particles rain down on his head when he finally stops hitting me. They are either too distraught to notice, or they don't care anymore. Benny sits on the floor and rocks back and forth, holding his ankles. Griffin sucks his teeth with his tongue and stares at the new girls. I have nothing invested in them yet— no feelings either way.

He slaps Benny's shoulder on his way out of the room. I imagine he's fetching Ari and Audrey. They helped me carry out this plot, after all.

Griffin drags Ari into the room by her hair. Fresh blood runs from her nose. He hoists her up to her wire, attaches her, then leaves the room again.

Audrey doesn't fight. She walks solemnly in front of him and stands by a wire. She will need serious counseling after this ordeal. Even then, she will never be the same. At least she didn't eat the stew.

He hooks Audrey up, strolls over to the utility closet, drags the hose from inside, and drops it at Benny's feet. Benny makes no move to take it or stand.

"Get up, Benny. I'll find you another Jenny." Griffin curls his lip at the undigested Jenny meat on the floor.

Benny wipes snot from his nose and follows Griffin's eyes to the regurgitated Jenny stew. He gags and covers his mouth. "I don't want another Jenny. It won't ever be the same. We had a connection."

"If you didn't before, you do now." I snort.

"Shut up," Benny yells as he leaps to his feet.

I grin broadly at him and glance at Griffin. "Look at the way he hurts. Look at the way he cries for her. Look at how much he loved her. Do you remember what that was like, Griffy?"

Benny charges me and grabs me by the throat, cutting off my airway. "You are a disgusting excuse for a human. If the Egyptian ends up taking you, I hope he cuts you up in tiny pieces and feeds them to his dog."

Griffin rests his palm on Benny's arm. "Let her go."

Benny flares his nostrils and jerks his arm out of Griffin's grasp, releasing me.

I take several deep breaths and continue taunting him. "Like I did to your little bitch, Jenny."

Benny huffs through his teeth, his body stiff with rage.

He wants to kill me. I know how he feels. The knot in your stomach twisting so tightly that one wrong move by your prey and snap, it's over. You can't stop the rage once it floods your veins like lava from a volcano.

"Wait, what do you mean you made Jenny into a meal?" Ari asks from behind me.

Oh, fuck. I probably should have told her after she taste-tested the stew what the meat inside was. I rotate around to her and raise my brows. "Sorry about that, Ari. I never intended for you to taste the stew—just stir it."

"So that meat was…"

I give her a sly half-grin and nod. "Yep."

She's either going to hate me after this or not. I'm hoping for the latter.

Ari furrows her brow and stares at the floor. "Really?"

I grimace and nod a second time. I mean what else can I do? I can't change the past.

There's a long awkward silence. They're all thinking about the stew. Griffin swallows hard and covers his mouth. Benny sucks his tongue and spits on the floor. Ari assesses the leftover flavor in her mouth, smacking her lips together.

Staggering breaths escape Audrey's quivering lips. She inhales a massive breath and belts out an apocalyptic scream. "You're fucking crazy," she screams at me. "I hate you. I hate all of you. Kill me now. Kill me," she yells at Benny and Griffin, who cover their ears.

Snap.

Her volcano has erupted. If she were free, we would need to evacuate the bunker.

Another round of incoherent expletives howl from her lips.

Griffin grits his teeth and stalks towards her. He's had enough. His fist raises, and Audrey shuts up at once, muting her horrific sound effects. He glares into her distraught face. "Not another fucking peep out of you."

Silence befalls the contaminated space. The vomit on the floor emanates a putrid and unmistakable odor.

Ari stares at a coin-sized piece of carrot that tumbled away from the rest of the stomach contents. She hasn't blinked for almost a minute. Her eyes are stuck. I've had that happen. It's annoying. You want to close them so badly, but your brain is buffering, and you have to wait until it reconnects to your systematic Wi-Fi.

Her lashes flutter and flick a tear off them. "Huh. I always wondered what human flesh tasted like," Ari finally says, pursing her lips. "I must say, it's not that bad."

That's my girl.

She turns and smiles at Audrey. "Like, seriously it wasn't that bad. I think I liked it better than regular stew."

Audrey grimaces, and her chest heaves in and out rapidly. She's trying to hold it together to avoid a punch in the face. Hyperventilating finally takes its toll. Her eyes roll in the back of her head as she passes out.

I smile at Ari. "I make a mean steak, too."

Her head whips in my direction. "I love steak."

"Jesus Christ." Griffin covers his face with his hands.

Benny gags and drops to his hands and knees. His mouth waters and drips onto the floor. He stuffs two fingers down his throat but only bile comes out. His stomach has already ejected all of Jenny, yet he still feels her inside him. He pushes his fingers so far into his mouth his hand nearly disappears.

"No matter how many times you do that, she'll always be there, haunting your dreams, speaking inside your head, and churning inside your stomach. Her DNA is a part of you now. You never planned to let her go, and now she will never leave." I tilt my head slowly with an expressionless face. "You're welcome."

"Enough!" Griffin yells, making me smile. "Benny, do what you must but don't kill any of them." He turns his back on us, rubs his head, and walks towards the door.

"Where are you going?" Benny asks, sniffing snot higher into his nose.

"To call the Egyptian."

He's going to try and bargain to keep me.

Ha, ha, ha. It will never work. We have an agreement, and he is a businessman.

I am one of a kind, like a single-printed, signed copy, special edition book.

Femi will never let me go.

I'm fucking priceless.

Chapter Nineteen
Marley and Gina

Benny wipes tears off his face with the back of his hand and stares at the new girls. He pushes off the floor, grabs the hose by his feet, and blasts them with freezing water while they scream.

They have no idea what's coming—torture, rape, starvation, humiliation. Possibly death.

I can't help them. Not yet.

Marley's legs thrash back and forth, trying desperately to kick the hose nozzle from Benny's grasp. He doesn't see Gina coming. She runs on her tiptoes, slamming her hip into his shoulder and knocking him to the ground.

Attagirl.

Ari and I nod to each other. She can take what's coming, but Marley and Gina can't. They're too new, too young, and they don't know Benny's weaknesses.

I laugh aloud, taunting him as he staggers to his feet. "Damn Benny, you got knocked down by a little girl."

"What a crybaby. Crybaby, cryyyyy baaaaaby…" Ari sings.

Benny's face contorts with rage, seizing the hose nozzle from the floor. He yanks up Ari's nightgown and positions the end of the hose between her legs with shaking hands. "I'll do it." His eyes pan the room and land on each of us.

"Wussy," Ari murmurs, staring down at his idle hand.

"Wussy? No, Ari, he's a pussy. Have you seen the size of his cock?"

Marley and Gina exchange glances. "Schmuck," they say in unison.

Benny whips his head around and blasts the girls in the face with the hose. "I'm not a schmuck."

Griffin strolls in with a smile. The color in his face has returned, and his hands are loose and relaxed. "Benny."

The water stream slows to a stop as Benny closes the valve and drops the hose. "What did he say?"

"He said he'll be here in a couple of days to see the new merchandise, then decide." Griffin stops before me, seizing my thighs roughly. "As much as I wanted to keep you all to myself, I'm looking forward to allowing Benny to have his way with you now that I know who you are."

"I'm looking forward to it as well." I wink at Benny.

"The Egyptian will take the deal." Benny walks over and stands beside Griffin. "And when I'm finished with you, I'm going to feed you to the others."

I tilt my head at him. "I'll give you the recipe for my stew in laymen's terms, so you don't fuck it up."

"I tasted the stew when no one was watching..." Audrey sobs and glares at me with watery eyes. Snot runs down her lip and lands in her mouth. "...and I liked it. I'm a cannibal now—a people eater, a sick fuck." She wails to the ceiling.

Oh, my. What's this? A new addition to the Maneaters Club. Well, in her and Ari's case, a woman, but that was a one-off. Men have more meat to offer, so that's what I prefer. I gaze at the ceiling, picturing our potential future. Like vampires ravishing a small town, our numbers will grow. We will spread like locusts around the world, punishing men like Griffin and Benny—their meat will be our reward.

Griffin rubs his temples as he leaves the room, returning moments later with a roll of tape, which he tosses to Benny. "Shut her up." Griffin orders, pointing to the still-wailing Audrey.

Benny rips a long piece off the roll and wraps it fully around Audrey's mouth and head.

No one speaks. It's like we all forgot what we wanted to say. The words are there, but we can't decipher them into audible speech.

"Can we have Jenny stew for dinner?" Ari asks, breaking the silence.

Everyone stares at her.

She raises her eyebrows. "What? It tasted good, and I'm hungry."

Benny chucks the tape at Ari's face, striking her in the mouth, and bloodying her lip. "I'm going to kill you." He storms towards her, grabbing her throat and crushing it with both hands.

Ari's face pales, turning an ashen shade of blue.

Griffin squeezes Benny's wrist. "Stop." He shakes his head. "Let her go."

Benny thrusts Ari's head back, releasing her from his grasp. "This isn't over." He turns his back and marches out of the room.

Ari looks at Griffin, takes a deep breath, and blows out a staggering breath. "I'm still hungry."

"For fuck's sake." Griffin scoops up the tape and presses a piece over Ari's lips. "Shut the fuck up for once." He walks over to the door by the galley, turns around, and sets eyes on each one of us. "No one's eating tonight."

I smile as he closes the door behind him.

Gina tilts her head at me. "So, you killed Benny's friend too; the one in the trunk?"

"Not just his friend."

"How many people have you killed?" Gina glances at Marley and then back to me.

I smile at her inquisitive face. "Including Jenny, thirteen."

Gina clears her throat and stares at the floor. "Who were they?"

"People who deserved it."

Her head raises high enough to look me in the eyes. "How did it feel the first time?"

"Gina." Marley's eyes widen as she shakes her head.

I nod my head. She's curious but afraid that if I answer I will then have to kill them.

"You don't have to be afraid, Marley." I glance at Audrey who's staring at me with hollow, solemn eyes.

Audrey breaks eye contact and studies the floor. Her hands shake above her head and her heart pounds beneath the fabric of her top.

The light above the door flicks to green.

Perfect timing.

They can hear the whole story in order as it occurred—even get my confession on tape if they choose.

"The first three people I killed was during my time in the military. Two were enemy soldiers I killed in self-defense and the third was a sergeant in my unit who liked drugging and assaulting women. I thought it would have been harder, but squeezing that trigger was the easiest thing I have ever done." I feel my eyes glazing over as I remember.

Marley's voice staggers. "But what about the people eating part? When did that start?"

I shrug the best I can with my arms above my head. "When my sister died, I had no reason to hold back my desire for human flesh."

"What was her name?" Marley asks.

I glare at the camera. "Amelia. Amelia Genevieve Parks. But we called her Lia. And as for the first human flesh part, that honor went to Griffin's estranged best friend from childhood. It's so bizarre. I tried to tell him if he just told me everything he knew, I would let him go. But he still protected him. Even after all this time, he wouldn't give up his friend. His mistake, I guess. He tasted amazing in a pot of beans over a massive campfire."

The door slams open, and Griffin enters with balled-up fists. "You fucking cunt."

I bat my eyelashes at him and grin. "Oh, come on Griff, you didn't even like those people anymore."

"Who else?" Air blasts through his nostrils like a bull ready to charge. "You said *those people*, indicating there's more than one."

"I did, didn't I? When I arrived in Virginia, I found someone who heard about a newer doomsday shop that a dipshit guy started up not far from his while his brother was in some institution. Despite not caring for the competition Benny's shop caused and even though he thought Benny was a moron, he still didn't want to tell me where you guys were."

"Todd," Griffin says more to himself than to me.

"Yes, that's it, Todd. What a dumb ass name. Well, after some significant torture—waterboarding, stress positions, starvation, and walling, that one's my favorite, he finally told me what city you were in."

"Jesus." Griffin rubs his temples.

"No, Jesus wasn't involved in any of this." I shake my head and grin. "I visited two larger doomsday shops, which, let's face it, both were fronts for this sex trafficking ring you all are a part of, but neither of them was yours. When I went to the third shop, I met someone interesting. He was buying supplies for his men when he spotted me talking to the cashier.

I close my eyes and take myself back to that evening. Everything I started to say, he'd finished my sentences. He knew me, despite just meeting me for the first time. I could tell him anything. My pussy moistens, remembering the moment he thrust his sizeable cock into me.

Griffin snaps his fingers in front of my face. "Get to the fucking point, Odeya." He crosses his arms and glances at Benny as he enters the room.

"I felt my sister in the room with us. Amelia sent him to me like a gift straight from heaven. I fucked the shit out of him, and I mean fucked. We did things I'd never done before." I grip the wire above my head and straighten myself. "I told him everything. From what you did to my sister, the people I've killed so far, and my plan—every nitty-gritty detail. He had connections and vowed to help me."

I smile at Benny. "It took a little time, but we enjoyed each other's company while his people hunted you down. You know, keeping your shop off the grid along with yourselves, made finding you more difficult, but not difficult enough." I gaze around the room and set my eyes on Griffin. "You should be careful who you talk to and confide in when you're on the inside. Not all doctors keep things confidential. Your Dr. Morgan was more than happy to share the stories you would tell him about Benny and his buddies starting up their network of sex slaves and using the dark web. I mean, it took a little time, of course, to get him to talk, but when I threatened to cut off his cock and shove it up his wife's ass, he was more than happy to share what he knew." I smirk at Griffin. "You and I both know that Benny wasn't the brains of this operation. At least, that's what your medical chart says."

"Fuck you. I played a big part in getting this whole thing set up before Griffin got out and took over for Edward." Benny puffs up his scrawny chest, trying to appear intimidating and strong.

How comical.

"You didn't take over for Edward, he never left. Edward got this place set up, and Edward ran the show with you until Griffin got out because he knew you weren't strong enough to manage it on your own. He didn't leave this place until he knew Griffin was out, and on his way here."

Griffin glares at Benny but says nothing.

I smile at the uncomfortable silence between them. Benny must have told him an amazing tale of how hard it was for him to set this all up and find all these buyers, when the truth was, that he did nothing on his own. Griffin knew about Edward but thought the extent of his help was minimal. Benny may be good with math and making sales for the business end of things, but when it comes to dealing with the customer, no one likes Benny.

Not even a little.

Benny pulls his collar away from his neck and gives Griffin a half-hearted smile. "That's a lie. You can ask Edward."

I shake my head at him. "Oh, Benny. When was the last time you spoke with your mentor?"

Benny sends me a horrifying glance as he does the math inside his head.

"Ding, ding, ding. He's finally worked it out."

Griffin steps towards me and squeezes my chin. "Is he dead?"

I lick his finger, and he releases my face. "Of course he is, along with his father, and that other guy who was torturing women in that hole in the ground. But don't worry, the girls he held captive down below are safe."

"Fuck." Benny rubs the top of his head. "Just fucking kill her Griffin."

Griffin stands a foot from me. "Who's your lover? The one helping you. What's his name?"

I cackle at him. "I'll die before giving him up."

"You're dying either way." Benny points out.

"Not before I kill you and your brother. It's the end of the line for you and your family. You're the only two left. The bloodline stops here."

Benny's eyes grow to saucers as he turns to Griffin. "Pop and June."

The brothers turn white, like mirroring ghosts, before racing from the room.

"Who are Pop and June?" Marley asks.

"Pop is their whore of a father, and June is the young slut he married. Who do you think told me how to find Benny's friend, Georgie, who was in the trunk?"

"Holy fuck. They're going to kill you for sure," Gina says.

"They value their own lives more than anything else. They know they can't kill me."

"But they can kill us." Marley glances at Audrey, Ari, and Gina.

"No, they can't." I grin. "They need you as leverage—to trade in my place to the Egyptian."

"What if your plan doesn't work?" Gina's voice cracks.

"Don't worry. No matter what happens, no one in this room is going to die."

Behind the door, a great hollering gives way to agonizing silence. They don't come back as I expected them to. Perhaps they knew that's what I wanted—to see their faces, to see their anger.

To see their pain.

I tilt my head down and cast my eyes across the room at Ari. She smiles with her eyes at me. She too knows the end is near, and we are mere days away from blowing this hole right out of the mother fucking ground.

Chapter Twenty
Avoidance

It's been quiet for too long. Marley's head bobbles as she struggles to keep her eyes open. Gina snores softly. Ari's been trying to get her gag off by pushing it with her tongue. Even if Audrey could talk, she wouldn't.

I stare at the green light above the door and wonder what they are doing. My guess is they're planning a couple of funerals and answering a bunch of questions the police are asking.

Muffled words stagger from Ari's mouth. The tape rests on her upper lip like a mustache. She blows it upward with forceful breaths, and it shifts under her nose. "Cheap ass duct tape. At least I don't have to have my lip waxed for a while."

I chuckle and shake my head. She's always looking at the bright side of things.

"So, what's the plan?" Ari walks in circles and then starts running. She lifts her feet and swings in a counterclockwise rotation then stops.

"Ari, don't do that now," I say under my breath—my eyes locking on the surveillance equipment.

She stares at the camera and frowns. "We can't wait. If they let the Egyptian take us, we're toast."

"Let's talk about something else. Where are your parents?"

"Well, my douche of a dad left my mom because she's kind of a bitch and moved to the Philippines. Last I heard, he got married again. As for my mom, she took off to Florida to enjoy the warmer weather as soon as I turned eighteen."

"Leaving you behind?" I raise my eyebrows.

Ari nods. "She knows I'm an independent woman. Being the youngest of seven, you learn to take care of yourself."

And there it is. The reason she does whatever she can for attention. When people have children, the first child always gets the most of everything—attention, schooling, extracurricular activities, and the best clothes. When the second child comes around, they get a little less, because now there are two children to care for and money gets tight. By the time Ari was born, she was wearing the hand-me-downs of the hand-me-downs, and her parents had nothing left to give, including attention.

"Where does your mom think you are?"

"University of Virginia." She accents her voice and gives it a southern twang. "I went to the beach over the weekend and ended up at a party with a bunch of rich dudes right on the ocean. Next thing you know, I wake up in the woods with these assholes." She nods at the camera. "Rich people are sick and twisted fucks."

She's not wrong. I am rich and twisted.

A family friend helped me sue the trucking company responsible for my parent's death. Between the insurance payout and the settlement, I could buy an island if I wanted. But why spend money on frivolous things? I'd rather use it to further my cause—ridding the world of these abusive fucking men and filling my chest freezer while doing so.

Ari sways side to side on her tiptoes. "Can I call you Odie?"

A flake from the ceiling lands on my forehead when I turn to face her. "I thought you liked Willow better."

"I do, but you're like a badass, and Willow feels more like a goodie two shoes. Odie sounds more gangster. Like a street name."

I chuckle softly. "You can call me whatever you like."

Ari frowns as she looks at the camera. "That thing just blinked yellow, and the light went off."

Air stops flowing through a vent in the wall, and the little bit of light shining beneath the galley door disappears, leaving us in complete darkness.

"Either they shut down the generator or it malfunctioned," I say.

"Won't we suffocate down here?" Ari's voice elevates.

"If they don't make it back in time, yes."

"How long?" Gina asks.

"About an hour, maybe two."

Breaths quicken across from me. It's Audrey, panicking. If she keeps this up, she'll pass out in no time, which might not be a bad thing under the circumstances.

They'll come. They have to. Losing us would cost them too much money.

Worst case scenario, I'll yank myself out of the ceiling and open the doors to the other rooms, releasing trapped oxygen and buying us more time. But if they don't get the hatch open or fix the generator, no one will come out of this room alive.

"Girls, we need to all loosen our wires."

"I'm working on it," Ari says in a breathy voice.

The air shifts the hair on my arm as she swings by.

"Ouch," Gina cries out as Marley thumps into her. "Be careful. We have to take turns swinging."

"Sorry."

If the lights came on now, Griffin and Benny would see a bunch of swinging monkeys floating around the room.

"Fuck," Ari murmurs. "I got something in my eye."

"Don't look up while you swing," Marley says.

I came to this place with a purpose—to satisfy the hunger inside me.

By killing my sister, Griffin brought me out of hibernation, and he's the ultimate prey—the one that got away.

But these girls need me and have helped me. I owe it to them to make sure they get out of here alive.

Everyone needs to stop talking and conserve their energy and the air.

"Girls, I need you to stop everything you're doing and be still."

"What are we going to do?" Gina asks.

"If too much time passes, I'll yank myself out of the ceiling and open the doors."

"Why don't you just do it now?" Marley's voice cracks.

"Because I don't want to lose the opportunity to take them both out if I don't have to." I sense their unspoken words. They think I'm being selfish, and that's fine. They don't know me well enough to trust that I will keep my word. If I were them, I wouldn't trust me either.

The Green-Eyed Monster. That's what some kids called me in elementary school. Just because I played a little rough on the playground and wasn't afraid to stand up for myself doesn't make me a monster. Does it?

I mean, I was the only student in my grade with green eyes, and with my jet-black hair, I stood out even more. Of course, sucking my bleeding wounds when I'd fall on the pavement at recess probably didn't help.

By the time I made it to high school, no one knew what my real name was. I was just '*Monster*' by then. They weren't wrong. I am a monster in the eyes of the law and civilized society. Perhaps if they were kinder to me, I wouldn't have turned out the way I did.

Nah.

I like who I am—who I've become, what I am that they aren't.

Free.

When I'm finally caught, everyone who sees the news will say they aren't surprised and bring up all the things I did and the signs that were always there. But where were they when they could have stopped me?

I can feel everyone's thoughts, filtering through their heads—sense their fear in the room. Audrey sniffles every few seconds as she whimpers.

No one speaks for what seems like hours—afraid talking will suck what little air we have out of the room. Beads of sweat run down Ari's forehead into her eyes. The hair around Audrey's temples sticks to her moist skin.

"I can't breathe," Gina says, inhaling and exhaling rapidly. "There's no air."

I rotate to the sound of her voice. "You need to stay calm, or you'll pass out. Take slow deep breaths and exhale. Do it with me. In…out." I breathe in slowly and exhale, and she does the same.

I'm getting dizzy.

"Fuck." I yank my wire multiple times.

Ceiling crumbs rain down on my head, pelting me in the dark like hail. With every yank, my heart sinks a bit further.

The air in the room stales, and the strength I need to break free becomes less and less.

"What are you doing?" Ari asks. "I thought you wanted to wait?"

"I can't. We are losing air too fast."

I wrench and wiggle the wire hard, but it doesn't come down. I need to swing.

"Girls, move as far away from me as you can."

I start running in a circle as fast as I can, lift my feet, and slam into Audrey. She never moved—her feet planted like they were stuck in fresh concrete.

"Audrey, please. I know you're upset, but you need to move back. I can get us out of here."

Feet shuffle in the dark, and I can no longer smell her breath. I walk backward to my original position, run, and lift my feet.

Woohoo. I think to myself as I float around the room.

A glimpse of light appears out of the corner of my eye, but it takes my brain too long to figure out what I see.

I stop moving abruptly as someone seizes my legs, holding them tight. The light in the room flickers on, and metal scrapes against metal as the ventilation fan starts spinning.

Griffin glances at the debris on the floor, then the ceiling. "Someone has been busy."

I slam to the floor with a violent yank as Griffin rips me down, wire and all, detaching me from the ceiling. He wraps the loose wire several times around my arms, securing them to my chest. I kick my legs as he drags me from the room.

We enter the gas chamber. I bite my tongue as he throws me on the bed, yanks off my pants, removes several lengths of rope from the cabinet above me, and secures my ankles with a unique knot.

His red face and huffing breaths tell me everything I need to know.

He's pissed. How dare I try and escape.

"You can't save them." He reaches beneath me, grabs the eye hook from behind my back, and starts unwinding me.

Under, over, under, over, all the way to my waist. I punch his face once my hands are free. I land one blow after another while he struggles to grab my quick-throwing jabs.

Blood drops on my nose as he seizes my wrists and pins me down. "Stop Odeya. Just fucking stop. I don't want to fucking kill you."

"You already did, the moment you pulled that trigger in the restaurant that day."

His brow furrows and his mouth turns downward. "She left me. Don't you see?" His eyes glisten as his mind floods with memories of what he did, what he had, and what he lost. He squeezes my wrists tighter. "I couldn't let anyone else have her. I needed her like I needed air. She dumped me, and I felt like I was suffocating without her." He gasps for air as he chokes on his words, desperate for me to understand—for me to feel his pain. "She was my everything."

His *everything*? How dare he?

"She was my everything!" I scream at him, my spit landing on his furious face. "You took the only person in the world who understood me. The only person keeping my demons at bay." I buck my body, trying to throw him off.

"I loved her, and so did you. We have that in common."

"We have nothing in common. I'm going to fucking kill you, you mother fucker."

He shakes his head slowly. "No, you won't. I'm the last thing tying you to your sister—your revenge, the memory of her. If you kill me, you have nothing left. No purpose. Nothing."

"Fuck you," I hiss at him. "Do you think revenge is the only reason I'm here?"

He leans down and kisses my lips tenderly. "I miss her, but I have you, and I don't care about your reasons."

His fingers caress the side of my face and his eyes peer deep inside mine. The way he's looking at me, it's as though he's not seeing me, but seeing her—seeing Amelia.

I slap him across the face with the hand he released to touch me—to touch *her*. "You don't have me. I'm going to kill you, then fuck my boyfriend on your corpse."

He seizes my hand, crushing my fingers in his grasp. "That's enough out of you." He reaches into the cabinet, removes a roll of duct tape, and presses a piece over my mouth. His forehead leans against mine as he whispers. "I don't care how long it takes. You will be mine. You will be my girl the way Jenny was Benny's." He rocks his head across mine and pushes off me as he stands. "I love you, Amelia."

My face drops at the mere mention of her name. I picture myself cutting out his tongue. How dare he? The headboard bangs into the wall. I know throwing a tantrum will do no good, but I need to release my anger somehow.

Griffin stands by the door with his hand on the handle, watching me. I glare at him, growling through my sealed lips and thrashing about on the mattress.

He smiles at me. Not a gotcha smile, more like, I just caught an exotic animal and it's all mine kind of smile. He intends to keep me here on display for his viewing pleasure.

Well, I am not his surrogate, and he will not use me as such.

He opens the door, turns off the light, and walks out, leaving the door open.

Good riddance. Dickhead.

My mind drifts backward to the day I bit off Benny's ear. Fuck.

An eye for an eye. Or in that case, it was an ear for an ear. Anything I do to them, they will do to one of the girls as punishment.

I stomp the footboard with my heel.

No one comes.

I stomp harder.

Nothing.

He's ignoring me. I killed his father and stepmother. The cost of their deaths will be high, and I have no one to blame but myself.

Someone's going to die today, and I won't be able to stop it.

I close my eyes and turn my ear to the door.

My breath catches in my lungs as it starts. The unmistakable screeching of someone being tortured pierces the door and slams into my eardrums. My pulse leaps from my neck, and my heart vibrates in my chest. The rage inside me burns through my veins.

The ropes may keep me captive like a caged animal, but even animals break free from their captures, and I am no ordinary animal.

I am a Monster.

Chapter Twenty-One
Don't Answer

He wants me to hear them scream. That's why he left the door open.

Gina's voice echoes through the entire space as she yells my name. They're making her do it—plead for me to come and save them, knowing I can't. Ari continues defying them—yelling for me to 'kill these mother fuckers.' She doesn't care what happens to her as long as the brothers die.

Marley slams into the room naked, falls to the floor, and crawls to my side. She digs the ropes around my ankles frantically, trying to free me from the bed. Her eyes are wide with fear and her face is, bloody. I thrash about on the bed but barely move. Griffin tied my wrists and ankles in a constrictor knot making escape impossible.

Benny strolls in, tiny dick jiggling, wiping blood from his mouth. "Where do you think you're going?"

"Stay away from me, needle dick." Marley staggers to her feet and pushes him back.

I couldn't have said it better myself.

Benny grabs her arm when she swings a punch at him and throws her on top of my legs belly first. He punches her several times in the upper back. She tries to pull away from him, but he drags her back and enters her from behind.

"No. Please, stop." Her body presses further into me as he fucks her.

I've never seen such fear in someone's eyes like I do now. I look away, no longer able to stand the sadness on her traumatized face.

Benny rests his body on her back, crushing her further into me as he rocks back and forth. "Be a good girl and hold still." He closes his eyes and rams hard into her.

I can't help myself. I sneak a quick look at her.

Tears wet my thighs as she wails and pleads for help with her eyes.

I'm useless. I want to help her but can't. Everything inside me screams with her. Every time she shouts my heart breaks a little more for her.

Benny finishes inside her, panting heavily as he looks at me, and smiles. "Her friend is next."

I buck on the bed, bouncing Marley off, and scream through the tape. When I get free, I'm going cut that dirty cock of his off and stuff it up his sweaty, hairy ass.

Griffin enters wearing nothing but black boxer briefs. "We've got company."

"Who the fuck is it?" Benny lifts Marley by the back of the neck and tosses her on the floor between them.

"The fucking rich kid."

Benny glances over his shoulder at me. "He wants her, doesn't he?"

Griffin smiles at me and shakes his head. "He wants Audrey."

"Really? Didn't see that coming."

"Yeah, me neither. I guess there was an incident with one of the girls, and she needs to be patched up. He's willing to pay double for her."

Audrey isn't in any shape to treat injuries, but at least she'll get out of this hole in the ground and be one less person they can use against me.

Griffin picks Marley up by her forearm and shoves her into Benny's chest. "So, what do you think? Could she be your new Jenny?"

"No one can replace my Jenny. But she can keep me company for now." He spins Marley around and pushes her into the hallway, leaving Griffin and me alone.

He traces his fingers from my bound ankle, up my calf and thigh, then stops between my legs where he flicks my lips. "You and your sister have a lot in common—both pretty, both have the same ass, both a good fuck." His fingers enter me and move in and out. "You are staying here with us."

Us.

I furrow my brow and glare at him. He intends on letting Benny have me. My stomach churns at the thought of Benny touching me. At least Griffin has charisma and a fuckable body with edible meat. Everything about Benny repulses me, including his voice. Even if he had good muscles, I wouldn't partake.

I don't eat junk food.

Griffin's rhythm picks up the pace as he continues talking. "I'm going to fuck you every day for the rest of your life. You will never leave this place. You'll be my slave." He pulls his fingers out fast and wipes them on the blanket. "And as for the Egyptian, he's as good as dead."

They plan to kill him and keep me. I can't let that happen. Everything I have gone through would be all for nothing if he kills Femi. I knew this would be hard, but I didn't realize how hard. Getting close to these girls was never my intention or part of the plan, but here I am feeling guilty—responsible for their well-being now that they are being used against me.

Benny knocks on the doorframe. "The kid's in the galley."

Griffin sighs and tilts his head at me. "We'll finish this later."

He pauses before joining Benny in the hall, smells his fingers that were inside of me, and closes his eyes. "You even smell the same." He continues through the door and disappears.

Fucking pig.

I stare at a smudge on the ceiling. Images of my sister flood my mind. Guilt has made me reckless. I'm no better than these men or any of the others I have killed. I could have stopped this sooner and saved these girls earlier, but I'm selfish. My need for revenge far outweighs the lives of these women. At least it did until I got to know them.

Arguing roars from the hallway.

The rich kid strolls in and stuffs his hands in his pockets. "There she is."

Griffin spins him around to face him. "I fucking told you, she's not for sale. You're here for Audrey and that's it."

"What's the harm in getting a little taste? I'll pay you five thousand right here and now to let me have five minutes alone with her."

Five minutes? Fucking minute men.

"Ten," Benny says from the doorway.

"Done."

Griffin swipes his face and stares at me. "Five minutes but keep your cock to yourself." He glances at his watch. "Starting now."

The brothers leave, closing the door behind him.

Rich boy walks slowly to the side of the bed and stares at my naked and bound frame. He fucks me with his eyes and then glances at the door over his shoulder.

Air launches from my lungs as he dives on top of me. He whispers in my ear as his soft pudgy fingers make entry. "Oh, yeah baby. You like that don't you?" His tongue slips inside my ear, muffling his heavy breaths. He unzips his pants and circles the outside of my pussy with the head of his penis.

Fuck, he's going to take me.

"Just the tip?" The head of his cock bounces around my hole but doesn't enter. His moaning grows in intensity.

I've never known a single man who can stop at 'just the tip.'

"Fuck it." He announces and stuffs his dick inside me.

For an overweight youngster, he's not half bad. His rhythm, depth, and speed are spot on.

Get it, boy.

I move my hips towards him. I need to release. I should feel guilty for wanting him to finish, but I don't. His cologne turns me on even more. The sandalwood and musk scent brings back pleasant memories. Right before these dopes snatched me from the side of the road, my boyfriend and I fucked in the rain on an old private airport runway. The smell of him slowly washed away as the storm soaked our half-naked bodies.

Rich boy moans louder and louder as he grinds himself into me. "Fuck, you feel good," he murmurs in my ear. "You're so wet."

Damn right, I am.

My eyes roll into my head as an orgasm works its way to my pussy.

Almost there.

He rips the tape away from my mouth. "Tell me you like it. Tell me to fuck y—"

Metallic liquid lands in my mouth, choking me, and my throat and chest warm. My orgasm retreats inside me somewhere unknown, ruining the moment. The kid's head drops onto my collarbone as Griffin releases it. The cut in his throat runs from one ear to the other. His eyes roll back, and Griffin seizes his waistband, yanking him off me and dropping him on the floor.

I lift my head and stare at the space between my breasts.

So much blood.

If only I were an anteater. I could whip out my sticky, lengthy tongue and lap up the metallic juices.

Blood gargles through the hole in the rich kid's throat, splattering upward as he takes his last breath.

Griffin wipes his bloody hunting knife on his green fatigues then slides the knife back into its black leather sheath. "Fucking entitled little prick."

I need to get out of these knots and off this bed. Griffin swears under his breath as I pee. What did he expect? I've been stuck here for hours. He has to let me up now.

Benny charges into the room and stares at the motionless lottery winner and then at the wet, soiled comforter between my legs. "Gross. Maybe she has a problem."

Yeah, you two.

Griffin takes his knife and cuts my bindings. "No. She's just being an asshole."

He's not wrong.

He lifts me to my feet. I fall into his chest, rub the side of my face against his skin, and moan. "I wish you could have waited another minute to kill him" I gaze up into his eyes and smirk. "He was about to make me cum in a way you never could."

"Get the fuck off." Griffin grabs both my shoulders and jolts me violently. "You need to comply, Amelia."

I pull my arms away from him and take a few steps back. "Don't you say her name."

"Amelia?" Benny furrows his brow. "That's not Amelia. She's dead. You killed her, remember?"

Griffin pushes me to the floor and shoves Benny into the wall. "You think I don't know that? Just like you're looking for another Jenny, I've been looking for another Amelia. Why do you think I've never hung on to anyone and am always willing to let them go? Odeya may not be her, but there is no other woman who will ever come through that hatch that can get this close to being her." Griffin presses his pointer finger into Benny's bony sternum. "This is the end of this discussion. Now, dig through the rich kid's pockets and find out where he lives so we can bring the twins back here and resell them."

No, no, no. They can't come back here. I have enough to worry about with the other girls.

"Maybe you should wait to get them. You can stay here and help finish what the rich kid started." I gap my legs open and clap at Griffin with my bony knees.

Griffin licks his lips and bites his bottom lip. "The longer the twins stay there unattended the better the chance they get away. I can't let that happen."

Benny moves Griffin's hand off his chest and digs through the pockets of the dead man on the floor. "You're making a mistake keeping her alive."

I grin at Benny when he looks at me. "Your parents made a mistake not aborting you when they had the chance."

Benny kicks me in the hip. "No, your parents should have aborted you."

I smile at the red spot where he kicked me. "Don't be childish Benny. You and I both know Griffin is better off without you."

Griffin steps between Benny and me, stopping him from kicking me again. "That's enough." He reaches his hand out to me, and I accept his help off the floor. "She's baiting you. Don't fall for it."

Griffin's right. I am baiting him. I grab my pussy lips, one lip in each hand, and wiggle my goods at Benny like a worm tempting a fish. "Eat me, Benny." I open and close them, so they are doing the talking. "Here, fishy, fishy, fishy. Come and sink your cock into my net."

My head snaps to the side as Griffin backhands me in the side of the face. "Knock your shit off, or I'll strap you back to the bed."

I pinch my lips shut, closing their filthy mouth, and wink at Benny. "We will talk more later."

Griffin smirks at my twisted sense of humor. He pulls the soiled sheet off the bed and tosses it in the direction of the bathroom.

I stare at the blood puddle beside the rich kid, gingerly dip my toes in it, and make a smiley face in a clean spot on the floor.

Benny's eyes fixate on my crimson-colored toes then slowly raise to meet mine. "You are a sick fucking woman."

I place my hand on my chest and smile. "Awe thanks, Benny. That's the nicest thing you've ever said to me."

"Fuck you." He pulls the kid's wallet from his back trouser pocket and opens it. "He lives like an hour from here."

"Go get the girls. Take his body in case he has any high-tech security that needs his biometrics."

"Why can't you go?"

"I need to be here in case the Egyptian shows up."

Benny nods as he bends over, seizes the kid's wrists, and drags him away, leaving a red path in his wake.

Griffin walks me to the shower room and positions me under the showerhead. "Stay."

I raise my hand to my forehead, saluting him.

He sighs and disappears around the corner. Cold water splashes over me within seconds, making me gasp and hardening my nipples to stone. My body stiffens against the freezing shower. It slowly turns warm, relaxing me.

Griffin moseys toward me, cock swaying back and forth. Oh, how I'd love to grab it, swing him around the room, and launch him into the wall.

Wee.

My boyfriend and I have a bedroom swing in our room and various other adult entertainment items. I even have an inflatable sex pillow that fits my dildo so I can pleasure myself when he's not around, or when he is, it doesn't matter to me as long as I get mine. My voracious sexual appetite needs constant fulfillment.

Griffin steps in front of me, bows his head, and rests his forehead against my chest with his eyes closed. "Why do you have to make this so hard? Can't you see how much I love you."

What in the sweet ass fuck is he talking about?

"You and I are meant to be together forever. You're my soulmate. That's why you came back to me, through her."

He's not talking to me. He's talking to my sister.

Oh, hell no. He's not reliving some moment they shared long ago before he murdered her.

Time to poke the bear and break his heart. "She's dead. You killed her. I'm Odeya, not Amelia, and I'll never let you forget th—"

He grips my throat, cutting off my airway, and glares into my eyes. "You are who I say you are. Now shut the fuck up and turn around." My breathing restores as he lets go.

I plant my feet firmly, pressing them hard into the floor as I push him into the opposing wall. "I'm Odeya! I'm Odeya! I'm Odeya!" I scream in his face.

He crushes my shoulders in his grasp, forces me to the floor, and steps out of the shower, leaving a path of watery footprints behind him as he leaves the room.

I stare at my unrestrained hands and cup them in front of me. Water bounces off the puddle filling my palms. I throw the liquid into my face and scrub the blood from my skin. Tainted reddish-brown water swirls down the drain by my feet and disappears into the abyss.

The cascading water distorts Griffin's appearance as he enters with a roll of tape and a dry towel. He kneels beside me, dries my mouth so the tape will stick, unravels a six-inch piece, and presses it firmly over my moist lips.

I could have fought him, but he would have won, so I let it happen. He hoists me to my feet and pushes me face-first into the wall opposite the shower head. My arms crank behind my back as he grabs one and then the other and holds both of my wrists with one hand. He spreads my thighs with his fingers from behind and pushes his cock inside me slowly. His fingers wrap around my throat, and he thrusts into me hard, then relaxes, hard then relaxes, hard then relaxes.

"You're so fucking beautiful. I missed you so much." His voice is low and seductive. "You are my everything, and no one will ever come between us again."

He turns me sideways, facing the outside of the shower, grips me around the waist with one hand, and pushes my back towards the floor with the other, folding me in half like a piece of paper. "Don't move."

His cock pokes the wrong hole first then slams into the right one. I tilt my head up and watch us in the mirror across from the shower. With every violent thrust, my head jerks in the reflection and inches us slowly out of the enclosed space.

I concentrate on his face. He's picturing my sister as he fucks me with his eyes closed.

Two can play this game.

I throw myself backward into him. He slips onto his back, and my ass ends up on top of his thighs. I flip myself around, mount his waiting cock and close my eyes, picturing my boyfriend.

His hands grip my hips as I grind them in a circle— around and around and around.

I'm enjoying this.

He's enjoying this.

We are enjoying this.

Taking control of the moment gives me a sense of power. I could rip his cock off with my teeth and watch him bleed out, but I need to release the trapped orgasm inside me. I may not understand blue balls because I'm a woman, but I know if I don't release a pent-up orgasm, I get frustrated, irritated, and sometimes, violent. It's like having all the symptoms of a menstrual cycle without the bleeding part.

It's coming. I collapse onto his chest, rest my face on the side of his, and grip his hair with both hands.

Oh, God. This one's going to hurt.

I clench my jaw and press my pussy into him, forcing his cock deep inside me.

Oh, damn. Here it comes.

Motherfucker.

I explode onto his cock, and he unloads into me at the same time—both getting what we wanted.

I rest my head on his chest, listening to his heart pound while I catch my breath. My eyes follow a bead of water that rolls down his bicep and lands on the floor. He presses his palm into my ribs and pushes me off him. We stare at the ceiling, side by side, panting.

I strip my lips of the loosely attached tape, crush it into a ball, and toss it over my head.

"I love you, Amelia," he says without looking at me.

I hold my breath and my tongue. I want to say, *'fuck you, Griffin.'* and pound his face repeatedly for saying her name, but I won't. I'm the last person he will ever fuck, and he'll be in a to-go container very soon. I smile at his shiny, muscular thighs, and my mouth waters.

So…much…meat.

I turn my head to face him with a bright and sexually satisfied smile. "I love you too, Femi."

Meow.

Chapter Twenty-Two
Roll Play

Griffin's face goes blank as he turns it to me. A slight smile twitches just under the surface as he shakes his head. "Your fucking nuts." He exhales noisily as he stands, grabs a towel off the bar, and wraps it around his lower half. "You love Femi. The Egyptian? That's funny. As if you're even capable of love." He saunters out of the room, shaking his wet hair as he exits.

I'm capable of love. What a mean thing to say. He hurt my feelings.

Not.

I turn on my side, rest my arm on my hip and thigh, and smile at the doorway.

Benny rounds the corner, covered in blood, and stops abruptly. His jaw drops and his pants bulge with an instant mini hard-on.

His eyes watch me from their corners as he strips off his soiled clothing, steps in the shower, and rinses off the rich kid's blood.

He wants me so bad he can taste it.

When his eyes close to rinse his face, I twist my body to face him, gap my legs open, and play with my lady lips.

Hands grip me under the armpits and yank me to my feet. "Not funny," Griffin whispers as he flips me around and shoves me out of the room. "Are you trying to piss me off today?"

He's wearing the same jeans he did the day he gassed me. I stop in front of him and run my fingers over his washboard stomach, stopping at the tab on his zipper.

"What's for dinner honey?" I unzip his pants slowly, seducing him with my eyes.

He grips my wrist, throws it out of the way, and zips his pants up. "Stop it."

I bite my bottom lip. "I thought we were playing our roles. You can be my boyfriend, and I'll be my sister. You can make me a nice dinner, and afterward, I can fuck you on the table of dirty plates."

Or I kill you when your guard is down, chop you up into tiny pieces, and make a gourmet burger out of your tender leg meat.

Mmm…burger—a little cooked onion, some ketchup, a dollop of barbeque sauce, topped with a slice of tomato and green leaf lettuce on a slightly toasted butter-coated brioche bun.

Damn. I'm starving.

All this talk of food is making me horny. I stop walking, lean against the wall outside of Griffin's bedroom, rub my breasts, and moan. "I'm hungry, baby. Can I eat you for dinner?"

"For Christ's sake. Get in here and put some clothes on." He pushes me into his bedroom.

I crawl onto his mattress and lie face down with my ass up facing him. "How about you just get me an apron from the kitchen, and I can just wear that? We can warm up some stew, and I can make some homemade bread."

His eyes get stuck on my bare behind. "I threw the stew away. And you're never cooking for me or anyone ever again."

I flop onto my side, breaking his focus. "So, you are cooking dinner?"

He hesitates like the question came out of my mouth in another language he didn't understand.

I rub the comforter with my palm. Furry things make me smile. Any time I go to a fabric store, I run my fingers across all the different textures. Someday, I'm making a quilt with all my favorite materials so I can touch them any time I want.

Griffin pulls open his dresser drawer and removes a white silk nightgown with spaghetti straps as I stand. It hits me in the chest and falls to the floor. This is the first time he's made me wear such attire. I pick it up by the strings and sling it back to him. "I'd like to wear sweats and a T-shirt please."

He balls up the gown and pitches it in my face. "You wear what I tell you to wear."

My cheeks inflate as I exhale. There's no use fighting with him about it. It's either wear this or nothing. I swipe it from the floor and pull it over my head. It feels cool and silky against my skin. The bottom of it lands at my feet. I adjust the straps by my shoulders and smooth the wrinkles around my abdomen.

Griffin takes a step towards me and pulls my hair over my shoulder. "Turn around."

I comply.

His breath warms my exposed neck, and he kisses it softly. "We'll make dinner together." His arms wrap around me from behind and squeeze me gently. "But I'm only going to say this once..." his arms crush around me like a vise taking the air from my lungs. "...you will behave. No funny business. Okay?"

The side of my cheek rubs his forehead. "Okay, baby."

I gasp as he lets me go and walks in the direction of the galley without me. I'm unbound and free to move about the space.

It's a test to see what I will do.

I leave the room and join Griffin in the galley. Benny's sitting on the bed where they first held me when I arrived, pulling on a pair of muddy boots. Griffin opens the fridge and motions with his hand to look inside.

Benny's eyes turn to saucers. "Oh, hell no. She's not cooking. Have you lost your fucking mind?" Benny taps the side of his temple with his middle finger. "She'll fucking poison us."

"Benny, we are making it together, and I'll be watching her the entire time."

I smirk at Benny then peer into the fridge. Someone needs to go grocery shopping. We don't have much to work with. I open the cupboard to check out the canned goods. We have egg noodles, canned chicken, carrots, and peas. On the bottom shelf is one stray onion in a mesh bag, a can of creamy chicken soup, and a single sleeve of crackers.

"Well, I can do a chicken casserole but that's about it unless one of you wants to take me grocery shopping."

Griffin shrugs his shoulders. "I like casserole. Benny?"

Benny rolls his eyes and stalks out of the room.

He's mad. Poor baby. He's probably going to cry in his room. What a pansy.

Griffin turns his attention back to the fridge. "What do you need out of here?"

"The shredded taco and mozzarella cheeses, mayonnaise, butter, and some of that coffee creamer."

He takes them out and sets them on the counter beside the canned goods. "I need a boiling pot for the noodles."

Griffin reaches in front of me, smacking my knee with the lower cupboard door. I shift out of his way. He sets the pot in the sink, so I can partially fill it and set it on the hot burner.

Bubbles form in the bottom of the pot after several minutes, making my nose twitch as I remember the first time I tried to boil human meat. The smell, like spoiled garbage, was intolerable. Now I either use a frying pan to sauté it, barbeque over an open fire, or break out my crockpot.

Griffin takes my hand away from the pot of boiling water. I stare at the red spots that slowly begin to blister. My mind was so focused on memories, that I didn't notice the water spilling outside the pot and burning the back of my hand.

"Your disorder is a blessing and a curse, isn't it?" Griffin asks, removing the boiling noodles from the stove and draining them in the sink.

I smile but don't answer as I reach across his chest. He snatches my hand, crushing it in his grasp, forcing me to let go of the chopping knife. "I'll dice the chicken."

"Of course." I step back and lean against the counter.

With every strike of the knife against the cutting board, my smile grows. It's the same knife I used to kill Jenny, and I never washed it—just wiped it with a wet paper towel.

Griffin dumps the chicken into the bowl with the rest of the ingredients, stirs it, and pours the contents into a thirteen-by-nine pan. He sprinkles crackers on top and rubs his chin. "I think it will be good."

He rubs his chin a lot when he's deep in thought or uncertain of something. Playing poker is something he could never do. His tells are too obvious.

"Oh, it's going to be delicious." I open the oven, and he slides the food inside.

Benny enters, opens the fridge and cracks open a beer. He takes a small sip, sets it on the counter, and eyes me suspiciously.

"The new girls are all cleaned up, and the other two are finishing getting dressed." His intense glare doesn't leave mine.

"Good. Bring them in. Dinner will be ready in…" Griffin glances at me.

"Thirty minutes." I stand, smile at Benny, and wash my hands in the sink with lots of soap. I dunk my hands in the dirty, soap-filled bowl we used to combine ingredients.

Griffin leans on the counter beside me and sighs when Benny leaves the room. I push off the sink, wrap my arms around Griffin, and drip dirty, soapy water into Benny's beer. "So…" I smile at him. "…are you going to eat my pussy for dessert?"

He pushes me back onto the bed across from the stove. "I've had my fill of you today."

I lift my gown and spread my legs showing him his juices dribbling from my pussy. "But I need you to clean up your mess." I open and close my legs, moving the air between us.

He grabs my knees and slams them together. "Keep them fucking closed."

The door opens beside us and Audrey, Ari, Marley, and Gina shuffle inside.

"Move over," Benny says pushing me towards the foot of the bed.

Even with me at the very end, there isn't enough room for all of us.

Benny grabs Marley's arm, and his beer, sits in the chair, and pulls her onto his lap. Our hips all touch as we wedge ourselves together on the mattress. Griffin sits across from Benny in the only other available chair. He interlaces his fingers and watches me over his knuckles.

"It won't be long now," I whisper to Ari who's sitting on my right.

"No talking." Griffin slaps the tabletop with his palm.

Benny takes several gulps of his beer and then smacks his lips. "This beer tastes funny." He eyes me and stands up fast, dropping Marley onto the floor in front of him. "What did you put in it?"

Griffin drops his face into his hands and vibrates his lips. "Benny, she didn't touch your drink. I was watching her the whole time."

Sorta.

Benny snatches his beer from the table, nearly spilling it, and dumps it in the sink. "Fuck that. I don't trust her at all." He opens the fridge, grabs a second beer, and takes a swig. "Now that tastes right."

I tilt my head and smile at him. "Maybe your tastebuds are off from eating too much Jenny."

Griffin slaps my mouth without warning, knocking my head against Ari's. "Shut the fuck up, Odeya."

I wipe the blood from my smiling lips with the back of my hand and nod. "Oh, I'm back to being Odeya, huh?"

"You are who I say you are." Griffin points in my face and furrows his brow. "Now shut up and listen." He sits back down. "You're all here so I don't have to repeat myself. The twins are coming back. Their buyer is dead and Benny's going to be leaving to get them after dinner. When they get here, Benny and Marley will be staying in his room. The twins will stay in the holding room with Audrey and Gina." He goes out of his way not to look at me.

I look around the room and then back to Griffin. "And what about me, Griffy?"

He frowns and points to the mattress beneath me. "You're staying here, tied to the bed, in case I need a late-night snack."

Great. I get to listen to the soothing sound of the droning refrigerator and a dripping sink.

I drop my hands into my lap and flick my fingernails back and forth.

Flick, flick, flick.

Griffin sits back down and drums his fingers on the table.

Flick, flick, flick. Drum, drum, drum.

Ari scratches the front of her teeth.

Scrape, scrape, scrape. Flick, flick, flick. Drum, drum, drum.

Gina sucks air through her front teeth.

"Stop!" Benny yells. "You sound like a bunch of annoying children making bodily noises for attention."

His knee bounces up and down when he sits making a swooshing noise against his track pants.

Ari giggles, and so do I. Benny opens his mouth but the timer dings and he says nothing. I stand and walk to the stove.

Griffin places his hand across my chest. "Sit down. I'll take the hot food out of the oven."

He's afraid I'm going to toss it on them. I could, but I'm not one to waste a good meal on anyone. I take the plates from the cupboard and scoop a heaping spoonful of steaming casserole onto two plates. I pass them to Ari and Audrey. Then drop some on another for Gina.

Benny swipes two plates off the counter. "I'll get mine and Marley's."

His stomach gurgles noisily, and I smile. "You must be starving Benny. You should take a little extra."

He glares at me, drops two globs of food on his plate, and shakes it off the spoon like a lunch lady. I take a small corner of food from the opposite end of the dish and drop it on a plate for myself. The crusty edges are my favorite.

Griffin puts an empty plate over the pan. "One from the corner for me too."

I scrape out the corner across from mine and spread it on his plate.

No one eats at first. They all stare at each other and then at me. They're waiting for me. They think I would poison everyone just to get the two brothers. I don't take the easy way out like most female killers. Using poison is for the weak who don't want to get their hands dirty. I like the hard, rough, messy, up close, and personal way with lots of blood.

I open my mouth and shovel the flaming hot food inside. Mmm. Delicious.

Benny nods and takes a big bite, scorching the roof of his mouth. The food tumbles out of his mouth onto his plate as he waves the air in front of his lips. "Fuck. That shit is hot as fuck."

"Well, duh, it just came out of the oven, dummy," Ari says rolling her eyes.

I slap the side of her leg and laugh through my nose. She needs to behave, or they'll string her up for the rest of dinner.

Griffin rounds his lips in front of his fork and blows his food. A piece of cracker crumb falls onto the floor as he takes a bite.

We eat in silence for several minutes. Benny's stomach bubbles loud enough for everyone to hear.

It's working.

He holds his hand over his stomach and stares at Griffin. "She poisoned us."

Griffin scrapes the last bite of his casserole into his mouth, drops his fork in the sink, and his paper plate in the trash. "No, she didn't Benny. You ate too much as always."

Benny groans and unties his pants. "Fuck. I have to shit." He gets up and exits the room quickly.

Griffin turns to me and places his hands on his hips. "He did eat too much, right?"

"You saw how much he put into his scrawny stomach. What do you think?"

Griffin lets his hands fall to his sides and stares at the ceiling. "Looks like I'll be going to get the girls." He walks around Marley, who's still sitting on the floor, and starts picking up the mess left on the table.

Perfect. I need time alone with Benny Boy.

Ari stares at the side of my face. I turn to her and wink. She smiles broadly and wipes her nostrils with the side of her pointer finger speaking quietly so Griffin doesn't hear. "What did you do?"

I cough and cover my mouth. "A little soapy contaminated dishwater in his beer."

We giggle, and Griffin stops before us. "What so funny?"

"I can hear Benny shitting from here." Ari chuckles.

He grabs Ari by the bicep. "Get up." He nods to Audrey, Gina, and Marley. "And you three. Come on. Back to your rooms."

I stand to follow.

Griffin rests his palm on my shoulder and forces me back onto the mattress. "Stay here and don't fucking move."

I raise my eyebrows and nod.

Perhaps we will have dessert after all.

He leads the girls through the doorway. When he comes back through, he enters the hanging room and closes the door behind him.

I sit quietly while I wait for his return. My wrists are red and brush-burned from the restraints. The skin feels like rough sandpaper. I rub my fingertips over it several times. It's not rough enough to exfoliate off my fingerprints. I'll have to buy more paper for my orbit sander when I get out of here.

I lean sideways on the mattress with my head resting on my palm and put my feet up. A bubble fights its way to the surface of the casserole on the stove. How lucky the air is to be transparent and unseen. It squeezes its way into any available space and can escape easily when trapped given the opportunity. The bubble pops silently as it reaches the surface of the casserole.

Unlike the air, when we escape this place, we will not do it silently.

We are not invisible.

We are not going to disappear.

We are not empty.

Chapter Twenty-Three
Dessert

Griffin never comes back. Instead, Benny comes through the door with a set of handcuffs and throws them at me. "Put these on."

"Where's Griffin?" I peer behind him.

"He went to get the twins and bring them back." He crosses his arms and spreads his legs shoulder-width apart. "Put the cuffs on."

I slide back on the bed and put my feet up. "Come on, Benny. Now's your chance. Fuck me."

"I promised Griffin I wouldn't." He looks away from me.

I crumple my gown in my grasp as I lift it high and let my legs fall to the sides. He stares between my legs, and I moan. "Fuck my ass, Benny. Come on, baby."

He grabs his head with both hands and grits his teeth. "Fuck. Please just put the fucking cuffs on so I can secure you and go to bed."

I slide my fingers between my legs and stick two inside me. "Oh, Benny. Can't you see how wet you make me?" I remove my fingers and suck my juices off.

"Fuck, fuck fuck." He turns away from me and faces the wall.

The mattress rises as I stand and open a kitchen drawer. He turns back to me as it scrapes open, and I remove a plastic ladle with a fat rubber-coated handle and leave the drawer open.

"What are you doing?" He takes a step towards me.

"Well, if you won't fuck me, I'll just fuck myself." I turn the spoon around, open my legs wider, and insert the handle inside me.

His breath quickens as I glide it in and out of me. "Oh, Benny. I wish this were you." I turn my back on him and bend over. "Don't you want to put your cock in me while I fuck this?" I peer over my shoulder at him.

"I can't." He bites his fist in frustration.

I back my naked ass into his poking pecker. "Do it, Benny. Fuck me."

His pants rustle behind me.

Here we go.

His fingers dig into my hips as he pulls me to him, grabs his micro penis, and sticks it in my ass. I let the ladle fall to the floor and thrash my body away from him.

I lean against the counter beside the open drawer. "Fuck me on the counter, Benny."

I brace my palms on the counter, hop up, and slide my ass onto the hard surface. He slips his micro-sized, little boy cock inside me, holds my head with one hand, and places his other behind my lower back.

"Oh, fuck. You feel good." He pumps in and out of me rapidly.

He's so gross. Nausea creeps into my mouth. I knew sex with him would make me sick. I try and hold my breath, but it's not enough.

Fuck, this was a mistake.

My stomach churns and my mouth waters. I'm going to vomit if I don't get away from him.

It's the smell—sweat, bad breath, and musty armpits with a side of smegma.

Gag me with a fork.

I curl my fingers around a four-inch paring knife in the drawer and with his next backward motion, I seize his cock in my grasp and slice it off with one quick cut.

He screams and backs away from me holding his phantom dick. Blood pours down his legs as I wiggle his flaccid string bean in front of his face. His eyes widen at the site of his previously attached appendage. It wasn't much to look at to begin with, and now that it's detached from him, well…it's even smaller.

I set it gently on the counter and walk slowly towards him, backing him closer to the bed—bloody weapon in hand. "Put the cuffs on and I'll save your life."

His eyes dart to the blood dripping from the base of his severed cock. "Fuck you!" He screams as tears meet the snot on his face and blend.

"You already did." I stab him in the cheek with the blade, sending it through to the other side and then wrenching it through his face—giving him a wider mouth.

When he grabs his face, I push him onto the mattress and tighten the handcuffs around his scrawny ankles with a sinister smile. "Bleed, Benny Boy, bleed."

I head to the girl's room and open the door. "Come on girls. Let's have some fun."

They all stare at each other, no one wanting to move. Ari glances at the blood on my hands and lifts them in hers. "Is he dead?"

"Not yet." I smile and nod towards the galley.

Ari steps in front of me, but the others don't move. They're afraid—afraid this isn't real and there's no way I could have killed Benny so quickly after Griffin left.

I'm in a time crunch. What do they expect?

"Benny's not going to hurt you. He's restrained and bleeding profusely." I wave them over to me with a soft smile.

Marley runs to me and hugs me tightly, her body trembling. "Thank you."

I gently push her away from me. "Don't thank me until I get you out of here."

She nods and disappears down the hallway, with Gina following after her.

I walk over to Audrey. She stares at the floor, anxiously picking at her nails. I lift her chin and a tear slides down her face. "It's your time to shine Nurse Audrey."

She furrows her brow at me, not understanding what I mean. I tenderly guide her to the galley and point to Benny's bleeding, dickless wound. "I need you to sew up where his cock once was. Can you do that?"

Her eyes open wide, and she shakes her head furiously. "No, please. I can't."

I grip her forearms in my hands. "Audrey, think about everything they've done to you— everything they made you do—humiliated you, abused you. Think about what you can do to him now if given more time." I take the first aid kit off the counter and feed the handle into her right hand. "Do it for us." I peer at the other girls standing beside Benny, who's moaning on the bed. Every one of them has their hands over their mouths. Gina gags and looks away.

Ari takes her hand away and uncovers her smile of delight. "Where's his dick?"

I nod over my right shoulder. "Sitting on the counter."

She stretches her neck and giggles when she spots it. "Oh, my gosh. It's even small when it's disconnected."

Audrey stares at the lifeless appendage. "Should I sew it back on?"

"Hell, no," Ari says, turning her back to Benny. "Just sew him up as is. It's not like it's a big wound."

Audrey nods and walks slowly to Benny's side.

I am sure he would object to her touch if he could talk, but his new mouth makes it impossible. He digs his heels into the mattress and scoots away from her when she bends over him.

I love it. The panic in his eyes makes it all worth it. He's outnumbered, injured, and defenseless. No one can save him, not even Griffin, and he knows it.

Audrey pulls his hands away from his balls and pours a small bottle of saline onto his wound. Benny makes a snorting noise as air moves fast through his nostrils. The mattress lowers when Audrey sits down and opens a small sewing kit. He scoots farther away and leans his back against the wall.

I grab the joint of the cuffs between his ankles and pull him towards us. He shakes his head and howls. I bend his knees towards the ceiling and open his legs as far as I can into the butterfly stretch position.

Audrey rests the needle on his skin, ready to puncture, then takes it away and looks back at me. "This may not help. He's lost a lot of blood already."

I nod at her encouragingly. "We are just buying time."

Ari wraps her arm around one of his legs and sits on the bed. I sit on the opposite side, and we stretch Benny's legs far apart while he screeches.

Audrey turns back to Benny, releases a slow, staggering breath, and hooks the needle through the skin just above his balls where the cut begins.

He sits up suddenly and screams through his throat. Ari and I work together to push him back down and hold him flat so Audrey can continue. By the third stitch, Benny stops moving and passes out.

After making a knot, Audrey bites the suture thread, applies a sterile piece of gauze, and then applies two long pieces of surgical tape that run from his pubic hair to his balls, holding the dressing. "Best I can do," she says over her shoulder. "What about his face?"

"Leave it. I have plans for that after we clean him up."

"Oh, can I help with those plans?" Ari claps and jumps up and down at the foot of the bed.

"Of course, but first, help me get him strung up." I grab Benny's ankles and yank him onto the floor. His eyes spring open, and he stares helplessly at the ceiling.

Ari grabs one arm, Gina takes the other, and we half drag, and half carry him to the hanging room. We drop him beneath a secure wire. He grabs Audrey's legs and begs for help with his solemn glassy eyes.

Ari skips across the floor and kicks his arm away from Audrey. He lands on his side, and she stomps his ribs. The cartilage crunches under her foot and he gasps for air— soundless cries come from his yap. She stops and kneels beside him. "What's the matter, Benny? Does it hurt? Remember when you asked me that?" She punches him in the temple and spits on his head.

I clap my hands together and bark orders at them like they were a part of my military unit. "Marley, pull the hose from that utility closet, and Audrey, go check the cabinet where the red button is that opens the hatch. If it's unlocked, we can leave. Ari, find us another set of cuffs."

Benny rolls back and forth on the floor, groaning. Blood seeps through his dressing, and his bloodshot eyes stare at the light buzzing above him.

Ari spins a set of handcuffs on her pointer finger. They make a whirring noise as they gain momentum, launch off her appendage, and fly across the room, striking the wall. Ari holds her shoulders high and grimaces. "Oops."

I chuckle and shake my head. "Bring them here."

She speed walks to the cuffs, scoops them from the floor, and skips back to us. The cuffs click several times as she secures them so tight that the skin on his one wrist buckles.

Gina and I lift Benny to the wire, and Ari attaches him.

"The cabinet has a padlock." Audrey wipes a tear from her face. "There must be a key somewhere."

I rummage through Benny's pants, checking all the pockets.

Nothing.

The button to freedom sits inside a locked steel cabinet and someone hid the key.

"We aren't going to get out of here, are we?" Audrey whimpers beside me.

Ari puts her arm around her shoulders. "Of course we are. Odie has a plan, don't you?" Ari grins at me and I nod.

"By this evening, you girls will be free."

Marley stands a few feet from Benny and blasts him in the face with the hose. "How do *you* like it, fucker?"

Benny pinches his eyes shut, protecting them from the blasting water.

Gina wraps her hands around Marley's, and they pummel his frame with high-powered hatred from head to toe like two firemen battling an out-of-control blaze. Redness plasters his bare skin.

Ari holds her hands up, stopping them from spraying. She takes the sprayer and walks slowly around Benny several times before stopping behind him. Benny shouts and his body bucks forward as Ari shoves the nozzle into his ass. He shakes his head *'no'* several times. Ari smiles at him and turns it on full blast. His body stands taller as he gets on his tiptoes, trying to relieve some of the force and pressure, but it does no good. Vomit pours from his orifice and drains down his chest.

Ari cranks the hose off and turns Benny around to face her. "How'd that feel? I bet it's like having your asshole douched by a firehose." She snorts several times, and the hose slips from her grasp. A loud fart echoes around the room the second she bends over to pick it up.

Our laughter starts as a quiet giggle but quickly escalates to full-on uncontrollable hilarity as the smell of putrid poultry fills the space. Audrey gags and runs away from us, disappearing through the galley door. The rest of us choke and laugh until we cry—tears of joy mixed with tears of pain. Our brokenness hides behind walls of laughter, and the smiles that come with it.

Marley and Gina stop laughing and hold each other while they cry—the reality of what's to come settling in. Griffin will return and punish us for what we've done.

We know the truth. All of us do. What we are doing to Benny is wrong in so many ways, but right at the same time. The scales of justice could never balance what they did to us. No court of law will punish them the way they deserve. It's up to us to right this wrong.

I rub Ari's head on my way past her. "Try not to kill him."

"Where are you going?" Ari starts to follow me.

I put my hand up. "Stay here. I'm just going to talk to Audrey."

Ari nods, turns around, and strikes Benny in the diaphragm, knocking the wind out of him. "Cunt." She smiles up at his barely open eyes. "Since you don't have a dick anymore, I can call you that, and it makes sense."

Gina and Marley sit on the floor a few feet in front of him, and Ari joins them. They lean against each other and stare up at Benny's motionless frame.

I enter the galley and stop abruptly. Audrey stands motionless, gawking at Benny's penis still sitting on the counter.

I stand beside her and place my hand on her back. "It looks like a worm."

Snot flies from her nose, splattering on the counter and the worm as she laughs and cries at the same time.

We hold each other, trying not to fall as we become hysterical. Our heads bump when we buckle at the waist and slide to the floor. Her tears of sadness and fear slowly melt away as tears of laughter take their place.

But it's not just any laugh.

It's the cackling laugh of an unhinged, traumatized lunatic.

I...love...it.

I join her, and our paradoxical laughter echoes around the space.

Ari pokes her head into the room. "What's so funny?"

Audrey and I glance at each other and cackle even harder. Audrey points at the counter and tries to talk but the words come out incomprehensible. She takes a few shallow breaths and tries again. "It's a worm." Her upper thighs slam together, and she holds her knees tight as she rolls onto her side. "Oh my God, I'm going to pee my pants."

Ari picks up the wiener with her thumb and pointer and wiggles it at us. "We should hang it in the hanging room, so Griffin sees it as soon as he comes back."

"I think we should cook it." The words just spill out of my mouth. I can't help but say what comes to mind.

"And make what out of it, a chicken fry?" Ari curls her lip. "That's boring."

Audrey continues laughing—her face wet with tears. "A chicken fry?" She folds in half and rolls across the floor. "More like a mini corndog."

I raise my eyebrows. "Now *that* I can do." I open the drawer and remove a twelve-inch wooden skewer.

"You're joking, right?" Audrey stops laughing, grabs the edge of the counter, and pulls herself to a stand.

"Nope." I smile and slide Benny's dick onto the tip of a skewer.

Audrey gags, covers her mouth, and runs from the room.

Ari stands beside me. "What do you need?"

I retrieve some premade pancake mix from the cupboard and set it on the counter. "Grab a frying pan and the oil." I fill the pancake container with warm water and shake it violently.

Ari spins the frying pan in her grasp and then drops it on the burner. "Now what?"

"Heat me some oil, would you?"

"How much?" She holds the open oil over the pan.

"Enough to cover this." I hold the dick-kabob in front of her face.

"Got it." She pours the remnants of the oil into the pan, which turns out to be the perfect amount. I fill a small bowl with batter and evenly coat Benny's former dipstick. The oil bubbles on the stove. I drop the corndog dick into the hot oil and rest the end of the skewer on the edge of the pan.

"What smells so good?" Gina walks in, sniffing the air.

"Benny's corndog," Ari says over her shoulder, not wanting to take her eyes off the cooking appetizer.

She peers in the pan. "It's kind of small."

"That's because it's Benny's dick wrapped in pancake batter." I glare at her.

"Oh, I understand. That makes sense. So, who's going to eat it?"

"No one. We are leaving it on the counter for Griffin." I take a small plate out of the cupboard and set it beside the pan.

"Do you think he will eat it?" Ari asks, turning the corndog over.

"I hope so." I glance at the clock. Griffin should be collecting the girls at the rich kid's house now. A few minutes to load them, and then the drive back—leaves me with little time. I lift the corndog cock from its pan and set it on its plate. The end curved slightly during cooking, making it look like a side smile. I shift it to the edge of the plate and grab the ketchup and mustard from the fridge. I place two large dollops of ketchup at the top and a blob of mustard in the center of the plate.

"Awe, it looks like a smiley face." Ari holds my shoulders from behind and smiles at the food.

I slap my hands together in satisfaction of a job well done. "Time to clean up. Ari, help me get Benny to the gas chamber. Gina—you and Marley clean up the hanging room the best you can, then come in here and do the same. Ari and I will come to help you when we finish prepping Benny."

Benny's sopping body drips discolored water onto the floor. I rest my palm on the red and angry welts dotting his chest and push him. He doesn't move, but his eyes dart beneath his lids, confirming he's still alive.

Ari grabs him from behind in a bear hug and lifts him high enough for me to unclip him.

She makes no effort to hold Benny. Once he's free from the wire, she lets go, and his body lands hard on the concrete. The saturated dressing between his legs dangles by a single piece of medical tape stuck to a stray pubic hair. I grip it by the corner and yank it off, taking the hair, root and all.

Pluck the dick-less duck.

Benny groans through his throat as Ari and I drag him from the hanging room into the galley and down the hall to the gas chamber—crying out loud when Ari and I swing him onto the mattress. His eyes barely open when I secure his hands and feet with cuffs to the headboard and footboard.

I stare at his paling and ashen skin and then turn to Ari. "We need some supplies." I steer her to the girls' holding room.

Audrey stares blankly at the wall beside her bed.

"Audrey, I need your makeup kit," I say to the back of her head.

She points to her mattress but doesn't move. I peer under her bed, remove the bag, and nod at Ari for us to go. She shakes her head and points at Audrey.

She wants to stay and talk to her—console her, reassure her, make her feel better. It's fine with me. I'm used to working alone.

I jog to the gas chamber, swing the door around, and flop on the bed beside Benny. The ivory-colored foundation sputters out of the container into my hand. Benny turns his head away from me, and I hold it still, spreading a creamy coating across his pale face. Using a blush brush, I dot white eyeshadow all over his face, giving it a ghostly appearance. Benny's eyes wiggle under my fingers as I make his eye sockets match his black heart.

Now comes the smile.

I don't put the lipstick on his natural lips. Instead, I draw a giant red smiley face on his jagged new mouth and fill it in. If only I had green paint, I would color his hair green.

Ari enters as I put the cap on the lipstick.

"Oh man, I missed it." She traces the red border around Benny's new mouth. "He'd look like the joker if you had a little green paint for his hair."

"Yeah, I thought about that. Right now, he looks more like a deranged clown."

I stand on the mattress, open the cabinet above his head, remove a gas mask, and set it gently on Benny's face.

I scan Benny up and down and sigh. I don't know what I'm going to do with myself once my mission is complete—learn to knit or sew, maybe? If I did that, I would make a bikini out of some man's flesh and flaunt my creation at a local beach. I wonder if my skin suit would tan if I laid in the sun.

Making clothes and other items out of inedible, useless skin is another perfect way to dispose of them. I could sell them at the Oddities and Curiosities Expo in Buffalo. No one would bat an eye at a purse made of skin—lined beautifully with red satin and a finger bone fed through a hole in the purse flap keeping it closed.

Hmm. Now I must try it.

I take the mask off Benny's face and purse my lips. "I have an idea. See if there's dental floss in the bathroom."

Ari shuffles from the room and returns a few minutes later. "Here." She passes it to me. "What are you going to do?"

"You'll see."

I take the canister of gas from the cabinet and secure it tight to the side of Benny's neck. The floss glides between my fingers as I loop it through the pull pin on the container, tie one end to it, and wrap the other end of the thread several times around the inside mouthpiece, leaving just enough room to slide my fingers inside.

Ari raises her eyebrows and smiles. "Oh, I see what you're doing. You're creating a booby trap for Griffin."

"You got it. Pass me the tape behind you on the table." I point over her shoulder.

Benny turns his head to the side, trying to keep me from setting the mask on his face. "Ari, tape his head down."

She grabs the roll of tape, unfurls the end, and secures it to the metal bed frame. I press Benny's head firmly into the mattress as she runs the tape over his forehead, around the back of his head, then back over his forehead, making it so he can't shrug the mask off his face.

Ari and I stand back and cross our arms. The cheap clock on the wall ticks loudly.

Tick, tock, tick tock.

We step out of the room and swing the door around. I twist the lock on the knob, before closing the door behind me.

The girls are finishing cleaning the floor and dishes when Ari and I step into the room. Ari helps Marley flip the stained mattress on the bed but leaves it bare of sheets. A small droplet of blood under the bed catches my attention. My knees crack as I kneel and swipe the tacky liquid with my finger. Gina taps my shoulder and hands me a damp cloth. After scrubbing the stain, I toss the rag back to Gina, stand up, and close the hanging room door.

The galley appears the same as it did before Griffin left. The only difference is the happy corndog on the counter and the sheetless mattress.

I nod, open the door, and wave the girls inside. Once we were all in the next hall, I locked the galley door.

"Why are you locking all the doors?" Ari asks as we squeeze into the holding room.

"So it takes longer for Griffin to get to us."

Audrey stands from the bed. She wipes tears from her eyes and glances at each of the other girls, but not at me.

Ari places her hand on Audrey's shoulder as she begins to sob. "Don't worry. Odie's getting us out of here, tonight."

She steps away from Ari and bites her thumbnail. "What if you're wrong? What if Griffin comes back and kills one of us because you killed his brother?"

"I told you. The Egyptian is coming to take you away." I step towards her.

She steps back and puts her hand up. "You don't know that he will take the deal."

I move her hand out of my way and step within a foot of her. "Audrey, I know for a fact he will." I pat the side of her face and flop onto her bed putting my arms behind my head. "Either way, Griffin dies."

"What if you are wrong?" Marley asks, standing beside Audrey.

I close my eyes with a smile. "Ladies, I am never wrong."

Chapter Twenty-Four
Welcome Home, Ladies

You could hear a pin drop. We hold our breaths as the hatch echoes when it opens a few rooms away.

Griffin's coming.

Audrey shakes violently beside me. I take her hand and steady it with mine. Another door opens violently.

Bang.

Marley and Gina scurry to my side of the room and cower between the wall and bed.

My eyes land on each of the girls. Their faces all look the same.

Petrified.

They have every right to be. I'm counting on Griffin's fear of Femi's wrath if he kills me, and how much I remind him of the love he killed a few short years ago.

He regrets killing Amelia. I can see it in his eyes every time I say her name. But as for the girls, they would just be a monetary loss. He could always find new ones. If my plan doesn't play out as I hope, we are all dead, including Femi, money be damned.

Inaudible streams of curse words filter through the sound of another door crashing open. Audrey yanks her hands out from under mine and curls herself into a shuddering ball at the room's far corner. Ari steps away from the closed door.

"Why the fuck are all the doors locked, Benny?" Griffin's voice pierces the door.

He doesn't know yet. How exciting.

Crying penetrates the partition and shadows appear under the door, blocking the light.

Keys jangle, and the door handle twists without hesitation.

The twins enter first, wearing matching satin red lingerie. Ari runs to them and hugs them simultaneously. Their bodies stiffen.

In the short time they were away from us a lot had to have happened. Although they smell like cherry blossom body wash and appear clean, they've endured something dirty—something so awful it changed them. Eve has a fresh five-inch cut on her arm crudely held together with butterfly strips. Bruises dot their once-perfect skin, and both of their wrists have raw, pink skin showing—weeping onto their palms. The ropes the rich kid held them with were too tight and unforgiving.

Leah grabs Eve by her elbow, and I catch a glimpse of her arm. The rich kid did not cut Eve, she did it to herself. On Leah's arm, in the same location as Eve's cut, a tattoo reads, 'Property of Matthew Fields' in fancy cursive.

Griffin stuffs the keys into the right front pocket of his jeans and gazes around the room. His eyes lock on mine, and I smile. He steps further into the room, and Audrey's quiet whimpering becomes louder.

Griffin furrows his brow and then turns to me. "What the fuck is her problem?"

"You," Ari announces wrinkling her face. "What a dumb question." She rolls her eyes and sits on the bed beside me sinking the mattress further to the floor.

I stare down our line. Eve, Ari, Leah, and I all have our hands resting on our laps like a group of obedient children waiting for our teacher to give us instructions or an assignment. Marley and Gina hold each other against the wall behind us. I stretch my legs in front of me and cross my arms over my chest.

I'm not obedient or like them. If he were to produce a ruler and slap my knuckles, I would glare at him like I used to do to the nuns at the Catholic school I attended. They thought I was the devil. Perhaps they were right.

Air blasts from Griffin's nose. His eyes sag with fatigue and his face reddens with irritation. "I take it you made the corndogs," Griffin says to me.

"She did," Ari smiles. "They're so great. You should try it."

"I won't be eating anything she makes unless I watch her make it."

A metal-on-metal noise echoes down the hallway from the other room.

Clank, clank.

The hair on Griffin's arm raises.

Clank, clank—quieter this time.

I peer down at Ari's bicep. Goosebumps plaster her skin and her knee bounces beside me. I rest my palm on her leg and steady her nerves. In the corner, with every clank of metal on metal, Audrey jerks and presses her hands over her ears a little tighter. The twins glance at each other and then both look at me. Behind us, Marley and Gina breathe rapidly.

The air in the room shifts and becomes dead quiet. I can't even hear anyone breathing. We all wait and listen.

Clank—barely audible this time.

It's Benny. He must hear Griffin and is trying to get his attention. I thought he'd be dead by now, but the scrawny little fucker is holding on. Perhaps Griffin will try and save him and take him to the hospital. Of course, if he did that, he would risk the police finding out about this place, so he wouldn't have a choice but to try and help him himself or call the Egyptian's doctor.

Griffin peers down the hallway to the source of the noise, closes his eyes and listens.

Clank.

His eyes spring open and his head whips in my direction.

I tilt my head and smile softly at him.

If regret had a face, it would be Griffins at this very moment—pale, glossy-eyed, staggering breaths escaping his barely parted lips.

He grips the upper right side of the door jamb with his right hand, rests his forehead on his arm, and pinches his eyes closed. "What did you do?" His head rocks back and forth over his forearm reddening it. His jaw clenches, and the color of his face changes from ashen to a lovely shade of red. "I know you did something. I can feel it." He opens his eyes and glares at me.

I stand from the bed and take a few steps towards him. "There's still time to say goodbye if you hurry."

Clank.

Griffin's face drops. He pushes off the door jamb and moves quickly down the hall.

Eve flicks a piece of butterfly strip with her finger. Leah grabs her hand, interlaces her fingers with her sisters, and whispers a prayer to Jesus for protection—tears dripping from their eyes.

Audrey presses her bare feet into the floor and tucks herself tightly into the corner. She holds her bent legs against her trembling body and sobs on her kneecaps.

Ari gazes up at me with hopeful eyes. "Are we leaving soon?"

I rest my palm on her unruly and tangled hair. "Yes."

Gina and Marley move out from behind the bed and closer to Audrey.

Shouting, like that of an animal being torn apart by wolves, carries down the hallway from the gas chamber room.

Griffin has made a gruesome discovery. How tragic.

I place my arms behind my back, interlace my fingers, rock my body side to side, and close my eyes—swinging my neck in rhythm with the song I'm humming.

She's deadly, man.
She could really rip your world apart.
Mind over matter.
Ooh, the beauty is there but a beast is in the heart.

Oh-oh, here she comes.
Watch out, boy, she'll chew you up.
Ooh, here she comes.
She's a maneater.

—Hall and Oats

Coughing and gagging grow louder as Griffin staggers into the room with snot draining from his nose—eyes swollen into slits of tear-filled rage, sorrow, and tear gas.

The gas mask boobytrap did its job.

He charges me, still gasping for fresh air, seizes me by the throat, and throws me to the floor.

I land on my back, knocking the air from my lungs.

Ari steps between him and me. "Take him to the emergency room or call the doctor. You can still save him."

Griffin punches her in the temple without hesitation, and she lands on her side motionless beside me. Her hair covers her face. I can't see whether she's still alive or not.

I take a deep breath and crabwalk away from Griffin.

Audrey slides up the wall and runs towards the open door.

Griffin stretches his arm out in front of her, and his forearm strikes her in the throat, clotheslining her. Eve and Leah stare at Ari's motionless body on the floor and Audrey's shocked face and hold each other tighter.

The blade of Griffin's hunting knife scrapes slowly out of its sheath. His steps, slow and careful, come closer and closer to me. Marley dashes through the doorway and disappears. Audrey rolls on her side and crawls out into the hallway, vanishing around the corner.

I clamber to my feet and dodge the blade of Griffin's knife as he charges me. Gina jumps on his back, jarring the blade from his grasp, and yells, "Run!"

Griffin grabs the fabric of her shirt on her back, yanks her over his shoulder, and tosses her away from him. She lands in front of me, partially on Ari, and scrambles to a stand. I swing her behind me and use my buttocks to bump her out of the room. "Go to the galley," I shout to her over my shoulder.

I'd lock Griffin inside but that would leave the twins and Ari trapped along with him.

He barrels towards me, grips my shoulders, and slams me into the doorframe. "I don't need a knife to kill you."

He wraps his hands around my throat and squeezes. I kick my legs as the floor disappears beneath them.

Clank, clank.

Benny's calling for Griffin again. The noise seems quieter this time. He's losing strength.

Blood leaks from the holes my fingers create in Griffin's arms, but he won't loosen his grip. I let his arms go and swing at his face, landing one punch after another, but it doesn't faze him. Blind rage and adrenaline fuel the anger burning through his veins. His eyes are open, but he doesn't see me.

Stars and black specks dance together in my field of vision, and the room darkens slowly. I raise my knee and nail Griffin hard in the nuts, but his grip only loosens long enough for me to gasp one breath. Rage blocks the pain of my groin strike. Now he knows how it feels for someone to hurt you and not feel it. It's like adrenaline rushing through you all the time with no relief in sight. You just hold your breath and hang on for the ride that never ends.

I relax my body, making myself heavy in his grasp, but that doesn't work either. In the corner of my eye, I catch a glimpse of my sister. Her outstretched hand reaches for me as the wall between the world of the living and the dead becomes transparent. My parents stand behind her with their hands on her shoulder. I reach for them—fingers only an inch away from Amelia's.

Griffin releases me suddenly. I take several gasping breaths and Amelia and my parents slowly dissipate. I caress my neck and stare at the corndog and skewer sticking out of Griffin's bicep.

Marley's hand slowly lets go of its wooden handle, and she backs away from us.

Griffin's eyes follow the blood draining down his arm until it reaches the floor and glares at her. "Fucking bitch."

He grips the appetizer in his palm, crushing it in his grasp before yanking it out and throwing it on the hallway floor between him and Marley. He takes a step towards her but stops abruptly. His brow furrows and his eyes squint as he stares at the impotent cock resting limply in its center. Inaudible words tremble from his lips as he stares at Benny's previously attached appendage. Marley slides sideways away from him. He doesn't move to stop her. The dick dog holds his attention as he mumbles to himself.

Clank, clank.

"Benny's running out of time," I pant, rubbing my neck. "You need to take him to the hospital." I glance at the hole in his arm. "You should go too. You might want to get some antibiotics."

I didn't even see the swing coming. He spun around so fast and hit me so hard that I had no time to react. Griffin's blurry silhouette folds over me, and his fingers twist around my hair, tightening it to my scalp. Something wet smears into my spine as he drags me across the floor, into the hall, and down to the hanging room where he drops me beneath a dangling wire. I shake my head several times releasing the fog from it. My body bounces up and down as he rips my clothes away from my body, leaving me naked.

He paces before me, unsure of what he wants to do with me—keep me, kill me, get rid of me, or sell me.

The frustration I'm causing wears on him—ages him, weakens him. He must wonder why I haven't taken the opportunity to kill him already.

Well, my dearest Griffin, that would ruin my plans for you. Like a game of chess, the pieces must fall in place in a specific order, and the moves just so to ensure a successful win—a checkmate.

His face changes from anger to sadness and back again as he reasons with himself under his breath. He needs revenge, but I remind him of Amelia, and killing me would be like killing her all over again. Keeping me will be a constant reminder of what I've put him through and done to him and his brother. Selling me to the Egyptian only gives him monetary satisfaction.

Griffin walks away from me but stops with his hand on the galley door handle. Quiet crying comes from the ladder to the hatch. He glances at Audrey sitting on the floor, leaning against the bottom rung of the ladder leading outside.

He leaves her there and exits the room. She's not a threat to him. Marley on the other hand, is in trouble.

Her screams echo through the halls but fade within seconds. He's either killed her or dragged her back to the holding room with the others. Several minutes go by before Griffin saunters in, wound tied off with a piece of fabric, dragging Marley's motionless body behind him. She moans as he hoists her up and cuffs her to the wire above me.

A small knife slides out of his ankle holster, and he points it in my direction. "This is on you."

I reach for her and try to stand, but dizziness drops me back to my knees. The blade staggers over her chest, scratching its way down to her leg, where Griffin stops and smirks. He jerks Marley's head back, and she screams as the knife sinks deep into her upper thigh, severing her femoral artery. Griffin rotates the blade and then pulls it out, leaving a gaping hole. Blood gushes onto my head and lap. I reach up and press my palm over the hole, squeezing her leg as tight as I can, but it's coming out too fast.

Marley's face drains of color as her heart pumps all her blood between my fingers and onto the cement.

I take a deep breath and screech at him. "I'm going to fucking kill you." My hands grip Marley's leg tighter.

"Good luck with that." He smiles and wipes the blade of his knife on his pants. He glances at Marley's pale face one last time and strolls toward the door.

I need him to stop. I need him to stay here with me and leave the others alone.

"Benny and I fucked while you were gone."

It just came out. I tried to think of the only thing that would upset him, and Benny breaking his promise was the ultimate betrayal.

Griffin stops walking but doesn't look at me.

"He fucked me in my pussy and my ass, and he enjoyed every minute of it. I told him we shouldn't because you would get mad, but he said, 'fuck it' and took me right in there on your kitchen counter."

His shoulders raise to his ears, but he still refuses to look at me. "Liar," he murmurs.

"Liar? How do you think I was able to cut off his cock? Do you think he just dropped his pants and let it happen?" I grin.

Griffin slowly turns around and looks at me. "You incapacitated him somehow and did it after."

I smile broadly and laugh through my nose. "Oh, Griffin. You have no idea how easy it was to convince him. He's wanted me for so long and you..." I cackle at the ceiling. "...you deprived him for your own selfish reasons."

"She's telling the truth." Audrey uses the ladder rung to brace herself and stand. "He put us all in our rooms like you asked but when it came to her..." Audrey glances at me. "...he couldn't help himself."

I nod my head at her, thanking her for coming to my defense, and smile at Griffin. "See, I told you."

"Fuck you, Odeya." He turns away from me, glares at Audrey, and storms out of the room, slamming the door behind him.

I frown at Marley's open, dilated eyes and release her leg. Blood drips from the tips of her toes landing soundless in the shallow puddle on the floor. Gravity, and a slight slope in the floor, carry the stream of crimson to the base of the ladder and around Audrey's bare foot.

She walks slowly to Marley, leaving a trail of bloody footprints, and rests her fingers on Marley's neck. "She's dead."

I sigh heavily and sit back on my heels.

Her death is on me. It's not like I knew her, so it isn't that much of a loss to me, but it's still sad.

Audrey turns and faces me. "She was brave and died protecting you."

Tears no longer fall from her eyes. Audrey has nothing left. Her emptiness takes over, leaving her a hollow and fragile shell.

Griffin's voice carries from the next room, and she doesn't even flinch. She sits on the floor between Marley and me in a puddle of blood.

The door separating us whips open, and Griffin walks over and stands between Audrey and me. He tucks his phone back into his pocket and glares at me. "The Egyptian is on his way and bringing the doctor with him. You better hope for your sake she can save my brother. Because if he dies, then you die, and I don't give a fuck..." His voice rises, and he grips my chin. "...what the Egyptian has to say. He can take the other girls, but you, you are mine." My body tumbles backward as he shoves me onto the floor.

He steps back and nearly trips over Audrey. His eyes widen as he looks from her to me over his shoulder. "Jesus Christ, what did you do to her?"

What did I do? Has he gone mad?

I didn't understand what he was referring to until he stepped out of the way. On the floor, beside Audrey, a bloody sad face with mouse ears frowns at the ceiling.

Audrey hums and her head bobs in tune with a nursery rhyme as she draws a second face.

Hmm...hmm...hmm. Hmm...hmm...hmm.

"*Three...blind...mice. Three...blind...mice,*" I sing in a low, sinister tone as she hums. "*See...how...they...run. See...how...they...run.*" I tilt my head and grin broadly at Griffin.

Bang, bang, bang.

Benny calls Griffin to the gas chamber.

Griffin walks backward towards the door, with an expressionless face, as I continue singing. *"I cut off his cock with a carving knife. Did you ever see such a thing in your life..."* The door slowly closes. *"...as the...three...blind...mice?"*

"*The...three...blind...mice,*" Audrey whispers on the floor.

I know her sadness shouldn't make me happy, but I feel like she's working her way closer to my level of crazy, and it makes me ecstatic. She's one of us now. Fear has evaporated from her body like the hot sun in the desert. She has nothing left to lose. They have taken everything from her, and I have given her something to look forward to.

Revenge.

The light on the camera above the door flickers green.

He's watching us.

Audrey draws the third mouse.

I lick my lips and smile at the camera.

"*The...three...blind...mice*," Audrey sings in a low, demonic tone with a devious smile, slowly smears all three mice with her palm, and glares up at the camera lens.

I smile at her. This sharp change in behavior, brought on by treacherous circumstances, fills me with joy.

She has crossed over to the dark side. The little voice inside her head that tells her she's doing something wrong no longer exists.

I tilt my head down, my evil eyes staring into hers as she looks at me, and I wonder.

What kind of monster she will be?

Chapter Twenty-Five
Don't Speak

Waiting.

It's the hardest part of all of this.

Well, that, and trying not to fall asleep when your body and mind are exhausted. Instant gratification is much more tolerable than this slow-burn scenario I've put together. Playing the long game has never been my strong suit.

My eyes fixate on the dried blood on my hand. Marley's death is partly on me. If she hadn't stabbed Griffin trying to save me, she may still be alive. Then again, Griffin was out for blood after what I did to his precious brother. If it wasn't her who died, it would have been someone else.

Probably Ari.

I think back to when my life changed forever.

The moment I received the phone call that Griffin killed my sister, all the promises I made to her didn't matter anymore. Her death granted me permission—to be who I've always wanted to be, to behave any way I like, and to eat what I desire.

I still remember the day my mother called and told me to come home right away. I kept asking her what was wrong as words staggered through her crying lips. When she finally collected herself enough to tell me, I didn't believe her. I remember stopping in the middle of the college campus walkway and swearing at her. 'What the fuck did you just say?'

She wailed on the other end of the line as she repeated what she just told me. "Your sister is dead. He killed her."

My phone slid from my hand as I lost the strength to hold it. The screen shattered as it landed beside me on the cement. Other students weaved around me, not caring why I was there, only that I was blocking the path to their next class. One person stepped on my phone, nearly falling, swore, and then kicked it into the grass to his right before he continued walking—his muscular thighs mocking me as he storms away bitching about how much his day sucked. He had no idea how lucky he was that my brain was still absorbing the news I just received. Otherwise, I would have grabbed my number two pencil and stabbed him in the neck right then and there. But I needed to get home and making him my official first meal for what he did was not a good enough reason.

I sit up and my head teeters. The constant blows to the head are taking their toll.

Three...blind... mice... Ari hums softly to herself.

She appears older now than she did when she first arrived. Her eyes carry more bags beneath them, and her hair is frizzy from lack of conditioner.

Trauma can change you. How you interact with people, manage your emotions, and facial expressions become less genuine. You force a smile even though you're dying inside. Slowly, you don't react to people at all and withdraw from family and friends. Nothing makes you smile; nothing bothers you anymore. You become numb to the world around you. Soon just being around people is too much. You stay in and prefer your own company over other people. Being alone, even when your thoughts chatter inside your head, is preferable.

But that's not who Ari is. She's not going to hide inside her house, alone and cut off from the world. I have no doubt she will spread her wings and fly from this cocoon they hold us captive in. The world will burn to the ground as she punishes it for what the universe allowed to happen.

Griffin must have taken Marley down and brought her in when I fell asleep. The nursery rhyme is stuck inside Ari's head like a vinyl record that keeps skipping and repeating the same chorus over and over.

Three...blind...mice.

She stops humming when she catches me staring at her.

"Well, look who finally decided to wake up."

I continue looking at her but stay quiet.

"What?" She furrows her brow. "Do I have a booger hanging from my nose or something?"

"No. I'm just wondering what your plans are for when we get out of this place."

She purses her lips and glances at the ceiling. "Well, I thought about staying with you for a bit and learning how to cook."

"You want me to teach you how to cook?" I raise my brows and grin.

"Well, yeah, I thought maybe we can trade expertise."

Huh. There's no downfall to learning other ways to kill people. However, explosives tend to blow the human body into bits, rendering their meat useless and contaminated. There's no harm in learning, just in case, but I don't play well with others out in the real world.

"We can do that." I smile at her eager face, knowing it will never happen.

Audrey's not here with us and the bloody artwork on the floor is gone.

"Where's Audrey?"

Ari stops humming. "Griffin took her out but made her clean the floor first."

She starts humming again.

I hum with her.

Three...blind...mice.

The door beside us screeches open, and Griffin enters holding his phone.

We hum louder.

He stops walking and glares at us. "No more humming. That damn song has been stuck in my head for a fucking hour."

I smile at the thought of Griffin humming his destiny, except it won't be his tail I cut off.

Ari stops humming, raises her eyebrows, and follows Griffin for a few steps on her tiptoes as he strolls by. I shake my head at her, and she nods.

She just can't help but stir up trouble.

Her mouth opens, and I shake my head again.

Oh, God. She's smiling. She's about to say something stupid or irritating to piss him off.

Don't do it, Ari.

"How's Benny Boy?"

Fuck.

Griffin stops walking and stares at her with gritting teeth. "Don't say my brother's name again."

Ari holds her head high and huffs. "Can you at least tell us if Benny is still alive?"

Oh, Ari. She'll do anything for attention.

The air fires from Ari's lungs as Griffin punches her in the abdomen.

Pounding comes from above us. Griffin steps over to the ladder and stares up at the steel entrance.

Stomp, stomp, stomp.

He slides his phone from his pocket, punches a few buttons, and nods at his phone screen. His hands work quickly to unlock the cabinet and press the red button, unlocking the escape route above.

Metal scrapes against metal as the hatch lock slides open.

A woman's designer ankle boot steps onto the first rung. The doctor makes her way down and stops in front of me.

She's an unbelievably beautiful woman. I don't know why she doesn't wear her hair down. I'd prefer it.

I close my eyes and picture myself swooping the hair away from her perfect, firm neck. The scent of her perfume sending wave after wave of pulsating desire between my legs. My fingers gliding over her trim, muscular abdomen and into her waiting, wet pussy while my boyfriend watches us. He would then fuck her while I fuck myself with my realistic, flesh-colored, vibrating, and thrusting dick that runs on batteries and has a remote.

I love that fucking thing.

"No." Griffin's voice startles me away from my daydream. He grabs the doctor's bicep and steers her away from me. "My brother is your only priority."

I smile up at her, fucking her with my eyes. She raises her brow. A tiny smile creeps into the corner of her mouth as she turns away from me and looks at Griffin. "Very, well. Where is he?"

Griffin glances behind him as bodyguard number one climbs down the ladder wearing tactical attire, black boots laced up tight, and a Glock within easy reach on his hip. "Gas chamber." He sighs with his hand on his stomach and turns his back on the guard.

The change in the type of guard should have been Griffin's first clue that something wasn't right. His concern for his brother clouds his judgment, and he's ignoring the pit that's brewing in his stomach.

The doctor nods at Griffin and glances back at me. "I heard you did a number on him."

I cackle and glare at Griffin. "I just removed his insignificant appendage."

The Egyptian's steel-colored suit jacketed arm hooks around Griffin's mid-swing, stopping him from striking me. "Don't fucking touch her."

Griffin's eyes widen as the Egyptian releases him and two bodyguards each grab an arm. "Femi, what the fuck is this? I thought we had a deal. You take the girls in exchange for me keeping her."

Femi removes his black leather gloves, pulling them off one finger at a time. "We do. I'm taking all the girls…" He smiles at me then twists his neck to face Griffin as he removes his jacket, unbuttons his cuffed wrists, and loosens his tie. "…but I want her by my side until I leave."

He reaches his hand out to me and pulls me from the floor. His arm wraps around my waist, and my pussy smolders as he pulls me close to him.

I'd like to wrap my legs around his tan face and let him eat me for breakfast, lunch, and dinner while running my fingers through his silky black hair.

Fucking release, me, Daddy.

"This isn't part of the deal." Griffin yanks each of his arms away from the bodyguards and blocks us from entering the galley.

Safety's click behind his head. The barrel of a gun presses into his temple.

I wish Griffin were naked at this very moment. I bet his asshole is puckering tighter than a hand carrying a bag full of dogshit after a long walk.

Don't let go.

Griffin grimaces and raises his hands. "This is bullshit."

"Griffin, I suggest you step away so I can finish my business here. I am taking the other girls as agreed and then leaving the bunker. I think…" He places his hand on Griffins' shoulder and shifts him out of our way. "… you can appreciate the fact that I didn't kill you and your brother for tarnishing what's mine."

What's his?

No one owns me.

I own you.

"But she's not yours anymore. That was part of the agreement," Griffin points out.

"I know what I agreed to." Femi pulls me in front of him and uses his lower body to bump me into the galley entranceway.

He steps into the room, pulls me back by my arms, and holds his body tight against my back, trapping me in his tight embrace. His cock hardens to stone beneath the fabric of his dress pants.

"Perhaps I could spend a few moments alone with her before I go." His dick rocks against my butt cheek, massaging it with its stiffness, and his hot breath warms my neck as he speaks softly into my ear. "So, fucking beautiful."

Pussy juices dribble down my inner thigh.

Griffin wedges himself between us and the doorframe and stumbles into the galley. "That's not going to happen."

Femi spins me around to face him and stares deep into my eyes ignoring Griffin's furrowing brow. He's fucking me with his mind, and I'm returning the favor.

Griffin slides his hand between our faces, breaking our eye contact. "Can we get on with it?"

Air bursts through Femi's nostrils, making me blink. He turns to Griffin and frowns. "I don't know Griffin, can we?"

The bodyguards stand on either side of Griffin.

He glances to his left and right and sighs heavily. "Look, I don't want any more problems. I just want the doctor to treat Benny, and then you take the girls and go."

Femi steps away from me and stops before Griffin. "Take me to the girls."

Griffin walks around him, stops beside me, and whispers in my ear. "Soon, we will be all alone." He continues walking and disappears through the doorway.

I smile at the thought of being alone with him.

Femi gestures to the space in front of him. "After you."

My face flushes. A knife couldn't cut the tension between us. He rests his hands on the small of my back and holds it there as we venture through the bunker heading to the holding room where the girls are. We pass the gas chamber room, and I stop walking.

The doctor is sewing up Benny's face. It's not going to matter. Even if he doesn't smile ever again, his scar will.

Femi smells the back of my neck and rubs my ass. "I love the way you smell."

My breath quickens, and my face prickles. I slide my hand behind my back and grab his cock tight, turning my head to peer up at him. "Do you like that?"

He grunts and exhales slowly. "Yes."

I rub his shaft rapidly and friction warms my palm.

Femi pants louder and louder.

The material of his pants swooshes beneath my palm. My fingers pass over a small wet circle spreading on Femi's pants near the tip. I grab his cock in my hand and use my thumb like a Jeopardy clicker, pressing my finger into his moist tip through his pants making the wet spot bigger.

Griffin yanks me sideways away from Femi, pulls me against his chest, and wraps his arm around my waist. "That'll be enough of that. She stays with me while you get the girls."

The bodyguards stand on either side of Femi. He adjusts his manhood and raises his eyebrows at Griffin. "If that's what she wants." His eyes drift to mine.

"It's what I want." I grin.

Griffin squeezes me tighter, increasing the pressure on my chest. "I don't care what you want." He loosens his hold slightly, and walks forward, using his body to push me into the gas chamber room with Benny and the doctor.

He tightens his arm around me once more. I gasp several times and push down the arm wrapped too tightly around me. "I can't breathe."

"You're talking, so you're breathing just fine." Griffin stuffs his hand into his pocket, removes a single key on a keyring, and passes it to Femi. "The girls are down the hall to the right."

Femi curls his fingers around the key and winks at me. "See you later."

I wink back. "I look forward to it."

He steps out of view, and Griffin relaxes his hold on me.

I feel like a giddy schoolgirl whose crush just announced to the entire playground that I am his girl no matter what anyone else says.

Griffin places his hand on the door handle to close it, but Femi returns and stands in the way. "I prefer it if you left the door open."

"No disrespect, but you have the key to take the girls. I have no intention of keeping your doctor, despite how beautiful she is. Once she helps my brother, she can go. Now if you don't mind, I'd like some privacy." Griffin slowly moves the door, intending to close it.

Femi doesn't move. His presence creates an awkwardness in the space between us. He's supposed to be getting the girls. Instead, he stands in the doorway with his hands in his pockets with a smile lingering in the corner of his mouth.

Griffin presses his palm into my abdomen, tightening his grip. He's not releasing me until the door's closed.

They're in a standoff.

Great, we could be here all day.

I smile with my eyes and shake my head at Femi. This is an unnecessary display of masculinity at an inappropriate time.

Femi's eyes soften. He removes one hand from his pocket, gives me a subtle nod, and takes a small step back.

The tension between them lifts and Griffin's hold on me relaxes, but I can feel his anger. It emanates away from his body, thickening the air around us.

Femi glances to his left, holds the key over his shoulder, and nods at his armed men. One of the men takes the key from him as he passes behind Femi and heads for the holding room where the girls are.

Griffin didn't notice the extra manpower, but I did. All of Femi's men are in the bunker now not just the original two.

I count four.

Griffin's too preoccupied with keeping his eyes on Femi and his hold on me. He doesn't realize the tides are turning.

Femi takes a slow step backward out of the doorway, turns on his heels, and strolls away.

Griffin lets go, swings the door around, pushes it close with his fist, and glares at me.

He knows.

If he doesn't, he must sense something isn't right.

I glance over Griffin's shoulder.

The doctor looks up from tending to Benny and smiles at me.

Griffin's hands open and close repeatedly as my eyes dart back to his, and he eyes me suspiciously.

He wants to hit me.

I smile and lift my chin, making the offer.

He grabs me, spins me around, pulls me against his chest, and points at Benny. "Everything you've done to him; I'm going to do to you."

I glance up at him over my shoulder. "I don't have a cock, Griffin. Maybe we can cut off yours instead. It would certainly make a bigger kabob."

The doctor stifles a laugh.

Griffin opens his mouth to speak but says nothing.

I thrust my ass into him, breaking myself free, and flop into the chair beside the bed. "What's the matter, Griffin? Cat got your tongue?"

"Get up," Griffin orders, fingers roughly gripping my hair. "I didn't say you could sit." He lifts me from my seat and drops me on the floor by the doctor's feet. "Stay down there like the bitch you are." He pushes my head down, and my mouth strikes the floor.

I glare up at him and wipe the blood from my lips. "You're going to regret that."

He pushes my head a second time, scraping my cheek against the textured floor, and growls in my ear. "The only thing I regret is not killing you sooner."

He releases my head and turns his attention back to Benny.

I touch the side of my face, pick a tiny pebble of concrete embedded in my cheek off, and flick it under the bed. I watch it skip across the floor and land on the other side.

I should have kept it. I could stuff it into Griffin's penis hole later as a form of torture.

Oh, well. I guess I'll have to abuse him some other way.

Griffin takes Benny's hand and holds it in his.

How touching.

"You're going to be okay, brother." Griffin holds their conjoined hands against his forehead.

Oh, dear. That's so sad. He thinks Benny's going to survive this. I clear my throat and chuckle.

My body slams into the floor, and Griffin pins me beneath him, nostrils flaring and face red. "Do you think this is funny?" He twists my head to the side, forcing me to look at him. "If he dies, I will fucking cut your heart out and mount it on the wall. Then, I will exhume your sister and decorate my walls with her fucking bones."

Wow, so aggressive.

My head bounces off the floor. Black stars and blurry vision obscure my view. I shake my head several times but still have a hard time seeing. He lifts my head to slam it again.

"Excuse me." The doctor interrupts him and removes a syringe from her bag. "I'm giving him a shot of Morphine.

It will help him with the pain." She draws the liquid inside the needle and flicks the tip to remove the air.

Griffin releases me and sits back down beside Benny.

I sit up, and my head bobbles. My eyes adjust almost back to normal. A few floating black specks remain. Something wet trickles down my temple. I touch my head and smear blood on my fingers. My hand shakes, but not from fear.

It's rage.

My eyes burn through the side of Griffin's head as he watches the doctor flick the needle one last time.

She hesitates to inject Benny as the door swings open across from her, and Femi saunters inside. "Are you about done?"

"Yes," the doctor and I answer in unison with a smile.

Griffin glares at me as I roll my lips inside my mouth trying to contain my laughter.

Femi chuckles to himself and slides his hands into his pockets. "Well, let's get on with it."

The doctor winks at me as she stabs Griffin in the thigh with the needle and plunges the medication into his leg.

The look on his face...priceless.

He stares with wide eyes at the needle sticking out of his skin before slapping it away. Like a tree struck with a final blow from an ax, he tips in slow motion to the side, and falls off the bed, landing beside me.

Timber.

His eyes roll back in his head as he struggles to remain conscious and I tenderly place my palm against his cheek, leaning to whisper in his ear. "It's my turn to play."

Femi stands beside me and rests his palm on my shoulder. I kiss the back of his hand and smile up at him. "Don't go far, my little pussycat. I've got plans for us."

He leans down, cups my chin in his palm, and kisses me tenderly. "Don't worry, my love. I'll be right outside, waiting for you on the surface."

Chapter Twenty-Six
My Turn

The girls cry in the hallway. I kept my word—my promise that they'd be free, and Femi would take them out of the bunker.

Audrey shuffles into the room with her head down and stands in front of me. She fiddles with her shirt, and stares at its material, before finally making eye contact. "Are we really leaving?"

I reach out to her and take her trembling hands in mine, steadying them with a gentle squeeze. "You are going home today. No one will ever hurt you again."
I glance at Benny's wide-eyed and shocked face as he hyperventilates through his nose. "I'll make sure of it."

She stares at Griffin's motionless body on the floor. Her foot raises, and I thought she might step over him. Instead, she stomps on his cock hard with her bare foot. She covers her mouth, shocked by what she just did. "I don't know why I just did that."

I grip her right hand and tug it slightly. "I do."

She collapses into my arms sobbing uncontrollably. I stroke her tangled hair. Ari steps into the room and places her hand on Audrey's shoulder, pulling her away from me. She smirks at me and steers her into the hallway.

There's work to do and Ari knows Audrey shouldn't be here to see it.

The doctor's bag drops on the floor by my side with a thud. I stand in front of her, move a lock of hair out of her face, and wrap it around her ear. She leans in and kisses my cheek. "Do your worst."

I stroke her jawline with my fingertip and grin. "I always do."

She laughs through her nose and twirls my hair one last time before continuing through the door. Since I met her, I've always called her Doc. I don't know her by any other name, nor do I want to. Getting too close to her will only make it harder when I leave.

For her.

I, on the other hand, can't allow such attachments. Losing my sister was enough loss to last me a lifetime—superficial relationships are all I have left to offer. My fractured mind doesn't allow anything more than that.

I kneel and unzip her leather bag. She keeps a variety of items necessary to conduct minor surgery, suture wounds, sedate patients and treat infections. A scalpel has a sharper blade than your standard kitchen knife. I squint as the light from above reflects off the blade and into my eyes.

Benny stirs on the bed and moans. I should have made the others help me put Griffin on the bed, but I can just torture them on the floor. First, I need to move Benny.

I detach Benny from his bindings, and he swings half-heartedly at my face. Even if his fist struck me, there wasn't enough force behind his attempt to do any damage. I place my palms, one under his waist and the other under his shoulder blade, and roll him off the other side of the bed. The floor vibrates when his body strikes it.

He's even uglier when he cries—eyes red and puffy, face scrunched and twisted in despair, his second mouth I created for him tightening as it tries to heal.

His fingers scratch the floor, trying to spell something. I leave the room and grab a pen, and a Post-it note from the kitchen junk drawer. When I place it in his hand, he scribbles two barely legible words.

Kill me.

I lift the note from the floor and place it on his forehead. "Now why would I do that, Benny Boy?"

I want…no, I need him to see everything I do to his brother. He's always looked up to him and counted on his strength and leadership. Benny will see that Griffin is nothing special.

He's nothing more than a man. A man about to die.

I remove a roll of duct tape from the cabinet above the bed, rip off several pieces with my teeth, and stick them on my leg.

Benny whimpers as I push him from his back onto his side. I roll a bloody blanket up behind his back and prop him up so he's lying on his side facing away from the bed. He scissor kicks his feet and flails his hands, trying to grab me. I take two long pieces of tape and secure his ankles to the leg of the bed by the footboard, and his hands to the leg by the headboard. He bucks his body in the middle, but he's not going anywhere.

I peel a piece of tape from my leg, crank his eyelid up with my thumb, and tape it open. I do the same with the other eye and add a few extra pieces to make sure they stay open.

I let out a throaty laugh at his appearance. "You look surprised to see me, Benny." I take my pointer finger and trace the new smiling mouth I gave him earlier. "Happy, too."

I drag Griffin's flaccid body parallel to Benny, sit on his chest, and drag the flat of the scalpel over his carotid. Benny makes throat noises beside me as he tries to talk. I smile at him. "You want me to spare him after what he's done to us? Done to my sister? Done to me?"

Benny nods his head and more garbled noises come from his oversized yap.

I tilt my head and frown. "He killed my sister, Benny. He needs to die."

Tears dribble from his eyes and land on the floor. I press the sharp edge of the blade against Griffin's throat. Benny shakes his head rapidly, pleading to me with his eyes not to kill his brother.

"Okay, Benny. You win for now. I will let him live. But it's not without consequence." I smile, slice Griffin's shirt down the center, and yank it from beneath him.

His chest is so defined, so sexy.

So meaty.

I trace my fingers down his abdomen, stop at the top of his waistband, and unzip his pants.

Benny's head shakes, and he moans again.

"Now, you can't have it both ways. This was your decision, remember? You wanted him to live. Now you must accept the consequences of your choice."

I shimmy Griffin's pants and underwear down, revealing his soft cock, and hustle down to the hanging room. Rain drizzles through the open hatch. My pussycat wanted to make sure I could get out if something happened.

How sweet of him.

He's always so thoughtful and thinks two steps ahead. It's probably why he's so good at chess and always beats me. Well, he doesn't technically beat me. I usually let him win. It's such a long, boring game, and I don't have the patience for it.

I still remember the last time we played. Femi reached for his king, and I snatched it and stuffed it down my pants. He reached into my pajama bottoms to retrieve it but didn't take it out. Femi's dick wasn't the only thing that ventured inside me that night.

I shake my head, clearing it of the fond memory of that evening, grab several lengths of rope from the utility closet, and drag them back to the gas chamber.

Benny hyperventilates through his nose, blasting snot everywhere. I drop the length of rope on the floor and begin wrapping Griffin, starting with his legs. Griffin's head twitches and his eyeballs shift under his lids.

He'll be awake soon. I need to hurry. I seize his arms and secure them to his sides.

"What the fuck," Griffin slurs trying to lift his heavy head.

Benny squirms beside him and grunts.

Griffin's eyes widen when he sees his brother. He bucks his body but barely moves. His face reddens with anger. "Let him go, Odeya. He's had enough."

"Enough?" I smirk and climb off his chest. My feet tuck beneath my thighs as I sit cross-legged beside him. "You are trying to tell me he's had enough? Have you had enough too, Griffin?"

"I…" Griffin's head lifts, then drops back down. "…I deserve it, but Benny, he—"

I cover his mouth with my hand. "Benny deserves to die, just as much as you do."

He screams as I press the blade through the skin covering his pectoral muscles and slice off his nipple. I balance it on the side of my pointer finger like a coin about to be flipped at an NFL game. "Bloody side up, I take the other one—flesh side, I leave it attached to your body."

"No, Odeya, please don't." He begs.

I flick the flesh coin in the air, and it lands bloody side up on his abdomen. "Both it is."

"No, no, no." He scoots his body away from me, but Benny keeps him from moving too far.

His scream catches in his throat before staggering out like a wounded animal. The second nipple slices away just as easily as the first, thanks to the precision of the scalpel's blade. I hold one in each palm cut side down. "They look like two brown eyeballs staring back at me. Look, Griffin, see?" I hold them by his tear-covered face, and he turns his head.

"Please, just leave us and go." His voice comes out shaky and defeated. "I'm sorry I hurt you and for what happened with your sister. I wasn't in my right mind, just like you aren't now."

"*I'm* not in my right mind?" I furrow my brow at him. "You do know that you gave me a reason to choose you."

I curl my lip at Benny's puny frame. "I only wish your brother had some meat on those fragile bones of his. Taking anything from him would be like peeling the remnants of meat left on a chicken wing after someone ate all the good parts."

Griffin thrashes beside me and flips onto his side. Blood drains from where his nipples once were, staining his chest with lines of crimson.

I close my eyes and slap his nipples on my lids. "How do I look with brown eyes?"

He groans and tries to roll away from me. I let the nipples fall from my eyes. "What are you going to do, roll your way out of here?"

I push him onto his back and straddle him, resting my pussy on his cock. "Want to fuck one last time for fun?" I grind myself into him.

"Fuck you." He wiggles beneath me as his cock hardens without trying.

"Oh, yes. Your cock wants to play with me." I rotate my hips around and around. It gets harder and harder.

"Fucking stop." Griffin whips his body side to side then launches me off him with one big thrust of his hips.

I land beside him and glare at his penis pointing at the ceiling. "Fine, you don't want to give it to me willingly, I'll fuck your cock another way."

I swipe the scalpel from the floor and crawl to his side.

"No," he screams and rolls his body away from me. "Please don't, Odeya. Anything but that. Chop off my hand if you have to, just don't do that."

"Now, Griffin…" I force his body face up, and his dick swings side to side, starting to soften. I stand and grab a length of rope from the cabinet above the bed, tying one end around Benny's waist, and the other end around Griffin, securing them to each other and limiting his movement. "…I can't fuck a hand. But this…" I grip his cock in my hand and stroke it up and down several times, hardening it back up. "…this I can fuck."

Griffin's mouth stretches open and screams as I rest the scalpel at the base of his cock. "Please! Please don't!"

I tilt my head to the side, smile at his pleading eyes, and saw his dick off at the base with the razor-sharp blade. His body rocks back and forth, trying to move away from the tormenting pain between his legs. Benny sobs beside him and tries to speak.

What are you going to say to him, Benny? Are you going to tell him everything's going to be, okay? That life will continue despite his lack of cock, and you can still be happy.

I cackle at the ceiling. "Ha, ha, ha." I raise the dick above my head like a sword, warm blood draining down my arm, leap to my feet, and place it gently on the chair by the bed. I grab the doctor's bag and remove a suture kit and several bandages.

Griffin writhes back and forth. I press my palm onto his hip, holding him still, and stab his gaping wound with a needle. He cries out and tries to move away from me, but I hold his hip firmly. "Hold still. I know it hurts, but if I don't finish, you'll bleed out."

"Let me die." His lips quiver and tears stream down his face. "Just get it over with and kill us both."

"Now where's the fun in that?" I smile and stab the needle just above his balls a second time.

The jagged and uneven stitches look awful by the time I finish, but they will hold for now. Griffin's eyes are heavy, and he's one blink away from passing out. I squirt a blob of triple antibiotic ointment onto a clean gauze pad and slap it onto the sutured area.

Griffin's head pops up. He clenches his jaw, suppressing his bellowing.

That will wake him up.

I dismount him, swipe the cock from the chair, and jog to the galley. The kitchen drawer scrapes open and my eyes light up as I grasp the wooden skewer. The wooden point of it squishes into the severed end of Griffin's penis, and I stop it about an inch from the tip. I open the freezer door and place it gingerly inside. What better way to use and reuse such a magnificent appendage? A cocksicle; woohoo, I can't wait to ride that frozen pop later.

I wash my hands in the sink and head back to the gas chamber. Griffin stares into Benny's wide-open eyes— face twisted in despair. "I'm sorry," he cries. "I should have listened to you."

"Yes, you are. And yes, you should have." I kick Griffin onto his back and smile at the brothers who for the first time, are equal—dickless, beaten, bloody, and bound. "Let the games begin."

I open the cabinet above them and remove the gas mask. "Remember this?" I wave it over their heads. "You put this on and raped us." I slide the mask over my head and walk into the hallway. "Now, it's your turn."

The dildo Benny and Jenny used on me sits clean in his sock drawer. I stare at it and smile. "Ready to play?"

Griffin is by the door when I return. The rope around Benny came undone. I push him back away from the door so I can close it. I slap him, then Benny, in the forehead with the twelve-inch purple silicone dick. "Who needs it first?" My voice muffles behind the mask.

"Please, Odeya, don't do this," Griffin pleads with me.

I gaze at his pained and desperate face. His puffy eyes and pointless tears do little to soften my heart.

Benny stares wide-eyed at the ceiling. They must look at each other for this.

I want them to see how much pain they've caused. They need to see the suffering in each other's eyes to understand the severity of their crimes. I want them to witness their transformations from perpetrator to victim.

I grab the duct tape and sit on Griffin's neck. He bounces beneath me as I tape his eyes open like Benny's, and turn him onto his side, facing his brother.

Griffin shakes his head as I crawl over Benny and position the dildo between his ass cheeks. "No, don't."

"Okay," I smile and tilt my head.

Griffin sighs and relaxes his body.

Did he really think it would be that easy?

I push the purple toy into Benny's asshole.

He screams through his double mouth and tears race from his helpless eyes. It takes more pressure to get the full length inside him than I thought it would, but I guess it makes sense since it's unlubricated and dry as fuck. I pull the dildo out slightly, spit on it, and shove it back in.

There, that's a little better.

The tension on the tape around Griffin's eyes tightens as he tries to close them so he can't see Benny's pain. I keep my eyes on his as I ram it into his brother's ass harder and faster. It gets easier and easier as his anus stretches beyond its natural capacity.

"Please stop," Griffin begs.

In and out I go, ignoring Griffin. I continue my assault until blood covers the entire surface of the dildo and dribbles freely from Benny's torn rectum.

I yank it out and stare at the gaping hole. Blood drains from it, over his ass cheek, and onto the floor. I should sew it shut and feed him a bunch of Jenny soup, but Griffin threw it out.

What a fucking waste.

I bounce the fake cock off the side of Griffin's bare hip, smearing Benny's blood on his skin. "Your turn, Daddy."

"Please…" Griffin weeps. "…don't."

I slither over his body until I'm behind him and whisper in his ear. "You know you want this, baby." I rub his bare, sexy ass gently. "You're going to love it," I say with a smile as I walk my fingers across his buttocks and down to his crevice. "Just wait and see."

His ass cheeks tighten together, and I separate them with my fingers. "Be a good boy and let me in." He tightens them further and scooches forward. I grip the ropes on his thighs with one hand and jiggle the tip of the dildo on the outside of his anus with the other. "All this playing is making me horny. I can't wait to fuck your cock later."

I push the blood-covered dildo with a steady pressure into his anus. It slides in easier thanks to Benny's blood donation.

His screams start quiet then increase in volume as I go in deeper. "Stop! Please, have mercy," Griffin shouts.

I hesitate and take it back to the entrance of his rectum—small amounts of fecal matter escape from his hole. The mask on my face stretches my eyes back as I rest it on my head and furrow my brow. "Mercy? Did you show my sister mercy?" I clench my jaw and ram the full length of it hard into his asshole then bring it back slowly—feces and bits of blood roll across his ass cheek. A staggering scream bursts from his lips. The stench of his bowels releasing gags me.

"Did you show the girls mercy, you nasty mother fucker?" I ram it a second time. Griffin's screams pierce my ears, and they ring like the annoying stand-by channel that my father used to use to set the color on his television for the fifteenth time.

Benny sinks his head further into his shoulders. You'd think he'd appreciate me breaking his dominant and abusive brother down after the way he treated him.

A layer of fresh blood coats the dildo's surface, joining Benny's as I draw it back to me and Griffin screams again.

I need to invest in earplugs. For such a manly man, he sure has a high-pitched scream.

"Did you show Marley mercy when you fucking killed her?" I thrust it violently inside him one final time, jarring the mask off my head, and partially obscuring my view.

His face, red, distraught, and filled with pain, twists away from his brother, trying to hide his traumatized expression. I hold the dildo deep inside his rectum, and grab the duct tape, taping the dildo so it would stay in place.

Griffin rocks himself trying to discharge the foreign object obstructing his shit shaft.

I reach for his jeans, remove his cell phone from his pocket, and place the phone over his face to open it. Once I find Femi's number, I Facetime him.

He answers at once. "Is that you behind the mask, my beautiful Odie?"

I slide the mask on top of my head. "Hello, my pussycat."

"Are you enjoying yourself?" He grins at me.

I turn the camera to face Griffin and Benny making sure their whole bodies enter the frame.

Griffin's eyes widen as Femi waves at him and laughs. "Looks like you have them right where you want them."

I stand and walk across the room, glancing over my shoulder at Griffin as he lifts his head for a brief second and drops it back down.

He's beaten.

I have won.

We have won.

But I'm not finished with him yet.

We are not finished.

Oh, no.

I set the phone down across the room against the wall. "Can you see us?"

"Yes, my love."

I back away from the phone slowly. "Are the girls still with you?"

"They are. They didn't want to leave without you, especially Ari."

I chuckle and stand beside the cabinet. "Are you ready to watch the show?"

Audrey's expressionless face comes into view, blocking Femi. "Is that the third mouse I see next to mouse number two?"

I peer over my shoulder and smile back at her. "I didn't use a carving knife, but this little mouse…" I wave my hand over Griffin's bandaged cock. "…no longer has his metaphorical tail."

She nods her head and smiles wickedly.

Her bright side no longer exists. She only sees the darkness inside her that the brothers created. The once caring nurse is replaced by a formerly caged monster trapped deep inside her by what's considered normal and acceptable in the eyes of society. She's now free, like me, from their cages—from their laws.

From guilt.

We all have a bit of darkness within us but make the conscious decision not to use it.

It's only when someone pushes us, do we cross over the line of what is acceptable.

Griffin and Benny created us—me, people like me, and like them. Some say it's nature versus nurture, but I say it's both. We are naturally born with the propensity for violence, but society and family nurture and choose how we use it or if we use it.

We either stuff it away and take what life gives us and follow the rules or we don't. I choose the latter.

Always have.

Life pushed these girls into the darkness with me.

And now that they're here, they'll never be the same.

Chapter Twenty-Seven
Dinner for One

I came into this bunker hunting for a tasty meal with a side of justice, but I am leaving with something else.

Knowledge.

Seeing these girls and experiencing this with them has taught me that psychological and emotional pain is more damaging than physical. Bruises disappear, scars fade, and for the most part, bodies will heal.

But your mind, your mind once fractured will change who you are for good. You become a shell of your former self—become someone else. These girls may be able to go back to their former lives if they choose, but who will they be? They won't be the college student, or housewives from before.

They're tainted.

I can see it in their eyes when they look at me. They no longer see me as a killer. They see me as a friend. Someone they depend on and trust. If I showed up at their doors before Benny and Griffin kidnapped them, introduced myself honestly, and told them who and what I was, do you think they would have welcomed me into their lives?

Hell, no. Well, maybe Ari.

The point is, I'm a killer, but they don't see me as the villain in this situation. I'm their hero.

Me.

The person who's about to torture and kill their torturers is the hero.

Go figure.

I retrieve a gas canister from the cabinet and stand with one leg on either side of Benny and Griffin. Sliding the mask over my face, I pull the holding pin, releasing the gas.

I can't imagine how it must feel. They scream, each in their way—coughing and gagging while they writhe in pain. Neither can close their eyes to protect their vision. I bring my masked face close to theirs and stare at them, one then the other. "How does the pain feel? Describe it to me." I hover over Griffin.

Snot shoots from his nose onto the mask, blocking my vision on one side. I swipe the mucous with my hands, rub it on his face, and shove the dildo deep inside him while he screams. "You like that, don't you Daddy?"

His whole body shakes as he rocks his body wildly, trying to break free. Benny lies motionless beside him. His wide eyes drip tears but don't move. He's stopped fighting. I press my fingers into his neck and check his pulse. It's weak, but he's alive. Just passed out. I need him awake.

Rising to my feet, I turn on the fan to ventilate the gas from the room.

"Is he dead?"

I jump at the sound of Ari's voice forgetting they were watching me.

"No. He's passed out."

Shiny mucus covers Griffin's face. He takes several shallow breaths and coughs. "Odeya, please just let us go."

I furrow my brow at him. "Let you go? This place..." I gaze around the room. "...is your mausoleum. You're never leaving."

I slide the mask off my face and toss it on the bed frame. My knees pop as I kneel beside Griffin. "So, how does it feel to be a victim?" I scan his body, reach for the dildo, and yank it from his ass, tape and all, ripping a bunch of pubic hair with it. "Or should I say victimized?"

"Fuck you." He grits out through clenched teeth.

He has fang teeth that sit in front of the rest. I never noticed this before. Perhaps if he smiled broadly and more often, I would have.

I strike him across the face with the dildo. It vibrates in my hand as I bonk him in the head with it several more times, bitch slapping him for talking back.

Boing, boing, boing.

Particles of feces and dried blood shed off, floating into his eyes.

Here's a side of pink eye to go with your trauma, Griffy.

"No, Griffin. Fuck you." I strike Benny in the head with it, waking him. "And fuck him too."

Boing.

I stare at the fake penis in my hand. It has a good amount of texture and perfect stiffness to it. I may have to buy one. Mine is true to the real thing but sometimes doesn't feel fully hard enough like a rock-hard cock does. Some dildos are too hard. I might as well be fucking myself with a plastic doll's leg. So cold and stiff.

I've had one that was too life-like before. The fucking thing kept bending when I tried to ram myself. If it was a real man's dick, I may have broken that fucker in half.

Good grief.

Who designs these things anyway? A man?

"Hit them again," Ari yells through the phone's speaker, unlocking my eyes from the purple appendage.

I gaze over my shoulder. "How many times?"

"I don't know. Whatever feels good to you."

I nod my head and turn back to Benny and Griffin. Griffin's eyes widen further as I raise the purple cock over my head and smash it down on his nose, crushing the previously broken cartilage even more.

Blood gushes down the side of his face and his eyes water excessively as he shrieks. I grip the dildo tight in both hands, lean over Benny, and smash it into his double mouth, ripping it open. A throaty howl comes from his bloody mouth that's wider now that I have smacked it open.

I kneel between them and bounce the purple cock off each of their faces one, then the other, back and forth, blood splattering across the room with each blow.

Bong, bong, bong.

Double tap.

Ba-boing.

"It looks like you're playing whack a mole except you're not getting any points or winning a prize." Ari laughs then snorts and laughs even harder.

I stop striking them, stand, and pick up the phone. Ari's glassy eyes reduce to slits as she continues cracking up.

"It's not about prizes or points, Ari," I say without smiling. "It's about humiliation."

The phone muffles and Femi's face appears. "She's pouting."

"Let her."

Griffin's phone pings with an incoming text message, and I read it to myself.

Femi's head bounces in the frame as he walks and talks. "Who is it?"

"Barnes, the old man." I take a deep breath and blow it out as I walk over to Griffin. "Looks like your buddy Barnes wants to know if I'm ready for purchase." I cut the tape securing him to Benny and turn the phone so he could see the text. "Who am I to deny someone the pleasure of my company?"

The phone beeps with every stroke of my thumb as I reply.

'She's ready. I'll even have her prepare a nice meal for your arrival. Come in about an hour. Bring cash, one hundred thousand.'

Three dots appear and then disappear. He's likely trying to object to the price, but I feel like I'm worth at least that much. The three dots appear...

'See you in an hour.'

My mouth twists upward as I stare down at Griffin.

Femi clears his throat. "I know that face. What are you planning?"

"Are you close?"

"Yes, we are about a mile down the road. Why?"

"Ask Ari if she wants to help me prepare a nice dinner for our guest?"

Femi opens his mouth to speak when Ari snatches the phone away. "I'm in."

"Femi, can she borrow your car?"

"Of course." He nods to his bodyguard who fishes the keys out and passes them to Ari.

He turns back to me. "Look how excited she is."

Femi turns the camera so I can see Ari.

She's leaping up and down while crushing Audrey in her grasp.

Audrey holds her at arm's length. "Go."

Ari runs to the car behind Femi, cranks the engine up and floors it. Mud flies up and dots the bodyguard's pristine attire. They shake the sludge from their hands and glare in the direction of the camera. Femi comes back into frame and shrugs his shoulders. "I'll pay for dry cleaning," Femi says to his men with an unapologetic smile.

He stops smiling and eyes me sideways. "Please be careful."

"Always."

I hang up and head to the kitchen space to find a meal to prepare for our incoming guest. Now that I'm having Ari help me, I will have fulfilled my promise to teach her how to cook.

Kinda.

A loud thump comes from behind me. Ari's on her ass at the base of the ladder. She peers through the doorway and smiles at me. "The fucking ladder is slippery." She staggers to her feet. "I think I broke my ass bone." Her right hand kneads her buttocks.

I wave her into the room. "Come on, we have to throw this dinner together in an hour."

"What do you need me to do?" She hobbles towards me still rubbing her butt.

I grab an assortment of ingredients, set them on the counter, and give Ari quick instructions, before grabbing a filet knife from the drawer and walking away.

"Wait. Where are you going?" She steps towards me.

"Stay here. I'm going to get our meat."

"Meat?" She furrows her brow, opens her mouth, and nods. "Ooh, meat." She winks at me. "Can I watch?"

"No." I stroll away then yell over my shoulder. "But you can listen."

Griffin's by the door when I enter, having wormed his way across the floor again, leaving a trail of smeared blood.

I sigh and place my hands on my hips. "Well, I told you to get groceries, and you didn't listen. Now we have a guest coming and no meat." I kick him onto his back. "But you, my dearest Griffin…" I slice the ropes covering his deliciously muscular right thigh. "…you have plenty."

One of the pieces of tape sweats off allowing one of his eyes to move freely. When the free eye closes, he looks like Cyclops. "You can't do this." His voice cracks as he pleads and tries to remove his leg from beneath my grasp.

"I can, and I will." I rub his meaty thigh, massaging it with my hand as I hold it firmly against the floor. "I just need…" The blade slices into him, passing through a tiny layer of subcutaneous fat, a smidge of fascia, and into the main ingredient, muscle. Griffin howls in agony and thrashes about but does little to deter my progress "…I just need a couple of cutlets for dinner."

My tongue sticks out the side of my mouth as I saw through his flesh. His thigh shakes beneath my blood-coated hand. I try and grip it tighter, but my hand keeps slipping. I glare at him. "If you stop wiggling around, this will go faster."

There's so much blood—on him, under him, all over me. It's hard to see what I'm doing now, but I still need one more hunk of meat. I cut blindly into the stained skin about five inches above the first hole and shave off another piece as another round of screaming echoes around the room.

I should have taped his mouth shut before I started.

A painful lesson learned.

I gaze at his angry, distraught face.

Sweat pours down his temples and beads on his forehead. The two slices of meat cover my palm with blood. I wave the five-inch lengths of crude-cut meat before Griffin's face. "Thank you for your kind donation."

He lifts his head slightly and screams with every ounce of strength he has directly in my face. I wipe a dab of his spit from my brow, purse my lips, and smack him across his vile, foul-smelling mouth with one of his leg cutlets, leaving streaks of blood across his face.

His face drops suddenly, and he falls silent. I don't know whether the shock of what's happening to him is finally sinking in, or if the slap across the face with his leg muscle was the last straw. Either way, he's stopped screaming, and I'm thankful for a few seconds of silence.

I grab the doctor's bag, take out several bundles of gauze, and stuff them into his bleeding wounds. "I'll be back shortly to dress those properly. I wouldn't want you to bleed to death."

His silence is short-lived.

I roll my eyes and exit the room as Griffin wails and hollers inaudible words at my back.

Ari smiles when I enter the galley. "Is it Griffin's?"

"Of course. You can't get good meat from Benny's scrawny ass."

She rubs her hands together. "So, what are we making?"

I drop the meat into a clean bowl, set it in the sink, and rinse off the blood. "Beer battered thighs with mashed potatoes and corn." I remove the rinsed meat and drop it on the counter. "Hand me that big metal spoon with the holes in it."

Ari passes me the spoon, and I smack the cutlets in the center multiple times, flattening them out and making them even. "Put some oil in a pan for me."

She spins the frying pan in her hand, drops it on the burner, fills the bottom with oil, and sits on the bed, flicking her fingernails while she waits. "You make me feel safe."

Safe. I, of all people, make her feel safe. I pause with my hand on the handle of the frying pan.

Her hero.

Perhaps her home life was more complicated than she let on. She's tough on the outside but has a tender heart when she lets her guard down. "Come watch."

Ari leaps to her feet and stands beside me. I dangle the breaded protein over the bubbling pan and drop it into the boiling oil. We watch Griffin's thighs cook together. The steam floats above the pan and enters our nostrils.

What a glorious smell.

I hold the fork out to Ari. "Keep an eye on these. I need to finish patching up Griffin's wounds."

Ari nods and takes the utensil from me.

Griffin hasn't moved since I left him. The tape around his eyes no longer holds them open.

I scan the small space, and my eyes fixate on the dried blood on the floor by the bed.

It's mine—the last time he would ever hurt me or anyone else.

My face twists as I glare down at Griffin.

How dare he close his eyes and try to rest.

There is no rest for the wicked, not according to the bible.

Who am I to go against the word of God?

I kick his unmoving legs, and his eyes flutter open.

"Let me die." His voice comes out barely above a whisper.

"I can't do that yet. You need to suffer the way we suffered. The way my sister suffered." I remove the gauze from his leg holes.

"She died instantly. There was no suffering." His eyes look at me in a daze as he chuckles. "I pointed the gun at her head and pulled the trigger."

I dig my thumbs deep into his wounds. He screams at the ceiling. "Fuck you!"

My thumbs dig in deeper. I leer into his eyes.

He wants this.

He wants me to react. He's trying to get me to kill him.

No.

I need more time.

I remove my thumbs, grab more gauze, and stuff it in the holes, using tape to pull the skin together. I pile a bunch more gauze on top and tape it around his leg. "This should stop the bleeding for now." I tear off a piece of duct tape and press it hard over his lips. "I can't have you giving anything away."

I step over him and kneel beside Benny.

What a sad, little man. His face is unrecognizable and who he was before, is just a memory. There's no fight left in him. He can't talk anymore, scream, or react to my torture.

He's nothing but an empty shell of a human, shattered, like an egg on the sidewalk.

I no longer have a use for Benny.

Griffin mumbles through the tape and shakes his head rapidly as I rest the blade of the scalpel against his brother's throat.

I nod my head. "It's time to put this dog down, Griffin. He's suffering."

The blade squishes deep into Benny's neck, puncturing his windpipe and allowing the air stuck inside to escape. His eyes open wider, and his head falls to the side, staring emptily at Griffin. Blood puddles around his neck and drains onto the floor. A small amount escapes his mouth.

My fight with him is over. His death is on Griffin, not me.

Tears plaster Griffin's sobbing face, and the wrinkles in his forehead deepen. I remove the blade slowly, swipe the blood from Benny's throat with my finger, and squat beside Griffin. He screams through his gag, his face red with anger.

I paint a perfect heart on his cheek with his brother's blood. "This is your doing, Griffin," I say calmly, looking deep into his eyes so he can know the truth of it.

"When you killed her, you unleashed me on the world. In a way, I am your creation, and you are my origin story."

Blood from Benny pools beneath him, and Griffin closes his eyes—inaudible words stagger from his lips.

I stand and tower over them. "Look at us now—both condemned to die for what we've done. The only difference is, you're not the one who will take my life." I step over him into the hallway and then turn back around to face him.

"If you would have just walked away from her, Griffin, just let her be and moved on to someone else, I wouldn't even be here, and all your friends and family would still be alive."

His head tilts up high enough for him to fixate his distraught and hopeless eyes on me.

I laugh. His defeated-looking face has me on the edge of hysterics. "I am a plague with no cure, a virus with no vaccine—a deadly army of one. And you…" I point at him. "…you killed the only thing preventing me from ravishing this world. You freed me, Griffin. And for that, I thank you."

A massive toothy grin spreads across my face, nearly closing my eyes as he tries and fails to lift his head—his body too weak to support it.

"I'll be back."

I need to take a quick shower, get all this blood washed off, and put on something sexy for our guest. I search for Ari and find her in the hanging room, swinging on the wires. I shake my head and smile "I'm taking a quick shower. Can you set up a table in here with tablecloth and utensils?"

"Yes. I put the food on a plate and covered it."

"Thank you. You should go stay in the holding room. I'll come grab you when it's over."

"Can't I be your waitress or something? I want to watch."

I shake my head. "I can't risk him grabbing you as a hostage."

Ari puts her head down and swipes the floor with the bottom of her foot. "Fine."

"I can record it for you though."

Her eyes light up. "That'd be awesome." She runs to me and hugs me tightly.

"Alright, alright." I pat her shoulder. "Get this stuff done and get out of here. I only have about fifteen minutes to get ready."

She skips to the utility room and disappears. I pad down to the bathroom and turn the shower on. When I step under the showerhead, rust-colored water washes down the drain. I scrub all the blood from my hair and body, pat myself dry, and hustle to Griffin's room. There is an assortment of dresses in his wardrobe. I grab a short black cocktail dress and shimmy it over my thighs. My hair is a tangled mess from lack of conditioner. Pieces stretch and break off, filling the teeth of the comb. I twist my hair into a bun, securing it with a thick rubber band.

Ari passes me in the hallway as I head for the hanging room to wait. She raises her hand for a high five. "Everything's ready. I even taped a knife to the underside of the table for you, just in case."

I ignore her hand and smile. "Great. Go wait in the holding room."

She nods her head and jogs away from me.

Such a cheerful, spirited girl.

A little too spirited.

I step into the hanging room, sit at the table with my hands on my lap, and smile while I wait in silence.

Chapter Twenty-Eight
White Rabbit

I drum my fingers on the tabletop and roll my eyes.

He's late. It's been an hour and fifteen minutes. Perhaps the exorbitant cost made him reconsider.

I stand and adjust my dress. The scratchy material reddens the skin on my upper thighs. The things I must suffer through for my art. When I get out of this dress, I'm going to burn it, so no one's ever plagued by its uncomfortableness again.

Griffin's phone vibrates on the table. It's Femi.

'Anything?'
'No.'

He sends a heart emoji, and I send one back. I flub my lips. This is ridiculous. I head to the galley, unwrap Mr. Barnes's dinner, and pop it in the microwave. It won't taste as good reheated, but I don't like eating anything cold.

"Hello?" A voice echoes through the hatch opening.

I take his meal from the microwave, hustle back to the table with it, and put the phone on my seat. "Mr. Barnes?" I peer up at him.

He furrows his brow. "Why is this open? Where's Griffin?"

"It's a test. He wanted to show you how ready I am." I adjust my breasts higher in my dress. "Come down, I've made you dinner."

He hesitates and then places his leg on the first ladder rung. His outfit resembles the White Rabbit's—gray pants, a red jacket, and a bowtie. On his head, rests an out-of-place brown leather cowboy hat and leather boots to match, caked with mud. I should kill him now just for wearing such an outfit.

He shifts his bifocals up on his nose as he reaches the floor. A briefcase rests at his side. "Well, don't you look beautiful, young lady?" He strokes my arm with his wrinkly hand.

"Why, thank you." I rub my hands across my abdomen and smooth my dress. "Come and sit. I just warmed your food."

The chair scrapes against the floor. He sits and scoots himself to the table. "Looks good. What is it? Beer-battered fish?"

I smile. "It's beer-battered boneless Griffin thighs."

"Oh, my. Is it a family recipe?" He cuts a piece and stuffs it in his yap.

"No, just Griffin." I rest my elbows on the tables and my chin on my interlaced fingers. "So, how is it?"

"It doesn't taste like chicken, but it's delicious." He takes another bite and moves it around his palate. "What is it, pork?"

"I told you, it's Griffin's thighs."

He scoops up a heap of mashed potatoes. "Fine, don't tell me." His eyes scan the room. "Where's Griffin? I need to pay him." He slurps the potatoes off his fork.

"He's resting."

"Resting?" He dabs his lips with a napkin. "Well, tell him to get out here. I don't have all day, and I want to get you home."

I rest my palm on the back of his hand. "Yeah, about that. What are your plans for me?"

"Well, I know I may look old, but I can still get it up."

I take my hand away and put it under the table. "And what if I don't want that?"

He sits up higher in his seat and furrows his brow. "Well, I don't care what you want. You're my property, and you'll do what I say."

I nod my head and curl my lip. "And if I refuse?"

He seizes my hair and slams my head into the tabletop, holding it there as he whispers. "I don't know what game you're playing here, young lady, but I don't like being tested. There will be no what-ifs or refusals in my home. When I tell you to do something, you don't hesitate, you just do it." He pushes off my head and returns to eating.

You gluttonous fuck.

I make no move to lift my head. I use my fingernails to pick at the tape holding Ari's knife to the table. The rubber band around my bun pulls a wayward hair on my scalp, making it itch. I remove one hand from under the table, use the pad of my finger to scratch my head, and then sit up in my seat. I roll my eyes as he shovels another bite of mashed potatoes into his mouth dropping half of it on the white tablecloth.

"Perhaps you should pay Griffin now so we can get going."

Barnes tosses his napkin on the table and stands. "I think that's for the best." A burp rises in his throat, and he covers his mouth as it escapes. "Excuse me. Compliments to the chef."

I cup the handle of the knife in my palm and rest the blade against the inside of my wrist when I stand. "Right this way." I walk quickly around him and hold the blade in front of me.

He's staring at my ass. My stomach churns at the thought of his wrinkling cock touching me. At his age, he probably ejaculates dust instead of liquid.

Benjamin Button, mother fucker.

I swing my arms behind me and turn around at the gas chamber door. "He's inside."

His knuckles rattle the door.

Inside my head, I tell myself a joke.

Knock, knock...

Who's there?

Dead and dying men...

Dead and dying men who?

Dead and dying men whom you will be joining shortly...

No one responds to his knocking.

He rests his ear against the door. His oversized lobe stretches as he adjusts the positioning of his head and knocks again.

What a fucking idiot.

"Why are you knocking? Just go in." I turn the knob and crack the door.

"I thought I heard something." He grips the briefcase tighter in his hand.

"Yeah, it's Griffin, duh." I cross my arms. "What are you, scared?"

"How dare you? I'm not scared of anything." He huffs through his nose, pushes the door open, and storms inside.

His foot slips in a smeared blood trail and his legs split wide, ripping his pants at the crotch. "What the fuck?"

The long awkward pause that follows brings a pleasant and welcoming smile to my face. If he wasn't scared before, I bet he is now.

Barnes's feet slide out from under him, and he falls sideways on top of Griffin and Benny, dropping the briefcase in a puddle of crimson.

Griffin's head launches to the ceiling, grunting, and growling through the tape, as old man Barnes uses his wounded leg to push himself upright—his feet sliding around in Benny and Griffin's blood.

I giggle as the old man fumbles to gain his footing and stares at the blood covering his hands and the patches on Griffin's legs. "What's this?" He looks up at me, his face paling, and then back at Griffin and Benny with wild eyes. "Who did this?" He covers his mouth and swallows hard. "Was it you?" His eyes focus on mine.

I tilt my head and smile.

He reaches down to the floor slowly and picks up the case filled with money. It springs open, spilling bundles of hundred-dollar bills all over the floor.

I pick up a packet, partly covered in tacky blood, and fan the bills. "Mr. Barnes, I think we are done here."

He raises his hands in front of him. "I don't want any trouble." He shuffles sideways towards the doorway. "I'm just going to leave. You can keep the money." He slides the open briefcase towards me.

I rip the currency strap securing the money and toss the bills in the air. They float and flutter slowly down to the floor.

One lands on old man Barnes's shoulder. He glances at it and slowly turns his head back to me. "Look, I'm just going to go."

I hop forward, landing on a clean spot on the floor.

Barnes backs up into the hallway.

"But wait, you came here for me, remember?" I side-skip onto another clear space.

His lip quivers. "I changed my mind."

I suck my teeth and shake my head. "Now, now, Mr. Barnes, a deal is a deal." I kick the open briefcase hard, striking Barnes in the shin. The rest of the money dumps out by his feet. "Pick it up."

The sole of my foot steps in tacky blood, making a peeling noise when I lift it and take another step. Fear keeps him from moving. I'm within a foot of him now. The rancid smell of mashed potatoes, Griffin thighs, and unbrushed teeth tarnishes the oxygen entering my sinuses. I wrinkle my nose.

"I don't want it. You can keep it." He turns his body slightly in the direction of the galley and points down the hall. "I'm just going to leave."

I sigh heavily and place my hands behind my back, concealing the knife in my grasp. "Well, if you'd like to go, and I'm not coming with you, then at least take your briefcase. I have no use for it."

He glances at the crocodile black leather and nods. "It is a nice briefcase." His eyes brighten. "You can have it. Call it an apology."

"An apology? Oh, that won't be necessary. Please, take it with you." I take a tiny step backward. "You can have it." I stretch out my empty hand, gesturing for him to pick it up.

He bends down slowly, keeping his eyes on me.

Griffin shakes his head rapidly.

He doesn't trust me, and I don't blame him.

Barnes takes his eyes off me, only for a moment, to snap the briefcase closed.

I drop to my knees, and swing the blade under his chin, stabbing him just to the right of his Adam's apple. The knife saws through his neck like a tough piece of steak as I push it in deep while holding his greasy gray hair.

I yank it harshly out of his throat and blood squirts straight out of the hole I created.

He lifts his head to look at me. His eyes, staring at me like the idiot he is, widen to saucers, desperate and betrayed. The briefcase drops from his hand and blood seeps through his fingers as he tries desperately to cover the hole in his neck.

I rest my palm on his elbow, stare deep into his tear-filled eyes, and yank his arm down. Arterial spray warms my face, and I smear it like cover-up.

He collapses on the floor beside Griffin. I stand over him, smiling a sinister smile as he chokes on his last breath.

Warm liquid seeps between my toes as I shuffle through the crimson river and walk to the holding room. Ari's sitting on the bed, staring at a far wall.

"Ari?"

She turns her head slowly in my direction with an expressionless face. Her spirit must have been wondering again.

I smile broadly at her. "Want to come paint with me?"

Ari's face brightens. "Really?"

"Of course. Come on." I nod toward the galley.

I remove a basting brush from the drawer and then search for something else to draw with.

Toothbrush.

I jog to the bathroom and take the toothbrush belonging to Griffin. I swipe the bristles with my fingers.

Perfect.

I hold the basting brush and toothbrush out to Ari. "Choose your instrument."

She grabs the basting brush and smiles. "I like big bristles."

"Let's go paint some masterpieces." I twist my body away from her, and we waltz down the hallway to the gas chamber.

Ari stops in the doorway. Her mouth drops open with a half-hearted smile and her eyes lock on Griffin. "Damn, Griffin. You look like shit."

Griffin's eyes sag with fatigue—growing tired, losing strength, dying. We must work quickly.

Ari slips sideways on her way to a blank wall, nearly falling on Barnes. "Odie, you made a mess."

"Jealous?" I glance at her over my shoulder as the smooth wall receives the first bloody stroke of my makeshift paintbrush.

"Kinda. I could have helped, you know." Her painting instrument staggers over a nail in the wall.

I jam Griffin's toothbrush into Benny's neck, and swirl it around, coating the bristles evenly.

Griffin stifles a cry in his throat—tears glisten in his ear canal.

I wink at him and continue painting.

On the other side of the room, Ari paints a massive head of a dog and writes, 'Benny's Bitch, Jenny' over it in Barnes's blood.

I chuckle to myself and finish my artwork. A silhouette of a naked woman with wings. Her hand rests on top of my red-painted head. The toothbrush falls out of my grasp. I use the small amount of wet blood on my fingers to handwrite the words I wish I could hear from my sister. 'I forgive you.'

My pointer finger sticks to the wall when adding the period after 'you' and stretches the skin on my fingertip slightly as I force it off the surface.

Ari stands beside me and takes my hand in hers—our bloody hands like pieces of tape adhering to each other.

She squeezes my hand. "You have nothing to be forgiven for."

I glance at Griffin and lock eyes with Ari. "Time for you to go."

"What about you?" She tightens her grip.

I peel her fingers off. "I'll be up shortly. There's one more thing I have to do. Besides, I need you to pick up Femi."

She drops her hands and walks slowly to the door.

I've noticed that despite her strong personality, she pouts when she doesn't get instant gratification or something she wants. Redirecting her mood takes little more than mentioning explosives, and she lights up like fireworks bursting in the night sky.

"Ari?" My voice comes out happy and welcoming.

She turns and smirks at me. "Yeah?"

Flakes of dried blood shed off onto the floor as I swipe my palms together. "Have the concoction ready to blow this bitch to the surface."

"Hell, yeah. That's what I'm talking about."

Griffin moans on the floor by my feet.

"What are you going to do with him?" Ari steps on his stomach.

I place my hands on my hips and exhale an exaggerated sigh. "I'm going to fuck his cock and cum on his face."

Ari stares at the place his dick used to be. "Is that like a metaphor or..."

I grab her by the shoulders, turn her around, and lead her out of the room. "You should get going. I'll be up shortly."

She disappears around the corner. I bend over, pick up the old man's hat, and brush off the debris and smears of blood. I place it on my head and smile at Griffin. "It's just us now. Whatever will we do?"

He says nothing. His eyes open and close, but he's barely coherent. I stroll down the hall and whip open the freezer door. Griffin's frosted cock glistens in the frozen space. I lift it by its wooden handle and caress my exhausted face with it. In my head, I hum *Old Time Rock and Roll.*

I run down the hallway into the gas room and slide in the blood across the floor like Tom Cruise in Risky Business. Griffin's dick is my microphone. The frozen dick bumps my lip, and I get stuck like Flick in The Christmas Story. I peel my mouth away, leaving a small amount of flesh on the makeshift microphone.

My eyes cross as I focus on the little crystals starting to melt on my man-made dildo.

It's time for us to get acquainted.

I straddle Griffin's body, tip my hat, and stuff his cold cock inside of me. "Oh, yes, daddy, fuck your cowgirl."

Griffin's brows furrow. "Psycho." The words stagger out of his mouth barely above a whisper.

Psycho? Me?

The nerve.

I leap away from him, using his face to push myself to a stand and gallop around the small room, riding his dick like a stick horse. "Oh, yeah. Fuck yeah. Giddy up, you mother fucking stallion."

My legs take me into the hallway and down to the bathroom where I catch a glimpse of myself in the mirror. What a hot mess I have become—rusty dried blood covers nearly every inch of me, my hair in shambles, perfect skin scarred for life, a wooden skewer dangling from my pussy hole.

But my face tells an entirely different story. Although I'm not smiling it looks happy, relieved, and brighter despite smudges of blood here and there. Perhaps because the end of Griffin is near. The wheels of justice finally catching up to him.

My wheels.

I rotate his cock inside me, and a pocket of air burps out.

Oh, my. Here comes the prickling.

I hustle down the hallway back to Griffin and collapse just inside the doorway.

This one's going to be a gusher.

I crawl on my hands and knees towards Griffin. "Oh, Griffin, your cock's going to make me cum." I mount his body, place my ass under his chin, and slide his melting dick out of me. He flexes his jaw down on my pussy and tries using it to push me away, but it only arouses me more.

My fingers slide on either side of my labia and pinch my lips between them. I rotate them around and around, grinding my pussy juices on his chin.

"It's coming. Oh my God. It's coming hard. Fuuuuuuuuuuuck baby, yes." I bounce my hips, and he closes his eyes as my juices squirt all over his face.

I grab his cheekbones, crushing them in my grasp. "Open your fucking mouth."

Griffin clenches his jaw refusing to drink my fountain of youth.

I leap to my feet and cross the room. The bloody handle of the scalpel sticks to my fingers.

I straddle him. "Open your mouth."

He shakes his head and purses his lips.

Stubborn fucker.

The blade sinks deep into his rotator cuff and stops at the clavicle. I twist the instrument and holler at him. "Open."

His teeth grind together. He growls and keeps his mouth shut, stifling a scream.

"Open you're fucking mouth."

I wiggle and yank the scalpel from his joint and slice him deep across the ribs.

Muffling screams vibrate in his throat.

Fuck this.

I stab his chest, not deep, in multiple locations. "Connect the dots, la, la, la."

Stab, stab, stab.

Poke, poke, poke.

Dot, dot, dot.

The blade drags from one bloody dot to the next, drawing a massive 'O' on his chest. "Connect the dots, la, la, la…"

I move down to his stomach, rest the blade on his belly button, and slice it from his belly button down between his legs, working my way to his anal dot.

Griffin's mouth flies open with a desperate bellowing scream for mercy. "Noooooo…"

I don't do mercy.

The blade tears his asshole like butter as I connect my final dot.

I seize his softening dick when his mouth stretches open—his final blood-curdling scream filtering out as I ram his previously attached weapon into his mouth.

He gags and tries to push it out with his tongue. I place the hat on my head on his face and pound my fist against the end of the stick through the hat.

I repeatedly strike. Even after he stops moving.

Stop, Odie. My sister's voice chimes inside my head.

I hold my hands above my head and slam them down on the now bloody cowboy hat like a sledgehammer.

Wham.

The memory of her funeral flashes before my eyes, blinding me to anything else.

Wham.

My brain begs for me to stop, but I can't. My upper extremities are set to autopilot on a plane, and I'm just along for the ride.

Wham.

The motionless corpse offers no reply as I scream, "Why? Why did you pick her?" I grip Griffin's partially decapitated and flattened skull, and shake it violently, partially knocking the hat off of it. "I fucking hate you. I hate you."

I toss his mangled head away from me, open my mouth, and shriek.

Griffin's dead, but I find myself wishing he would come back to life so I could kill him over and over again.

I punch his blood-stained chest.

He's dead, Odie. My sister whispers in my ear.

My legs barely hold me up as I stand, one leg on either side of Griffin's body—toes coated in bodily fluids. I steady myself on my left foot and stomp Griffin's abdomen with my right.

If only I had on a pair of boots. I'd "Boot Scootin' Boogie" all over this mother fucker's corpse until the wee hours of the evening.

I stand beside him, raise my heel, and stomp hard on his ribcage. The cartilage crunches and partially collapses.

I stomp them a second time and murmur the lyrics. "Heel toe, dosey doe…"

A throat clears behind me.

"Heel toe, dosey…" I raise my foot and purse my tremoring lips.

"Odie, he's dead."

My heel strikes a third time, ignoring Femi.

I raise my foot a fourth time, making small circles above Griffin's semi-mushed body as it hovers. "Heel-toe…" My words elevate and catch in my throat. "…dosey dooooe," I scream at the body before me.

With every raise and lower of my foot, his body flattens closer to the floor.

I don't know if I can stop. It feels almost like all the energy I have left in me runs straight into my leg providing me with the force I need to flatten Griffin's body into a pancake.

Do I need to stop? Can I do this every day until he's nothing more than a pile of ash?

The pressure in my head rises from tolerable to a pounding nuisance as my pulse skyrockets to dangerous levels.

This needs to end, but if I stop, where does that leave me? I started this journey to get justice for my sister while simultaneously satisfying my urge for a most unusual preference in meats.

Do I still need an excuse to continue?

Can't I just keep hunting people like him for others like a two-for-one special?

I can get paid to kill the perverts and eat their meat too if the quality is desirable.

My legs are getting tired, but I'm still stomping.

"Odie?"

Femi's voice seems so far away, yet I know he's in the same room.

My stomping slows to a step on and off but doesn't cease.

A gently placed palm lands softly on my shoulder.

I stop moving and cover the back of Femi's hand on my shoulder with mine.

His hand slides slowly from beneath mine. And without another word, he wraps his arms around my blood-coated body from behind, holds me tight, and brings my outburst to a quiet and peaceful close.

Chapter Twenty-Nine
Commitments

I don't know how long he plans to hold me for. Perhaps until my heartbeat slows to a normal sinus rhythm. I turn to him, covered in Griffin and Mr. Barnes's blood, cum draining down my leg, and my pussy twitches.

He's so fucking hot.

I still remember the day we met at that doomsday shop. I didn't intend on using him to help me find and kill them. It just kind of happened. We had an instant and undeniable connection. I could tell him anything, and he wasn't surprised. It was almost like he'd seen and heard everything I said to him before. Most men would have freaked if you told them you're a cannibalistic serial killer, but not Femi.

His response to me was, "*I like exotic meats as well.*"

Cupid shot me right in the vagina with his arrow as soon as those words spilled from Femi's lips.

Meeting him changed a few things, it changed me.

I never relied on anyone for help before. But I must admit, this whole plan would have been much harder without him. If it weren't for him, this may never have been possible.

I want him.

I want him here and now.

He senses my desire, leans down, and plunges his tongue far into my mouth.

My stomach flutters as he reaches his hand down and stimulates my pussy lips with his thumb, arousing me— another reason I allow him to live.

I take my mouth away from his and whisper in his ear in a breathy voice. "Eat me."

My body leaves the floor and lands hard on the bloody mattress. I grip his black silky hair as he rams his tongue inside me. He sucks my lips like a gourmet lollipop as I cum into his mouth.

His zipper digs into my bare flesh as he rips it down and pulls out his stiff cock, jamming it inside of me. His arms hook under each of my legs, sliding them over his shoulders and stretching them out of their normal anatomical proportions.

He thrusts into me over and over, panting like a rabid dog. "I fucking love you, Odie."

I know what he wants. He wants me to say, 'I love you too,' but we just aren't there yet.

I fish my hands under his shirt and dig my nails into his spine, marking my territory. "Fuck me harder."

He grips the hair on either side of my head and rams me, retreats, and rams me again, harder and faster until we rupture together—our time apart making things quick, efficient, and satisfyingly short.

My breathing becomes shallow as he collapses on me, crushing my body beneath his frame. He rests his face on the side of mine.

Benny's discolored corpse rests beside us.

We pant and stare at his empty eyes.

I feel his face, smiling against mine. Both are satisfied, not only for the orgasms we both just achieved, but for this part of our lives to be over.

"Marry me?" His breathy words shift the skin on my face.

Air catches in my lungs.

What an unexpected turn of events. I hope he doesn't think if we get married, I won't one day break down and eat him for dinner.

I stroke his thigh with my pointer.

So…muscular.

I lick my lips.

Like a well-packed filet mignon tightly wrapped in cellophane, they wait for me to take them home and toss them on the grill.

I wish he didn't please me so much in other ways. He'd make a fantastic meat bundle—filling my freezer like a delivery of Omaha Steaks.

But the way he touches me, understands me, and provides me with the resources I need to continue my work holds me back. He serves a purpose and that's what keeps him safe.

How lucky for him.

I turn my head forcing him to lift his. His eyes, dark and sultry, gaze deep into my soul.

He's serious.

He wants to marry me.

What a brave man.

I stroke the side of his face with my palm. "You know I may not have a lot of time left."

He moves a lock of hair that fell from my bun and curls it around my ear. "Is that a, yes?"

"It is."

"Good." He reaches for his pants and pulls a ring box from the front right pocket. "If you didn't say yes, I would have to give this to Ari."

I smack him in the chest.

He laughs, opens the box, and removes a multi-carat, trilliant-cut diamond ring.

I present my left ring finger to him.

He slides it over my knuckle and then kisses my hand. "I love you, but…"

"But what?" I sit up on my elbows.

"…we need to get out of here. It's starting to smell like rotting corpses." He waves his hand in front of his face.

I wrinkle my nose. "More like spoiled meat. Such a shame."

He climbs off me and stands. "Come on. Let's find you some clean clothes."

"Found some." Ari's voice startles us both.

"Ari, how long have you been standing in the hallway?" Femi hikes up his pants and zips his fly.

"Long enough to know that I better be your first choice as maid of honor." She smiles wickedly and leans against the door frame, holding pink clothes. "And to confidently say you two should record a porno."

"A porno?" Femi chuckles and looks at me. "I don't think that's a good idea."

I grimace and raise my eyebrows. "Probably not, but we could always wear masks."

Snot launches from Ari's nose. "You could wear Benny and Griffin's masks." She wipes her face on her sleeve as she continues laughing.

What a twisted and fantastic idea.

Ari furrows her brow, bends down, and lifts the cowboy hat partially covering Griffin's face. "Is that his dick in his mouth?"

"It is." I step around her, take the clothes, and head for the bathroom.

"I guess that's what the phrase, 'eat a cock' really means," she says to my back as I walk away.

She's crazy but in a different way. Ari's more like funny crazy than psycho crazy.

The sweatpants and shirt Ari found must have been Jenny's. I don't see them belonging to anyone else. None of the girls, including me, have any of our clothes from before. Perhaps, because they did to them what they did to me when I arrived here and cut them off. Jenny received preferential treatment because of Benny.

I picture Jenny in it the day they picked her up. I bet she looked like a Barbie girl—head to toe in pink, hair in a ponytail, boobs bouncing up and down as she jogs down the road or wherever the hell they kidnapped her from. Benny must have had some sick Barbie fetish. It's probably why the outfit is still intact. He probably beat his dick off while she wore it and called him Ken.

I drop the outfit on the ground and step into the shower.

As blood washes down the drain, I think about all the other women and children trafficked and trapped elsewhere in places like this—scared, afraid, hopeless. Sold from one person to the next until nothing remains of them but an empty shell.

They are my reason—my excuse to continue killing, and I'm going to use it.

I step out of the shower where Femi's waiting with a towel. The scratchy material exfoliates my skin, making swoosh noises as he makes his way down to my feet, dabbing them dry. He kneels in front of me, holding Jenny's sweatpants open and keeping his eyes on me. I slide my battered and bruised limbs into the pantlegs, one then the other, and hike them up to my waist. I take the sweatshirt from his grasp and hold it to my nose. It has a slight scent of Griffin, and I may never wash it. He must have been the last person to touch it.

What a fitting souvenir. When I feel nostalgic, I can take the sweatshirt, inhale its scent, and reminisce about this very day.

Femi grips my hair trapped under the shirt, pulls it over my shoulder, and straightens the hood. "Ready?"

He takes my hand, but something's missing. There's a sudden emptiness there that wasn't there before. My body doesn't react the same to his touch.

"What's wrong?" He pulls me into him.

I don't need to explain myself. It's not like he has any say in what happens next, but I want to give him the respect he deserves by telling him the truth and being honest. "I'm not going back with you. Not yet anyway."

He takes his hands away from me and plunges them into his pockets. "What do you mean, not yet?"

"You know, as well as I do, that this place isn't the only one out there." I turn away from him and walk towards the galley.

He grabs my arm and spins me around to face him. "Odie. I think you and I both know it's not just about the other potential victims that may be out there."

I glare at the hand gripping me and flash a devious smile up at his furrowed brows. "Of course it is. What else would it be about?"

His hand falls away from me and I continue to the galley without him.

Ari smiles when she sees me. "Did he tell you?"

I turn and wait for Femi to appear from the hallway. "Tell me what?"

Ari leaps from the chair and drums her fingers on the counter next to a small Igloo cooler. "Can I show her?" she asks Femi, barely able to contain her excitement.

He lets out a breathy laugh. "Go ahead."

Her hands work quickly to depress the buttons on the side of the cooler lid. She whips it open, pulls out a plastic one-gallon freezer bag, and shakes it. "We got doggie bags. Well, technically it's leftover Griffin meat. As soon as you got in the shower, I asked Femi if we could save any of it for you. I know you've been stalking those legs and don't like good meat to go to waste. So, I figured you'd like a to-go order."

I take the bag from her grasp. The slices are thin cutlets perfect for a lovely stir fry. I turn to Femi and give him a genuine smile. "Thank you for this."

He folds his arms around me and shakes his head. "Don't thank me. It was all Ari's doing. She cut the slices off and everything. She's a natural butcher."

"No, shit," I say in an elevated voice.

"No, shit." Femi smiles down at me and kisses my forehead.

Who would have thought Ari could process a corpse better than I can?

We glance back at Ari who's now wearing the devil mask and holding a machete.

I stifle a laugh and stroll over to her. "What the hell are you doing?"

She raises her weapon up and down and yells. "Off with their heads. Off with their heads. Off with their heads." The mask scrapes against her face as she lifts it, stretching the skin around her eyes making her look like a deranged Pokémon.

I can't trade her, so I guess I will use her for battle just like the game.

"Ari..." I shift the mask on her head, returning her face to normal. "...it's time to blow this bitch up."

A joker-like smile spreads across her face as she walks around me, into the hanging room, and pauses at the bottom of the steps. "Hey, Odie?"

I peer through the hanging room doorway. "Yes?"

"I'm going to make a big bomb," she smiles broadly.

"Good. Just don't drop it in here before we're out."

She cackles at the ceiling, starts climbing the ladder, and stops halfway. As her eyes scan the room, her face changes from light, airy, and cheerful, to bitter and angry. "A really big fucking bomb," she reiterates before disappearing through the exit.

I stand there—not moving or speaking, taking in the room much like Ari did.

Femi rests his hand on my lower back. "What is it?"

My mind wanders to the few short months we spent together in his ten thousand square foot oceanfront mansion learning each other's deepest and darkest secrets. It was a nice hiatus from all the killing and interrogating. But he knew I couldn't stay there forever and not finish what I started.

The day I left, we had a plan, but we also knew anything could go wrong. So, before I walked away from him, he held me tightly in his arms and told me he loved me for the first, and perhaps the last, time.

I didn't say it back.

I'm such a dick.

It's not that I don't love him. I'm just not in love with him. To be in love means something much deeper.

Deeper than the desire to hack off his limbs and slap them on a spit roaster over a campfire like a pig roast— handle cranking, round and around, barbeque sauce poured on from a plastic Kool-Aid pitcher.

Mmm, barbeque. I can almost smell it.

I gaze down at his legs and my mouth waters.

Fuck.

"Femi, I need a minute." I take a step away from him.

His lashes flicker and his mouth slightly parts. "You want to eat me, don't you?"

I smile and tell him the truth as always. "Yes."

He raises the cooler and shakes it between us. "Well, I'm glad we have this." He kisses the side of my face. "I'll make you something delicious for dinner."

It's nice to have someone else cook for me for a change. Sometimes his meals taste better, but I think it's because I didn't have to prepare it.

His shoes scuff the floor by the ladder. A ray of sun casts through the opening. He squints and closes one eye. Dust particles float in the rays as he rests his designer leather shoe on the first ladder rung. "Take all the time you need."

I think what he meant to say was to stay down here until the desire to eat him passes. I laugh internally at my thoughts.

You're safe.

For now…

Chapter Thirty
Hollow

The hanging room feels different. I curl my toes into the blood-stained concrete and sigh. This is no longer a place where tortured women hang, or the men who bid on them sip wine and make their selections.

It's just a room.

A room with random wires dangling from the ceiling waiting for the catch of the day that will never come.

I place my hand on the ladder rung and gaze at the overcast sky above. A single drop of rain lands on my cheek. I know it's just rain, but it's so much more than that. It's the feeling of freedom moistening my flesh. I haven't seen the sun or the sky in, well, I don't know how long it's been.

My legs wobble slightly as I ascend the metallic escape route and emerge on the earth's surface just as a rain cloud ruptures. I raise my arms out to my sides and spin slowly in a circle. I'm already clean, but this is a different kind of shower—natural, refreshing, and sent by the heavens to wash away the bullshit I just went through and carry back to the hell I just climbed out of.

I drop to my knees and squeeze the soggy grass in my hands, turning them green as I rip a clump from the dirt and smell its muddy roots. The hole from which the greenery came fills rapidly with water. I press the turf back into its rightful place and swipe the debris from my hands.

It will survive. It will reconnect to the soil and grow; despite the trauma I just caused it by tearing it from its foundation.

People are like that too. Not everyone, but a good amount.

Ari approaches the hole with a backpack slung over her shoulder. The weight of the bag presses down on her skin, leaving a red spot.

She's a survivor.

A crazy, hysterical, kind-hearted, and dangerous survivor.

I take the bag from her and almost drop it on the ground.

Fucking thing must weigh thirty pounds.

"Jesus Christ, Ari. What the hell is in this?"

She places her foot inside the portal into the bunker and takes a few steps down. "Oh, just a few chemicals, some experimental things I've been wanting to try. Femi's men collected them for me."

I hold the bag away from her outstretched hand. "And what kind of reaction should we expect out of these experiments?"

She pushes off a ladder rung, snatches the bag from me, and pulls it inside the opening. "How the hell should I know? That's why it's called an experiment."

I raise my eyebrow. "Well, I hope you only blow up this bunker and not the entire property, taking us with it."

She opens her mouth, closes it, and sighs. "We should be alright."

"Should be?" I place my fists on my hips.

"You might want to tell Femi to back up." She takes a few more steps down.

"Ari?" I kneel and peer into the hole as she places her foot on the concrete. "How far back?"

A sinister smile spreads across her face.

"Oh, for fuck's sake, Ari."

"You know for a cannibalistic serial killer; you worry too much." She twists away from the ladder and disappears.

"Worry? Me? Ari?"

And she's gone. I can't stop her now. Trying to keep her from what she's about to do is like trying to keep me from eating stir-fried Griffin cutlets later this evening.

She doesn't even know what her concoction is going to do. She may blow us and the entire state into a new location on the fucking map.

Femi waits for us in the back seat of his car. His distorted image shifts behind the rain-coated glass. I wave my hands at him, signaling for him to move back.

His driver moves the vehicle backward a few feet.

I swoop my hands at him again.

He moves back a little more.

The rain slows to a trickle. I squeeze the moisture from my sopping hoodie and shake my dripping locks.

So much for keeping the smell of Griffin on it.

A gas mask flies over my head and lands behind me. I turn around and stare at it. My stomach quivers at the memory of my time with Griffin in the gas chamber.

Fucking loser.

He could have done without the gas part. I cough and clear my throat, temporarily unable to breathe—trapped in that gas-filled room all over again.

I inhale the clean scent of freshly washed leaves and forest.

Close your eyes, breathe in deep, stagger a slow breath out…and repeat.

Ari's head, wearing the devil mask, surfaces from below startling me when I open my eyes. She stumbles to the surface, grabs my hands, and pulls me to my feet.

She swipes the gas mask from the ground, wipes off some loose blades of grass, and passes it to me. "Here, this should protect your face and eyes." Her voice muffles through the mask.

I glance at her and swallow hard. "Protect my face?"

"Should, not would." She points at me. "Don't forget I said that."

I slide the mask hesitantly over my face.

She's going to kill us all.

In my head, The Purge siren blares.

I tighten the mask on my face.

Ari strikes a match and drops it in the opening.

Femi's driver backs the car up a few more feet. I don't blame him. It's a nice hunter-green Maserati.

Nothing's happening.

Ari raises her wrist to her face and checks her imaginary watch. The devil mask on her face shifts up and down as she shows me the fake time on her non-existent watch.

Any minute now.

My stomach churns and I start feeling ill. "Ari, I think we should move away from the h—" I didn't get to finish my sentence.

A whooshing sound followed by a massive explosion rocks us off our feet. I land hard on my ass, my teeth sinking deep into my tongue, making it bleed. We rip the masks away from our shocked faces and pant heavily at each other with massive smiles while covering our ringing eardrums.

"That was freaking awesome," Ari shouts leaping to her feet.

Her face drops as the ground cracks around us, and a chunk of earth nearby sinks several feet.

"Oh, shit." I jump to my feet and stare at her. "Is that it? Is it done?"

She rubs her palms on her outer thighs. "I don't think so."

"What do you mean you don't think so?" I grip the gas mask in my hand tighter and stand in front of her.

She wrinkles her nose and grimaces. "Well, it definitely should have been bigger." Her disappointed eyes lock on the devil mask sitting on the ground by the sinkhole. "Maybe, it's because I put the one in the oven, and it's just not heated up to temperature yet?"

I place my hand on Ari's elbow. "Ari, did you put a bomb in the oven?"

She nods. "I set it to self-clean because I know that gets the hottest."

"We should run," I say, pulling her towards the car. "Like, right now."

I turn and sprint towards the car, and she runs behind me holding the devil mask against her face.

My fingertip just touches a raindrop on the door handle when another explosion vibrates the entire car, creating a sinkhole a few feet away. I stick my finger in my ear and shake the canal trying to hear anything, but only a buzzing sound rings through it.

The door flies open, and Femi waves at us wildly. "Get in."

I dive inside, head first, landing partly on Femi's lap. Ari crashes into my hip and slams the back door shut.

The driver stomps on the gas, launching us backward in reverse.

Another explosion sends the bunker ladder high into the air, just missing a crow. Flames and smoke billow from cracks and sunken earth in multiple locations.

Femi and I both stare blankly at Ari.

She shrugs her shoulders and shouts. "What? I told you it was going to be big."

Femi winces. Ari doesn't realize how loud she's talking, still partially deaf from the explosion. She leans her head against the window, fogging the glass with her breath, and watches the fire and smoke grow as we drive away.

I drop my head against the headrest and close my eyes.

My eyes flicker open as Ari flicks a muddy particle off my leg with a smile. Femi puts his arm around my back and taps her shoulder. "You did good, kid."

"I know." She smiles and gazes out the back window, watching the smoke float into the sky and join the clouds.

The fine hairs in Femi's nose shift as he laughs through it, and turns back to the window, watching the trees fly by.

I stare through the windshield, eyeing the road ahead. The bodyguard makes eye contact with me and smiles with his eyes. I chuckle and smile out of the corner of my mouth. He knows I'd never eat him.

He's too skinny.

We discuss it all the time when I tell him he needs to bulk up.

He's no dummy. His chicken legs and meatless ribs make him nothing more than an unappetizing cracker.

Not worth my time.

Gravel kicks up from the small hotel parking lot as we pull in front of our rooms.

A firetruck screams by. No doubt heading to the place we just left from. The motel room door in front of the car opens. Gina emerges and leans on the frame with her arms crossed. Audrey joins her, holding her upper arm with the opposite hand and rubbing the chills from her skin.

The twins wedge themselves between Audrey and Gina and come to the car to greet us. Their compliance kept them from suffering so much damage.

Eve holds her hand out to Ari and helps her from the car. She nods and smiles at the black smoke in the air behind her. "Was that you?"

Ari looks over her shoulder and sighs. "Yep, that was me."

"Anything left of the place?" Leah leans on the window frame and peers inside at me.

"Just these." I pass my gas mask to her and pick up the devil mask from the floor of the car where Ari left it.

She takes them both from me and hands the devil mask to Eve.

They stare at each mask with a similar blank expression and glance at each other.

"Are you thinking what I'm thinking?" Eve asks her sister.

Leah sighs heavily and nods. "Garbage," they say simultaneously.

The twins hold each other's hands, carry the masks across the parking lot to the blue dumpster, and spike them over its rusty edge.

Femi climbs out of the car after me, and we lean against the back of the car, waiting for them to come back.

The twins swing their joined hands and smile at each other as they stroll back to us. They're going to be okay.

Two state trooper vehicles speed by, lights and sirens flashing and screaming. I peer over my shoulder. Ari's talking with her hands as she tells the girls what happened at the bunker after they left.

She talks a lot and has an overwhelming need for attention.

When you're a killer, drawing attention to yourself is never desirable.

Audrey glances at me and gives me a half-hearted smile. She threatened to kill me once. Sure, she was caught up in the heat of the moment after realizing she ate the Jenny stew, but still. What if her trauma causes her to turn on me?

In my head, I picture the twins sitting on a couch before a psychiatrist discussing what they went through—discussing me.

They are all liabilities, and I don't know how much time I have left. My condition has already far surpassed its typical life expectancy. Time is a precious commodity, and I can't afford to lose it.

Femi pats my ass, shifting me out of his way, and unlocks the trunk. He removes the red cooler. "Come on my love, we have some grilling to do."

"Stir fry," I say over my shoulder as he walks toward our room entrance.

Ari comes up behind me and loops her arm around mine. "Come on, let's get cooking them tenderloins."

"They're cutlets, and you go ahead. I'll be right there."

She shrugs and skips into my room.

I need to leave, and soon.

Doc stands in the doorway of the room next to ours, watching me. I give her a subtle nod, step on the sidewalk by my room, and sit in the outdoor chair. The shower sputters on in our room. I peek inside and catch a glimpse of Femi's tight muscular ass as his towel falls away when he enters the bathroom.

Nom. Nom.

I could slice off an entire cheek and toss it in my crockpot.

Mmm…rump roast.

"You, okay?" Doc asks, leaning against the wall beside me distracting me from my fantasy. "Want me to look over your injuries?"

"No, you've done enough." I smile over my shoulder at her. "I'm just thinking."

She steps closer, her minty breath floats into my sinuses. "About?"

I ignore the question and focus on a giraffe-shaped cloud in the sky.

She stands in front of me, and crosses her arms, blocking my view. "Thinking about what?"

"Everything."

Chapter Thirty-One
Come What May

When faced with the truth of what lies ahead, sometimes you need to make decisions that others may not agree with or understand. I was premature in telling Ari she could stay with me—agreeing without thinking.

Femi eyes me as he tends the grill. I smile at him and shake my head at Ari, who's waiting for a second helping of corn.

A plate slides in my lap, and Audrey smirks at me. "I brought you some stir fry."

Barbeque stir fry is usually one of my favorites, but my stomach is in knots. Too many people know who I am and what I've done. I glance at Ari—what we've done.

The wind shifts, blowing leaves and dust across the parking lot, carrying smoke from the fire with it. My eyes water. Audrey scurries down the sidewalk and disappears into the room she shares with Ari.

I gaze down at the twins leaning against the building. They squint their eyes and duck inside, retreating from the pollution tarnishing our barbeque-scented air.

One by one, the men join them.

Femi closes the grill and holds his hand out to me. "Come on. Let's get inside."

He holds me from behind inside the doorway, and we watch the storm intensify.

The clouds blacken out the sun and a plastic chair tumbles across the parking lot. I stretch my neck out of our room and peer down the sidewalk.

Ari grins at the sky with her hands raised in the air.

"Get inside," I yell down to her.

She waves at me and dances in a circle.

A pea-sized piece of hail bounces off the sidewalk by my feet.

"Ouch." Ari rubs her head and grimaces.

Another chunk of hail falls, striking the side of her cheek, and reddening it at once.

Audrey grabs her around the waist and pulls her into their room.

The hail comes down faster and in large amounts, coating the lot and sidewalk. The sound of it, a cross between a crackling campfire and crinkling paper.

"Do you think she'll learn to listen?" Femi asks, kissing the side of my neck.

I sigh heavily and rub Femi's arm that's resting against my chest. "I don't know."

The storm ends just as quickly as it started—going from hail to rain, to sprinkles in a matter of minutes. Tiny raindrops shimmer in the rays of sunshine beaming across the parking lot.

I pat Femi's hand on my stomach. "Time to go."

He spins me around to face him and holds me against his chest. "Where?"

I smile at his inquisitive face. "Out of this moldy-smelling room."

The soft touch of his fingertips dragging across my forehead sends chills down my neck. "And then?"

"I have to work some things out." I move from between his arms and step into the parking lot; the hail crunching beneath my feet. I use my thumb to spin the ring on my left finger.

Why the fuck did I say yes?

He walks towards me, hands in his pockets, and smirks. "Odie, we don't have to get married right away. Things with us happened so fast. I don't care whether it's a year from now or ten years, I can wait." He removes his right hand from his pocket, holds my left hand, and covers the diamond. "It's just a ring. It's not a binding contract."

I take his hand off mine and untwist the ring from my finger. "I have to go. You hang on to this." I place the ring in his open palm.

"Odie, what are you doing?" He reaches for me.

I step farther away from him. "I'm sorry."

Ari steps from her room and shields her eyes from the sun. "Are we leaving?"

I tilt my head at Femi, ignoring her question. "Take care of them, will you?"

He nods his head and swipes his face with his palm. "Don't do this, Odie. It will break her heart."

"They're safer with you." I place my hand on the door handle of one of his convoy SUVs. "I'll leave this at the airport with the keys in the glovebox. You can pick it up later."

Ari knocks on Leah and Eve's door in the background.

I climb into the vehicle and adjust the seat.

Femi grabs the steering wheel. "What about Doc? You need her to check the places you can't see."

Doc steps out of her room and smiles through the windshield at me. I smile back and give her a finger wave. "Who do you think packed the vehicle for me while you were in the shower?"

Femi looks in the back seat at the black leather briefcase and duffle bag Doc placed there for me and sighs. "How long?"

"As long as it takes."

"Fuck, Odie." He squeezes the windowsill with both hands.

I shift the SUV into reverse. "Don't worry. I'll stay in touch." I glance down at his hands still holding the side of the vehicle. "Move please."

"We were supposed to be doing this together."

I take my hand off the wheel and place it on his. "Come here." He leans in close, and I kiss his lips tenderly. "I love you too."

His hands fall away from the vehicle, shocked at hearing the words finally coming from my lips.

Did I mean it?

Okay, maybe not. But he let go, and I didn't want to have to run him over, so I call that a win.

I press the gas and back out of the parking space. He smiles and nods at me through the window as I straighten the vehicle and shift it into drive.

I hit the gas and slam on the brakes. "Jesus Christ, Ari!" I yell, shifting into park.

She stands in front of the hood with her hands on her hips. "Oh, don't you Jesus Christ me."

The back door opens, and the twins climb into the third row and Audrey and Gina plop into the back seat.

"No. Get out," I say over my shoulder.

I glance at Femi, who smiles at me. "Femi, come get them."

He turns his back on me and strolls away. "Sorry, they're safer with you."

Fucking dick.

I should have drugged them all and then left.

I grip the steering wheel tight. Ari crosses her arms and glares through the windshield.

Audrey's face draws my eyes to the rearview mirror. She doesn't have to say anything. I know why they got in. I know why they feel the need to come with me.

They want their power back, and they think I can help them get it.

Ari climbs in beside me and burns a hole in the side of my face with a fierce stare. "I can't believe you thought we'd be better off staying behind," Ari finally says after several seconds of silence.

"I just want you girls to be safe. Besides, traveling alone is much easier than with a group." I lock eyes with Leah in the third row as I pull onto the road.

She shakes her head and looks out the window.

"That's just an excuse. You don't want us coming because you are afraid you won't be able to save us if something happens like you didn't save your sister." Ari crosses her arms and huffs beside me.

I slam on the brakes, slide into the grassy area beside the road, and shift into park. "You're God damn right," I yell at Ari.

She presses her back against the door, her face draining of color as I take my seatbelt off and scan each of the girl's faces in the back. Audrey's hand shakes as she picks her bottom lip with her fingernail. A tear cascades down Leah's face, and she smears it across her cheek with her palm.

I steer back onto the highway and speed up without another word. The tense atmosphere in the vehicle squeezes me from the inside out.

Something glows in the door by my thigh. I reach into the storage space, and a disposable phone silently rings. I flip it open and hold it to my ear.

"Hello?"

"I know you didn't get the clean break you wanted." Static interrupts Doc's words, but not enough to keep me from knowing what she's saying. "I can help with that."

I glance at Ari, who's watching me intently. "Okay."

"There's a rest stop not far from you, stop there."

Click.

"Hello?"

She hung up.

"Who was that?" Audrey asks, leaning between the front seats.

"Doc. She has something for me." I smack the turn signal down, taking the exit for the restrooms on our right.

Ari looks behind us. "What did she do, follow us?"

"I don't know." I shift the SUV into park and turn off the engine. "While we are here, does anyone need to use the bathroom?"

"We do," the twins say in unison.

Audrey climbs out and moves her seat forward for them.

Ari reaches over the console and takes the keys. "I do too. But I'm not leaving you with these." She dangles them in my face with a sinister smile and hops out, slamming the door behind her.

Little shit.

I step out and lean against a tree growing beside our parking spot. A cardinal swoops in front of me and lands on a low-lying branch. His mate joins him seconds later. They chirp back and forth to each other before taking off together over my head. I watch them fly to the next tree and smile at the approaching Maserati in the background.

"He let you take his car?" I say with a half-hearted smile, leaning in the open driver's side window.

She chuckles, shakes her head, and hands me the keys. "No, he's letting you take his car."

"Femi's letting me have it?" I raise my eyebrows, stand, and step away from the car as she opens the door.

"Of course he is." She unloads my briefcase and bag from the SUV and tosses them in the back seat of the Maserati.

I peer over Doc's shoulder. Ari skips towards us, spinning the SUV keys on her finger.

"They're going to try and follow." I nod behind her.

She removes a scalpel from her inside pocket, kneels beside the front tire, and stabs it. Air sputters out rapidly, flattening the front driver's side tire to the rim. "That will slow them down." She stands and hugs me. "Go."

I kiss the side of her face. "Thank you."

She rubs her blushing cheek. "I'll miss you."

I drop into the Maserati and smile at the open, empty cooler, sitting on the floor of the passenger seat.

Ari spots me leaving and starts running. I press the gas and take off through the lot, heading back to the highway. I glance in the rearview mirror and watch Ari give up on chasing me and chuck the keys to the SUV at the back of my car.

I feel bad for leaving them behind, but I work better alone.

I adjust the rearview mirror and gaze into the eyes of the monster staring back at me.

A brutal, torturous, and painful death awaits the men who chose the same life as Benny and Griffin—their fate, sealed in a tomb beneath the grass and rubble.

I flick the turn signal and head towards the interstate.

The empty cooler bounces, partially closing its lid.

My hunt for fresh meat is never-ending…

…and I have a freezer at home to fill.

The End…Sike…

My head snaps to the left, and I swerve quickly to the right, avoiding the red sports car that nearly hits Femi's Maserati.

Ari.

I knew she would come for me. I shake my head and find a service road to turn into. The red sports car barrels in behind me and skids in the gravel. I chuckle to myself, climb out of Femi's car, and lean against the trunk, waiting for her.

She whips the driver's side door open, and it bounces back, smacking her leg as she places it on the ground.

"Son of a bitch." She grabs her calf, rubs it, and hobbles towards me, bitching under her breath.

I smile at her red face and clenched fists when she stops in front of me. "Hi, Ari."

She purses her lips and grips her hips—her head launching to the sky. "*Hi*? You ditched me at the rest stop and all you can say is *hi*?" She continues staring at the blue sky.

"Oh, come on Ari, you know I couldn't take all of you with me." I peer through the window of the sports car. A car seat sits in the backseat. "Who did you steal that from?" I nod behind her.

Ari continues looking at the sky as her mind wanders around somewhere trying to find its way back to the present.

She tilts her head down, blinks several times, and glances over her shoulder. "Some lady was taking her baby out to change his shitty diaper right after I chucked the keys at you." She looks back at me. "I figured it was fate, and I was meant to chase your ass down."

"Ari, why did I leave?" I ask, raising my eyebrows and wiping the sweat from my neck.

"Because you like to work alone." Her voice raises an octave as she gives me an uncertain, and incorrect answer.

I cross my arms, waiting for her to think about why I left, and ask me again.

She puts her head down, kicks the dirt with her bare foot, and grimaces. "Because I draw too much attention."

"And why is that bad?" I tilt her chin up with my pointer finger, forcing her to look at me.

"Because that's how you get caught."

I let my hand fall away from her. "Exactly."

She won't look at me.

Here comes the pouting.

I vibrate my lips and turn my back on her. "Get rid of the car." Even though my back is turned, I can feel the smile spreading across her face.

This is temporary. I will teach her what I know about cooking and killing, and she can teach me about blowing shit up.

The end.

As I flop behind the wheel of Femi's car, I already regret my decision. Ari skips towards me as flames shoot from the windows of the stolen sports car.

Jesus Christ.

She yanks the passenger side door open, slides in beside me, and points at the flaming car through the windshield. "This is the last time. I promise."

"Ari, what did you do?"

She whips Griffin's cellphone between us, turns its camera until our faces are in the frame, and snaps a picture as the red car explodes in the background between us."

I scrunch my shoulders and glare at her as she quickly types, '*Don't worry I'll keep her safe,*' and hits send.

"Ari," I say calmly.

"I know." She passes me the phone and smiles. "No phones."

I roll my window down and chuck it as it pings with an incoming message.

"Odie?"

The Maserati moves slowly in reverse as I back out of the service road and pull it back onto the highway. "Yes, Ari?"

"I'm hungry."

A smile twitches in the corner of my mouth "Well then, let's go find someone to eat."

To be continued…maybe.

If you enjoyed reading You Should've Kept Driving, please don't forget to leave a review.
If you didn't, reread the last line of the story.

With love,

Odie a.k.a. Willow

Other books by this author

Libitina
The Prickling
No One Leaves
The Unnerving
Sidero (Book 1)
The Carpenter's Chameleon – Sidero (Book 2)

Special thanks to the following beta readers

Taryn Davis
Kim MacPherson
Meriah Gutterson
Gabbi Hodge

Printed in Great Britain
by Amazon